D1432295

PURE
WILDFIRE
Sunfire
LYNNE
CONNOLLY

ELLORA'S CAVE
ROMANTICA PUBLISHING

What the critics are saying...

80

5 Stars "On a scale of 1-10 I give it an 11! I was hooked on *Sunfire* from the first paragraph and couldn't put it down until I finished it. [...] Lynne Connolly has created a masterpiece! I hope that this book is only the beginning of a series for the Pure Wildfire band. [...] Even if these sexy beasts weren't shape-shifters they'd be hot enough to melt a girls panties. This book is a keeper. I've got my eye on Lynne Connolly."
~ *Euro-Reviews*

5 Angels "Ms. Connolly has created an incredible story that ensnares the reader in from the very beginning. [...] The descriptive way in which the transformation scenes were written brought them to life for the reader. I for one hope that there will be future books about the other members of Pure Wildfire. Thanks go to Ms. Connolly for an incredible story."
~ *Fallen Angel Reviews*

4.5 Stars "Lynne Connolly writes a masterful story that leaves the reader wanting more of her characters. Without a doubt this is a top-notch novel. The fresh take on paranormal society and the details she imbues in her story make this author one to watch out for. This is definitely a fabulous book and I can not wait for more." ~ *Senual EcataRomance Reviews*

An Ellora's Cave Romantica Publication

www.ellorascave.com

Sunfire

ISBN 9781419958984
ALL RIGHTS RESERVED.
Sunfire Copyright © 2008 Lynne Connolly
Edited by Briana St. James.
Photography and cover art by Les Byerley.

This book printed in the U.S.A. by Jasmine-Jade Enterprises, LLC.

Electronic book Publication January 2008
Trade paperback Publication February 2009

With the exception of quotes used in reviews, this book may not be reproduced or used in whole or in part by any means existing without written permission from the publisher, Ellora's Cave Publishing, Inc.® 1056 Home Avenue, Akron OH 44310-3502.

Warning: The unauthorized reproduction or distribution of this copyrighted work is illegal. Criminal copyright infringement, including infringement without monetary gain, is investigated by the FBI and is punishable by up to 5 years in federal prison and a fine of $250,000.
(http://www.fbi.gov/ipr/)

This book is a work of fiction and any resemblance to persons, living or dead, or places, events or locales is purely coincidental. The characters are productions of the author's imagination and used fictitiously.

SUNFIRE

Trademarks Acknowledgement

જી

The author acknowledges the trademarked status and trademark owners of the following wordmarks mentioned in this work of fiction:

Amex (American Express): American Express Marketing & Development Corp

Armani: Ga Modefine S.a. Corporation

Dolce & Gabbana: Gado S.A R.L. Corporation

Gibson guitars: Gibson Guitar Corp

Iron Maiden: Iron Maiden Holdings Limited

Led Zeppelin: Joan Hudson, Plant, Page, James P., Baldwin, John Aka John Paul Jones

Levi's: Levi Strauss & Co.

M&M's: Mars, Incorporated

Perspex: ICI Chemicals & Polymers Limited

Porsche: F. Porsche AG

Rega Planar 3: Rega Research Limited

Rickenbacker: Rickenbacker International Corporation

Roland keyboards: Roland Corporation

Rolling Stone Magazine: Straight Arrow Publishers, Inc

Rolling Stones: Rolling Stone Licensing

Savoy: Los Angeles Entertainment, Inc

Stratocaster: Columbia Broadcasting System, Inc

Toyota: Toyota Motor Corporation

Zippo: ZippMark, Inc. Corporation

Chapter One

so

It was the kestrel's lucky day. The small bird below him soared through the atmosphere, the fresh spring day lending it a carelessness that gave the larger bird of prey its chance. Small birds should be more aware of their surroundings.

With a swish of wings and a silent swoop, the kestrel made a dive, wings folded tight to its body, the air rushing past its sleek body. Claws sank into the bird's soft body, seating their hold firmly before the hawk spread its wings to prevent hammering into the ground.

The bird sighed, a soft whisper of air in its beak. Birds didn't usually sigh, but this bird, while small, felt like a good meal to the kestrel, so it ignored the unusual sound. The trees cleared and the kestrel slowed its flight, searching for a likely branch to land on to devour its meal. It spied one and plummeted down. Before it hit the branch, a strange sensation ran through its body, starting at the claws.

A rippling sensation and a pull, as though the little yellow bird had suddenly become heavier. Swelling in the kestrel's grip, it grew larger. At first, the bird of prey gripped harder; after all, a larger bird would make a bigger meal, but the little snack became a banquet, then something that threatened the kestrel instead of the other way around.

The bird of prey released its burden with a shriek and, spreading its wings, escaped as quickly as it could.

The bird's plumage altered as it grew, the red breast developing and glowing, the yellow feathers taking on a golden hue. The short, sharp beak hooked, gaining a lethal edge with its increased size, and the beady brown eyes bled into a deep, dangerous crimson.

It had been the kestrel's misfortune to pick on the phoenix. There was only one in the world and luck didn't get much worse than billions to one. The kestrel had captured a sentient, singular bird, lethal to most other beings. The hawk had been lucky to get away. If he'd been of a mind to, the phoenix could have shaken it off as though it hadn't existed, killing without a thought. But he was feeling generous that day, the first flight he'd had for a while, the promise of spring lending him a lightness of spirit.

The phoenix took a moment to repair the wounds caused by the kestrel. He concentrated on closing the gashes on his shoulders before taking the short hop to the ground below. He shook out his feathers and leaned his head back to enjoy the sunshine on this fresh spring day.

A sharp sense of anticipation tinged the air, of something coming, something new, but the phoenix felt no hurry to go and find it. His golden wings gleamed as he rippled them and he enjoyed the sight of the bright plumage quivering in the light. His appointment could wait.

Or perhaps not.

The bright sunshine and the sharp spring air called to him, but he had things to do, people to meet. Landing in the secluded glade he'd scouted earlier, the great bird paused, letting his enhanced senses enjoy the day for just a moment longer.

Sighing, the phoenix furled his wings close to his body. He wanted to get this meeting over with. An early finish meant he'd have time for another flight later.

Under the curious eyes of a bird of prey soaring high in the sky, the phoenix shape-shifted.

His wings shortened and his feathers melted away to reveal the gold-bronzed skin beneath. His neck straightened, his head took the shape of a human.

In five minutes, a naked man stood in the grove of trees. The only reminder of the phoenix that remained was the swath of bright red hair reaching to his waist. The phoenix, whose other name was Aidan, picked up the pack lying in a corner of the glade.

* * * * *

Aidan found jeans, a black T-shirt, cowboy boots and a thick, black, studded belt in the pack, with several little plastic wallets containing money, credit cards and other bits and pieces. He cursed when he realized he'd forgotten a tie for his hair, but after dressing, bent and picked some coarse grass and twisted it into a makeshift thong. While he enjoyed keeping one of his phoenix attributes in plain sight, long hair was a bitch to keep tidy.

Aidan went over the upcoming meeting in his mind. He'd only promised to play on their manager's pet project, a charity album, because of the news he had for John Westfall. Once Westfall knew Pure Wildfire's second guitarist had walked out, there'd be fireworks for sure.

But then, who better to face fireworks than the phoenix? Aidan grinned and headed out the grove in the direction of the manor house.

Before John Westfall converted it into a business center, the house was a modest, but handsome, eighteenth-century gentleman's residence. Now offices occupied half the house, together with the heavily soundproofed studios, the acoustics in them honed to perfection. People came from all over the world to use them. Nobody liked Westfall, but he was a good manager and the studios were a dream.

Buttery cream stucco covered the house, giving an impression of continuity through the ages, which Aidan knew was entirely false.

As he got closer, the coarse grass changed to fine lawn, barbered as short as velvet pile. Aidan tilted his head back and took a lungful of the clean, fresh air. Nowhere in the world had the same crisp newness as England in the spring, the fresh, clean air he loved spiced with a bite of the chill of winter just passed. Just back from a visit to the States, Aidan savored the pleasure of being on home ground again. He loved America, but whoever said there was no place like home was right. Come to think of it, an American said that. Aidan grinned. To each his own. No doubt Chris and Jake Keys, the bass section of the band, felt the same about their native Texas.

Very few places heralded a visitor's arrival with a burst of Bach, especially played on the guitar. Drawn by the music, as always, Aidan changed direction and strolled toward the west wing, business forgotten for now.

The French windows lay open to the air, invalidating all the careful soundproofing in the studio behind it. Aidan reflected wryly that the staff always closed the windows when Pure Wildfire used the studios.

This was magical, a moment out of time. He stood outside, watching and listening.

A girl bent over a fine Spanish guitar, picking out a melody, spinning the counterpoint on the strings with agile fingers. Her long, straight dark hair fell over the polished wood and even her clothes seemed magical, the fine white embroidered lawn top and gathered skirt marking her as special, untouchable.

Unless Aidan was greatly mistaken, this was Corinne Westfall, the eldest of the three girls known in some circles as the Westfall Gold Mine. Since the age of sixteen, when the music press acclaimed her the latest wonder to hit the classical world running, Corinne Westfall dominated the classical music charts. Corinne's and Aidan's worlds crossed only through her father and the few times he'd seen her onstage, but now he wished he'd met her before. He'd never felt drawn to a human like this before, the music, her slender form, calling out to him to touch, to explore.

Aidan watched her fingering with a connoisseur's eye. Her hands were large enough to form unusual bridges on the fret. He hadn't considered her level of skill before, distracted by Corinne's ingénue appearance. Onstage she wore skimpy clothes, which gave him uncomfortable feelings of underage sex the one time he'd seen her, curious to know what drew people to her performances. He'd turned away from the pictures on her many album sleeves. Looking at her now, mentally calculating her current age, he was pretty sure this was the effect Westfall wanted and he mentally labeled any man a slimeball who turned his daughter into an underage sex symbol just to sell a few albums.

But this girl was now a twenty-eight-year-old woman — no ingénue. But the memory of his distaste stayed in the back of Aidan's mind, however much he tried to dispel it.

Today, Corinne Westfall was a purely lovely woman, lost in a world of her making. Hers and Bach's.

The sight of Corinne in the sunshine, lost in her music, took his breath away. Why did she waste her talent on second-rate classical pop?

Westfall wanted them to play a feeble track for his charity album, an artsy folksy number written by another of Westfall's signings. Watching her now, Aidan knew she could play it in her sleep. Westfall wasted Corinne's talent for money and fame, used her to push his own career.

Corinne looked up, and her dark eyes widened when she saw him. She frowned, then the creases went, faded into the soft skin on her forehead, skin he had a sudden, crazy impulse to taste. "Splinter?"

He grinned. "Call me Aidan."

"Oh, oh yes." Her use of his band name seemed to confuse her, or perhaps it was the sensation of returning to reality. He knew that feeling well, coming after a long solo, or a writing session with his brother Ryan.

Interesting that she recognized him immediately. He hadn't marked her for a fan of rock music. He stood with his back to the sun, so she must only be able to see him in silhouette. The hair, the clothes, the stance must have told her who he was.

She stood up, holding her guitar. Not the clear electric plastic monstrosity she used onstage, her trademark, but a beautifully made acoustic guitar, the wood so smooth it begged for his touch. Perhaps he meant her, because up close Corinne Westfall had soft, silky, touchable skin. Now that she was standing, her slight figure seemed entirely womanly. Any remaining images of a little girl vanished from his mind. This was a woman. A woman in her prime.

He took a step forward, pleased she didn't take one back. He smelled her now, a light floral perfume and her, teasing his nostrils. Delicious. The scent made him want to lick her, add taste to the mix. Lick her everywhere, especially in the place he could almost sense was wet for him. His fingers itched to touch her, smooth his hands over her skin, feel her inside and out. He curled them a little, pressing his fingertips against his jeans to give himself some tactile sensation, just not the one he craved.

"I thought you were coming by later this afternoon, after you'd seen my father," she said, her voice as musical as her instrument.

He had to stop this feeling of need, of wanting her. "I decided to come here first and discuss what we're going to do." He'd meant it to sound innocuous, but what he wanted to do with Corinne had nothing to do with the charity album he was there to record.

"Does my father know you're here?"

"Not unless he was watching me out the window. I walked across from the road, left the driver to bring the car. Too good a day not to."

"Perhaps you should tell him you're here."

"Not yet." Was she so obsessed with her father? Westfall controlled her career, but seeing her face-to-face for the first time, Aidan became startlingly aware of the waste. To immure such a lovely woman in perpetual childhood, to throw her talent away on popular classics seemed shameful.

What was he thinking! One part of his brain, the Splinter rock guitarist part, told him not to be so stupid. If it got out that he'd connected with her any other way but professionally, the music press would hang him out to dry. The other part, the core that was Aidan Hawthorne, told him she was the loveliest woman he'd ever seen and his body yearned for hers as though she was made just for him.

Aidan won. He took another step forward. She held her ground, standing just inside the open French windows, glowing in the light of the sun streaming over her from behind him. He smiled, just a small curve of his lips. "Do you tell your father everything?" He lowered his voice to an intimate purr, heading straight for her mouth.

"Pretty much." The practical, sharp tones hadn't come from Corinne.

Startled, he raised his head as someone else moved into view. Another girl with the same long, dark hair, but with a rounder face, stepped out of the gloom. She stood before him, feet apart, hands on hips, and he felt the aggression in her attitude, saw it in her stance. One of the Westfall twins, Corinne's sisters.

With a smile for Corinne, he stepped past her into the room. Then he realized that by moving away, he'd put her into the full glare of the sun. He turned to see her blinking, dazzled by the bright light. He felt a wave of protectiveness, so unexpected he nearly took her in his arms. *Stupid.*

This rehearsal room and recording studio was older than the suite his band usually used. The room reminded him of many other rooms he'd inhabited in the past the planked wooden floor with the long scrapes showing where heavy items like speakers had been moved, the instruments resting in custom-made stands, the plain walls. Almost like coming home. *So much for the glamor of a career in music.* He gave a wry grin.

Almost. It smelled different somehow. He took a moment to taste the air. Perfume, that was it. Corinne's light scent blended with the heavier perfume the Westfall twins used.

One of the best things about being a rock guitarist was that no one expected him to smile all the time. So he didn't. The twins stood before him now, the brown eyes he found so appealing in their older sister somehow cow-like in them. Their rounder faces made them more childlike in appearance, although Aidan knew they'd just reached their twentieth birthday. They wore jeans and light tops, the colors and styles clashing, a relief to see, since they always dressed either identically or in carefully coordinating clothes onstage, in that vaguely eerie way twins often used.

The Westfall twins sang. Or tried to. When he heard them on the radio, Aidan always switched it off. While their older sister had real talent, the younger two owned hothouse voices, forced into early maturity by expensive voice coaches, made to sing arias their delicate, physically immature vocal cords couldn't quite cope with. They wouldn't last long, their voices would die before they reached their thirtieth birthday, but by then they'd have moved on to something else. Pop probably, chart singles that didn't require as much effort or quality of voice.

Two familiar cases sat on stands. "I see my guitars arrived."

"Your chauffeur delivered them just now. Where were you?"

Flying.

He turned to the girl, one of the twins. "I got him to let me out early. I walked the last mile. It's a beautiful day, a shame to waste it all indoors."

The twins looked at each other and smiled in a knowing, sly way. "You don't see many mornings, I'll bet," one of them commented.

He shrugged. "Some days I do, some I don't. Depends what the schedule is. You must know that, you're in the business too."

"Our concerts tend to end before midnight."

He grinned. "So do ours. But we don't." He couldn't resist. He leered at her in his best lascivious rock star manner. The girl nearest took a half step back before putting up her chin. Then she horrified him by smiling and he definitely saw the spark of interest in her eyes. Oh no. He'd fuck her in a minute if he didn't want her sister so much, but it was too late—he knew which Westfall he wanted.

The door opened to admit a young man. Extraordinarily handsome, dark hair cut short and neat, very blue eyes, a feminine, rosebud mouth. Aidan searched his memory for a reference, but one of the girls stepped forward and put a proprietary hand on his arm. "Hi, Tom."

Thomas Albright, he recalled with an effort. He'd read about him in one of the gossip columns. Once engaged to Corinne Westfall, now attached to one of the girls. Ashley. Oh well, it was a way to tell them apart. The one attached to Albright was Ashley Westfall.

He turned in time to see the anguished look in Corinne's eyes before she dropped her eyelids and bent to place her guitar carefully on its stand. His heart went out to her, and he sent mental daggers of hatred to the man who'd hurt her, instinctively protecting her.

Thomas Albright gasped and dropped like a stone, one hand clutched to his throat. He landed on the planked floor with a reasonably satisfying thump.

Aidan knew he shouldn't project violence quite so strongly, but he couldn't bring himself to give a fuck. Almost dispassionately, he wondered if the man was dead.

* * * * *

Why did he look guilty? Corinne caught sight of the expression in Aidan's amazing eyes. Guilt definitely stamped them for a moment before he smoothly erased it and moved to where Tom lay unconscious. Just as well he'd moved, because Corinne found it hard to stop staring at him—the most beautiful man she'd ever seen. And sexy as hell in that outfit, his t-shirt and leather pants clinging lovingly to his body.

He must think her crazy, staring at him like that.

Part of her knew she should keep away from Tom, the part that protected her from the ache when he callously informed her he'd be dating Ashley from now on, the part that responded coldly to her sister's continued taunts.

Paige sobbed noisily and Ashley moaned low in her throat. Corinne recognized the sound as a vocal exercise, equally effective as a sign of grief when her sister needed one.

Aidan remained the only person in control. He coolly bent over Tom and listened to his heart, his ear to Tom's chest. He dragged Tom's tie down so it sat at half-mast. Corinne had never seen her ex-lover so untidy before—even in bed, Tom was immaculate, pin-neat. And boring as hell.

With the realization came relief, freedom from Tom's superiority and Ashley's veiled taunts that she couldn't keep a man. The sight of Tom Albright, his carefully maintained immaculate appearance so messed up, gave her a moment of childish delight. Why had she wasted one moment in grief when Tom told her he was leaving her? Next to Aidan Hawthorne, Tom melted into nothing. He'd never been worth the waste of her time.

Aidan looked up. His golden eyes met hers without a blink. "He just fainted. He'll be fine in a minute."

"Sh-shouldn't we put him on a sofa or something?" Ashley said, her voice quavering.

Aidan looked down at the man on the floor, eyebrow crooked. Even they were flame red. Corinne wondered if he dyed them too. On another man, they'd have looked wrong, but not on him. "He seems comfortable enough where he is." He didn't say he couldn't lift him. Despite his spare figure, Corinne had no doubt Aidan Hawthorne could lift her ex-fiancé easily if he wanted to. The impression of easy strength she got from him was too natural to be assumed.

Aidan sauntered over to the two battered guitar cases. Corinne held her breath. Splinter's guitars were the stuff of legend, and ever since his chauffeur had brought them in, her fingers had itched to look inside the cases.

She used a succession of Perspex guitars in public. All the same, with the same soft tone, no individuality, no distinction. She couldn't tell the difference between them, perhaps because there *was* no difference. It didn't matter to her public. Sometimes she got the feeling she could play *Mary Had a Little Lamb* and it would climb to the top of the Classical charts. She knew how George Harrison felt when he insisted he wouldn't tour with the Beatles anymore. They could have played anything or nothing, he'd said, and the reaction would have been the same.

She was "The Girl with the See-Through Guitar" and that was all.

Aidan lifted the first guitar. A Rickenbacker, with a flame mahogany finish, like the ones bands used in the sixties. He concentrated on checking the tuning before he turned to the amplifier, plugged in his instrument and switched it on.

For the first time, Corinne noticed which amplifier the girls had chosen to bring in today. She should have been suspicious when they'd said they'd take care of it. It was the amplifier no one could work with. It produced discordant noise and all attempts to fix it met with failure. That, plus the twangy Rickenbacker sound, made for disaster. She had no doubt the twins wanted to amuse themselves and laugh at the stupid rock star.

Aidan glanced up, straight at her, his expression bland, but he knew all right. She managed a wavering smile. After he struck a few very Beatle-like chords, Aidan replaced the guitar in its case and turned to the other one. He made no comment but lifted a Stratocaster from its padded nest.

Corinne held her breath. A choke from the floor as Tom woke up hardly distracted her from the sight of one of the greatest living rock guitarists with one of his favorite instruments. So close she could almost touch him. *Starstruck!*

He hit a note. The amplifier made the sound a travesty of what it should have been but, amazingly, he managed to coax something out of it. Frowning, concentrating on his work, Splinter played the first few notes of one of Pure Wildfire's ballads. With a few tweaks in the sound booth, it would sound almost like the one on the album.

That was true skill. Splinter could take a piece of equipment everybody despised and make it work.

Not that anyone but Corinne paid any attention. The twins were helping Tom to his feet, clucking over him like fussing chickens. She shot him a look of scorn she was sure nobody would see.

She turned back to Aidan and caught the sympathetic expression in his eyes. He knew what she was thinking. Her cheeks burned in shame.

He put his guitar down. "I don't think this is going to work."

She expected he would leave, perhaps in a tantrum. Everyone knew rock stars were notoriously temperamental.

Mildly he said, "Have you an acoustic I can use?"

Her startled expression must have surprised him, because he laughed. "You think I learned on an electric guitar?" The laugh drove a dimple into his left cheek, adding flashes of amusement to his eyes.

Corinne felt herself falling even deeper for him. She smiled back, the moment of intimacy strong. "No." She crossed the room and lifted down her second-best guitar. Another custom-made acoustic, the wood gleaming palely. Briefly, she wondered how she knew she could trust Aidan

Hawthorne with such precious instruments when she'd never seen him play an acoustic. But she just knew.

She handed him the guitar and he took it from her carefully but didn't take his gaze from her face until he held the instrument fully in his hands. Then he gazed at it and tested its weight before he slipped the strap into place around his neck. "Thank you." His soft words sounded more intimate than they should have. "It's a beautiful guitar."

He played a few notes of her transcribed Bach piece. Almost without thinking, Corinne reached for her own instrument and picked out notes in counterpoint to his, spiking the mathematical complexity with magic.

"Are you ready now?" Ashley's hard voice broke into their idyll and reminded them of the task they had come here to do. Aidan's lip quirked in a wry expression that made Corinne laugh, but she turned away, ready to play for the twins.

A folk song, designed to show off the twins' voices, nothing like the true, raw voice of England, but a bowdlerized, prettified piece. Aidan and Corinne were supposed to provide accompaniment, be the frame for the voices. Tom went to the long sofa placed against one wall and slumped on it after assuring everyone he was quite all right, really, he'd just felt a bit faint, perhaps he had a cold or something. They were to "just ignore him and get on with it".

With a few doubtful glances at Tom, the twins took their places. After checking the tuning, Aidan declared himself ready and found a stool to sit on. Corinne took her place by the French windows. Aidan nodded and they began to play.

It was awful and magical at the same time. Awful from the twins, wonderful from the guitars. Corinne found herself playing the melody, while Aidan wove notes in and out of hers, enhancing and deepening the tune. They almost drowned out the voices, but sadly, not quite.

Corinne watched him and knew this must be the first time Aidan heard the twins raw, without benefit of studio enhancement. Paige probably sang better than Ashley, but the competition for last place was close. The volume they could raise together formed their best asset, the worst being their pitch. Endless rehearsal, double tracking and great backing voices made sure their public performances came up to scratch, together with hour upon hour of lessons from expensive teachers. They performed their concerts by rote, always enhanced by "special guests", including Corinne herself more often than not. She'd promised herself she wouldn't do it anymore, and now here she sat, accompanying her sisters again.

Aidan's jaw clenched after the first bar and remained clenched through the piece.

They managed a run-through somehow. Once. When they finished, Aidan got to his feet and put the guitar carefully down on a nearby stand. Too carefully.

"I have to see your father. Do you need me to come back before the actual recording?"

He addressed Corinne, as though the girls didn't exist. Through Tom's sycophantic applause, she answered him. "I don't think so. Thank you for coming."

He didn't give a conventional response. How could he, after such a performance? Instead, he flashed her a grin before he left the room, closing the door with a quiet click. She stared at the closed door, blinked and turned to her sisters.

"I thought you'd practiced this one. You were out of tune, both of you, though it's hard to say which of you followed the other. You can't expect a musician of his caliber to waste his time on you if you're not ready."

"His caliber?" echoed Paige, her voice even shriller than during the song. "The man's a rock guitarist! Where's the caliber in that?" Corinne stopped herself telling Paige and Ashley their voices were the kind of shrill soprano that would never take them to the top level in classical music, but would serve them better in the pop arena. She'd told them before, even talked to her father about it, but he shrugged her aside as if her opinion meant nothing.

Paige paused and smiled, one finger touched to her chin in a practiced gesture of provocation. "I wouldn't throw him out of bed though. He's very fit." She touched her tongue to her lip.

"Don't talk about him as though he's an object." Corinne's words came out too sharply, only because she'd thought the same and because Paige's constant "onstage" gestures irritated her.

Up close, Aidan Hawthorne was more of an icon than he seemed from far away, not less, like many performance artists. She'd attended a concert on the quiet, free to admire the sweat-slicked skin that accentuated every muscle in his half-naked body at the tail end of the performance. She pushed away the vision of her tongue catching the sweat, knowing he wasn't for her. Different worlds, different expectations, different everything. After a concert, he probably had a dozen groupies lapping the sweat from him and catching it in little vials to sell later. She shook off the image. "Did you listen to him play?"

Paige shrugged. "I was too busy singing. I thought you missed a few notes."

Typical of her sister to try to turn the blame. "I played fine." She turned away, on the pretext of putting her guitar on its stand, and fought an unexplained desire to hug it to her, as though the warm wood was her only friend. *Foolish!*

Ashley joined Tom on the sofa and he curled his arm around her. The demonstrations of affection between them became more blatant every day, provoking Corinne to respond with jealousy. Both Ashley and Tom would get off on that. "I thought you played a bit flat," Ashley commented, leaning into her fiancé.

"I wasn't," Corinne said tonelessly, not prepared to get into a pointless argument. "We've got a week before we're due to lay it down in the studio. Plenty of time to get it right."

"A week!" Paige bounced over to the sofa and sat on the other side of her sister's boyfriend. "We have a gala tomorrow night and a guest appearance on that TV show! There's another track to record —"

"Which TV show is that?" her twin interrupted.

Paige turned to Ashley with a toss of her hair and a bright smile. Corinne felt sure Ashley already knew. "'Divas', that program about women in music. They're doing a classical edition." Now came the part Corinne knew would arrive — inevitable, and probably the reason for the whole conversation. "Are you on that one, Cor?"

She shrugged. "I went on it a couple of years ago. They do a classical special every year. They probably don't want to repeat themselves and have me on again."

Ashley sniggered. "I didn't know you cared about repeating yourself. You do it often enough."

Corinne couldn't win this one. The twins liked attention too much to give it up. They made sure they went to all the right parties, all the right premieres, even more than Corinne had in her brief career as classical music's latest *wunderkind*.

"Time we went somewhere else," Ashley remarked.

Corinne picked up the sheet music for her transposition of the Bach piece and immersed herself in it. No more discussions, no more humiliations. When the door opened and closed behind Tom and the twins, she didn't look up. Only when sure she was alone and unobserved did she let the tears come.

* * * * *

Feeling the tense atmosphere of the house in every pore of his body, Aidan made his way to the office wing. He knew this part of the house well, though the family areas were usually no-go. Studios in one wing, offices in the other, family rooms in the middle, all connected by the great showpiece hall. Not that he'd want to venture into the family area. Those poisonous sisters, the younger two, didn't attract him one bit, although he'd caught some blatantly admiring fuck-me leers from them during the rehearsal. He got a different feeling from Corinne.

She definitely appealed to him physically. He thought the feeling was mutual too, though he wouldn't have an opportunity to test that. She probably despised him and the rock world he came from. Classical musicians usually did. She did have talent, much more than her sisters, but she wouldn't have to try hard for that. Forcing himself into his usual air of detachment, trying desperately to ignore the passion for a dark-haired guitarist flaring inside him, Aidan headed for John Westfall's office. His manager, Corinne's father.

Photographs of the bands and musicians Westfall represented lined the corridor. Every aspect of the music world, from classical to rock, country to jazz, came under the close scrutiny of John Westfall, manager and Svengali. Most entrepreneurs concentrated on one genre, but Westfall handled all genres. A shame he used the sleaziness and cheapness of pop as his selling tool and ignored the best of all genres.

The secretary waved Aidan through after one startled glance of recognition. He didn't knock but went straight in, the heavy Georgian paneled door opening silently at his touch.

A large, mahogany partner's desk faced him and behind it stood John Westfall — short, dressed in black t-shirt and trousers. Aidan briefly wondered, as he always did, where Westfall bought his trousers. He didn't think anyone made that kind of high-waisted, pleated front any more. He took Westfall's hand, extended in welcome, and shook it briefly, sprawling in the seat before the desk at Westfall's expansive gesture. After he'd refused coffee, Westfall asked Aidan how the rehearsal went.

Aidan shrugged. "Okay, I guess. It went."

"You must have found it a bit different, working with my girls."

"Sure is." He assumed the surly expression of the stereotypical rock star, lip curled slightly, eyes half closed, his position in the chair slumped and careless. He'd been in the business long enough to learn most of the tricks. He had no intention of letting Westfall into his private life or giving him any clue about his thoughts. "Sexier than the band."

Westfall frowned, as Aidan hoped he would. Off balance now, no longer in as much control as before, he snapped, "They're my daughters, Hawthorne!"

Aidan shrugged again. "That makes it even more fucking amazing."

"You're not fit to be left alone with them."

Better and better. At least riling Westfall would provide him with some amusement and an outlet for the anger he felt when he thought of how his manager had ruthlessly used his daughters for his own purposes. He didn't know how much they were paid, but he'd bet not as much as he was, with his battery of lawyers to check his contracts. "I could fuck all three in an afternoon." He let his eyelids droop a little before he raised them and gave Westfall a flash of fire. Just a spark. Then he drooped again.

Westfall growled, but the moment passed and the man regained control. Or seemed to. It was all games, anyway. Westfall was no more close to losing his temper than he was. Aidan's empathy, the only part of his psi powers he used all the time, detected no crackle in the air, no disturbance. The man had his emotions under iron control. His anger was all show, which turned this encounter into a game. Westfall cared very little about the personal welfare of his daughters. Aidan wouldn't be so angry if Westfall had genuinely believed he was doing his best for the girls.

Anyone who used his daughters with that kind of single-mindedness selfishness shouldn't be trusted. Westfall would use anyone else the same way. Wring the profit out and toss them aside when the parade passed by. There was a word for people like that. Many words, now he came to think about it. Perhaps he'd write a song about it.

"When will you be ready to record?"

His biggest advantage in this encounter was his Psi sense, but the uncouth image he always cultivated with this man proved a big plus too. Aidan let the pause grow for a full half-minute. "The twins still need to rehearse, but when they're ready, we're good to go." He paused again. "Pure Wildfire has the three big concerts in London next month, and until then we'll be writing and resting. I can come back when they're ready. But make sure they're in tune this time."

"Resting?" Westfall sounded as if he didn't know what the word meant.

"Resting," Aidan confirmed. "At undisclosed addresses. Taking time out. Although we'll stay at the end of the phone if you need us. We're meeting the week before the concerts to run through the order a couple of times, then we'll be ready. In case you've forgotten, you don't get any say in that side of our business. Only, one thing's gone wrong."

He knew Westfall would hate having to ask, which was precisely why he hadn't told him. "What thing?"

"Matt walked out."

Matt, the second guitarist and the only member of the band not a shape-shifter. But that didn't have anything to do with why he quit. "We're not heartbroken and neither should you be. Matt's a junkie and that doesn't fit the way we are now. He's unreliable, doesn't turn up for appearances and rehearsals and doesn't contribute anything useful when he does show. We planned to sack him after the concerts anyway, but he said he'd got a better offer. He must have realized the way the wind was blowing and got out before we threw him out."

Thunderous clouds seemed to gather around Westfall. Better. Unnerving Westfall was the best way to win this encounter. "He stayed with you how long?"

"Nearly a year. He played on the first album, *Sunfire,* and the last tour. We liked him when he started, but he went downhill real fast after he discovered the junk. We won't miss him. But we need a guitarist for the London gigs."

Westfall glared at him. "No chance of him coming back?"

Aidan mentally reviewed the scene when Matt left. "No. We wouldn't have him, anyway."

"Don't you know anybody?"

Aidan allowed the corner of his mouth to curl a little. "Yeah, fucking truckloads of 'em. None of them we want are free and we don't want to poach from another band. I don't know anyone who's unhappy where they are and nobody of real talent's shown up in the last few months. We want a new band member, but failing that, we'll take a reliable session man. Better than poaching. We're planning to ask one of the people who covered for Matt on *Sunfire* when he was too stoned to stand up."

Westfall sighed heavily and pulled his chair closer to his desk, reaching for his computer mouse. "If that doesn't work out, you can leave it with me. I'll get something sorted out for the concerts. Does this mean we need to scale the promotion down?"

Aidan grinned and shook his head. "Nope. We can fill in what's missing. As long as the new kid can add some sound. You need to do the publicity about Matt leaving. It's what we pay you for, after all. We don't want Matt dissed. Just say he left to join Radical Tomatoes and hint at a row."

Westfall spluttered, his attention back on Aidan. "Radical Tomatoes?"

Aidan's grin broadened. "Sixties revival stuff. Fucking crap band, fucking crap name. But Matt gets to be lead guitarist and make like he's Hendrix. We've decided to play down the drug addict thing and go with the lead guitarist line, if anybody asks. He might see the light, even now and kick the drug habit. The row's a backup, in case Matt doesn't play along. We've got enough dirt on him to keep him down if he tries to fuck us about."

"Glad to hear it." Westfall turned back to the screen. It reflected palely in his reading glasses as he flipped through his portfolio. "I'll get back to you in a day or two."

Aidan shambled to his feet, deliberately clumsy, as though he'd spent the last few days in a nightclub instead of at home. He knew that habit annoyed his manager.

Westfall had the band wrapped up in a contract that would end soon. They wouldn't renew. Not that they'd tell him yet. Aidan had foiled a few attempts by Westfall already to make them do things that they didn't want to do. The track for the charity album was his last concession, keeping Westfall sweet up to the end of the contract.

Without another word, he got to his feet and headed for the door.

His way out of the manor led past the rehearsal room, he made sure of it. Maybe Corinne might still be there. Maybe he'd have another chance with her.

The waves of grief hit him like a wall of icy water on his way past. He couldn't ignore such anguish, so he turned the knob and went in.

The door opened silently, like the door to Westfall's office, gliding on well-oiled hinges. She stood with her back to the door, head bowed, shoulders shaking in quiet pain. Her sobs filled the room with sorrow.

At first, Aidan wasn't sure which sister wept so heartbrokenly, but the white clothes and the feel of the atmosphere soon told him. Guessing her wish for privacy, he closed the door quietly before he walked forward and placed his hands on Corinne's shoulders to tell her she was no longer alone.

"What is it? Is there anything I can do? Who made you cry like this?"

Her shoulders froze, tensing under his touch. She drew a deep breath and her hand went up to wipe away the tears. Only then did she turn.

Her eyes, made even darker by her tears, gazed steadily into his. Her cheeks were still wet but she'd composed her face before she turned to him. She looked ethereally beautiful and heartbreakingly lovely. Aidan caught his breath in wonder.

"You," she said. "You made me cry."

Chapter Two

ᏚᎧ

Immediately, Corinne felt sorry for what she'd said, even if it was the truth. When she'd seen Aidan play and knew him for the best in his field, it linked all her feelings of dissatisfaction together. Corinne knew she fell short. Not much, but enough. She wasn't good enough.

The realization hit her like a brick in the stomach. She found it hard to face after so many years of trying. Aidan was good. Superb. He handled his instrument with such ease, but even with a bad amplifier, he coaxed out notes that put her crisp, defined playing to shame. Happy with the fame, the money and the acclaim, Corinne spent years hiding from the truth. Now, with horrible clarity and a demonstration of the skill that she'd always strived toward, Aidan Hawthorne took all that away from her.

Now the reason for her distress drew her into his arms. Hating her weakness, hating that anyone should see her like this, she couldn't stop her tears.

He said nothing, just held her, but after a moment, he pulled her closer and lifted her. She didn't resist, but allowed him to take her down onto the large, squashy sofa and hold her against his shoulder. The warmth of his body seeped into hers and suddenly Corinne didn't feel so alone anymore.

This wouldn't do! Pulling away, she took a few deep breaths and sat up. "Sorry." By some miracle, she found a handkerchief in one of the pockets of the ridiculous peasant skirt she wore. What was she thinking when she dressed that morning? She'd been nervous but excited, determined to make an impression on her idol. *Stupid*!

His skill made her realize how much she fooled herself. His absorption in his music showed her what she wanted. Corinne wept for her lost dreams, the way her father drew her away from her real goal in life—to play the guitar to the best of her ability.

Never in her wildest dreams did she imagine she'd be cradled in Splinter's arms, her back softly stroked by those hands that created such magic on the guitar.

"Just a stupid moment. Perhaps it's PMS," she ventured weakly. "I'm all right, really I am."

He caught her chin in one hand, held it steady and wouldn't let her look away. His eyes were really amazing close-up. Golden with streaks of orange and deep crimson. Not bloodshot at all, although with all the reports of the band's antics in the tabloids, it wouldn't have surprised her. But clear intelligence gazed back at her. He took the handkerchief from her nerveless fingers and gently wiped away the remains of her tears.

"Is it really just the time of the month? It doesn't seem like it to me."

"No." She couldn't lie to him, not when they were so close.

He bent his head and kissed her. Not in a passionate way, but the way a friend might comfort another, a gentle touch of lips, softly caressing. But at the contact, her senses stirred into life, reaching for more of him.

Her eyes flickered open. She had no recollection of closing them. He drew back and watched her with a slight smile in his eyes. "Better?"

She nodded. "Now I feel stupid. Everybody gets down sometimes."

"We both know it was more than that. Feel like telling me?"

Why should she? How could she trust him? She had no more reason to trust Splinter—Aidan—than anyone else in her life. Even her father.

But she had to tell someone, and she'd probably never see him again after recording the track for the charity album. "I've lost it. I'm not as good as you on the guitar, not as good as I might have been if I'd studied properly. You know that, don't you?"

"You're a hell of a lot better than some people I could name."

He didn't deny it then. Second rate wasn't good enough for her. Not anymore. "I'm not as good as people say I am. I don't feel the music anymore. I can't get into its heart." She sniffed.

He dabbed her cheeks with the handkerchief. "Don't say that. You're very good. You must know that."

Slowly she began to draw the pieces back together. When she recovered her shield, the one she lived behind most of the time, she'd shut him out. But not yet. Not quite yet. "I can play the notes in tune and my timing is never off. So can any number of music students."

"You sell the music. That's always half of it."

She shook her head and dropped her gaze to avoid those perceptive eyes, but he wouldn't let her. He put his finger under her chin and tilted it up.

She met his clear intelligence and told the truth. "My father taught me to sell myself. Trained me. Those plastic guitars are terrible acoustically but I'm welded to them because they're part of my image. I thought about retiring long before now, but I just let it go on. I can't do it anymore." She bit her lip. "I'll go away somewhere, learn to play well and come back low key."

"Is that what you really want?"

She smiled shakily. "It's better than what I have now." Childhood dreams shot through her mind. Dreams of playing a Stratocaster to an adoring crowd, people going nuts in the mosh pit for her solos. Ever since she'd heard her first rock album, daydreams filled her mind. She could play air guitar with the best practitioners of the style. "It's a start."

"Won't you find it hard?"

"Maybe." She paused. "I never really wanted to do it enough before. The money, the adulation, it's all addictive, isn't it?"

He grinned. A dimple flashed and disappeared in his cheek. "I never thought of it like that. I've always put music first, everything else second."

"It shows."

"Thank you." Then he quirked a brow. "You know our music? I thought you classical types looked down your noses at us rockers."

She chuckled. She still felt tearful, but now that she'd made her decision, the world was slowly settling into place again. "I've got Pure Wildfire's album. I can't wait for the next one."

His turn to laugh. "You're joking! A classical brat like you? I never suspected!"

"I went to one of your concerts. Dad doesn't like us to go, says we should be busy working, so instead of provoking him into hours of nagging, I resorted to a little trickery. There was a Brahms concert on at the Albert Hall, so I bought tickets for that and for yours at Brixton Academy, and then I went to yours."

His laugh broadened and he gave her a quick hug. "Sly! Did you enjoy it?"

She smiled back. She found it difficult not to join in with his infectious laugh. "I loved it. I loved the power and the energy most of all. Everything that's missing from my music. I need to move people like you do, bring them something more than a carefully learned piece I don't really care for."

His laugh faded and he stared at her, a new intensity in his gaze his eyes. "Can you play any of our stuff?"

"Most of your solos, and I can play some of them straight through. I pick up tunes very quickly."

"Show me." He got to his feet and went to the case, pulling out the Stratocaster. He set it up then held it out to her. "Come on."

"Father might hear."

He snorted derisively. "On this amp? Hang on, take this and I'll lock the door." He shoved the guitar at her and strode to the door, turning the key in the lock. Before indulging in tears, Corinne had already closed the French windows, so now they were effectively soundproofed.

She could hardly believe she held Splinter's Strat in her hands. Close up, she saw the scratches and signs of hard use. He handed her a plectrum from a stack in the case. "Do you use these?"

She nodded and took it. It felt different, but she wasn't totally new to electric guitars. She'd experimented with them until her father declared it a waste of time. He didn't know she had a Fender stashed in her room, concealed in her wardrobe behind a swathe of white dresses. She played it sometimes, even plugged it into an amplifier when everyone was out or on the rare occasions when she had a studio to herself. She wasn't afraid of being caught—she could cope with that. More the knowledge that she was terrible. She couldn't bear anyone she knew hearing her make such a noise.

Slowly she'd improved and begun to wonder if she might add an electric guitar to her repertoire. Do a Dylan, outrage her fans and get some new ones. Now she held the Strat closely to her chest, watching its owner stand in the middle of the floor, feet well apart, waiting for her to begin.

The very familiarity of the pose, seen so often in engineers, sound technicians and concert goers, put her at her ease. So what if she made a racket?

She struck the first note of one of Pure Wildfire's ballads.

Five minutes later, she came out of her reverie to find he'd moved closer to watch her fingering. "You're not new to this, are you? You've got a few things wrong, but it all works." Corinne sighed in relief and pleasure. She enjoyed working with other musicians, unless they happened to be her sisters. "It's your timing," he continued. "You've got to get used to the off note, the syncopation. Here. Try the sixth bar again."

She counted herself in and played it. He took the guitar off her and played it himself. "See?"

Corinne saw. When he gave her the instrument again, she played the bar, feeling the difference for herself.

The grin came back. "Much better. Try it right through again."

She began the ballad again, playing "Tearing Me Apart", murmuring the words as she played.

Hardly aware of him moving behind her, when she felt his body behind hers, she carried on playing. He reached over and touched her fingers on the strings. "Let me," he whispered to her. "Make the chords." Heat burned all along her back.

Never had she felt closer to anyone in her life before. He seemed to breathe the timing into her mind, and they played as one person. She soared, daring to vary the strict timing, holding and sustaining when he pulled and twisted a note out of shape. It seemed so easy when he did it.

His technique added an extra dimension to the playing. Up close like this, she saw how he worked, his strong fingernails pulling the notes out of the guitar. He must strengthen his nails. Perhaps he used superglue, many guitarists did. They seemed so strong. Like claws.

The sound faded away, echoing in the room, and in her mind she heard the last words of the song. "I'll stay until the pieces fade."

She hadn't been aware of her singing until she heard his voice, mingling with hers. She turned her head and he captured her lips in a searing kiss.

Openmouthed they explored each other. Corinne had never kissed like this before, as if it really mattered. His tongue entered her and she tilted her head to accommodate him better. He licked the roof of her mouth, sending shudders down her spine, waves of languorous desire sparking into glowing flame. They caught fire from the moment their lips touched, driving Corinne into a hot state of desire.

He withdrew his tongue from her mouth, and she felt the loss, as though he'd left her body empty. Then he returned, plunging his tongue deep again, curling the tip against her, inviting her in to share his taste. She reciprocated, touched her tongue to his lips, then the soft skin inside and his mouth. He gave a soft groan, the little puff of hot air against her lips urging her to do more.

She hadn't realized how wonderful a man could taste. The slight tang of mint with a taste all his own, one so unique she couldn't begin to describe it, with elements of spice and sugar. But having tasted him once, she would know Aidan Hawthorne for the rest of her life.

She jerked back at the startled realization of what she was doing and who she was doing it with. "We can't."

His voice came to her in a low murmur. "We can. If you want to stop, we'll stop. But this is too good not to carry on a little further. Just a little. Please, Corinne."

His seductive tones made it impossible for her to resist him. She didn't want to resist. He felt too good, smelled too good to stop now.

Besides, why not? She'd exposed herself to him in one way, played the way she wanted to, so why not do this too and see where it took her? Corinne wasn't exactly the well-behaved classical princess her public thought her, but she'd been celibate since Tom abandoned her and now she realized how much she'd missed sex. She'd see Aidan once more, when they recorded the track for the charity album, unless he chose to lay it down separately, then she'd probably never see him again, except in public. So why the hell not?

He moved back slightly to lift the guitar strap away and put the Fender carelessly down, the instrument falling with a dull thump and a twang of strings. Aidan turned back to her without looking where it landed, although she knew the guitar must mean something to him. He studied her, unsmiling, sparks of desire flashing in his eyes. She lifted her arms to him and he accepted her invitation.

It would be foolish to pretend she didn't want him. Ever since he walked through that door, she'd been aware of a growing physical attraction and her desire increased with every moment. She'd wanted him since she saw him in concert, since she first heard the *Sunfire* album, but that had been general, the kind of desire she knew would never be fulfilled, just like most other dreams, something to fantasize over in her more indulgent hours. And she had. But her vibrator didn't compare with Aidan. Not even close. Every inch of him was alive, his large hands stroking her back as he kissed her, the long sweeps caressing her, drawing her in.

Now here he was and she wanted him more than ever. No longer Splinter, the rock god whom she fucked in her dreams, but a man. A man she wanted very much. His hot kisses made her yearn for more, and she reached for his t-shirt, shoving her hands under it to touch his chest. Skin to skin. His tongue in her mouth, he drew her closer and she felt the hard bulge pushing his jeans out. He moved so that his cock slid into one side of the V created by her crotch, pushing it into her body, the rough fabric of his jeans catching on the open weave of her skirt. The fabric slid between her legs, and she felt her pussy dampen and soak through her panties into the white skirt.

His fingers feathered up her neck and he speared them into her hair, cradling the back of her skull so she couldn't move. Not that she wanted to when he invaded her mouth, filling her with his presence. He caressed her, licked her lips as if he couldn't get enough of her taste, and touched the base of her throat, the barest caress of his hot mouth.

Suddenly he was gone, leaving only cold air where his body had pressed so hotly against hers, a chill striking her neck where he'd left damp, heated touches. Corinne blinked, momentarily disoriented.

Aidan strode to the sofa and threw the loose cushions down on the floor. He turned back to her, one eyebrow quirked in query. "Your choice, Corinne." His voice had roughened and deepened with passion. She looked at him, long hair rumpled by her fingers, t-shirt rucked up at the front, jeans tented by his erection. No choice. No choice at all.

He waited for her to make her decision, his mouth slightly open, his face flushed with passion. He didn't have to wait for long. She almost stumbled in her haste to join him, slipping off her low-heeled sandals on the way. Smiling at her, he swept her into his arms and lifted her off her feet, before he took them down to the makeshift bed on the floor. "How about the sound booth?" he murmured. "Can anybody get in there?"

She shook her head. "It's kept locked."

"Don't say you've not been warned." He rolled so she lay under him, her skirt tangled around their legs. He lifted his head, and rested his weight on his elbows. "You're fucking lovely, Corinne Westfall." Then he bit his lip. "Sorry."

"What for?" She smiled when she realized. "Swearing? You think I never heard a man say 'fuck' before? And I thought I was old-fashioned!"

His laugh reverberated through her lower body, where they pressed together intimately. It felt delicious, even through their clothes. She could feel his cock hard against her pubic bone. She couldn't resist wriggling a little against him.

An abrupt end to the laugher and a low groan rewarded her. He bent to take her mouth again, surrounding her with heat. She reacted eagerly. His opened his mouth wide and slanted it across her lips, devouring hers, and she responded, as wild as he, squirming under him to reach more, feel more. When he pulled away, she stared at him, dazed with need.

"Too many clothes," he gasped, and put his hands on the hem of his t-shirt, dragging it over his head. His chest was broader than she'd expected, his shapeless t-shirt somehow hiding the definition of his muscles. His light tan and the easy way he moved spoke of strength and fitness.

Not taking her gaze away from him, loving the sight of Aidan's fit body, Corinne pulled at the tie of her drawstring top until it came loose and he watched her tug the neck wider until it became useless, his eyes branding her every move. She glanced down at her top to find somewhere to grasp it so she could drag it off. Her plain white bra came into view and she wished she'd worn something seductively lacy, but he didn't seem to care.

He touched the underside of her breast, making her shiver in response. "Do you need this bra?" Taking her light gasp as a response, he unclipped the front fastening and impatiently pulled the material aside. "Fuck. Oh fuck."

Corinne had never thought her breasts attractive. They were heavy and full, tipped with large nipples the color of a damask rose. From the look on Aidan's face, he didn't think they were unattractive. He stared, his gaze so heated she could almost feel it burning her already hot flesh. He covered them with his hands almost reverently, gently massaging, lifting them and pressing them together, making Corinne twist up to him in pleasure. With a groan, he moved his hand to curve around her back, pulled her up to where he knelt above her and took a nipple into his mouth. He didn't stop to touch or kiss, but sucked her in as if he was starving and she had the only sustenance he wanted. His single-minded need ripped through her body.

The wet suction created a response that shot through her and she cried out softly, her voice breaking. He lifted his head, a wicked smile curving his full lips. "You're gorgeous. I can't believe you've kept all this hidden from the world."

"But not from you." And not from all of the world either. There were half a dozen men who could confirm that.

The smile broadened. "No, not from me." He moved up her body, back to her mouth and claimed it in another searing kiss.

Skin to skin with Aidan felt like no other encounter had ever done. This wasn't how she'd imagined an encounter with a rock musician. In her dreams, Corinne let her most sordid fantasies run wild, imagined a knee-trembler backstage between the show and the encores, let herself become the skankiest groupie, the most predatory fan. She still harbored that at the back of her mind, but this wasn't the fulfillment of that particular fantasy.

This was different. A man and a woman exploring each other's bodies, nothing between them except a few inconvenient clothes.

As she thought this, she felt his hand between them, at the buttons of his fly. She reached down to help, eager to feel his whole length stretched naked along her body.

Aiden went commando. When she helped him unfasten his jeans, his cock fell into her hand, hot and hard. She gasped at the speed of the contact, the way events were escalating, her voice blending with his low cry when he felt her touch him. She took her opportunity and gripped him, squeezing him, then sliding her hand up to the tip and down again. He was fully erect, hard for her. She moved her hand down, then up, loving his reaction as he pushed into her grasp.

"Wait. Stop. Carry on like that and I'll come in your hand. Give me a minute." He sounded breathless, as breathless as Corinne. He leaned back and she feasted her eyes on him while he dragged her skirt and panties out of the way.

They looked at each other. Corinne gazed at his hairless chest, with flat brown nipples she longed to taste. When he moved, his muscles tightened, bulged in response, but in repose she could hardly see them. An athlete's body, with lightly bronzed skin. Every wet dream she'd ever had, personified.

She reached out hungrily to him, but he smiled and drew away, dragging her skirt and panties down her legs and away, shoving his jeans off to join them. When he knelt to return for her, she saw his erect cock properly for the first time. It reared out of a bed of bright red curls that were only slightly darker than the hair on his head, more red than copper, flaming with gold and orange highlights, but unmistakably red. She stared, fascinated.

"Like what you see?" he murmured huskily.

"Oh yes." She dragged her gaze back to his face and grinned. He smiled back. "I wondered what color your hair really was. Everyone does." There were rumors that he dyed everything, but surely not there!

Speculation entered his gaze. He stared at her for a full half minute before replying. "It's not dyed. People just assume it is and I let them."

"Oh, but nobody has hair that color!" she was shocked enough to blurt out.

"I do." He reached back and loosened the tie, letting his hair fall loose around him, blazing red in a halo cast by the sun streaming in through the windows.

The sight pushed her over the edge Aidan, like a living flame, hers for the taking. "Come here," she whispered.

His body covered hers, surrounding her with living heat. He slipped his hand between them, down to her crotch and into the dark curls there, searching and finding her inner lips. His faint groan when he slid inside her labia made her arch up, trying to persuade him to push inside her, but he slid his finger up instead, searching for her clit. And finding it. His mouth once more took hers in a deep kiss as electricity jolted her up to another level of bodily awareness. He circled her clit then pinched it between thumb and finger, the slight pain only enhancing her need for him.

For a second time he pulled away, leaving her gasping her need. His sudden departure pulled her out of the hot mood his seduction had drawn her into. "What is it? What's wrong?"

For answer, he reached for his discarded jeans, delving into a pocket and bringing out a foil packet held between two fingers, one of which had just a few seconds ago been touching her. It still glistened with her juices. He waved the packet at her. "We can't forget this."

"I'm on the Pill," she said.

He paused, staring. "Baby, you have to take care." His voice softened to a low, intimate tone, caressing in its intensity.

She felt a thrill, hearing him use a word of endearment and smiled up at him. "I trust you." She knew she shouldn't, but when she looked into his eyes she saw honesty and concern, and she knew he wouldn't hurt her.

He caught his breath in a sharp gasp. "You know what I am, what I've done? Do you trust all your lovers like this?"

"I know some of it. But no, I don't trust 'all my lovers' like this." All six of them as opposed to what—hundreds? He'd probably had a lot of women. The rock star lifestyle would see to that. She couldn't explain why she felt this way about him, that she could trust him. It had nothing to do with her lurid fantasies about the guitarist Splinter and everything to do with a man called Aidan Hawthorne. "I've never trusted anyone like this before."

"I'm glad to hear it." Tenderness replaced the faint anxiety in his amber eyes. That was the last thing she'd expected when she'd decided to let this encounter take its course. She'd expected a fierce fucking to help chase her blues away, but it seemed to be mutating into something else. Something deeper and far more unsettling.

She watched him smooth the condom over his cock, one-handed. Part of her wanted to help him, part of her wanted to watch, so she let the voyeur win. She admired his expertise.

"What is it?" So sensitive to her already, he'd even noticed her moment of regret. "Do you want to stop?"

"God no!"

Her vehemence made him chuckle and he came down to her again, covering her body deliciously with his long one, surrounding her with his heat once more. His lips met hers, inciting all the fire simmering just underneath the surface. He dipped his tongue into her mouth, caressing her softly. "Then we won't stop," he murmured against her lips. "Open your legs wider, sweetheart. Let me in to that sweet pussy of yours."

She opened them slowly, making him groan in frustration, then he laughed when he realized she was teasing him. She joined in and they were laughing together when he entered her. His broad head pushed her flesh aside, but he entered slowly. She felt every touch, surrendering to his invasion only to clasp him tightly as he entered her.

Her laughter faded into a moan. He felt so good, sliding gently deeper, that she couldn't stop arching her back, pressing her ass against the chair cushion under it in an effort to get closer to him.

"Ready for some magic?" he murmured, his mouth heating her ear.

A long drawn-out "Ohhh", barely articulated, followed by a startled "Oh!" of surprise.

Surely—impossible though it seemed—*surely* he'd lengthened, swelled, *grown* inside her?

"I didn't know if I was right, but now I'm sure." He sounded awed. His words made no sense to her, but she was sure of one thing. He *had* grown.

He moved from side to side, making her feel even more full, even more wanted. "This is impossible," she whispered.

He breathed a kiss to her temple, the tip of her nose and her mouth, feather light touches of his lips. "Why is it impossible? I wanted to fuck you very much, and when I came inside you, I wanted you more. I'm responding to you, sweetheart, that's all. Don't ask questions. Just enjoy."

He lifted up and watched her while he moved harder, drew out to plunge in deep and deeper yet. The wet sounds of their joining told them both how much she wanted this, what he was doing to her. She couldn't keep still. She arched her back, moved to try to get closer and lifted her legs, hooking them around his backside to drag him in with her heels. His hair flowed down around them, strands of bright red mingling with her dark brunette, touching her shoulders and waist with whispers of sensation.

They kept their eyes open. Gazing up into his golden eyes, deepened into bronze, Corinne thought she saw glints of red, passion lighting the depths to revelations of awareness.

His strokes deepened, lengthened, and he smiled down at her, the smile not a sharing of pleasure, but an invitation to enter a world she'd only glimpsed before.

She was seeing things that weren't there. Corinne desperately tamped down her imaginings, reminding herself of the reality. *This is only a pity fuck. I'll never see him again after this. It's just comfort. He saw me unhappy, he fancied me and this suits us both. For God's sake, don't get involved, Corinne. He has dozens of women at his beck and call. Don't become one of them.*

She felt him call to her, felt it although he didn't speak. His voice echoed in her head. *Enjoy, sweetheart. This is yours. All yours.*

The beginnings of an orgasm stirred inside her, nerve ends tingling in awareness, woken by his insistent, pounding strokes. He showed her no mercy, and when she tensed a taut smile tightened across his lips, baring his sharp, white teeth. Corinne always found it hard to orgasm from regular sex, needing extra stimulation on her clit to come, but Aidan seemed to know what she needed before she needed it.

He came down to her, resting his weight on his elbows, changing his angle of entry so he rubbed against her clit with each stroke. "Oh God!" No longer able to think, she arched hard so that only her shoulders and ass touched the cushions under them. She climaxed so quickly she hardly realized it was coming. No slow build-up, this. Another orgasm followed on the heels of the last one, and then she felt as though she was climbing in a series of sparkling climaxes, each one greater than the last, small explosions like an expensive firework, building to the big one at the end.

He put one hand under her back, supporting her, and continued pounding into her body, not stopping until she'd reached the top of the cascade, where she burst in a deluge of passion, coming with an intensity she'd never known before.

They pressed so closely to each other that she felt the moment his orgasm started, the sac holding his balls tightening. She opened her eyes to see him. His head was thrown back, his body drove hard inside her, and his lips opened again over his clenched, white teeth. With a strangled cry he came, his whole body tensing in a delicious symphony of muscular strength.

She felt the pulsing and then another orgasm hit her, an echo of the mighty climax that had climbed through her body a few moments before. The strength of his had roused her again.

So when she came to herself, she was still shuddering slightly, held safely in his arms, twined around him still, but on her side now.

She lifted her head to receive a soft, sweet kiss and let her head fall against his shoulder. He folded her close and at last closed his eyes. She joined him, but not before she glimpsed something she couldn't remember seeing before on his body. When she slid her leg down his, she felt heat under her thigh, even more heat than they'd generated together and looked down to see what burned her.

A tattoo-like mark glowed on his thigh. A tiny bird, each feather perfectly drawn in red, but burning like fire, shades of orange and gold shimmering on his leg.

She stared at him, knowing he'd felt her flinch. His smile drove straight into her heart. "Don't worry about it. Sleep now, just for a while."

She obeyed him, letting herself slip into a beautifully restful doze.

* * * * *

John Westfall was working in his office when he felt it. Something was in his house, something he'd waited for years to contact. Psychic strength, massive waves of it, pulsed through the atmosphere. He'd only felt strength like this once before, on his wedding night. Ever since then, he'd searched for it, knowing untold power lay there. The only constant need in John's life was power.

He couldn't generate the power, but he could sense it and he knew when a psychic was around. Sometimes he'd made contact, but always the psychic refused all knowledge. They lied in some cases. He'd even married one, once.

Now here it was. The power drew him with seductive intensity. John stood up and left his office, murmuring something to his secretary as he passed her.

Outside his office in the thickly carpeted corridor, he paused to take his bearings and then turned left.

He was right. The feeling got stronger. This was no imaginary power, this was real. This was awesome. He strained toward it.

It led to the door of the rehearsal room.

When he cautiously tried the door, he found it locked. It didn't matter. He had keys. He turned to go back to his office and then paused at the small door next to the one to the rehearsal room. The sound booth.

When he tried the door, it opened silently. Normally he would take steps to discover who left the door open and sack them. These rooms held too much expensive equipment, not to mention the recordings bootleggers and thieves would love to get their hands on, for John to take chances with security. But now he silently blessed the careless cleaner who hadn't locked up after herself.

The booth lay shrouded in darkness, but John knew the layout well. He insisted that the staff kept the booths tidy, although not every engineer obeyed this dictate. He had to pay extra if a cleaner found syringes, rolled-up paper tubes or vestiges of powder clinging to the inside of self-seal plastic bags, just to keep her mouth shut. When had cleaners got so wise to drugs?

No one had used this booth for a while. He stood well back from the large window so they wouldn't see him.

They'd thrown the sofa cushions on the floor and lay there, bodies entwined. Splinter had his back to the booth while Corinne lay cozily in his arms, breathing deeply in sleep, her dark hair mingling with his flaming red shade, her limbs twined between his longer, stronger ones.

John knew Corinne wasn't a virgin. He'd thrown men at her in the past in an effort to keep her with him, men who did what he told them to do. Now Corinne was playing into his hands again, although he hadn't instigated the move this time, hadn't suspected what Hawthorne could be. But the strange symbol he saw on Aidan Hawthorne's upper thigh threw his plans for Corinne and her sisters into the back of his mind.

A bird, a glowing red bird that faded as he watched until it disappeared. Unusually for a rock star, the only other tattoo Aidan possessed was a burning rose on his upper arm, the same one all the band sported. The other—that was a brand of power.

John hardly believed what he'd seen, but he knew what it meant. He'd seen that mark before, in an old book, one of the grimoires he kept under lock and key.

He'd caught himself a firebird.

Chapter Three

❧

Thursday arrived quickly, together with Scott Marsh, the engineer who was to mix the charity album. When informed Splinter was to join the track, he grimaced. "Don't like working with rock and pop stars. Rock stars are usually better though. At least they know one end of a guitar from another. You should have said before then. I wouldn't have come until dinner time. Chances are he won't turn up until then." Drawing a crumpled pack of cigarettes and a Zippo lighter from the pocket of his worn and torn jeans, he glanced at the other occupants of the sound studio. The girls grimaced, but Corinne shrugged and he took that as permission. He flicked the lighter open with a metallic ting and lit the cigarette. Scott Marsh was an unreformed smoker, but he'd worked with Corinne on two of her previous albums, and they understood each other. The twins used a different engineer, someone who had a lot more input into the final product, someone who could turn their adequate voices into angelic ones, but Corinne never needed much tweaking to get her sound right. That was only when she used the gimmicky Perspex guitars onstage.

Scott went through to the sound booth and flicked on the light. They were in the new recording studio suite, several rehearsal rooms and three separate recording studios. This one was the smallest, but the one at the end of the corridor had room for a full orchestra. It brought John Westfall a great deal of money, since several large orchestras paid handsomely for the privilege. Corinne loved sitting in on the sessions, taking no part but enjoying the music, giving her soul a chance to fly free.

She sat on a stool and lifted her guitar from the stand. A craftsman in Spain had made it to her specifications. Its pale spruce top gleamed, a beautiful contrast to the polished rosewood body, and the mahogany neck fit in her hand like another limb. She would always have this—always have the solace of music. Even if her audience turned its back on her tomorrow or she turned her back on it, she'd make music to her dying day.

What chance was there to improve when she churned out album after album, performing to audiences so deeply uncritical they compared her to Segovia? She needed a change, audiences that didn't accept her as perfect. She needed to move on. As usual when her mind turned in this direction, she felt something like a small electric charge, turning her from her thoughts. It was so normal she hardly thought about it anymore, but now she wondered if it wasn't just a little odd.

Enough. One thing at a time. She tuned the guitar and stilled her hands, waiting for the girls to stop fussing and Tom to quiet. He was performing a few scales. He'd always played the flute and was good enough to play with an orchestra but didn't need the work. His family was well off, owning property in London that brought in a very comfortable income. In fact, Tom's family was stinking rich. It didn't make him any more attractive to Corinne. When he smiled at Ashley in the private, intimate way he used to use with her, Corinne was surprised to find she didn't feel a qualm. He turned that look on and off like a spotlight. At least Splinter had done that for her, freed her from any feelings for Tom.

"Your father's forming a band."

He'd mentioned as much. Corinne shrugged and continued to tune her guitar.

"The girls, me—and you. And a few session musicians."

That was news. Lifting her head, she met Tom's defensive stare. Defensive because he must know what she felt about that. She smiled. "No."

"Fuck no," Ashley said and tittered a laugh as if the expletive was somehow clever. "You're in, big sister. He's calling it the High C's, says it's because our income's down and he needs to repackage us."

Like parcels. "No way."

"Yes way." Paige came to stand in front of her, hands on her tightly denim-clad hips. "Dad says you're in and you have to do it. You're contracted to him. Every note you play in public is under his control."

Her heart sinking, Corinne realized it might just be true. She had signed the last contract seven years ago, when she was still euphoric with success and admiration, still believed everything the critics said about her. Critics, nothing. Her father probably had those in his pocket too. Still, she wouldn't do it. She had no intention of doing anything until she'd had that fucking contract checked by an independent legal professional. If her contract was really watertight, she'd walk away and record nothing if she had to.

She checked her watch. Another fifteen minutes and she'd excuse herself and leave her phone on so that they could call her when they wanted her. She needed to think. And in any case, she couldn't bear sitting there waiting for him, as though this was just another recording session, just another guest artist. Thank goodness they weren't using the same room they used last time. She wouldn't have been able to bear it. Corinne tended to use the old studio as a rehearsal room, but she hadn't set foot in it since—since last Monday.

She had no idea how she'd react when he came—if he came.

Without fanfare, the door swung silently open and he stood in the opening. He carried two guitar cases, one in each hand, he wore torn jeans and an old concert t-shirt—not his, but an Iron Maiden one—and a worn leather jacket.

His attention went straight to her, not bothering to pretend interest in anyone else. He strode into the room and straight across to her. "How are you?" He murmured the words, obviously meaning them only for her.

Corinne tried to breathe. His entrance robbed her of thought for a moment. None of her boyfriends had affected her like that before, even in the first throes of the affair. "I'm fine," she managed weakly. Her voice sounded thready.

He frowned. "You don't sound fine. Later. Tell me later."

There'd be a later? Corinne had psyched herself up for the recording, didn't know if she could stand a later. But if it ended like last time—oh yeah, she might force herself to stand it.

A hush fell over the room. Even Tom stopped forcing notes through his flute. Suddenly aware of the silence, Corinne blushed and looked away. Aidan's chuckle was taunting, aimed at Tom and the twins. "Hi, I hope I haven't kept you waiting." He didn't sound as if he cared much.

"Well, actually—" Tom began self-importantly, but Splinter talked right through him.

"It's just as well Ryan's staying with me, because I'd have slept right through it. He's started going on early morning runs, but it won't last long. Still, he woke me up and here I am. Otherwise you wouldn't have seen me this side of noon." He put down the cases very carefully, unlike when he'd dumped the Strat down last Monday.

The twins devoured him with their eyes, voraciously assessing his shape and the outline of his form in the well-worn clothing that fit him like a second skin. Not at all put off, he stared back. They wore carefully selected casual clothes, ironed jeans with a Dolce & Gabbana label clearly prominent on Ashley's, Levi's on Paige's. Their tops were designer, their jewelry coordinated to match their outfits. Their personal outfitter had trained them well. Corinne had long since developed her own style, with what amounted to two wardrobes—public and private. It was rare she chose a public outfit to wear in private, but she'd done that last Monday.

And look where that ended. Fucked in every sense of the word, mooning over a man who probably hadn't given her a second thought since he walked away through the studio door.

She'd get over it. When she fucked a man, Corinne knew from experience that she would adore him for two or three weeks, then begin to see the person underneath the glamour. The sex seemed to give them a sense of specialness that often didn't exist past the first month. This was no different. At least, that was what she tried to tell herself, but inside, honesty told her there was far more to it than that this time.

"Who's Ryan?" Tom asked, chin out. No longer the sole alpha in the room, he showed signs of belligerence. An alpha challenged on his own turf.

"My brother." Ryan, the singer and lyricist with Pure Wildfire, incredibly hot, but in an androgynous, Bowie-as-Ziggy kind of way. She'd stick with Aidan. Not that she'd have much chance of that, she recalled, her mouth twisting in self-denigration.

Supremely at ease, Aidan shrugged out of the jacket and let it drop to the floor before hooking a stool with one long leg and dragging it closer. He meant to sit with her, Corinne realized. She would have to sit here and smell that gorgeous scent of male and light cologne, play her guitar and pretend not to care. She wanted to hear him call her "baby" and "sweetheart" again in that breathless, intimate way he'd used last Monday. She wanted to touch him, lie with him in the relaxed but contented mood he'd evoked in her. After the hot, passionate mood of a few minutes before, of course.

None of that was going to happen. While he unpacked his guitar and settled himself, then tuned the instrument with an expert touch, she held her peace and looked anywhere but at him.

Paige wanted him. Corinne could tell from the sideways glances her sister kept shooting at him while she pretended to study her music. Well, she couldn't have him. Corinne couldn't stop Aidan from having any woman, but she was damned if she would let her little sister take this from her without a fight. The experience was hers and she'd fight to keep it.

The voice in her head, so like his, soothed her with a gentle *Shhhh*. She looked around, startled, the heavy wings of her hair slapping against her cheeks, but no one had spoken, no one else had noticed the sound. She wondered if she were going mad. It wouldn't surprise her in the least.

Aidan glanced across to the big window and his mouth tightened when he saw Scott Marsh sitting behind the desk, but he said nothing. He glanced around. "Ready when you are."

They did it in three takes. On the first, Paige was so engrossed with Aidan she fluffed her first line. On the second, it was Ashley, trying to cover up a bum note from Tom. The third wasn't perfect, but it was adequate. When they were done, Aidan stood up and put his guitar down, propping it up against the keyboard that stood ready but not needed on this session, indicating either a break or that he'd done. "Play it back," he commanded Scott. "Let's hear what that one sounded like."

Better than she'd thought. A lilting folk song, the twins reasonably together in their rendition of the lovelorn lass waiting for her fisherman lover to come back from the sea. They missed the point of the song—that the fisherman was never coming back—and sounded cheerful, emphasizing the wrong phrase in the last verse, the love instead of the loss. But it would do. It would probably feature high in the singles chart for a week or two and remain on a few shelves for a while. And it would help the charity, one of her father's pet projects, the PHR or Perfect Human Race, set up to fight poverty and starvation in the world.

Corinne leaned back. Aidan sat in front of her now, so she could watch him without seeming to, her attention ostensibly on the engineer in the sound booth. She watched his shoulders flinch ever so slightly at each misinterpretation, but he said nothing. At the end of the piece, he said, "That should do. A bit of a cleanup and we're good to go." He stood up and glanced back at the box. "Don't wreck it with strings, Marsh. It sounds better as it is." Without waiting for a response, he turned to Corinne. "I need to see Westfall. Is he in?"

Corinne nodded. This was probably the last time she'd see him so close. The next time would be on a stage fifty feet away, if she could bear to go. He'd probably forgotten the promised "later". She had a ticket for the second London performance and a story ready to excuse her absence, but she had no intention of telling him that.

Aidan glanced back at her, his hot gaze licking her from head to toe. "Don't go anywhere."

Corinne stared at him in shock. "Why?"

"What I have to say to your father might concern you."

"What about us?" Paige sounded a little shrill after her recent exertions at the microphone. She took off her heavy headphones and shook her head to fluff up her hair. The twins didn't have Corinne's heavy fall of black hair, but a lighter brunette shade that curled up prettily at the ends.

"I don't think you'll be needed," Aidan said, hardly giving Paige a passing glance. He turned back to Corinne. "If you need a retake, let me know and we'll do it before I leave."

He left. The brief eye contact sank down to her soul, searing, as though he knew what she thought, what she felt.

That was that then. They might, if she was lucky, get together for a video, even then they might film their different parts in different places, only to come together on the film.

Her encounter with a rock star meant more to her than she'd meant it to, but she couldn't be sorry. For a short while, she'd felt as one with someone else, enough to jolt her out of her pleasant existence and make her realize this life wasn't enough for her. Now, even if she never saw him again, she owed him for that.

So why did the thought of never seeing him again make her heart plummet into her shoes?

She listened to the vacuous chatter of her sisters and kept her head bent over her guitar, picking out a tune.

"That's one of Pure Wildfire's, isn't it?"

Corinne hadn't noticed until Ashley spoke. Now she realized what she was playing. She stilled her hands on the strings.

"Isn't that 'Tearing Me Apart'?"

She feigned nonchalance. "Is it? He played it when he came before, don't you remember?" Too late, she remembered he'd played it for her alone.

Ashley frowned, the creases on her brow making her look adorably vulnerable. Corinne had watched her practice that particular expression in the mirror. "I don't think he did. I heard it on the radio."

"Perhaps that's where I heard it." She lifted her guitar and took her time putting it back on its stand.

Paige's voice came tauntingly from behind her. "She fancies him! She wants Splinter!" Corinne looked up and met her sister's bold stare. "You do, don't you?"

She met this head on. "Don't you? You'd have to be blind not to fancy him."

"A bit of rough? Is that it?" That was Tom, adding his mite.

She regarded him for a short moment before answering. "After you, Tom, everything is rough." She was delighted when he blushed hotly and looked away.

The door opened to reveal her father's secretary. "Mr. Westfall wants to know if you can spare him a moment."

"I believe so." When the girls made to follow her, Miss Grantham held up a restraining hand. "Just Corinne for now, he says."

Corinne felt her sisters' glares all the way out of the room.

She followed Miss Grantham to her father's office, although she knew the way very well. Miss Grantham was the epitome of the secretary—middle-aged, smartly dressed, unobtrusive except when she was required to be otherwise. She'd been with her father for years, and still Corinne didn't know her first name. She seemed to prefer it that way. Normally Corinne would have walked with her and chatted, but this time she wanted to think. Why only her?

She was no nearer an answer when she entered the office and found her father sitting in his leather chair and Splinter on the couch, feet propped up on the coffee table in front of him. His attention moved to her when she entered and he gave her a lazy grin. Nothing of Aidan seemed to exist in this decadent creature. She'd have been afraid to meet him for the first time if he'd been like this. But it was also the image that excited her—the degenerate, anything-goes image he projected. His hair fell from its tie to the seat behind him like a tail, triumphantly red, challenging the tasteful blacks and grays of the office. He grinned. "Hi, babe."

Not "baby", but an insolent "babe". Bewildered, she turned her attention to her father. Tight-lipped, he sat bolt upright.

"You wanted to see me?" That sounded childish, like a schoolgirl ordered to the headmaster's study. Oh well, she couldn't help that now.

Her father heaved a sigh from the bottom of his soul. "We've reached an impasse, so I decided it was time to bring you in on the discussion. Sit down."

Splinter slanted her a look through half closed eyes and waved a hand. Corinne crossed the room and sat in the chair on one side of her father's desk—a soft leather chair, far more comfortable than the one he kept in front of his desk, which was slightly lower than his and straight backed, aimed at making the sitter uncomfortable. Splinter's low chuckle didn't bother her—at least that was what she told herself.

She looked at her father enquiringly.

He smiled, all teeth and sincerity. "I've suggested to Splinter here that you join Pure Wildfire. Purely on a temporary basis, of course, until I can organize the new band with your sisters and Albright."

The words, spoken so calmly, rocked her world. She clutched the arms of the chair. "What? How can I? That's not my market, not what I do!"

"But you know all their work, don't you?" There was only one way he could have known that. Splinter must have told him. At that moment, she felt only hatred for him and the way he'd casually revealed her secret. The knowledge that he'd betrayed her poisoned her memories of that interlude they'd shared. It was gone, nothing left to keep her warm in the long, cold nights ahead.

She glared at her father. "It makes an interesting exercise sometimes, yes."

"Don't get all stiff on me, girl. It could be useful." John Westfall leaned forward, hands curled around the edge of his desk. "Listen to me and use that brain. At least you have one, unlike your dimwit sisters. You know I want you in a new band. Folksy, less classical, though you can't junk all the classics. Older stuff, Elizabethan and medieval. You, the girls and Tom for ballast." Some ballast. She started to reply, but her father hadn't done speaking. "Guesting with Pure Wildfire will ease you into the pop world, give you a bit of cred and make the critics sit up."

Wildly, she glared at Splinter. What the hell was he thinking? A classical babe would be destroyed in the hothouse atmosphere of rock. True, they didn't play thrash, she'd be completely lost there, but sometimes the hard driving music verged on it. The fans would probably mob the stage and tear her apart. His only reply was an arrogant grin.

Her father continued to speak as if what he was saying wasn't the most insane proposal this side of the angel Gabriel rocking with the Rolling Stones. "You will join Pure Wildfire for the three concerts in London. They won't want you to do anything more than backup. Splinter," he paused fastidiously as though he found it hard to pronounce the word, "Splinter plays lead guitar. He informs me that he needs someone to—" he smiled faintly.

"To fuel the machine," came the deep voice from the sofa. He gave her that lazy smile again. "The sound behind me needs to be full. Do you know the second guitar parts?"

"Not really." She'd concentrated on the dazzling playing upfront, only barely aware of the solid backing below. Now that she thought about it, she saw how necessary it was. Matt had been only adequate, but their first guitarist had been brilliant, taking the occasional solo, filling the songs with sound and fury.

"Well, the first concert's in three weeks' time."

"We usually sleep between them," Splinter put in. His slurred words made him sound drunk. "Or do something else." The last words were definitely provocative. Corinne ignored them, but the irritation remained. "I've told him it won't happen. You'd have to pass an audition. We're a dem-democratic band and we all vote on new members." His stumble on the big word was deliberate, she was sure, but she didn't know why she knew.

"I can cope with that kind of concert schedule as long as I get the rehearsal time."

"We do things a bit different."

"I know." She kept her words bland and dry, although she felt like screaming at him. Didn't it mean anything to him? She knew their reputation, read about them and still she'd opened up to him. Corinne wasn't sure whom she was angrier with—herself or Aidan Hawthorne. Or Splinter, that arrogant, insolent man sitting not ten feet away from her.

She'd cope. Classical musicians weren't exactly angels. Or perhaps he thought they were. Then he was in for a few surprises, if she had anything to do with it.

What was she thinking of? This proposal was ridiculous. She said so. "This is stupid. Who's going to accept me as a member of Pure Wildfire?"

"It could be done," Splinter said. "If you go out with me."

Chapter Four

ဢ

"What?" Corinne couldn't have been more astonished if he'd asked her to fly to the moon with him. "What on earth are you talking about?"

He sat quite still, his lips curved in a smile she didn't know how to interpret. Was he sneering at her or inviting her to join in the joke? What fucking joke?

Her father heaved another great sigh. "I want to increase awareness of you at street level. I told Hawthorne about the band and he agreed you need more pop culture. More—"

"Britney?" offered a cool voice from the sofa.

He got a daggers look for his pains. "Hardly. But something like that."

"You want her to record with us too?" Aidan's voice dripped acid.

"No, not necessarily. Just play with you at Hammersmith."

"The Hammersmith Apollo?" Corinne mouth dropped open as the final dart hit the mark. Of course the ticket in her wallet said Hammersmith, but she hadn't thought of it before. She'd played at many important venues, in Britain and abroad, but the Hammersmith Apollo was one of the apogées of rock music. She couldn't possibly play there. Pure Wildfire's performances there were to be the finale to a long tour of Britain and Europe, the last three concerts before the band went into the studio to write the next album and plan their assault on America. It meant a lot to Pure Wildfire. They had to be perfect.

"Yeah, just that." Splinter sounded cynical and she didn't blame him, despite hating him for his betrayal.

"I can't do that, Dad."

"Yes, you can. I've planned it all out. At least, I had." Her father concentrated all his formidable personality on her. She would never get used to the sheer power in his gaze. When she was little, she'd read Trilby and convinced herself she was being hypnotized by her Svengali father. Of course, that was all nonsense. Nobody could do that, it was only a story.

"You'll play at Hammersmith. I've organized a backup session musician, so you don't even have to play the whole set if you don't want to. Just appear there. Then you can do a few interviews with the press, admit you've always loved rock and buy yourself an electric guitar. That should do it. Then you do a few more interviews and let slip that you're forming a band with your sisters. I'm getting somebody to do the first single and we'll get the first album out for Christmas."

"Jesus!" The exclamation made Corinne and her father look in Aiden's direction. "Can't you just let talent show through?"

John Westfall made a sound of disgust. "I could if I wanted midlist! Look, you know and I know that Corinne's talent is real, but I have to lead the girls. They can do it, but only after rehearsal and a bit of tweaking in the sound booth."

Splinter's mouth curled in a sneer. "I saw Scott Marsh in the booth."

"You don't like him?"

"He's good at what he does, but Pure Wildfire's music is better without strings. The one time you persuaded us to try him, he turned us into some kind of soft rock setup. We might as well have our hair cut in fucking mullets."

Corinne stifled a giggle, but the smile he flashed at her was genuine, just a little of the Aidan she'd discovered behind closed doors. She turned away. This was stupid and they hadn't even got to the most ridiculous thing of all!

"So I play at Hammersmith, astound the crowd with my skill and have a wild affair with Splinter?" Her scorn hid the longing she felt, the firm denial of her own "if only" daydreams.

Aidan's voice softened. "It's the only way the fans will accept you. If I've fallen for you, if I can't bear to be without you, they'll call me stupid until they see you onstage."

"So I'm to be Yoko to your John? Linda to your Paul?" Now it was her turn to drip acid.

"Something like that. Except you'll be onstage with us."

She snorted. "More like Courtney to your Kurt."

"You know that's out of the question." Corinne was glad her father had some feelings left for his daughter, but his next words put paid to that thought. "She's under my care, not yours. *I* control her career."

"I don't want to control her fucking career." The words were flat and somehow Corinne knew Aidan was about to say something else. Something that remained unsaid. She might never know what he wanted to say, because she meant to leave the room soon. The whole thing was ridiculous.

Splinter hissed between his teeth, a short sound of disgust before he spoke. "It's not up to me if she joins the band, even temporarily. It's in the contract we have with you, if you look for it. The existing members of the band have to agree on it. No voting, just a straight agreement. All in or none at all. So she'd have to play for them. But if you want her to join your girl band, I can help. I'll take her to London and take her around the clubs on the circuit. The press will love it. I'll romance her, show her off. It'll give us both some publicity. And I'll only do that because I like her, not because you want me to."

It was a travesty. What they shared on Monday had been wonderful, an hour out of time. Now he wanted to pervert all that, turn it into yet another fucking publicity stunt. Turn sugar to shit. She wouldn't do it. She wanted to keep her memories.

"When are you going to London?" she asked abruptly, breaking into the negotiations.

Aidan looked at her. Not Splinter, but Aidan, just for a moment. Then the eyelids dropped and he was the arrogant stranger again. "Today. As soon as you're ready. The car's outside."

She could never see him again, except when she watched from a distance.

Her father had fallen silent, his lips pressed tightly together, his hands clasped in front of him in a gesture she knew meant he was thinking. She chose not to break the silence and Splinter seemed happy with his own thoughts. Eventually the guitarist got to his feet. "I've said all I can. If you like, I'll take her to London and she can audition, but I don't know if she'll get into the band. It's not my call and it's not your call either. We'll go to the clubs, become an item." He turned his head and stared at Corinne, the rock star gone, only Aidan Hawthorne in his gaze. "You could always marry me."

Corinne's head spun at his sincere expression, but she forced herself to ignore his charismatic appeal. That last comment proved he wasn't serious. He was taking the piss, trying to trick her.

Her father's head went up at that, speculation sparking the dark depths. "It's a thought. I want it in writing, though, that you'll separate as soon as the concerts are over."

Splinter turned his head, one hand on the doorknob. "Not bloody likely. Can you imagine what the press would do with that if they got hold of it? The furthest I'll go is an interview with *Hello* magazine. That's the offer. Take it or leave it."

He opened the door and left. The door clicked behind him with a finality Corinne also felt.

She didn't know who angered her more—Splinter or herself. She'd allowed herself to dream, to put herself in a position she could never hold. Only when her secret daydreams were within reach did she realize how stupid they were. To think for one minute she could hold her own with a band as exciting, as musically proficient as Pure Wildfire!, The first two albums, *Sunfire* and the live one, *Pure Wildfire Live* had gone gold faster than any other albums in the past five years, even counting phenomena and fads. The third would take them into hyperspace, the Rock and Roll Hall of Fame and they would be invincible, creating a backlist that would earn for the rest of their lives. If they didn't blow it, like taking on an unsuitable new member. America beckoned.

She couldn't compete with that. Pure Wildfire was way out of her league. And what Splinter had done to her in this room made her so mad she might have called his bluff, just for a moment. Flaunting an affair as a publicity stunt! He meant it too. There was no subterfuge in his words, no hidden agenda. She'd been a good fuck, that was all. She'd bet he'd taken a few groupies to bed since then. Splinter was famous for his predilection for women and equally known for not getting involved with any of them.

The whole band was like that, except for Ryan's affair, which had ended with the woman's death five years ago from a drug overdose. It might have been Ryan's experience that put Splinter off long-term involvements or perhaps his drying-out session from heroin accomplished it. Either way, since he'd sobered up, the seediest clubs had missed his presence. Corinne had seen an article in the Sunday paper bemoaning spectacular rock star deaths. The members of Pure Wildfire featured in the list of deaths to come, but at the moment they were bucking the "live hard, die young" trend.

"You should do it." Her father had spoken, and like a god, he was usually obeyed. Not this time.

"No. I won't. It's grotesque."

"Normally, I'd let you make that decision, but there's something you don't know."

"What?" She couldn't imagine what would make the difference.

"He's a firebird."

She frowned, wondering what he was talking about now. "No, he's not, his band's called Pure Wildfire."

Her father got to his feet, pushing his hands on the desk. His knuckles turned white and Corinne guessed he'd prefer to clench them and hit something. He'd never hit them, but he had a punching bag in the gym. It was a shame he wanted her to do this stupid stunt, but she wouldn't budge. She wouldn't audition for the band, she wouldn't marry or even go out with Splinter for the publicity.

"Your error." John crossed the room to one of the glass-fronted bookshelves and took out a well-thumbed volume, a large book bound in blue, with one of the clear covers her father used to keep his favorite volumes clean. Corinne's heart sank. This was his obsession, his folly. Old grimoires, studying magic and mysticism. She knew why he did it too—the only thing that mattered to John Westfall—power.

Outside, a dull day had brightened up and a shaft of clear sunshine spilled across the desk. Her father returned, blocking the dazzling light, and put the book in front of her. "There," he said.

She looked. She read.

Firebird. A legendary bird. They are gregarious, whatever form they take. They are shape-shifters, able to move from man to bird at will. They control fire. They live for five hundred years and perhaps more. In bird form, they are larger than eagles and invincible. In human form, they are vulnerable to injury, but they will not catch diseases and they will not age.

They may be known by their coloring, which tends to the fiery. The sure sign is a tattoo-like symbol on the upper leg. It only appears during mating and only then to the woman they have a true affinity for. It takes the form of a glowing feather or a small firebird. It fades shortly afterward.

Firebirds prefer to mate for life, but they are not bound to one soul. They may convert a loved one to their own kind, but they may only do this once. They may bestow certain gifts on friends and lovers, but this writer has not yet discovered what they might be. See later editions for clarification.

The phoenix is a firebird. See under phoenix.

Corinne didn't bother turning to phoenix. She closed the book, slamming the cover down. "Dad, this is all nonsense. You've hankered after magic and sorcery for years, but it's never come to anything. When will you learn there is no such thing as magic, no such creatures as shape-shifters? You married my mother because you said she was a sorceress. It's a good job the press thought you meant in the general sense, because you could have been laughed out of court for that!"

"She still looked as young when she died as she did the day I married her," he pointed out.

"And you've never heard of plastic surgery?" Of all the reasons he could give for her joining the band, this had the least chance of persuading her. "Give it up, Dad. You've tried for years to find a real example of genuine paranormal activity, but there's never been any proof, never anything you could show, and you've spent thousands of pounds looking."

Her father's lips tightened in suppressed anger. "They don't give their secrets away, you have to trap them into it. You've seen that mark on Hawthorne, haven't you?"

She paused, shocked. Yes, she'd seen it, just after they'd made love—fucked, rather. No, rock stars had tattoos. All over the place. She hadn't noticed any, apart from the bird and the burning rose, but she should have asked him for the guided tour. "No, how could I have seen it?" She wasn't about to encourage John's stupid obsession with the occult. Splinter had a tattoo. Big deal.

He didn't answer her question, but she already knew. Only a couple of ways he could have seen Splinter's bird tattoo and she didn't think there were any pictures of Splinter in swimming trunks. Which meant her father had seen them last Monday. Shit, fuck and damn.

"Corinne, I want a feather."

Fury colored her words. "I'll go and buy you one. A great big pink ostrich feather."

"I want a firebird feather. I want a feather from his breast, one he gave to you of his own free will. It'll give me more power than I know what to do with."

Corinne tsked. "I doubt that. You could stand in for God if he got sick and not be overwhelmed by the experience."

She got to her feet. She'd made up her mind. If she stayed here, her father would nag and nag until she walked out or gave in just for some peace. No, on this matter she wouldn't give in. But she could go away until the storm passed.

Or perhaps she'd never come back. The only part of her life that her father controlled was her professional life. If she abandoned her career, there wasn't much he could do about it. This might be the chance she needed, a chance to take legal advice, sound out the music colleges and prepare to leave the business called show.

This time he'd let her go and he wouldn't expect her back for a while. Westfall kept as tight a hold on his investments as he could, and she and her sisters were less daughters, more valuable assets to him. It was just the chance she needed, to get away and to stay away. By the time she'd consolidated her financial position, changed her bank accounts, booked her ticket to the Conservatory or somewhere else, it would be too late for him to stop her. Especially if she announced her decision to the press. He could stop her performing for anyone else, but right now she didn't give a fuck about that.

She was furious, at her father's cynical exploitation of her, at Splinter's casual attitude toward an experience she'd considered special. "I'll go to London with him, but not for your bloody feather. Because I fancy him, Dad. I've already had sex with him and I want to do it again. If my own father's going to pimp for me, I might as well do it willingly." She might, at that. Before she left him in the dust.

When she crossed the room, her feet made no sound on the deep-pile carpet. "I'll go and pack. You can tell him, if you like."

An hour later, she was packed. She only took two cases, large bags on wheels, the kind she used on tour. After she'd found her two favorite guitars, she'd be ready to leave this house, perhaps for good. She left the Perspex ones. Hopefully, she'd never pick up another one again. Ever.

Disdaining calling for help, Corinne dumped the bags in the main hall while she went to the music room for the guitars. When she returned, the hall was empty. Splinter came through the outer door. "Your father told me you were coming. Ready?"

She nodded and glanced back at the hall. She would never come back here. When she felt the familiar twinge in her mind that appeared at every rebellious thought, it immediately went away, but she didn't block it. It felt as if someone had blocked it for her. Strange, that had never happened before.

Painted panels in ivory faced her and the irritating mix of old and new taunted her with its pointlessness. Well, she wouldn't have to look at it again, either the nondescript oil paintings or the abstracts and bland, but trendy, sculptures. She snapped her fingers at it all and turned to leave.

The car, as she might have expected, was an SUV, one of those large vehicles meant for many people, not just the two of them. The driver waited impassively behind the wheel. He wasn't wearing a uniform. When she stepped inside, she saw most of the seats were folded away. A TV was bolted to the chassis on an adjustable bracket, two speakers on either side of it and several gleaming contraptions below, which she assumed were CD players, DVD players and the like. She couldn't see her luggage, except for her guitar cases. He stacked these on a rack in front of his and used a strap to secure them. "I had this cradle designed for guitars. Before that, I used to use the safety belts."

Despite the fury boiling under her surface, she smiled, recognizing the man who loved his music. "I do that too." The smile made her even angrier. His easy charm, now back to the fore, must have been what fooled her the first time. He saw her expression but waited for her to choose a seat. She chose one by the window. He sat next to her but didn't attempt to touch her. Just as well. She might have hit him.

The car pulled away smoothly. The graveled drive to the manor was carefully designed, like the rest of the house. He spoke, very softly. "What's wrong?" The car slowed down while the iron gates opened softly on well-oiled hinges, silently setting her free.

"You can ask that?" She turned a face of fury to him, no longer able to hide her hurt and anger.

"What? You knew that scene was all playacting, surely?"

"Which? Oh, don't tell me, all that in the rehearsal room last Monday."

The car began to pick up speed. "No. That was real."

"Tell me about it."

Silence fell. After a few minutes, he looked up from his clenched hands and spoke again. "Your father said you agreed. Why would you want to be with me if you think that wasn't real?"

She turned to him, more in control now, her mouth a thin line of dislike. "I'm not going to be with you. The only reason I stepped into this car is that I need to get away from this fucking place. You can drop me at the Savoy when we get to London."

"I see." He looked away, at the green hedges marking the edge of her father's estate as they whipped past the car window. "I was hoping you'd consider it. You're good enough to pass the audition, despite what I told your father. You can do it, Corinne."

"Why do you want me? Do you need the publicity?"

71

"Hardly." He turned around and grasped her hand, not letting it go even when she twisted it. "Did you believe all that crap in your father's office?"

"What crap? I heard a rock star laying down the law. Let me go!"

"Not until you tell me what you think went on back there. Let's have it straight, Corinne. It's the only way we're going to get past this."

She stopped struggling. He was stronger than she thought. She was only hurting herself. "You and my father cooked up some kind of obscene publicity stunt. I'm supposed to fuck you so that he can start his damned band on the back of the exposure. Well, I don't intend to have anything to do with it. I'm going to Paris or New York or somewhere. I'm going to study."

"Good. But stay with me anyway."

She stared into those incredible eyes. They seemed to glow, deep inside. She could almost believe her father's nonsense about firebirds. "Why?"

"Because I want you. Because some of that nonsense made sense. Because if you do that, I can help protect you from your father."

Her eyes widened in shock. "Protect? I don't need protecting! I have money, I can free enough up, and I don't need babysitting anymore."

He released her wrist with an abruptness that made her fall back. He leaned over to stop her banging her head on the window and she ended up in his arms. Again.

"How could you live like that?" he murmured, his mouth close to her ear, his breath hot on the rim.

She drew back, but he didn't let her go. She didn't fight him, but strangely, she wasn't afraid. She was in a car with a man she hardly knew and she wasn't as afraid as she felt sometimes in her own room in the house. Something she'd long put down to paranoia. "Live like what?"

"Always being watched and monitored. Never being completely alone."

"I don't know what you're talking about."

He stared at her, the sparks in his eyes sharpening. "You don't, do you?"

She felt something gentle in her mind, something that didn't feel as though it started with her. As though he was *inside* her head. She blinked and the sensation went away. "I must be tired."

"Then you can get some sleep on the way to London. But we need to do something else first." He turned his head and raised his voice. "Mike, can you go back to the house? Corinne's forgotten something."

"No, I haven't!"

The car stopped at the next rest area and reversed into it.

"Yes, you have." He continued to talk while the driver turned the car and set out, back the way they came. "You haven't noticed. You probably live with it every day, but as a stranger to the place, I noticed. They must be better concealed in the recording suite, because I never noticed them there, but I saw them in his office and in the other sound room."

"What? What the fuck are you talking about?"

"The cameras. I'd like to bet there are listening devices too, but they're easier to hide."

Her world spun dizzyingly on its axis. "C-cameras?"

"It's something you learn to look for when the paparazzi are after you. But no sleazy tabloid planted these. They've been in place awhile. A few are painted over, decorated when the rest of the place was."

She didn't want to believe it. Seeming to feel her confusion, he held her gently but firmly. "That was the reason for the playacting in your father's office. I don't want him to know what you want, or what I want, until it's too late. You're going back so you can see for yourself. There must be something you need to collect from your rooms."

"I—I suppose so. Too late for what?" She felt numb with shock, unable to feel a thing.

"For Westfall to realize you're not going back."

Okay, so she'd trust him. For now.

They were at the gates at the end of the drive. The man in the security booth saw them and opened the great wrought-iron portals. They rolled back to the front door. Aidan took her face in his hands and forced her to look at him. "I'll come in with you, so find something heavy for me to carry out. I'll show you the cameras, but don't stare at them or even seem to notice them. I don't want him to know we know."

She nodded numbly. Before he unclipped his seat belt, he leaned forward and kissed her very lightly on the lips, and then, before she could respond, he moved away.

After taking a few deep breaths, Corinne followed him.

* * * * *

He was right. Back in the car again, after an excursion in search of a particular plastic guitar, which took them to the rehearsal room and up to her apartment, Corinne had seen enough.

He didn't ask questions or gloat. Once back in the car, he fastened her seat belt for her and sat next to her again. When he reached for her hand, she didn't move it away but let it lie in his while she absorbed this new information.

The presence of the cameras and recording equipment put a new gloss on the scene in her father's study.

Even her bedroom had a camera in it. She'd been watched all the time she'd been in that house. Every move, every cough. She was glad she hadn't seen anything in the bathroom, but despite a definite feeling, she hadn't wanted to use it. "May we stop at the next service station?"

"What for?"

"I need to use the bathroom."

His hand tightened on hers briefly, and then he leaned forward to give the order. He didn't ask her why she hadn't used her own bathroom. He didn't need to.

The next stop proved to be a standard roadside café, where they decided to have coffee. Corinne found a little bleak amusement watching Aidan put on his jacket over his long ponytail. It made his hair a little less distinctive, and since many people dyed their hair bright red, he might get away with it. Not everybody liked rock music or recognized rock musicians. Her image as the white-clad waif was so distinctive she often got away with dressing in casual, brightly colored clothes and pulling her hair off her face with a clip. Just as she had today, in fact.

He entered the place as Aidan, without Splinter's swagger and arrogance, holding the door for Corinne to pass through. They took a seat and their driver, Mike, went to get the coffees.

In the end, Corinne was recognized first. It was late afternoon, a natural time for people to stop for coffee. She stood in the bathroom, washing her hands, when she heard the hesitant voice behind her. "E-excuse me. Aren't you Corinne Westfall?"

She turned to find the drying machine. "Yes, I am." She'd learned it was best not to be forthcoming, but she rarely had the heart to be cruel or rude to people. They were her customers, her fans, it wasn't their fault she hadn't found happiness or fulfillment in her work.

The woman was younger than Corinne, fine blonde curly hair rioting about a face with a delicately pointed chin. She stared at Corinne, drinking in her appearance. "I love your music! I saw you last year at the Royal Albert Hall, I thought you were so good! You inspire me, you know? I'm a science student, but your music helps me to concentrate, it seems to put me in a different world."

Corinne forced her practiced smile. She had a mask every bit as good as Aidan's when she needed it. Hers was open and friendly, with a shy reserve that helped keep people at a distance. But it didn't work now. The other woman stepped forward and took her hands, turning them over to look at the palms. "I can't believe I'm touching the hands that make such magic! Will you be releasing a new album soon? I have all your backlist and I've nearly worn them out!"

The worst thing was to hear people like this, people who genuinely enjoyed what she did, especially when she'd made the decision to change. It would hurt them, but she couldn't go on hurting herself anymore, making music she didn't believe in. Again, she felt the twinge in her mind. Again, it disappeared, almost immediately.

The woman's avidity made Corinne feel nervous. "I've contributed a track to a new charity album with my sisters," she ventured, hoping the nugget would be enough to get her away.

The woman frowned and dropped Corinne's hands, which she was careful not to snatch back to her side. "Ashley and Paige haven't half your talent, but I suppose it's better than nothing. Will you sign something for me?"

"As long as it's not a check." The feeble joke, made so often in the past, did the trick. They smiled at each other, easier now.

The woman entered one of the cubicles and Corinne left the bathroom, hurrying toward the corner where Aidan sat with Mike.

Aidan stood up and let her take the seat nearest the window, smiling wryly. "My legs are too long to go under these tables," he commented, but frowned when he looked at her closer. "What's wrong?"

She shrugged. "A fan in the bathroom. She asked me to sign something, so she'll come over when she's done."

His expression of sympathy showed her he understood. "Perhaps we shouldn't have stopped for coffee."

She picked up the plain white cup and took a sip. "No, I needed this."

"We've got coffee in the car, but I thought you needed the break."

"I did."

The blonde woman came out of the bathroom and looked around the restaurant, her face lightening when she saw where Corinne sat. She didn't immediately come over to the table though. She crossed the tiled floor to two tables where several young women sat and chatted and leaned over.

The chatter increased and several people shot curious glances their way. "Give me some paper and a pen," Corinne said, accepting the inevitable. "I'll give her an autograph on the way out."

Aidan sighed. "It's not always like this."

"I know."

Then he groaned. It took her a few seconds to see why. Next to the coach already in the car park, another came to a halt and the door opened. Out of it poured a stream of young people, older schoolchildren or college students by the look of them. Many of them sported Pure Wildfire t-shirts. "Perhaps there's a back way out."

"They've blocked our car in," Mike gloomily observed.

Aidan put both hands to his forehead. "Nightmare! Why did we ever stop?"

"Could be worse," their driver, who seemed to be a philosopher on the side, said. "They could have been press."

"It's bad enough. Give that girl your autograph, Corinne, and we'll be off."

Mike pushed a piece of paper across the table and reached inside his jacket for a pen as the boisterous group entered the café. Some looked around, including one of the wearers of the t-shirts. "Perhaps he just likes the design," Aidan said hopefully.

Not so. The girl stared straight at him and screamed, a squeal of excitement. "It's him!" They heard the sound clear across the room, despite the excited hum from the seated girls staring at Corinne.

A man crossed the room and headed for the toilets. When he reached their table, he stopped. "I'm driving the coach. Is that yours?" He jerked his head at the car. Mike nodded. "Thought so. I'll move the bus so you can get out. My passengers are a bit pissed, they've been drinking all day." He stared at Aidan. "I don't recognize you, but they damn well do."

"Thanks, mate." Mike turned his attention to Aidan when the man moved away. "Will you be all right if I go and move the car?"

"Sure." With a sigh, Aidan leaned back and stretched his arm across the back of the seat. No point trying to hide now. Seeing the sense of it, Corinne leaned back and picked up her coffee. "Avoid eye contact," she murmured.

"Too late."

The girl who had spotted him crossed the room, another in her wake. People aimed several curious stares at them, not least from the staff behind the counter, who hadn't noticed them when they came in.

Aidan turned into Splinter, eyes hooded, mouth turned down in an arrogant sneer, and Corinne put on her mask of affability and shyness. She'd always valued her privacy, that was the main reason she'd chosen to live on her father's secure estate. What a mistake that turned out to be!

"You're Splinter," the girl declared. She had pink hair, but Corinne doubted it was real. It made a stark contrast with her milk-white face. The girl glared at Corinne but addressed Aidan. "What are you doing with *her*?"

"Why do you want to know?"

"She's a dork. A twat, a c—" The girl didn't finish her sentence, developing a sudden cough.

"She's none of your business." Menace lay underneath the drawled words.

"He's right." A masculine voice sounded just behind the girl, who continued to stare at Splinter. "Come away, Lissa. They deserve a bit of peace." The man put his arm around Lissa's shoulders, and turned her. He paused to glance back at Splinter. "Great music, man. You've given me some good times." Aidan smiled at him, the smile genuine this time.

The man led Lissa away, but she turned her head, staring. "She's got no right being with him," Corinne heard her say. "He's mine. He just doesn't know it yet."

"Come on, babe." Corinne glanced at Aidan, and made to stand, but before she could, the blonde girl confronted the pink-haired one, standing in the middle of the floor, blocking their exit. Corinne felt Aidan's hand on her shoulder and sank back in her seat. She felt tense, but it wasn't too bad. A shame the students were the worse for drink. At least some of them seemed to be.

The two women seemed to be discussing the merits of their favorite musicians. At the tops of their voices. An intellectual debate it was not and it soon degenerated into pushes. The man who had led the girl called Lissa away from their table glanced back at them and went over to the counter, leaning over to murmur a few words to the orange-clad man standing behind the coffee machine. The man cast them a startled glance then moved away. The rest of the staff seemed frozen to the spot, unwilling to interfere. "He's probably told the man to call the police," Corinne realized.

"They won't get here in time." A grim determination she'd never heard in him before entered his voice.

Now a man from the Corinne group confronted one from the Pure Wildfire group, demanding to know why their hero was in the presence of a goddess like Corinne. Corinne covered her face with her hands. "Oh God, this is awful!"

"Not so bad, sweetheart."

The furor grew and people were moving nearer to their table, blondie versus pinkie at its heart. A few half-hearted pushes followed and voices rose higher. Someone threw the inevitable first punch.

When someone fell heavily against their table, jarring the half-empty coffee cups, Corinne started back in alarm, straight into Aidan's arms. Aidan was growling now.

"Okay, that's it." He got to his feet and seemed to lift straight up into the air. Corinne wasn't sure how he landed on the table, but his booted feet flashed before her eyes then were gone and he was standing in front of her. It was so fast, it sent a hush over their end of the room.

By now, everyone was on their feet, and cups and plates crashed to the floor off the flimsy tables. Aidan ignored everything but Corinne, pulling her to her feet. He kept hold of her hand and turned to face the rabble.

By this time, the commotion had little to do with the instigators, but when Aidan stood, people took notice. Several fell back. "Out of our way!" Aidan said. He didn't raise his voice, but somehow, they heard him above the commotion. Corinne's heels slipped on the tiles when he pulled her hand and he immediately turned back, concern in his eyes.

She was quick to reassure him. "I'm fine." He nodded, and tugged her toward him, putting his arm protectively around her shoulders. She'd never felt safer in her life. In this roadside café, with the staff nowhere in sight and the way out through a mass of shouting, fighting people, she felt safe.

And nothing touched her. Not a shard of flying crockery nor a wayward fist. Nothing. It was as though he'd thrown up a barrier around her. Even the noise came to her mutedly.

Even so, it was a very long five minutes.

The fresh air outside hit her in a rush, but by now Aidan had tucked her under his arm, sheltered and unable to see much. When a door opened in front of her, she climbed aboard, helped by Aidan's thrusting arm, then he was behind her, slamming the door closed. "Okay, Mike, go!"

She fell back when the vehicle took off, but his arm stopped her falling and he pulled her against him, where she sat on his lap, cradled in his arms. After a moment, she took a few deep breaths and pulled away to see his eyes anxiously staring into hers. She gave him a rueful grin and slid off his lap on to her seat. "Pretty bad," she commented. "Do you get that a lot?"

"Do you?"

"Yes, but I've never seen it close up."

Mentally, Corinne drew the shreds of dignity around her, waiting for the trembling to stop. The goons her father employed kept all that away from her. She'd seen it at a distance, overexcited fans, but never so close. Never so visceral. She'd smelled the danger, the excitement, and for the first time realized what drove them.

He reached over and took her hand, helping her fasten her seat belt. He didn't let go of her hand afterward. "You felt the thrill and it excited you."

"How… no, of course not!"

When he turned his head to look at her, she found herself unable to lie to him. She wanted to pretend that it didn't matter, but he must know, even though she'd stopped trembling now. "I feel things and I can feel your emotions. I know you're scared, but that's natural. I wouldn't have let them hurt you, Corinne. You're safe with me."

She did feel safe, but he put her on edge at the same time, creating an inner tension she didn't know how to cope with. "How can you say that?"

He stared at her, not speaking. She felt warmth bathe her inside and knew he was causing it. For the first time in her life, she felt something otherworldly and recognized it for what it was. But it was a far cry from her father's mumbo-jumbo. She still couldn't believe all that.

Chapter Five

∞

Aidan glanced at Mike and, taking the hint, he slid up the privacy window, leaving him with Corinne behind one-way glass windows. He'd seen her first tear, and recognizing she'd had enough for one day, prepared to hold her. He couldn't tell her how he'd thrown up a psychic barrier, keeping everything away from them, or how he wanted to kill any of the fuckers who'd even dreamed of hurting her.

To be honest, his violent protectiveness scared even him. He'd never felt like that about a woman before. Love 'em and leave 'em had been his motto, though he never left them unsatisfied. Mentally bidding his carefree years goodbye, he set himself to the task of comforting the woman who'd driven a sword right through his heart. Or maybe that should be a plectrum.

Smiling at his own wry thoughts, he studied her. She half lay in his arms, where she belonged in his opinion, the armrest shoved up out of their way. Her lips, soft, pink and eminently kissable, still trembled a little. As he gazed at her, she looked up and their eyes met in a timeless, open confession.

He was kissing her before he realized he was going to. He stroked her lips with the tip of his tongue and she opened to him. Just like that. So natural, so easy, he hardly realized they'd gone from comfort to fire in less time than it took one of Ryan's superbikes to get from zero to sixty.

When he tried to drag her closer, onto his lap, he felt the resistance of her seat belt, but then it released and he had her. She must have unclipped it. Instead of lying across his lap, she moved to straddle him. Now he was toast. Complete and utter fucking toast.

Slanting his mouth across hers, he tasted her voraciously, opening up and easing his hands between them. He had to touch, feel her incredibly soft skin against his own.

But she seemed as hungry as he was, pulling at his t-shirt until he drew back. He let her drag his t-shirt over his head and then went for hers, managing to get hers off and to unclip her back-fastening bra in passing. He was good at this. Hot, fast, mind-blowing sex. He wanted to show her how good. His erection strained tightly against the zipper of his jeans. He felt every tooth digging into him.

His breath caught in his throat when he saw her breasts, so gorgeously, mouthwateringly full. He wanted to touch, taste, look. All at the same time. Then he stopped, trapped by the expression in her eyes. Remnants of hurt lingered there, not inflicted by him, but there. She needed comfort and reassurance, not this. He should stop. He shouldn't take advantage of her when she must be feeling vulnerable. Be a gentleman, be chivalrous.

Fuck that.

With her breasts in front of his face, her denim skirt hiked up to the top of her thighs and the scent of her arousal in his nostrils, Aidan breathed deep and enjoyed her. No way could he resist this.

A car sped past, illegally overtaking on the inside lane, but they couldn't see in through the heavily tinted one-way windows. Not that Aidan cared overmuch, but Corinne might. She didn't look as if she minded, staring down at his face, completely absorbed by him. "God, you smell so good!"

She shoved a small packet into his hand. Where the fuck had that come from?

Who cared? Panting, he tried his best to be good. "Baby, it might be adrenaline making you feel this way. Are you sure you want to do this?" Was he completely nuts to even think about asking her? Her breasts quivered in front of his face, but he took a deep breath and held off. If she didn't say something soon he'd be on her like a rutting bull.

"Are you insane? Would I be like this if I didn't?"

He was. Completely fucking insane and he feared it might get worse. Especially when she put impatient hands on his fly and undid his buttons. The relief when his cock burst free was short-lived when she swooped on it and opened her mouth right over the weeping tip.

"Fuck, woman!"

His head jerked to one side and he saw the passengers of another car as it passed them. Although he knew they couldn't see in, the way they stared at the SUV made him wonder if they could see vague shadows, him lying back in the seat while the hottest woman in the world gave him the best blowjob he could ever remember.

Fuck, where had she learned to move her mouth like that? Up and down, while her tongue did incredible things, dancing around the slit at the top, curving under the head to stroke the sensitive skin underneath. She drank him in, made appreciative noises at the back of her throat, driving him completely nuts.

At this rate, they wouldn't need the condom. He had to drag her off him, still wondering if she could make him come, then wait until he hardened again. But right now he didn't want to take the risk. He wanted inside her. Now. If not five minutes ago. She lay against him, moaning her need, her tits brushing his arm with every breath she took, her nipples so hard he wanted to bite them.

No, he decided as he rolled the condom over his aching cock. Not then. Then she was working him like she'd been doing it for years. Once he got her in a bed, he could let her do that all night long, and even better, he could reciprocate. The thought of lying head to toe and taking her into his mouth while feeling her sucking him down below had an effect that made him clench his teeth.

So when had he got so thirty-secondish? He remembered a competition with the guys in the band, seeing who would hold out the longest when they all had girls sucking on them. He'd won by about five seconds, with Jake close behind. That had been fun. This was raw, aching need. If he didn't have her now, he'd die.

When he'd seen her lips close around his cock, that was when he'd gone completely ga-ga.

Obviously, giving himself a few seconds to cool down wasn't working, but it had given Corinne time to slip out of her panties. The scent of her arousal struck him right at the back of his throat and, unable to wait any longer, he lifted her and slid her home.

Right home. She was as wet as he remembered from last time, wetter even, and unable to resist, he slid a finger into that hot warmth and touched her clit. She went off like a rocket, screaming her pleasure, writhing around him in a way that brought him so close he had to bite the inside of his cheek and give himself a shot of pain to stop himself from coming too soon.

He wanted another orgasm out of her before they were done. He wanted her soft and replete in his arms, purring her pleasure. Then he'd take her home and put her to bed. And they could start all over again.

She gasped and he lifted his finger, glistening with her juices, and tasted her. Her eyes went wide when she watched him suck his finger, then before she could recover, he dragged her close and kissed her, sharing her taste and his delight in her.

He knew he shouldn't, but Aidan wanted a taste of the closeness shape-shifters shared when they made love. So he opened his mind, just a little, and slipped into hers. The barriers her father had erected were softer now, more resilient, so he destroyed a few more before warming her with their closeness and the passion he felt for her. He entered her with his tongue, his mind and his cock, his hands at her waist controlling their slow, easy movements, soothing his beast just enough to stop him coming.

This time he wanted a slow burn. He wouldn't let her take control, although she shoved against his hands before sighing into his mouth and relaxing her upper body against him. When she did that, he slid his hands up and over her breasts, caressing their soft resilience. They were like the rest of her—amazingly soft, but with an inner strength she was only just beginning to discover.

Aidan wanted this woman. He'd do everything he could to get her, short of forcing her.

The heat inside her was rising and she softened around him, surrounding him with hot, wet Corinne, unlike any other woman, perfect. They fitted, this worked and he could stay there forever. He wanted her closer. He put his arms around her, against her back and pulled her close, opening his mouth wider to suck her tongue in, caressing her, letting his hands slip lower, down to her beautiful ass. Her position, legs wide apart and draped over his hips, meant she was open everywhere and he let his finger, still wet from her body and his mouth, slip inside the tiny puckered opening. Just inside, where a furnace greeted him.

Corinne flinched, and for a moment he thought she was going to pull away, but she sighed and relaxed. He felt her acceptance in her mind, but she left an edge of wariness, unsure whether she wanted him to do any more. Okay, this was good. He'd take her there slowly, gradually, see what they both wanted.

Meantime, keeping his finger where it was, he rotated it slightly and was rewarded by a flood of wetness in her pussy.

He gasped and drew back, returning to tongue her mouth, use his brute strength to speed up their movements. This time there was no turning back.

When she moaned, whimpers turning louder, he carried on, relentlessly shoving inside her, letting his cock grow to its full length, touching parts of her no one had ever touched before.

And finding another sweet spot deep, deep inside. Her scream echoed his yell as he erupted inside her, gave her everything he had and then some.

They lay together, panting with their exertions, and he pressed kisses to her forehead and temples, lifting her chin to kiss her, this time softly, gently. He lifted her off him so she lay lengthwise across his lap, her head on his shoulder.

"Sleep, sweetheart. You need the rest."

She did. Tiredness swept over her in a wave.

Aidan held her, a precious burden, all the way to London, managing to re-dress her without waking her. He was tempted to ask Mike to circle the M25 several times, just so he could hold her for longer. She felt delicious. Corinne fitted into his body as if she was made to be there. And he was made to hold this woman.

His species fell in love quickly, so his feelings were perfectly understandable to him. He hadn't needed the confirmation of the mark on his thigh to tell him he was right about her. It said they were compatible, he could convert her, love her, even bond with her if they wanted to. But Corinne wasn't a firebird or any other kind of Talent. She would have difficulty understanding or even believing him.

It was so tempting to show her, to shape-shift in front of her, but that might drive her away forever. It would help if he knew how much she knew, or believed, of his world, where Talents like shape-shifters co-existed with humans, knowing each other but not revealing the truth to anyone.

John Westfall was interested, perhaps more than that. He'd seen the books in his office and recognized them as rare, so Westfall hadn't picked them up casually. He must have sought them out and known what he was looking for. Aidan wondered who told Corinne's father about the books. Many grimoires and instruction books were deliberately useless, all the better to hide the good stuff, but none of the bogus texts graced Westfall's shelves.

But how much did Corinne know? How much did she believe?

Aidan knew he had to court her properly. He smiled at the old-fashioned word "court" but nothing else seemed to fit. Especially after the raw sex they'd just shared. It came of mixing with people more than a hundred years old.

Firmly turning his mind away from the seductive pictures of Corinne in his bed that he could conjure up with no trouble at all, he put the time to better use. Although he wouldn't invade her privacy, there was one thing he needed to do for Corinne. He'd removed some of the blocks in her mind, but Westfall had been working on her for so long, they were complex and long lasting.

Aidan entered her mind, deliberately removing all the blocks that were left, opening doors long closed, removing all the stimulants that Westfall had planted, stimulants that worked like deterrents on lab rats, shocking the subject away from unwelcome thoughts. It was a form of compulsion, banned by his kind, and it gave Aidan great pleasure to remove them. He made a thorough job of it, destroying everything not Corinne, everything her father had imposed on her over the years.

Corinne roused as they left the motorway and headed for the center of London. When she stirred, he took his mouth away from her hair and watched her slowly open her eyes, and look up at him. He smiled and touched her lips with his in a gentle kiss. "Welcome back. We're nearly there."

"Where?"

"London. I live in Covent Garden."

She stared at him, her eyes unreadable. He felt nothing emanating from her except gentle warmth. Although he could have probed further into her private thoughts, she'd had enough intrusion for one day, so he refrained and let her keep her privacy. He always thought reading minds was an invasion of privacy, cheating somehow. His brother and cousins had no such scruples, claiming humans would do it without thinking if they could, but he tried to respect other people's space.

Eventually she spoke. "Take me to the Savoy."

"I'm not sure I want you to be alone. Come and stay with me. I've got a spare room if you want to use that." He hoped she didn't, but he had to make the offer. She'd had so many choices taken away from her he didn't want to take one more. But he'd still have her. He couldn't think of any alternative to that.

She pulled away, sitting up on his lap, making him groan and his cock stir. "I'm not a child, Aidan. I want to be alone, I really do. I'll go to a hotel. I need to get away and I want to think things through on my own."

He looked away on the pretext of looking out of the window, blinking away his disappointment, then back at her. "We have things to sort out. At the very least, we need to talk about the band."

"I know." She reached out and touched his hand. It felt blissful, but then she removed it, taking the sunshine away. "I only want to think on my own. Make a decision, free and clear."

"I see." If he pressed her now, he could lose her forever. He had to let her go, properly let her go. No surveillance, however much he wanted to watch her. She'd had enough of that to last a fucking lifetime.

"You need a decision soon. I'll at least know about the band by then. Do you think I should do it?"

"I think you should give it a try." He made an effort and separated his feelings for her from his feelings for the group. "Listen, Corinne. You have to break away from your father. I know you're unhappy with your present career." She lifted away and with regret he helped her retake the seat next to him and fasten her seat belt.

"I know. I have two choices as I see it. To take the job with Pure Wildfire, if you offer it to me, or to go to Paris. I was studying there when I made my first album, and after that was such a success, Dad took me away for some publicity stunts and a few concerts. I never went back, though I always wanted to."

That could work. He could still have her, could still love her. It might even work out better. Something in his heart relaxed. "That sounds like a good idea. I won't try to influence you. If you don't want to consider it, Westfall's organizing a session musician we can use for the London concerts. We already have one for rehearsals and we could use him."

"What about your first guitarist?"

He grinned. "Dan? He has his own career now. Unlike Matt, he left with our blessing. We worked well and his talent is easily as good as mine, but we don't jam together too well. He's doing great, and he'll do better." And he was one of the few mortals to know about Talents, those specially endowed people who had hidden amongst mortals for so long. Sometimes a Guardian would give permission for a mortal to be told, especially when they lived together or worked closely together. Otherwise, telling without permission could result in the death sentence. Aidan, as the phoenix, was a Guardian and in the position of being able to give that permission but he rarely used his privileges. He positively avoided them. He hadn't asked for a position of power in the Talented community and had never felt ready to take them on. But they came in handy sometimes.

She reached out and he slipped his hand into hers, twining their fingers together. He deserved that little piece of paradise at least. "But these are important concerts. Showcases."

He shrugged. "We'd planned them that way."

91

"Why did Matt walk out? Even if he wanted to leave the band, wouldn't it have been better to do it after the Apollo concerts?"

He looked away. "Maybe. It didn't work out, that's all. The drugs got to him and we couldn't rely on him for anything."

Her cell phone rang and she reached into her pocket, pausing to see who was calling her. "It's Dad."

"Don't tell him what you're planning."

She shot him a look of disdain. "Do you think I'm mad?"

Aidan decided to listen in, using telepathy to touch her mind and hear what she was hearing to prevent any attempt Westfall might make to add more blocks to her mind. His protective instincts bristled. She would not face her poisonous father alone ever again.

"Corinne."

"Yes, Dad, it's me. Is there something wrong?"

"Nothing. I just thought I'd better let you know. This band engagement puts our dates out a little bit. The album with the girls was supposed to start next week, at least rehearsals were. We'll reschedule."

"Dad—can you give me a bit more time? I'd like a rest before I start something else."

The voice at the other end came softly crooning. "Yes, I'll see to it. You should have a rest. Stay in London for a while. The next three weeks you'll be socializing with Pure Wildfire, getting your name in the papers. Then the concerts. After that, go and stay at the Savoy and spend a bit of money. I'll have the arrangements made. But I need you fresh and ready to go two weeks after that."

"Dad—I'm not sure I want to team up with the girls."

Westfall's words grew even softer. "That's okay, Corinne. If you're not happy, we'll talk." Aidan felt the probe, even at a distance through the phone, the gentle words that would have persuaded her, had the blocks in her mind still been in place. He turned the compulsion aside and felt Westfall's mood harden. "You're contracted to do five more albums under my management and with my approval, so you'd better think hard about it."

Alarm shot through Aidan's mind. Westfall had to approve anything she did? Bastard! He could silence her. Five albums! Pure Wildfire contracted per album, but Corinne never had anyone to advise her. Her father made good money for her, probably never taking more than his fifteen or twenty percent agent fee, but it didn't matter. She was his creature, his money machine and she wasn't going to get away easily. With anyone else he'd wonder how the fuck Westfall had managed to get her to sign such a punitive, controlling contract, but he knew only too well how Corinne's father had done it. He'd used primitive but effective techniques to block her mind, to make her sign. Maybe even put her in a thrall. He'd give his best Strat to find out who'd taught Westfall how to do that.

Corinne, his clever Corinne, didn't pause. "Thanks, Dad. I'll let you know in a few days."

"Good girl!"

Aidan wanted to punch Westfall. Wanted it bad. Murderous thoughts filled his head, thoughts of pounding Westfall to a pulp before showing him his true nature, shape-shifting in front of him and then killing him.

Corinne hung up and took some time putting her phone away. She didn't tell Aidan what she was thinking or what her father had said. She didn't know there was a need.

There had to be a way.

They were nearly at the hotel. The familiar blue neon sign outside gleamed at them when they drew into the forecourt.

"I'll come in with you," he said, and wouldn't take no for an answer. He carried her guitar cases, feeling privileged to be allowed to do so. That was nothing to do with her. They were beautiful guitars. At least, that was what he told himself.

He waited while she registered, hoping there were no rooms available. She turned to him, her face clear of emotion, smiling as if to a friend. Not the man who'd fucked her senseless just an hour ago.

"Do you want me to stay for a while?" he asked, hoping above hope that she would change her mind.

She didn't. "No, thank you. I need to be alone." Corinne bit her lip. Here it came. "Thank you. For everything." Her face was perfectly composed. The blow her father dealt her was nowhere in her expression. Five albums was a life sentence, one he had to try to help her to escape. Before she could work for anyone else, she had to complete those five albums. Musicians had compromised before, to wait out the length of the contract or to deliver dreck just to get out of it. But five albums!

He took his lead from her and smiled back, his face clear. "I'll let you think. But Corinne, don't worry about anything. Please. I'll come and see you in the morning."

She smiled, perfectly tranquil. "No. I'll come and see you. Tomorrow, I promise."

He hated waiting for people, but he agreed. He had little choice.

* * * * *

Aidan got busy as soon as he reached his flat. Several phone calls made sure the band would be available to listen to Corinne's audition, and within the hour, Ryan arrived, slouching up the curved staircase leading to Aidan's apartment. "I remember when this was a whorehouse," he commented. He wasn't talking about anything within most people's living memory. The flat lay in a converted eighteenth-century house, but was now ultramodern, gleaming with toughened glass. The streamlined effect was somewhat spoiled by the CDs and newspapers strewn casually about the place, but Aidan preferred it that way.

"Yeah, but don't tell me any more."

Ryan shrugged and sprawled out one of the leather sofas, displaying the elegance he could never shake off. He cracked open the can of beer Aidan handed him. "I can't see her fitting in," he said, getting to the subject without preamble.

Aidan slumped in one of the large armchairs, reaching for his own beer. "I want to help her get away from her father. I don't want him on our case all our lives."

Ryan took a deep swig before he spoke. "Unlikely. He's mortal."

"It might be for most of her life."

"Unlikely again." Ryan took another drink and ruffled his hair, as red as Aidan's but cropped short in a spiky cut. "Unless you're not planning to make this permanent. If she takes you, aren't you planning to ask her to convert?"

Aidan sighed. "Yes. If she wants it. It has to be her choice. Not everybody wants to turn into what is in effect another species."

Ryan snorted. "Are you fucking kidding? She gets to live for a very long time, she gets to be a firebird, she gets to fly! Who in their right mind's going to turn that down?" A sneer crossed his features, very like the one he usually wore in public.

"She might." Aidan sipped his beer morosely. "She's not like us. I've proposed already, but she thinks it's to get her away from her father and get some publicity. Either that or she doesn't think I'm serious. It'll be a signal to the press that she's made the break. If it doesn't work out with the band, we can use a session man while we're looking around and she'll go back to her studies. She doesn't want to carry on as she is." He remembered what he'd seen in her room and the temperature went up by several degrees.

Ryan could hardly fail to notice. "What's got you so riled all of a sudden?"

Aidan growled. "Westfall's been spying on her. She has—had—an apartment in that manor house and every fucking room was bugged. There are cameras in the bedroom. I don't know how anyone can do that."

"Keeping his own kids under surveillance? Bastard! So does she know?"

Aidan grunted. "She does now. She had no idea before. I'm not surprised, someone hid them really well. I found them by extending my senses and feeling for the difference in heat where the wiring wasn't all it should have been. Some of the cameras were hidden in the sprinklers, they must have been installed at the same time the sprinklers were put in."

"That means Westfall knows what you did with his daughter." Ryan sat up a little straighter. "Did you do anything else? Did you shape-shift where he could have seen you?"

Aidan shook his head, remembering the little grove of trees. "No chance. I would have done a scan before I did anything in a house I didn't know. All the wiring in the rehearsal room must have stopped me noticing it before, but in her apartment, where you can more or less predict what should be there, it was more obvious."

"Fucking hell!" Ryan leaned forward, his beer cradled between his long fingers. "So you want to get her away. What about her sisters?"

Aidan shrugged. "It's up to Corinne what she tells them. I'm going to get her a new mobile phone on a different network, make sure nothing connects her with her father before she comes here."

"Is she coming here?"

"If I can persuade her to." He lifted his head and met his brother's grim expression. Ryan's eyes were darker than his, more toffee brown than gold, but they contained the same reddish glints. Ryan was angry. His eyes literally flashed. "The thing is, she's contracted to her father for five albums."

The pause that followed was tense with anger, but Aidan felt Ryan controlling it, deliberately turning his mind to studying the problem. "I think we might visit Corinne's lawyer in the morning."

Chapter Six

ಐ

The office of Grayson, Grayson and Clark lay near Lincoln Inn's Fields, a prestigious property, gleaming brass and mahogany the order of the day. The clerk, obviously not a rock fan, wanted to turn them away, so when their name spurred little but polite interest, Ryan put his mind to the problem and they were ushered through after a short delay.

Aidan didn't object to Ryan using his influence in this case. Scruples were okay where he was concerned, but it was time to put that aside to help the woman he loved. If Ryan failed, he would use his own skills without compunction.

Mr. Grayson Senior met them with a smile and a coffee neither really wanted. "You were right to suppose I handle all the Westfall business. Do you wish to engage my services?"

Unlike the clerk outside, Grayson obviously knew who they were and the value of the business they could bring to him. His affability was positively unctuous.

Both Ryan and Aidan assumed the rock star persona, sulky, slouching, garbed in worn black leather with plenty of studs and buckles. The rose tattoos on their upper arms were clearly visible under Ryan's sleeveless t-shirt and Aidan's leather waistcoat.

"We're thinking about it," Aidan told him, slumping gracelessly into one of the chairs in front of the big desk and dumping his almost empty backpack on the floor. "John Westfall's our manager, as you must know."

Not for much longer, came Ryan's voice, clear in his mind. He sent back his wholehearted agreement.

"What worries us," Ryan said aloud, "is the conflict of interest if we did sign with you."

Grayson frowned. "I handle Mr. John Westfall's account, and my partners handle Miss Corinne's, Miss Paige's and Miss Ashley's accounts. There will be no conflict of interest."

Aidan allowed one eyebrow to lift a little. "What kind of contracts do they have?"

"I cannot divulge details of anyone's contracts." Grayson's hand went to cover the portfolio on his desk, red tapes loose.

Aidan continued to bring up points. "We want a better deal with our next contract. We only contract per album and per tour."

"It is difficult for a manager to control a career like that and your career is just beginning," Grayson said. "Mr. Westfall prefers the contract to cover a number of albums and more than one tour. He cannot plan ahead if you aren't willing to give him that kind of trust. However, the terms of the contract are up to you and your manager. I merely facilitate the legal process. If you agreed to come to us, I would hand your accounts over to one of my partners."

Ryan gave his trademark shrug, guaranteed to drive figures of authority wild. Grayson didn't respond overtly, but the muscles in his shoulders tensed under his neat blue suit jacket. "We'll have to meet him first. Look at me." He went from one sentence to the other without changing inflection. Grayson obeyed and Ryan snagged his glare.

"I don't know about keeping them separate," Ryan remarked casually, "but all the contracts are in that folder." Aidan felt the thrum of power as Ryan exerted his influence. Westfall would kill for that kind of power, taken for granted by so many shape-shifters but only used in extremity.

Ryan leaned back, more at his ease, not taking his gaze away from the hapless lawyer's. "Tell me, Mr. Grayson, if one of the Westfall girls wanted to break the contract with their father, how would they do it?"

Grayson answered without pause. He must have been thinking about this already. Aidan hoped Corinne hadn't been in touch with him, because it would alert Westfall to their actions. He listened to the list, much of which was impossible to achieve or not desirable. Unfortunately, there was no time clause, such as the one Pure Wildfire insisted on in all their contracts, or a quick release clause. Then one item made him smile. He would have exchanged a grin with Ryan, but Ryan was busy holding Grayson in thrall.

Grayson got to the end of his list and Ryan released him with a quiet "Thank you." They left after thanking him for his time.

"Well, there's your answer," Ryan said quietly. "I'm going home now. Call me to set up the audition." They reached an alley and they entered it. Aidan kept his attention on the dog-leg turn in the alley that kept them out of sight, putting up a mental barrier to prevent anyone entering while Ryan shape-shifted.

Ryan stripped and handed his clothes to Aidan, who stuffed them into his backpack. They touched hands before Ryan transformed. Aidan watched him melt, his body becoming smaller, feathers sprouting over the white skin until it was completely covered, the nose seeming to grow longer, harder until it became a sharply pointed beak, hooked at the end like an eagle's.

Aidan never tired of watching his clan shape-shift. It was newer to him than to the others, but after thirty years, it was still a miracle. Ryan made himself small enough to be mistaken for a sparrow, but close up, the glowing red feathers and long, elegant form marked him as different.

With a whoosh of his wings, Ryan took flight, soaring out of the alley up toward the blue sky above. Aidan removed the barrier and walked out of the other side of the alley. The whole process took less than three minutes.

Ryan would fly in through an open window of his tower block on Canary Wharf, but Aidan had to walk. Somebody had to carry the clothes. He could have called a car, but in built-up London, driving often took as long as it did to walk. Besides, it was a fine day and he needed to think.

Nobody bothered him on the way back. The fiasco on the journey to London was an exception. People generally stopped for a quiet word, shouted at him across the street or didn't recognize him at all. Corinne had a wider audience, perhaps, or maybe the slight cloud of obfuscation he generally assumed helped. He increased the fuzzing, something he didn't like doing because there might be someone in the street who would recognize the magic.

The band was very careful not to project onstage. To anyone watching, they were a rock band, nothing more. What made secrecy even more important was the fact that Aidan was the phoenix — precious and unique.

And useless. All Aidan had to do was to exist. Without him, fire would be uncontrollable, flaring up to consume the whole earth. He was an Elemental. For years, he'd avoided the responsibilities his birth conveyed on him. Leaders such as the phoenix helped the community of Talents to conceal its existence. They gave advice, took on roles of leadership. Aidan always felt inadequate for this. It was too much, something he felt unable to give. With the power would come knowledge, of his previous lives, of others he was bound to protect and secrets he didn't want to own. So he'd always refused them and other Talents were forced to accept his decision.

Passing the restaurants and hotels on Great Queen Street, striding through into Long Acre, Aidan hardly noticed the bustle of the city, as much a part of him as his quiet cottage on the coast was. He let his mind drift to Corinne, remembering how soft her skin felt, how well she fit with him. Almost unthinkingly, he stretched out his mind to her.

No, stop. No more influence. Let her make up her own mind.

As usual, people thronged Covent Garden. Tourists, shoppers and regulars elbowed past each other, seemingly oblivious of each other's presence. Having stayed some time in the North of England, Aidan knew it wasn't so easy to pass unnoticed there. Strangers regularly got into conversation with each other and the mid-distance stare wasn't as common. Some Londoners would die rather than recognize the fact that they weren't alone.

Passing a florist's shop, spring blossoms rioting in the containers outside, Aidan reflected that this was a pale reminder of what this place used to be, the central London market for fruit and vegetables and flowers. Before that, it had been a place for whores and fashionable whorehouses. Before that, very briefly, a fashionable area to live, and before that — a convent.

Plus ca change, plus ca meme chose he supposed. The more things changed, the more they stayed the same. One of Ryan's favorite sayings. Considering "nunnery" was old slang for "whorehouse," it seemed appropriate.

He crossed the road to avoid someone who stared at him. He quickened his pace, but nobody followed him. He heard a female voice behind him in speculative interest. "Hmmm…" If he'd wanted, he could have pursued that voice. It held no appeal for him. Corinne might already be waiting for him. She said she'd call, but he didn't expect her so early.

His apartment was in a building with a deliberately discreet doorway. It opened with a plastic card, or in his case, since he couldn't be bothered groping through his pockets for it, with a wave of his empty hand in front of the detector panel. The door clicked and he went through to the lobby, passing from busy marketplace to hushed silence. The concierge looked up from his book and smiled a greeting.

She hadn't arrived yet then, or the concierge would have told him. Feeling slightly disappointed, like a child with an empty stocking at Christmas, Aidan headed for the stairs.

Chapter Seven

ࣔ

Corinne arrived at Aidan's flat in the middle of the afternoon. On a fresh spring day like this, it was hard to be depressed, so she didn't even try. Now that she'd made some kind of decision, she felt much better, even though there might be trouble ahead for her. No, she corrected herself. There definitely would be trouble ahead. No "might" about it. She took her time strolling through the piazza, glad she was still able to do so without fans stopping her. Aidan must find it difficult with his distinctive not-dyed hair. She'd learned to hold her head up, avoid direct eye contact, wear her hair differently and put on her makeup a different way to her stage makeup. No sunglasses, unless it was sunny, no floppy hats unless they were in fashion. Too obvious attempts to disguise herself always led to extra attention. And absolutely no tight, pseudo-adolescent, sexy white clothes of any description.

Never again. No Perspex guitars either.

Pushing the memories aside, Corinne stopped to smell the flowers outside a florist's.

"Camellias have no scent," a flat London voice informed her. She smiled vaguely at the woman, dressed in a green apron with gardening implements picturesquely stuffed in the large front pocket. That pair of secateurs would have counted as a deadly weapon without the overall and flowers. Strange world, where if she took her apron off and waved her secateurs in a menacing way, she could be arrested for being in possession of an offensive weapon.

She passed on by shops selling tawdry souvenirs. A small figure at the front of the window display caught her eye.

A rock band, all smiling sweetly, done in resin. One had long, red hair, the wrong color, but who else could the figure be based on? His companions looked nothing like the other members of Pure Wildfire, but that guitarist was Aidan. Brown eyes instead of his amazing amber ones, but tall and rangy, like he was, and with a tattoo on the upper arm. Not a rose, though, a guitar. For the first time she wondered why he wore a rose. Apart from the strange, glowing bird on his thigh, his only tattoo.

She'd be able to ask him soon. The one thing she hadn't been able to decide on was Aidan, where he fitted in her life, what she wanted from him. She wanted to see him again on her own account, maybe even sleep with him again, but she wasn't at all sure how he felt. How he really felt. She might be just another casual fuck to him, nothing more.

Other people had taken her in too many times for her to take Aidan's words at face value. Tom had hurt her more than she wanted to admit. It hadn't taken her long to realize her feelings for Tom were ephemeral and she was better off without him, but the way he'd seamlessly moved from her to her sister, with a bare few days between the change, had made her feel worthless.

The entrance to Aidan's apartment building was so discreet she walked past it twice, cursing at the lack of street numbers, which would have made things so much easier. But on her third pass, she saw the concierge sitting behind his desk through the glass-paneled window and realized this must be the place.

The man looked up when she pressed the buzzer and let her in without making her shout into the machine. "Good morning, Miss Westfall. You're expected. Could you go up to the second floor, please?" He'd recognized her easily enough. Perhaps she was fooling herself and people just weren't interested in her anymore. She smiled her thanks and took the stairs rather than the lift.

Aidan met her at the top of the stairs and it seemed natural to take his hand. A short flight of stairs from the small lobby led to the main living area.

Her first impression was of light. White painted walls and light-wood floors dominated, with two large black leather sofas set at right angles to each other. The large windows were undraped except for Roman blinds gathered at the top, letting the light stream in. At one end was an opening, presumably to a kitchen or perhaps a bedroom. A couple of doors led off the main area, probably to bedrooms, bathrooms or even closets. He watched her, smiling. "Like it?"

"Yes." A simple living space. Obviously expensive because of the size and situation of the apartment, but strewn with the evidence of everyday living. A newspaper lay untidily crumpled on the glass coffee table, CDs lay next to it and he'd obviously chosen the stereo for functionality rather than looks. Cables peeked around the back of the stand and none of the pieces matched. He followed her gaze. "It's a Rega turntable," he explained. She knew the make. It was very good, but old-fashioned records didn't feature in many people's lives anymore. He flashed her a grin. "Sometimes only vinyl will do."

"Can you take the roof off with that system?"

He grinned. "Probably. Do you want me to show you?"

She grinned back. "Perhaps later."

Between the windows soared tall, slender bookcases, filled with volumes meant for reading rather than displaying, titles sorted by topic, not by color or size. It made her wonder about the man behind the icon. "Is this your favorite residence?"

He laughed outright then. "Residence? What a great word! Yes, I like it here, so I spend more time here than anywhere else. I can be private without being isolated. I don't like being isolated. It makes you think too much."

The last words sounded too bleak, but when she turned her head to look at him, he was smiling gently at her, no trace of sorrow in his eyes. "Come and sit down. Coffee?"

She nodded and went to sit on one of the sofas, which proved to be marvelously comfortable. She breathed deeply and relaxed for the first time in days. He came through from an opening, which must be the kitchen, with two steaming coffees in large dark brown mugs. The scent permeated the apartment. She liked that too.

He sat next to her, not too close, and dumped the coffees straight on to the table without hunting for coasters.

"You don't look as though you slept." Swiveling to face her, he stretched his arm along the back of the sofa, not quite touching her shoulder.

"I didn't," she confessed. "I had a lot to think about."

"Did you bring your mobile phone?"

Blinking at the change of subject, she nodded.

"Switch it off."

"What?"

"Switch it off."

She frowned at him but pulled the phone out of her pocket and switched it off. Glancing up, she caught him watching her. He held his hand out and she put the phone in it.

He put it on the floor, got to his feet and stamped on it, grinding it under his heel, the sound of smashing plastic echoing through the large room. She gasped, shocked by his sudden violence.

"I'll buy you another one," he said, his voice not raised or agitated, and picked up the fragments when he sat down again. "See?"

Corinne saw a mess of plastic parts and circuit boards. He picked out a small object. "This has no place in a normal phone. *This* means he's been monitoring your calls."

"Fuck!" The exclamation was unthinking. Furious, Corinne grabbed the item. "Is it dead?"

"Dead as it can be."

She turned it over in her palm, a small, nondescript silver disc, looking a little like a watch battery. Even if she'd dissected her phone, she wouldn't have known what she was looking for. "Why would he do such a thing?" Despair filled her. Her father didn't love her, she knew that, but why would he violate her privacy as he had been doing? Why did he want to own her completely?

"To keep you under control. John Westfall's a user."

"Why did *you* sign with him then? Didn't you know about him?"

He bit his lower lip. "Not completely. He didn't seem to be any worse than any of the other sharks out there. Because he was good and his reputation was hard to ignore and we wanted to use his studios. He made the contract a part of the deal. But we only signed for one album and one tour, like our solicitor advised us to do. Our contract is up after the Hammersmith Odeon concerts and we're moving on."

"Where are you going?"

"We've been negotiating with Randy Norwood."

She knew Norwood, but he only dealt with rock and pop stars and his client list was very small and very exclusive. He devoted himself to his clients. Aidan's trust that she wouldn't tell her father, or anyone else for that matter, warmed her.

Aidan watched her closely. Corinne turned her head and stared back. Balling the phone bug into her fist, she made to hurl it away from her, but he held out his hand. "No, we might need it as proof if it comes to court. I'll shovel up the other bits of your phone and keep them with it. All the other surveillance equipment is in the house in the country as far as I can tell. This is all we've got as evidence."

Sighing, she gave him the bug and he put it on the table with the remains of her mobile phone. "Does this mean that he knows I'm here?"

"Probably, but it doesn't matter. He already has this address. And that was his plan, if you remember, to get to me through you, to get us to hook up. Pure Wildfire only has two albums out, but we toured like fuck for a few years, and we've got a solid fan base. We'll do well, or we'll do really well, and I know the agents are talking about us as hot property. So Westfall wants to tie us up to a few more contracts. With that contract of yours, he has an in."

She stared at him, but she saw nothing in his dispassionate gaze. "Why were you willing to go along with him? To put me in the band and let him build up the publicity?"

"We're not going along with him. I wanted to get you out, so I said what he expected to hear to buy a bit of time. But what I did say was straight up. You can have an audition with the band—I told them, and they've agreed to give you a hearing—but we always vote for new members and the decision has to be unanimous."

She nodded. "Don't think I don't appreciate the opportunity, but I don't want it. I want to go to Paris and study."

"What about the five albums you're contracted to do?"

She fought the tears. She thought she'd cried them all last night but they returned now, pricking the back of her eyes, taunting her for her own stupidity. She looked away. "I'll cope. I'll churn something out if I need to."

He leaned forward and put his hand over hers where it lay on her knee. "He's your father, Corinne. Who wants to think that of their own father?"

She gave a muffled sob and he dragged into his arms. "God, I can't let you do that. Don't cry, Corinne, don't cry. Just listen. I've come up with a plan. Hear me out before you say anything."

Choking back her tears, Corinne stayed in his arms. It felt right to be here, with the faint scent of man and light cologne taunting her senses, his shoulder muscles firm against her cheek. Although she wanted more from him, she was unwilling to let anyone take control of her, ever again. If she won her freedom, she wanted it on her own terms. She would never in her life allow anyone to have that kind of control again. Not even a man whose devastating charisma turned her into sexual jelly.

"I managed to read a copy of your contract." At her exclamation of surprise, he smoothed a hand over her head. "God, I love your hair. So soft! Listen. You're not only contracted to do the albums, you have to do all the support your father deems necessary. All the promotion, the tours and everything else. Westfall has the last word on production too and on any project you undertake. You're bound to him. But there might be a way out."

Surprise gave way to appalled numbness. Her father had made her his slave. She couldn't do anything without his say-so. College was as far away as ever. He could stretch five more albums over years, until she was no longer of use to him. Her father could squeeze her dry and leave her with nothing. But she no longer felt as despairing, although she should because the news was worse than she'd thought. "How could I have signed something like that?" She wasn't stupid, how had she let him persuade her? Although she thought hard, trying to remember when she'd signed, a kind of mist hovered over the memory, as if she'd signed it in her sleep.

"It's not your fault. He's your father, and you trusted him. There are sleazeballs in the world, we all know that, but you don't expect one of them to be your own father."

"So is there anything I can do? Is there an out clause?"

"There are a few ways the contract can be broken. One— you can die. That's not an option, so we need more. You can be maimed, rendered physically incapable of fulfilling your duties. I thought of getting you a doctor and claiming strain through overwork, but the problem has to be physical. So that's out." He paused and his hand tightened in her hair for a fraction of a minute before he began his rhythmic stroking again. "You can take him to court and sue his ass. You could, Corinne."

"And be dragged through the gutter by the media?"

He soothed her with his touch. "That's true. But that contract has some weak spots you could challenge. You have the money to pay the legal fees, and even if you don't, I'll loan it to you until you get your rights back. You will win, I'm sure. It would hold him for a while and you might even win."

"Yes. I could." Public family arguments became fodder for the redtops, the tabloid newspapers and the TV companies who loved nothing more than to see private scandal become public. But she'd be free of her father, and it might be worth it. The case could drag on for years, but since she had no intention of performing as Corinne the Classical Princess again, that might help her. But she'd seen the strain cases of that sort had caused. Careers killed stone dead, reputations ruined. She'd drag all her father's clients into the mess by implication, and she didn't want to do that either. But she would, rather than go back to him.

He cleared his throat. "There's one more possibility."

She looked up, her eyes dry, but she didn't try to hide the desolation in her soul. "Tell me."

"You can become somebody else, someone not bound by the contract. That's the biggest flaw. He thought he'd considered everything, but that escaped him. The contract doesn't say "the person known as Corinne Westfall", or any other phrase, it just names you. 'Corinne Westfall'."

He paused, holding her tightly in his arms. She felt his lips press against her hair. "Do you see what I mean?"

"I can change my name," she breathed.

"When you cease to become Corinne Westfall, that contract becomes null and void. Considering your engagement to Thomas Albright, I wonder why your father didn't spot it."

Light dawned. "Dad was preparing a new contract, he said so. I would have signed it too." She turned her face into his chest, breathing in the scent of the leather waistcoat he wore and something sinfully masculine. "How could I have been so stupid?"

"It started when you were sixteen. I saw pictures of you then. You were young, breathtakingly beautiful and innocent. That was your appeal. He kept you like that, didn't he?"

She nodded, not trusting herself to speak, too angry to articulate. Furious with herself, allowing flattery to take the place of true achievement, allowing her artistic flow to be dammed like that. How could she have let it happen?

"He'll try to get you to sign a new contract any way he can. There's a solution. You know there is."

She lifted her head and met his eyes, calmly waiting for her. "You suggested marriage. I thought you were joking, you said it to rile him."

"I wasn't joking, Corinne. It'll change your name legally and break the contract. I'll help you to stop signing another one. Cleaner and cheaper than a court case, but it'll mean you have to trust me. I wouldn't blame you if you were done trusting people."

"Marriage!" Deep inside, she knew this was the best way. It would be quick, and her father had already agreed to her liaison with Splinter. She had no doubt he'd try to make her sign a new contract, taking account of her new name first, and perhaps ensnare Aidan as well. "It's a bit drastic! It's like changing horses in midstream, just going from one to another." She leaned back and flicked the hair out of her eyes, deliberately straightening up. "I want to be myself, I don't want to belong to anyone else or be under anyone's influence."

He studied her, his eyes unreadable. "I won't force you to do anything. A month, give me a month and then we'll see. If you want to do this, we need to follow your father's plan. Go to the clubs, be seen, get into the media. Let him think it's his idea. Then we marry. Corinne, nobody should be enslaved, not in this day and age, and I won't see it happen without fighting against it. We can marry and divorce if you don't want me. I'll sign anything you want. I just want to see you free of this man."

She picked up her coffee, wondering if she dared do this. It might be easier for her to employ someone to marry her, find a new lawyer who would draw up a prenup. Hell, she'd need that anyway.

No, you won't. You can have everything I own if you want it.

For a moment, she thought he'd spoken, but it was that little voice in her head again. It sounded like Aidan, but it wasn't him. It couldn't be.

He sat, legs open, coffee mug in one hand, hair loosely flowing over his bare shoulders, tendrils teasing his navel, which was exposed by the bottom vee of his waistcoat, the only garment he wore on the upper half of his body. Anything more purely masculine was difficult to imagine. She wanted him, oh yes, she wanted him, but she wanted her freedom too.

"I want you to be happy and to have what you want. Everyone deserves that chance, and if I can bring that to you, I'll be privileged to do it." He took a long drink of coffee and stared into his mug. "But I want you." Chills chased each other up Corinne's spine. His voice gained a softer, lower tone. "I won't force you, I won't make you, but you should know this. The times we made love meant more to me than a casual encounter, a passing fuck. I want to do it again, Corinne, I want to do it a lot. But you have to know I won't force you." A smile flickered across his sensual lips. "So what do you want? To fight your father in the courts, try to break the contract that way? To marry and then divorce after the concerts? To stay married?" He flashed a grin. "You might help me too."

She frowned. "How will it help you?"

"It might keep a few of the fans away. Not many, but it helps. Or we can marry and try to make a go of it." He leaned forward to put his empty mug on the table. It made a click, the only sound in the room. Double glazing muffled the sounds from the busy marketplace outside, and neither of them moved. He straightened up but didn't lean back again. "Give me that month. Marry me and then make your decision, free and clear of your father."

It sounded like the best plan. It was the only one she had. Why did she feel she could trust him? The trouble was, she couldn't trust herself. She'd been so wrong in her judgment of her father, she doubted she'd ever trust her own judgment again. This scheme was the quickest way of getting out from under, a way of becoming her own woman, free of anyone and a way of avoiding being dragged through the gutter press. If she could trust Aidan Hawthorne.

He was still watching her. Nothing emanated from him—she was totally alone. He sat so still he resembled a waxwork of himself. It was as though he wasn't there, asleep or gone away, leaving this beautiful husk behind. He waited.

Corinne thought. Stillness permeated the room, something outside real life. Had he held back time for her? It certainly seemed so.

She couldn't measure her thought in time, but for the first time in her life, she realized she was alone with herself. Someone had always been in there with her, a shadowy presence, just like the cameras in her room.

She allowed all the facts to filter through her mind. She got up and crossed the room to look out the window. Life went on down there, people moving through the market, street artists performing. Nobody knew she was watching them. Nobody cared.

After all, what did it matter? Who cared what she did? Corinne faced hard facts. She'd been foolish to sign the documents her father placed before her. Reading the small print made her fall asleep, so she'd taken his summary of the contracts as the truth. She had nobody to blame for her dilemma but herself. Now she had a way out, from the unlikeliest of sources.

The one thing that worried her was that she might be entering something worse, so she took time to analyze it all. Her career no longer mattered—she had money enough, at least for the next few years. Her father had never been stingy with money. She didn't want to carry on being the light classical guitar player. Someone else could do that and undoubtedly would. There were already a number of wannabes.

What did she want? What did she *really* want?

She wanted a career of her own. To be better at her art. To make a crowd of people bay for her, so that no one else would do for them.

She wanted love. Blindly, she put her hand out and caught at the windowsill to steady herself. The realization came as more than a shock. No one loved her. Until recently, she'd thought her father at least cared, but the discoveries she'd recently made meant she was just a commodity to him. He wouldn't miss her once she stopped making money for him, adding to his prestige. She could do the five albums, tours and promotions, slowly fade from the public consciousness and probably get what she wanted eventually, with no trauma, no fight. That would give her peace, solitude, a chance to study. But she'd be alone, completely alone.

Her sisters cared even less than Tom, who'd declared his undying love, promised her what she yearned for, then done worse than turn his back on her. He'd shrugged and moved on, not bothering to shut her out, knowing she would "understand".

In the end, there was only herself. And she'd let herself down.

His hands on her shoulders came as a shock. She'd forgotten there was anyone else in the room, he'd been so still, and she hadn't heard him move. It wasn't unwelcome. He felt like home, in a strange way, but there was something else. He felt right.

She turned and moved into his arms, felt him close them around her, and looped her own around his back. Lifting her chin, she stared into his eyes. He seemed to enter her, not invading as so many other people, but sinking into a place where he belonged, where he'd always belonged. A place waiting for him. When he lowered his head and kissed her, she accepted and gave back. Not a kiss of passion, but one of acceptance.

"All right," she said. "I'll marry you."

Chapter Eight

ഇ

"So what did you do to make her agree?" Ryan turned away from him. "Screw her senseless?"

Aidan chuckled, too wise to let his brother rile him. "No, I just pointed out it was the only way to get out of her contract. Then I took her out for lunch and back to her hotel."

"Slavery," Jake commented, and he didn't mean Aidan. He crossed the room in the direction of the coffee machine.

It was the day of the audition, two days after Aidan had persuaded Corinne to marry him. She was due to arrive in half an hour, giving Aidan a chance to speak to the band before she arrived.

"We haven't been in the bedroom once since we arrived in London. She's been staying at her hotel. I didn't want to use sex to persuade her. She needs to make this decision on her own, because it's more than how I feel about her, it's her whole life. I saw her yesterday, when we went to the register office to arrange the paperwork, and then on to the lawyer's to sign the damned prenup. I've promised to let her go without a fight if that's what she wants. Anything she wants, she can have."

Ryan turned his head and regarded Aidan through half closed eyes. "You're growing up, little brother." Aidan couldn't read his expression. "I suppose you want us to come with you when you make this public. Make a splash."

Aidan sighed. "Yes. That part I don't like, but we have to draw a line between her past life and this one. Whatever we decide, she's not going back to her father."

Chris snorted. "You've not fucked her? How come? Losing your touch, Splinter?"

Seething with sudden anger, Aidan swung at Chris, but before his punch landed, Ryan was there, catching Aidan's fist in his hand. "Don't be a fuckwit! You want your lady to arrive in the middle of a fist fight?" Chris grinned and Aidan reluctantly lowered his arm. Ryan didn't let it go until he relaxed his muscles. He'd have trouble with Chris. The drummer's prickly personality didn't give easily and wouldn't now. He wished Chris was as easygoing as his brother Jake, the bassist with the band, but however different their personalities were, they were one of the best rhythm sections in the business. Already, the thought of allowing a woman into the band, and worse, a classical chick, made Chris itchy.

"Whatever you think, Chris, she's here to stay. You can have her sitting in the corner of the studio or you can give her a chance with the band. That's up to you. What isn't is the way she'll be part of my life."

"Is she a prima donna?" The question was real this time. Matt had behaved like a prima donna, demanding this and that, never happy. Once they'd discovered his secret—the ubiquitous white powder—the reason for his behavior became obvious and Matt was history. The last thing recovering addicts like the members of Wildfire needed was an unrepentant user around them every day.

"No. Her father never allowed it."

"Hmm." Chris moved away, picked up a cloth and polished the high hat on his drum kit. "Whatever. So if she's going to be part of our lives, I might as well give her a fair hearing."

"Thanks." Aidan let his anger seep away. "Unless she really blows it, you know my vote will be to let her in, but if we do, it's for the three concerts, then we'll see. We're due in the States next year, so we have to get somebody permanent by then."

The door opened and Corinne entered, bringing the sunlight with her, or so it seemed to Aidan. He went forward to take her hand. She was trembling, and for a moment, he didn't realize why.

A fellow musician she might be, but she was also a fan. He squeezed her fingers. *They're just people.* She looked up at him, startled. She'd heard. He didn't care anymore. He'd held off for two days and he'd hold off for longer if she wanted, but it was hard and getting harder, just like parts of his anatomy. His cock turned to stone, fucking granite, every time he saw her, every time he thought of her. He hadn't beat off so much in his life before. When he wanted to fuck, he beckoned and women came running, but he never fooled himself. They wanted Splinter, not Aidan Hawthorne. Now he didn't want to do anything with anyone except Corinne. His masturbation was for sheer relief, because he couldn't go around with a hard-on all the time.

So he couldn't stop every telepathic communication as well as fighting off his desperate need for her. Intimate communication was part of the relationship his kind had with their partners. He longed to link with her completely.

By the time he'd made the introductions, such as they were, she was her confident self again and when he put a guitar in her hands, she reacted like the professional she was. She tested the strings, hit a few notes and tuned the instrument. Aidan took his place on the other side of the drum kit, leaving her alone. He guessed she'd be better that way.

"You name the numbers," he said to Chris, the most skeptical member of the band. Chris's mouth turned up in a sneer, but he shook his head, his spiked blond hair flying up even more and took a few breaths. "A couple of fast ones, a couple of ballads. We'll start with 'Lost In Space'."

The obsession with Corinne was Aidan's alone, but the band belonged to all four of them and he wouldn't cheat his colleagues. He hadn't planned the audition and hadn't coached her. She'd claimed she could do it and she must prove it on her own. Chris counted them down and moved in, his decisive, quick strikes giving the distinctive opening of the number they all knew so well.

She proved it. The first number was shaky and Aidan found himself covering for her when she missed a few notes, but when she made a mistake, she skipped that part and carried on. She would need to do that in a concert if she fluffed, especially with the improvisations and changes in the running order the band usually used. They were sensitives, and could feel the reaction of a crowd, so they varied their program to please the audience, dropping some numbers and adding others. They didn't need words to explain, and since he could communicate with her mentally, she wouldn't need it either. So he'd have to explain the telepathic part of his other self, but he had no intention of revealing anything else. Not yet. She'd been through enough already.

"'Tearing Me Apart'," Ryan announced. One of their showpieces, a power ballad that started quietly and grew to explosive, agonizing power.

At first they kept to the straight version, the one on *Sunfire*, the one Corinne would know well. Then they began to fly. This was where she'd falter, if at all. But she didn't. At least not much, no more than Matt had done. She added nothing of her own, but did her job, filling in the sound, adding the background beats and flourishes that the audience might not notice but would certainly miss if they weren't there.

As the session went on, with Chris calling out the next few titles, they picked up speed, warmed up. Ryan began the sinuous movements he was famous for, dominating his space in front of the drum kit. Chris went into himself, attaining the semi-mystical state he entered when he played, the symbiosis with his instrument, reacting, creating, always there, never missing a beat. And Jake, the powerhouse bass, filled the room with thumping, driving muscle.

Aidan let himself soar. That was his job. To enhance, to brighten, to add new variations to the memorable riffs every fan knew by heart, sparking and setting the audience on fire.

It didn't matter that there was no audience once inspiration hit. It was enough to play. It was always enough, even when he'd been a skinny teenager using a tiny amplifier in his bedroom.

He felt her with him as he'd never felt Matt, supporting, encouraging, building on every flight, sometimes echoing him, sometimes cheekily foreshadowing. He felt secure, safe to soar, even his wildest fantasies incorporated, made part of the music by the rhythm section and by her. Corinne.

When Ryan sang, she curved her notes around his body, made him the center of attraction. At one point, after a passionate cry for help in one of their most complex pieces, Ryan turned to Aidan and spoke, mind to mind.

She's in. The other two chimed in, Chris's laconic agreement, and Jake's added, *She's better than Matt. She'll do fine.* Aidan silently blessed his shape-shifter cousin, a rock in times of trouble, always there, always solid.

Corinne wasn't perfect, and when they started one of the new pieces from *Icefire*, she faltered fatally and came to a halt. The band stopped playing and all felt the reaction. While they were playing little mattered, but when they stopped, thirst and tiredness swept over them all. Aidan stripped off his t-shirt and reached for a towel. He almost lost his breath when she stripped hers off too.

Underneath, she wore a sports bra, black and opaque. He grinned. "We'll keep that in."

Her face was a picture of astonishment. "You mean you want me?"

"With conditions." Ryan walked to her, and took her hands. Momentarily, Aidan wanted to kill him, but his surge of jealousy passed. The strength of the emotion shocked him.

Ryan turned her hands over and felt the pads of her fingers. "Well, these seem tough enough."

She shrugged. "I'll manage. I used to soak my fingers in vinegar. It's supposed to toughen them up."

Keeping her hands loosely in his, Ryan looked into her eyes. Aidan restrained himself. It was Ryan's right to look into her mind. They all agreed they would do this to any new candidate, spot any flaws, any addiction. Ryan was too vulnerable, worse than any of them since he'd lost the love of his life to drugs and nearly lost his own at the same time. They couldn't risk being so close to another addict again. Aidan knew Corinne was clean, but Ryan had to find this out for himself. He was right. He felt his brother's response. Pure relief.

"You'll have to rehearse and there are new numbers you'll have to learn. You're on probation, Corinne, and we're going to keep the session man on call in case things don't work out. Are you interested in joining the band full time or should we carry on looking for a permanent member?"

"I-I'm not sure." Corinne looked confused. Aidan guessed it was partly the experience of the last hour and he decided enough was enough. He allowed his senses to stretch out, and he entered her mind.

He was right. Confusion warred with excitement and exhilaration. Her head jerked around and she stared into his eyes, as though she'd sensed his presence in her mind. He let her look, let her know he did this deliberately, and started across the room toward her.

No sound except his booted feet on the bare floorboards of the dingy rehearsal room and her heavy breathing. He shoved his guitar aside and when he got to her, pushed hers out of the way, then he took her in his arms and clamped his lips to hers.

Enough with restraint. She was his.

She tasted salty with sweat and sweet with success. Aidan wanted to share, wanted to enter, wanted to be with her. He was so proud of her that his heart overflowed and this was the only way he could show her. Ravaging her mouth, he drew her tongue into his, sucked gently on it and let her go. She responded, taking his mouth, drawing him in.

He had no idea how long the kiss lasted, but a sound drew him back to his senses, and eventually he drew back when he could bear to do it. The slow handclap came from the direction of the drum kit. He kept his arms around her and turned his head to glare at Chris, who grinned broadly. "I think we should keep that in too," the drummer said, not a bit abashed. "It'll drive the fans wild."

Aidan wanted to take her straight home to bed, but no one else wanted to let them go. He knew for a fact his brother sensed his desire, and Ryan seemed to take great delight in delaying them. He had to agree to go out that night, to start the campaign to free Corinne from her father.

As far as he was concerned, she was already free.

* * * * *

Corinne's mind whirled with emotion, acceptance and the realization that her life was really going to change, for good. She let Aidan drive her to the Savoy, where she packed the few belongings she'd brought. He drove her back to his flat, parking the small Toyota convertible in an underground car park she'd never been aware of before. The little red car wasn't as flashy as the black Porsche parked nearby and, Aidan assured her, fun to drive around town. "The SUV's a bitch. I usually get Mike to drive that."

"Does Mike work for you?"

"Yes, and for the rest of the band. He's a roadie and driving is his thing. He tells me he loves nothing better than driving the tour truck. I couldn't imagine doing that. Our lighting rig isn't as complex as some, but it still takes up a lot of space in the truck. Or rather, trucks. There are two now."

"I have to learn all that, don't I?"

He turned his head and smiled. "After what you've been through, it'll be a breeze. Trust me—you won't have to go through anything that bad again."

He turned back to the road, leaving Corinne with her own thoughts. She was glad of a chance to get them in order. That morning's audition had been more than she'd ever hoped for. Her initial shock at seeing them all together, remembering they were there for her, was soon superseded by a professional summing up of the situation. The rehearsal room was familiar enough, one of those bare, scarred rooms filled with expensive sound equipment, cheap plastic chairs and bar stools vying for space with digital Gibson guitars and Roland keyboards, each of which could keep the average family of four in grocery bills for a month or more. Jake and Chris Keys, brothers like Aidan and Ryan, intimidated her with their sheer size and golden hair that made them appear like lions waiting to pounce on their prey. Their sheer presence, the charisma all four exuded, intimidated her with their power. How could she concentrate in their presence?

And when she'd started to play, the magic began. She'd reached out and felt the music, added to its power. She was never quite sure what happened, but it had to do with her level of skill and her confidence in herself. That was why musicians practiced so hard, so they didn't have to think about the mechanics of playing an instrument, just how to best get the effect they wanted. That process filled her with joy, and as someone called the numbers, all the trills and fills she'd practiced in her room came to life.

The hour passed so quickly she wasn't aware of the time. The kiss at the end seemed a natural extension of her exuberance. It worked, it fitted and when Aidan's mouth met hers, she finally realized what she'd missed through the session. She wanted him, with her, close to her.

Aidan swiped a keycard through a slot. "I'll get you one of these," he told her. "You'll need a couple of other keys too."

He'd been careful not to look at her after that one glance in the car and hadn't touched her, except for a brief, impersonal contact with the small of her back in the car park, showing her where the lift was. She knew why. It was the same reason she hadn't touched him. He carried her bags, one in each hand, and she had her vanity case and guitar case in her hands. That wasn't the reason why either.

Not until they were inside the flat, not until the door closed behind them with a satisfying click and they climbed the short flight of stairs to the living room and dropped their burdens on the floor.

They fell on each other. His kiss took over where he'd left off in the rehearsal room on the other side of London, as though nothing had come between. His arms went around her, tugging at her jacket, and she let it slide to the floor. They didn't need words. He stripped off his leather jacket and tossed it to join hers, then tore his mouth away from hers and took her hand, leading her to the spiral staircase in the corner of the room, each tread made of greenish toughened glass. She'd wondered where he slept but hadn't dared ask before, because stepping into Aidan's bedroom would have sparked scenes she hadn't been ready for. She was ready now. And then some.

The bedroom would have appeared as minimalist as the rest of the apartment if it hadn't contained clear evidence of ordinary living. A blue alarm clock that didn't at all match the rest of the cool, beige fittings, a colorful throw on the bed, and a pair of cowboy boots on the rug. He didn't give her much chance to admire her surroundings, but picked her up and laid her on the bed, falling on top of her to kiss her senseless. His tongue invaded her in a series of shattering kisses, penetrating her mouth to explore and caress her. His hands moved over her body, slid up from her waist to cup her breasts in his hands.

When he lifted his head, he spoke for the first time since they'd arrived at the apartment building, panting as though he was out of breath. "Do you want to stop? Am I taking too much for granted?"

She shook her head, curling her arms around his neck and dragging him down for another kiss. He kissed like an angel, or perhaps a demon might be better, invading her senses, heating her up to boiling point. When he shoved his hand under her shirt and forced it under her bra to touch naked skin, she didn't notice any discomfort, just the relief of his touch on her where she needed him. He let his hand rest on her breast while he kissed her, putting his whole being into the kiss, stroking and stoking her need to blazing desire. He drew back and she felt the loss of his touch, before he leaned over her, one elbow on the mattress to support his weight, the other busy unbuttoning and unzipping.

Corinne was equally busy, tugging at his black t-shirt until he stopped just long enough to drag it over his head, revealing his deliciously tanned chest, his nipples as hard as hers felt. She touched them, dragged her nails over them, loving his shuddering response.

Her hands went to his waistband, frustrated to find his jeans had a button fly, impatient at the delay. When she finally undid the final button and pushed her hand inside, he was waiting for her, his cock erect and pulsing.

He groaned and pulled at her so she half sat up and he could reach the clasp of her bra. She only had time to shake it free of her body before he bent his head and took a nipple into his mouth, sucking greedily as if he'd been starving without the taste of her. She gave an abandoned cry, pushing toward him, inviting his touch. His mouth busy at her breast, he didn't stop dragging her clothes free, unzipping the fly of her Levi's and pushing the material aside to touch her stomach, curve his hand around her bottom and draw her closer.

They broke away and, by mutual consent, dragged off what clothing they had left. He sat up to shake his hair away from his face, and his gaze, lit by fiery sparks of passion, softened before he bent forward to plant fierce open-mouthed kisses on her throat and her breasts.

Sensation built on sensation. Corinne's nerve endings were on fire, aching for his touch. She needed all of him on all of her, and he must have felt the same way, because he lifted up and settled over her. His mouth left her breast to cover hers in a deep kiss of needy longing as she felt his cock push his way inside her wet, eager pussy.

The same miracle occurred as happened in the rehearsal room during their first time together. His cock grew inside her, touching that spot she hadn't even known existed before. His place. She loved it, his hunger, the neediness he wasn't shy in showing her, and she responded by lifting her legs to hug him above his hips as he began to ride her.

Her first orgasm came quickly, sparkling like champagne through her whole body, leaving her shimmering with desire, wanting more. She called his name and heard his response. "Corinne, oh baby, don't stop, keep coming for me!" She pushed up, wordlessly inviting him to plunge deeply inside her, fill her up to the top.

Pain nudged her senses when he moved into a place unbreached by her previous lovers, deeper than any man had been before. He lifted himself up on his hands and drove hard into her. His eyes shot sparks, his hair streamed around him like living tongues of flame. Corinne should have been afraid, but she knew there was nothing to be afraid of here. Not for her. His passion was as deep as his guitar playing, as committed and as on-the-edge scary. She loved it. She couldn't close her eyes, staring into his as though salvation lay there.

The next jolt up into orgasm took her by complete surprise. She thought it would take her time to reach another climax, but he shoved her into it before she knew it was coming. She arched up toward him, hearing his groan, feeling his mouth on her breast, sucking, tonguing, driving her wild. She heard his voice murmuring endearments and encouragement, but only briefly wondered how he could suck and talk at the same time. She felt him at her breast, sucking hard, creating a connection between them, but she heard him clearly. *Oh God, you're driving me crazy! You feel so good, so right!*

With one last cry, she flung her arms around him and convulsed, arching up against his hot, smooth flesh. He fell into her, his arms around her waist, crushing her into the soft spread beneath them, and he jerked, filling her with his essence.

They lay together, gasping and breathless, until he found the energy to roll slightly, taking his weight off her. She moved to him and he gathered her in. Their skin slid against each other, wet with sweat.

His soft moan made her open her eyes. His were softer now, nearer to amber than red — glowing with something she was loath to give a name to. He lifted a hand and gently peeled a strand of hair off her face before leaning forward and giving her a kiss, soft and loving.

Yes, loving. For a moment, her mind filled with endless love, and she knew it wasn't her own. He slid an arm around her and drew her close. "You're amazing."

"I thought you were." She paused, bit her lip.

"What is it? Did I hurt you?"

She shook her head, feeling her long hair clinging to her body. Some of his mingled with hers, red and dark brown, twining together with their bodies. It seemed only right. "It was wonderful."

"Yes, it was, wasn't it?"

She felt like laughing but didn't. He smiled, but the moment between them was so tense that only laughter would have broken it. "Don't spoil it," he whispered. "This is a place I hoped we'd get to. I didn't think we'd reach it so soon."

"What place?"

"Love."

The word dropped like poison between them.

Corinne's eyes widened in horror. "Love?" She didn't know, she didn't think of that. "I just wanted something for *me*," she whispered. "You can't love me, you can't!" She jerked against him, trying to pull away, but he wouldn't let her, his grip on her firming.

"Hush, hush, it doesn't matter. I won't use it against you, I won't hurt you or try to keep you if you don't want it, I swear. It just is, that's all." He didn't sound upset or distressed. Her stupid comment broke the moment. Perhaps she should have laughed, after all. "Sweetheart, loving isn't a life sentence. It's something to be celebrated, even if it's only on one side."

"No, it's not, you can't love me!"

He touched her nose with his lips. "Believe me, it is. Unrequited love will give me great song material. If you return it one day, I won't ask for anything more. But I don't expect anything."

"You can't know it. I read about one rock star who told every woman he slept with she was the one. How many have you told?"

"None."

"But you've slept with lots of women."

He burst into laughter and rolled onto his back, taking her with him. "You betcha! Lots and lots!" He stopped to caress her, his hands running up her spine in a way that made her want to curl up, just to prolong the sensation. "I have, you know. But I need to apologize for something else. We didn't use anything, love."

The last word could have been an affectionate endearment if he hadn't just confessed his feelings for her. In any case, the sex was so spectacular it might be just the afterglow speaking. What he said concerned her, but it was done now. "I've only been with Tom in the last year or two. I'm fairly sure I'm okay, you know, clean and all that."

"I swear I am." He stared into her eyes and she felt him inside her head again, reassuring her.

"And I'm on the Pill. I just kept taking it in the hopes of — you know." What had just happened, in fact.

"That's okay." He grinned. "More than okay. Fucking fantastic."

"Aidan, are you psychic?" She lifted herself up on her elbows, staring at him. It was the only explanation, fantastic though it seemed. Used to years of her father's nonsense, Corinne had steadfastly refused to believe his voice in her head was anything but her own imagination but she couldn't ignore it anymore. This was real, this was happening.

Yes, I am.

She heard the words as clearly as if he'd spoken them aloud. But he hadn't.

Can I do it to you?

You just proved it. Yes, you can.

What about — she couldn't stand this. It was too intense, too damn weird. "What about other people? Is that how the band communicates?"

"Yes." He didn't try to explain or convert her — he just stared up into her eyes and waited for her questions.

The sweat on her body chilled and she shivered. Immediately he leaned over and twitched the covers back, lifting her on to the sheets and joining her, covering them both, but leaning up again to watch her solemnly.

"All that stuff scares me."

"It needn't." He sounded as if he knew what he was talking about, which was more than her father did.

"My father's been into it for years. Any kind of power, he said. He married my mother for it, said she was a special kind of person, but she always denied it and I never saw any evidence of it. I didn't know her well. She and Dad divorced and I didn't see her much after that, then she died." She'd never told anyone about her fears before. She'd always slammed the door shut on them. Now Aidan forced the knowledge on her with his pragmatic answers.

"He knows certain things." Aidan curled a lock of her dark hair around one finger, watching it as though he could find answers in the gleaming depths. He lifted his head and she saw menace in the set of his jaw, in the gleaming depths of his eyes. "He'll do anything for power, won't he? Did he send you to trap me?"

She quelled her flash of instinctive fear engendered by his harsh expression. "You know he did."

He blinked and shook his head and he was Aidan again, the disquieting fire gone from his eyes. "Sorry. I've lived with this for years and I guess I'm paranoid. He wants you to get something from me."

"Yes, but it's all nonsense. Not like that—telepathy."

His eyes gleamed with speculation. "Ah yes, the telepathy. They've done some scientific research in Russia and the USA. There does seem to be a rational explanation, if you believe it."

"Is there?" She relaxed. If there was a rational explanation, then it might be all right. The supernatural, the paranormal, terrified her. Corinne always suspected there was something buried deep inside her, but she'd kept the door firmly closed, afraid of what it might reveal if she let it go.

"They think every child is born with abilities, but evolution has developed barriers. It must have been too painful to be so open all the time. But some of us learn to drop the barriers and some don't develop them at all. It seems to run in families."

"So all of you can communicate?"

"Uh-huh. It's natural to us, so we don't think about it much. Chris and Jake are distant cousins of ours, so it seems to run in the family." He lifted a strand of her hair, pushed back the covers and traced her nipple with it. She sighed and moved toward him, unable to resist his sensual promise. "You have beautiful breasts." He bent and kissed one, tracing his tongue around the areola. "We'll practice."

Before he swept her into a world where sensation ruled, she managed to gasp, "There are a few things we should practice."

He chuckled against her breast. "Indeed we should."

This time he took his time and gave her breast one long lick. "You taste like chocolate, Corinne. I've always loved chocolate." She lay back and tunneled her hands in his hair, felt the silky strands caress the sensitive skin between each finger. He nuzzled her breast, licked her nipple like it was a sweet treat, before taking it into his mouth. She wrapped his hair around her wrist and cried out at the shock that arced from her nipple right down to her womb. "Aidan!"

"Yes, baby?" He lifted his head and smiled at her before he returned to her breasts, licked and sucked at them. He leaned back to admire his handiwork. "You know, I've shared women with Ryan and Chris and Jake before, passed them on with comments, even marks sometimes." He huffed a short laugh. "Rock musicians are so crass sometimes. But it's fun. Great fun, and the other three haven't really had fun before. Well, maybe Ryan has." He tweaked her nipple, twisted it to give her a sharp spike of pain that he kissed away, soft touches of his lips against her areola. "But if any of them asked me to do that with you, I'm pretty sure I'd want to kill them."

He glanced up at her face, his expression almost ashamed. "Not a good thing for a guy, but a hell of a thing for a man. I've never felt possessive before. As long as I got my share, that was fine by me, but this time I want you all to myself. Nobody will ever see you like this if I can help it. Nobody but me."

"So you don't like to be watched?" She flinched when she remembered the hidden cameras in her apartment at her father's house. Had he watched her with Tom or one of her other boyfriends? Then she realized what Aidan meant. If anyone watched her with him without their permission, she'd kill them. This belonged to them alone.

He cupped her breast, watching the generous, rounded shape intently. "It never bothered me before, or at least not bothered enough to make sure I wasn't watched."

The thought brought a gush of wetness to her pussy. Her secret fantasy, of being a groupie taken by each member of the band as and when they wanted her, filled her thoughts. First Aidan, who'd fuck her without kissing her, just shove his cock in and pound into her, maybe against a wall in the green room, then he'd walk away and leave the wetness trickling down her legs. Without bothering to wipe her, Chris would take over and fuck her senseless, his long cock a contrast to Aidan's short, thick one. After that, they'd leave her until Ryan grabbed her and shoved her over the nearest piece of furniture, a sofa perhaps, where he'd shove into her from behind. She could almost feel the hard ridge of the back of the sofa digging into her hips. He'd leave her there and maybe Jake would take her, or a roadie, anyone who wanted the convenience of a wet cunt. They'd make her suck them, shoving their cocks into her mouth to force her to deep-throat them, flooding her with their come.

"Mmm."

With a shock she remembered he was psychic. "Oh baby, you dream well. As long as you don't want to do it for real, I'm right with you." He lifted his head. "But what made you think my cock was short and thick?"

"It's better." Her embarrassment subsided when she saw the gleam in his eyes, how much she'd managed to turn him on with her sleazy fantasy. Wonderfully sleazy. "You're better. You were just a—fucking machine in my fantasies. Everybody treated me with such respect in real life, nobody wanted to tell me the truth about the mediocre rut I slipped into. Even my boyfriends treated me like porcelain. One said I was his porcelain princess, and he didn't want to sleep with me until we were married, but he assured me he would treat me with nothing but respect. I finished with him the next day."

He feathered her nipple with a fluttering touch of his fingers. "What made you wait that long?"

She laughed. "I couldn't believe he'd said anything so dorky. He was twenty-six when he said that. He wanted me to sign that pledge thing, you know about staying a virgin until marriage. I took great pleasure in telling him he was too late."

Aidan joined in her laughter this time, but his hand stilled on her breast. "On the other hand, I want everybody to see what a sexy woman I've managed to get for myself. Dress as provocatively as you want, show them what they're missing, Corinne."

His possessiveness no longer alarmed her, she realized. She'd arranged their marriage, read every clause and then signed the prenup, even had an independent lawyer go through it for her, to make absolutely sure her get-out clauses were watertight, and watched Aidan sign an agreement that he would let her go the moment she asked him to and not contest any divorce she might instigate. So he had nothing but himself to keep her with.

He'd probably be safe with just that.

A wicked gleam entered his eyes, and his hand firmed on her breast. "So do you want to know what it's like to be a groupie? To service a rock star?" He chuckled low in his throat and a chill burgeoned along her spine. Her mouth went suddenly dry and she nodded.

"You've got to say it, baby."

"Yes," she managed, though the sound was barely above a whisper.

He sat up above her, resting on his haunches. Her legs were spread wide and he could see all of her, opened for his appreciation. He took his time, his gaze traveling up her body to her face. He met her eyes but shrugged and concentrated on her pussy.

"A pretty cunt," he said, as if assessing an inanimate object. He brought his fingers to her and with a thumb and forefinger opened her up, spreading her lips so he could see everything. "A fat, hard clit." He licked his lips and she felt a gush of wetness flood her pussy.

Before she could guess what he'd do, he bent and swept his tongue over her clit but withdrew immediately, making her howl in frustration. "Quiet, bitch."

She moaned. To be nothing but one big cunt, to have only one purpose, to owe nobody anything, that was freedom.

He bent and licked her again, not trying to hide the sounds he made. He slurped and mumbled, after swallowing, "Shit, you're wet. Just as well, since I'm going to fuck you senseless. And then maybe pass you on to Ryan. If you're lucky." He drank from her, bending his head to suck up their combined juices, and licked her from hole to clit, his tongue a gently abrasive stimulation. Bringing his fingers into play, he pulled back the hood that protected her clit and pulled the nub, raw and throbbing, fully into his mouth.

She cried out, howled and tried to twist away reflexively but he held her down with one arm across her abdomen and continued to suck.

She came, but he didn't stop, didn't give her any concessions to the ultrasensitivity, continued sucking until she screamed out his name.

Then he was on her, leaving her to surge up to her and take her mouth, at the same time plunging his cock deep inside her. She gasped and called his name, but he didn't seem to be listening. Driving hard, pleasing himself, he pleased her, until he lifted off her and stared at her again.

He tweaked her nipple, bent to lick it then grabbed pillows from the head of the bed, piling them in the center of the mattress. "Up," he said, indicating the stack. She sat up and blinking, reached for the pillow to help.

"Not fast enough." He grabbed her around the waist and almost threw her over the pillows. Her breasts hung down on one side, and he nudged her legs apart. Hot air blew over her thighs and she realized he was looking at her. She wasn't sure about that, but when she tried to close her legs he inserted his knees and forced them apart again. "Stay like that, you," he said, as if he didn't remember her name or couldn't be bothered to remember it. "I think Chris would like you. He likes big tits and a round arse. And this—" A finger prodded her cleft and found the pucker of her anus. He wriggled a finger inside and swiveled it. Pleasure/pain spiked her senses, then his other hand came around her thighs and opened her up. With an animalistic grunt, he shoved his cock inside.

It felt bigger than it had before and she realized it was because she was swollen with desire and his suckling, aching for him to come inside her. His finger left her ass and a large hand landed beside her head as he bent over her. His body curved over her, taking her, offering her no mercy and no choice.

She loved it. All she could do was take what he gave her, and he gave her plenty. Consideration and tenderness gone, Aidan pounded into her, relentlessly thrusting and gasping to her. "Oh baby, you're good. Your cunt is deep and wet, just what the band needs. Do you want us to keep you here, tie you up so we can take you when we want you? You're here for our convenience, to serve us and do whatever we ask. Shall I come in your mouth, your arse or your cunt? Which would you like?"

She opened her mouth to reply, but he grunted and reared up, grasping her waist to hold her steady while he rammed his cock deep into her. His balls slapped her ass with every drive, vibrating her slit, the sensations spreading up to her clit, which heated in readiness for another orgasm. It grew and spread through her, as unstoppable as Aidan's drives, the growing heat finally exploding in fire and sound.

Dimly Corinne realized the sound was hers, screams blending with Aidan's cry when he came, his seed burning inside her.

She was only semiconscious when Aidan lifted her around her waist, moved the pillows and settled her in the bed next to him, cradled in the shelter of his long body. He pulled the comforter over them and stroked her. "Sleep for a while, Corinne. Rest. Then we'll begin again."

Chapter Nine

ͽ

"I think that will do." The hairdresser stepped back with a frown of concentration, viewing his work critically. Corinne was a thing, an object, to this man. Devastatingly attractive, with a shaggy blond cut that advertised his services, Steven Dorinda only did the hair of the most prestigious clients at his exclusive Bond Street studio. His excellent assistants dealt with the others. Corinne would have been pleased to have one of those, but Aidan insisted, and despite the six-month waiting list for Steven Dorinda's services, he'd had his way.

She had a good idea how he'd done it too, staring at the receptionist until she called the great man down and then giving Dorinda the same treatment, using gentle, persuasive language to get his way. And what he said made sense, that since she was joining Pure Wildfire, Steven's creation would be seen all over the place. Maybe that rather than any of the weird mind stuff persuaded him.

This telepathy stuff was scary, but Aidan hadn't used it on her. Her decision to sleep with him, to marry him, was all hers, she was sure of it. She'd been wrong before, but she felt none of the triggers or outside influences that had so disturbed her in the past and now seemed not to be there at all. The little shocks she'd taken for granted when her mind had drifted to thoughts of leaving her father's management or giving up playing in public, they'd all gone, and it was only now they were absent that she realized how pervasive they'd actually been.

Now Corinne tried to look at herself the same way Steven Dorinda was doing—as an object. Gone were her long, straight locks, replaced by a shorter, sassier look. He'd cut her hair in a shaggy style, curled at the ends, each tip enhanced by red highlights, curling up her hair like flames up a tree. "That long style wasn't doing you any favors," Steven said. "I've kept it shoulder length, but the layers and the feathering lift your face and draw attention to your eyes. You should play them up, you have gorgeous eyes." Corinne had assumed Dorinda was gay because of his fastidious way of dressing and the way he flirted lightly with people who spoke to him, but his reaction to her wasn't that of a gay man. She felt a masculinity under the exterior, a definite interest despite his dispassionate, artistic approach to her new hairstyle.

"New makeup's in the cards," Corinne said quietly. Aidan had taken her shopping earlier in the day. New makeup, new clothes, a new look. It was more than time she looked her age instead of a sweet teenager. She'd left her teens behind ten years ago and it was time to say goodbye for good.

"Is it true? You're marrying Splinter?"

"Yes. You can tell who you like. In fact, everyone who comes through the salon doors. We want people to know."

"Why?" Steven Dorinda was no fool. His hairdressing empire made him a millionaire, but it took more than the talent he undoubtedly possessed to do that. Just like the band, he had to work at an image, employ experts to sell his skills. He'd even agreed to put his name to a brand of shampoo and hair products. It was good shampoo. A bottle of it reposed in Aidan's bathroom, thanks to her.

She didn't evade his question but answered him straight. "I want to break free of my father. I'm joining the band, at least for the next few gigs. Matt walked out, so I'm taking his place. The news of our relationship will only add to the buzz." She didn't mention the other thing, the thing that scared her senseless when she allowed her mind to dwell on it. How Aidan topped sexy, reached fucking unbelievable and touched toward the L word.

"Good grief!" A slow smile curled the pale pink lips. "Thanks for that. I'll make sure to spread it around. I'll have to get tickets for one of the shows."

"I think it's sold out, but I'll see you get a couple."

Steven chuckled. "I can't miss this! You're a very brave woman, Corinne Westfall."

She smiled back at him in the mirror. "I had to do something. I was stagnating the way I was before."

He laughed aloud then. "I know that one. I spent ten years as top stylist with someone else before I struck out on my own. It took me that long to realize I could do it." Hard to believe now. He picked up the hand mirror and showed her the back of her hair with a flourish perfected over the years. "Go for it, girl. It won't be easy, but making your mind up is the first step."

Corinne smiled her thanks and stood, shaking the cut hair free of her new ready-torn jeans. She shook her hair, watching the red lights fly about her head. Then she stood to one side and looked over her shoulder in true model-girl pose. A camera flashed and she spun around in annoyance. Steven shrugged apologetically. "It's for my personal collection. I'll delete it if you want."

"No," said a voice from the top of the stairs. "Frame it and put it in the window. I want everybody to see her like this."

It annoyed Corinne to find she melted at the sound of Aidan's voice, but at least she didn't run across the room and throw herself at him the way her body urged her to. Steven gave Aidan the same kind of assessing stare he'd given her at the start of the session. "Your ends need doing."

Aidan grinned. "Sure they do. I'll get them done."

"I wish you'd tell me what color that is. I know clients who'd kill for those highlights."

Unseen by Steven, Aidan winked at Corinne and then turned back to the hairdresser. "I don't know, I just leave them to it."

Corinne suppressed her giggle and crossed the room, deliberately taking her time. Aidan took her hand, twining his fingers with hers. "We're going to the Maiden Mega Store."

She gasped. "We'll be seen!"

"That's the general idea." He nodded to Steven. "Great job, many thanks." Steven nodded back and Aidan went down the stairs with her. In the main body of the relentlessly open-plan salon, they attracted more attention. Onlookers could hardly miss them. Corinne knew Aidan's mind was free and clear today, free of the fuzzing he used when he didn't want to be recognized. He'd shown her, demonstrated it to her. It made people turn away after one glance. She'd seen it herself that morning on the way here. Now she knew of his mental powers, a few more things became clear. Why, in her father's house, she'd joined with him so completely, why she'd occasionally felt reassured when she needed it when she was with him and how he persuaded people to do things for him with a few quiet words. Awesome. But, he told her, he never compelled, never made anyone do something they didn't want to do. That, in his opinion, was a crime. Shit, if she had those powers, she could have broken free of her father years ago.

He took longer than he needed to at the front desk, paying the girl and flirting with her before turning back to Corinne and looping his arm around her waist. He bent his head for a quick kiss, which she returned before someone opened the door for them and they went through.

A few photographers stood by a flashy sports car Corinne didn't recognize. He stopped to touch her ear with his tongue and murmured, "Here we go, baby."

This was for her. Although she'd faced the press before, Corinne felt vulnerable and suddenly afraid. Aidan's arm held her tightly to his side, giving her some support. This was the first time she'd appeared in public without one or two of her father's minions, his paid assistants and bodyguards. That was what was making her nervous. She was on her own here.

The voice came clearly into her mind. *You're with me.*

Yes, but I won't be with you always.

Deafening silence greeted that comment.

The flash of cameras and loud voices greeted them. She was used to that. They used the decibels to confuse the unwary, trap them into saying things they shouldn't. So she would say something seemingly unguarded.

"New look, Corinne?"

She paused to preen and pose. "Yes, do you like it?"

"Where's the classical princess?"

She paused and looked at the man from under her lashes. "She died. Forget her."

Laughing, she blew him a kiss, waited for the inevitable flash and turned away, not waiting for Aidan to open the door. Since he was in character as the loutish rock guitarist, she had doubts about that, so she put one foot on the door of the car and leapt inside.

It wasn't really the weather for open-topped cars, so she paused to toss her new leather jacket over her shoulders. Not that it looked new, but the quilted lining was warmer than the sleeveless black silk top she wore. Aidan—very much Splinter at the moment, all gorgeous slouches and leers—gunned the engine into life and even though she knew it was special, the power under her gave her a moment's alarm. They pulled away from the curb and the traffic seemed to melt away before them.

"Yours?"

He turned his head and flashed a grin at her. "'Fraid so. I like a well-designed sports car. Ryan goes in for bikes, has a garage full of 'em. I was tempted to borrow one, for the press, but I thought you'd had enough shocks for one day."

"I can manage," she said.

He chuckled. "You need to perfect your slouch. I'll have to teach you."

"You've taught me enough."

"I've only just started, sweet thing."

A memory of lying face down across pillows on his bed flashed into her mind. She felt his arm under her, drawing her up, and knew he put these thoughts into her mind. His voice echoed her thoughts, a deep purr of desire. "Oh no, baby. I've not taught you nearly enough, not yet."

She sat up to allow the chill breeze to cool her heated face. "Do you have to do that?"

"As long as you let me, I do. Call it an addiction."

He made a sharp turn, the small steering wheel spinning back through his hands. She desperately tried to change the subject. "Have you ever been addicted to anything? I know what the press said, but I also know they make things up when it suits them. So, for real, were you?"

He shot her a sharp glance and then turned his attention back to the road. They were attracting not a few looks from passersby, but going too fast for anyone to confront them, although, this being Central London, not nearly as fast as the car could go. It seemed a waste of power and speed. "Yes, we were, for real. As real as it gets. We all were. Because of our gifts, we got arrogant, thought we could take anything, but an addictive drug works on anybody and it worked on us. That's why there was such a big gap between *Sunfire* and *Icefire* and that's why Matt had to go. We couldn't be around him, he'd have dragged us back. Or at least he would have dragged Ryan back. He was in it harder and deeper than the rest of us because of Maria. Matt didn't give up when we asked him, got unreliable, and if he carries on at this rate, he'll be dead in a couple of years."

His voice took on a note of real pain. Corinne heard it and, without thinking, reached across and put her hand on his thigh. She felt his pleasure in her response and it wasn't sexual. It was simple human comfort, given and received.

He took another sharp corner. "We were all into it. You must know the story from the media. A few years ago, Ryan fell for Maria and he fell hard. She got us all into the drug scene. Despite her habits, she was sweet, vulnerable and very lovable. Ryan adored her. We thought we could cope. We couldn't." He paused, but although she didn't press him, he carried on. "Then Maria died. The dealer sold them some weird shit and they OD'd. That was the night before they were due to go into rehab, you know, one last hit and then finish. Ryan lost Maria and he's never been the same since. Her death hit him badly. He's still vulnerable, so when we found how deeply Matt was into the stuff, we cut him loose. Though the press thinks we fought, the usual temperamental rock star stuff, it wasn't. It was a decision we made coolly and with regret, because he worked well with the band. But it did lead me to you." He spoke his last words in a softer tone and he covered her hand with his and squeezed. He didn't give her a chance to respond. "Nearly there. Get ready. We might have some TV there."

Foreboding filled her. This was more than a simple appearance. "Might? You told people?"

"A few."

He swung toward the curb and parked on a double yellow line. He threw a waiting uniformed security man the car keys, and came around to the passenger side to help Corinne out. This time she did open the door. As he helped her to her feet, he murmured to her, "Play it natural, baby. They'll love you."

She hated him for doing this, but it had been her choice, after all. She'd agreed to take part in all the pizzazz, to put her father off the scent and help the band with its pre-concert appearances. Aidan took her at her word and plunged her headfirst into this new world. People thronged the outside of the store, shouting, holding up t-shirts and CDs. A couple of reassuringly large men in blue uniforms stood waiting for them. Aidan ignored them, heading for the ropes holding the crowd back. Corinne had reason to know they kept the ropes in store and also knew someone had forewarned them. She'd been here before, signing CDs and giving away a fucking clear fucking plastic guitar. For the first time, she used her mental connection with him deliberately. *Why didn't you tell me?*

Aidan, some feet away from her, answered immediately. *It got a bit out of hand. I thought we'd come here and do a bit of shopping, perhaps do a couple of tracks, and I told a newspaperman I call sometimes. He must have rung Maiden to see when we were expected.*

If I find our guitars inside, I'll kill you.

Erm — I did drop a couple off earlier.

Argh! Her expression of rage only resulted in his laughter and he didn't keep it inside. She saw him throw back his head and let his mirth out, full and strong. After signing a few CDs, he turned back to her and slung his arm around her shoulders in a gesture that said, "Mine."

She tried to pull away, only to feel him drag her closer. "I'm not an accessory."

"For now you are. Trust me. You're on my territory now. I'll play the accessory for your fans on your home ground, I promise."

It was chaos in the store. Flashes popped, and there was even a man with a mike, followed by another with a camera. She couldn't see the side of the camera, where the name of the TV company was emblazoned. It didn't really matter.

Showtime.

"When did you and Corinne get together?" "Have you decided about the new member for the band?" "Is the new album on time?"

Corinne watched Aidan deflect all the questions and had to admit he was very good at it. And he had one weapon she didn't possess, or didn't until now. He could turn petulant and refuse to answer anything else. They expected it of him.

When he swung her around and headed for the stage, he took the bouncers by surprise and it was a few seconds before the burly men caught up with them. It didn't matter, Aidan didn't need them. Tucked under his arm, Corinne felt the power in him, a power she'd never been aware of in any other human being. It made him invincible. He didn't throw the fans aside like the star of a Yacuza film, but they moved when he pushed and they didn't grab at them. They watched him swing her up to the stage that had held so many music luminaries for interviews and impromptu concerts and follow her up, not bothering to use the steps, but leaping up in one lithe movement. He approached the mike. "If you shut up, we might do a couple of things for you." He waited, not even attempting to speak again, but located the guitars. They were electric, but not top quality. "Disposable, if necessary," he murmured to her.

"Hi." Unexpectedly, Ryan materialized at the stage. Like Aidan, he swung himself up.

Corinne gasped. "Where did you come from?"

He gave her a lopsided grin. "I fuzzed. They didn't see me until I wanted them to. Hello, little sister, I came to help." He tilted his head and examined her new style, taking his time, ignoring all the whoops and whistles from the crowd. "I like it."

She heard Ryan and Aidan exchange a brief mental word. *Don't give them any news about the band yet. Just that Corinne and I are together.* Ryan nodded and a wave of warmth swept through Corinne. Acceptance. She'd never felt that before. Never.

We'll do "Tearing Me Apart" and "Lost In Space".

Aidan grunted his agreement and turned to tune his guitar. Corinne was becoming familiar with his withdrawal when he played. At first, she'd thought it was rejection, but she understood now. She should have recognized it. When she found a piece she loved, she was capable of the same thing, of cutting herself off from everyone and everything. It didn't happen very often these days, but perhaps now she could get it back. Aidan had never lost it.

They played. It wasn't perfect, not even near the usual standard the band demanded, but it worked. To her sometimes faltering accompaniment, Aidan added a series of riffs and trills, winding around Ryan's vocals, creating a mood, plaintive one moment and raucous the next. They were masters at switching mid-song, keeping the audience on its collective toes.

After two numbers, Ryan and Aidan answered a few more questions from the media and Corinne attempted a few of the more straightforward ones. Was she joining Pure Wildfire? What about her classical career? She kept her answers vague. She was capable of far more than this, but not today. Her new vulnerability, the speedy change in her life, had left her reeling from the impact and she wanted some recovery time.

She could have forced her way forward, answered the questions in her own right without too much trouble, but she knew they were right. This was the beginning of a three-week campaign, not a sudden jolt. Although, by the end of it, she wanted to be answering the questions for herself. If she couldn't be an equal member of the band, she wouldn't entertain joining it on more than a temporary basis. Paris and her studies beckoned.

Aidan's sharp response took her by surprise. He lanced through her thoughts. *Give me a chance! Don't even think that, not yet!* He sounded vulnerable, and she knew that communication was for her alone. Ryan showed no sign of having heard.

How do you do that?

What?

Keep your thoughts private?

Ryan did hear her, though he hadn't heard Aidan. *Talking dirty, is he? You'll learn to block, little sister. It's not that hard.*

You keep out of this, brother. She's mine.

I hear and obey, oh mighty lord.

The last was sarcastic, but there was an edge to the comment that Corinne found puzzling, as though somewhere, deep inside, Ryan really meant it.

The pause was enough. The reporters were moving on, probably to another venue somewhere else in the city. Word got around so fast it must be hard to keep up with the special appearances, dinner dates and theater openings.

The fans showed no signs of moving though. The most fanatical were the moshers, dressed in black and leather, cramming themselves along the front of the stage, but behind were a motley collection of chavs, pop fans and emos, all with their distinctive style of dress, behaving as everyone expected them to behave. But every face turned up to the stage was happy and eager. Just because the press had left, there was no reason to break up the party just yet.

Corinne began to play the Bach piece she'd transcribed the first day she met Aidan. The music took her away with its magic, and when Ryan shoved a stool under her backside, she sat, not thanking him. She didn't notice Aidan coming to stand beside her until he started to play, supporting her, adding harmonies and counterpoint when she needed it. Whatever kind of music she played, he was there. He seemed to get inside the skin of it, understand it so he could add and adapt.

After that, they finished off with another Pure Wildfire number, a gentle ballad Ryan used to suck the audience into intimacy, then left Aidan to sweep them up to the heavens with a soaring succession of notes.

That was the end. The audience, while disappointed they weren't going to do more, realized they'd had very good value, and began to drift away after the last burst of applause. Aidan and Ryan signed a few autographs, and Corinne signed one of her CDs. The woman handing her the jewel case said to her, "You're going to carry on making classical music, aren't you? You make my housework go so much easier!"

A lump rose to her throat. Abandoning her career would mean something to some people, after all. This woman she answered with the truth. "I don't really know. I love all kinds of music, but I was planning to take some time out to study. I've been getting stale recently. And—" She glanced back at Aidan.

The woman's homely face creased in concern, but she followed Corinne's glance and brightened. "Yes, I see why you'd want to do that. He's a handsome man, isn't he?"

Corinne chuckled. "Yes, he is."

The woman put her hand over Corinne's in a sympathetic gesture that was mother to daughter in feel. Corinne tried not to allow the tears she felt pressing inside her eyes to spill over. It was a very long time since she'd felt a mother's touch. "You take care of him, dear. My daughter loves the band and she tells me all about them. They've had a bad time recently, by all accounts." She looked up, and Corinne realized Aidan must be standing behind her now. The woman's face lit up. "You'll look after her, won't you?"

"I surely will." The soft voice sent shudders through her, intimately connecting them. She stood and felt his arm go around her waist.

The woman left after a quick smile and several photo flashes went off. Aidan rested his chin on her head. "I've rung for the car. We can go in a few minutes."

Ryan walked across to them, a small case in his hand. "You did that well. Rehearsal tomorrow?"

"I love the way you sing. You seem to get inside a song and push it out."

Ryan grinned. "Glad you liked it." Leaning forward, he kissed her cheek and scrambled off the stage, plunging into the crowd. The bouncers followed him, but there were no fanatics around, just honest-to-goodness fans who wanted to hear the music and tell him they enjoyed it.

When she felt the tug on her hand, she followed Aidan. She felt she was beginning to belong somewhere. It was a strange feeling.

Rehearsals the next day were very familiar, apart from one thing. Only Ryan and Jake could read music, so they didn't have anything written down. It was a shock to realize that Aidan couldn't, but he turned her concern off with a smile. "I've never needed to." Earlier in the day, he'd shown Corinne his music room at the flat, a converted bedroom, now crammed with guitars, amplifiers, a drum machine and a couple of keyboards. He'd shoved a Gibson SG into her hands. "See how you get along with that one."

Corinne planned a visit to one of the city's well-stocked music stores later that day to buy her own electric guitar. She fingered the instrument, knowing it was one of the best she could find. "If this is special to you, I'm not taking it."

He grinned, taking a battered Gibson down from its stand and placing it in a padded case. "No, *this* one is special. You don't get this one, lady." To all intents and purposes, it was the same model as the one she held in her hands, but the body of his was dulled with use, and scratches marred the shiny black finish. The paint had peeled off the corners. Corinne knew he was telling her the truth. Why one instrument should be perfect and another, seemingly identical, fail to meet the standard, she had no idea, but she knew it happened. She'd only brought her favorite instruments, and although they had both been costly, so were her hated trademark Perspex acoustics. She'd left the only one of those she'd brought back at the hotel, and hoped she'd never see it again.

The band hired the same rehearsal room they'd used for her audition, one of a suite used by many musicians situated in a side street off Oxford Street. Aidan stopped on their way there to buy a newspaper.

Pictures of Aidan with his arm draped possessively around Corinne's shoulders dominated most of the gossip and entertainment pages. She hated to see herself subjugated by him, but he was larger and he projected more of an image than she did.

"Don't worry, you'll find your own space soon." She looked up, surprised to see Ryan so close. He grinned and picked up another paper. "A good picture of me, this one. My publicist will want a copy of that." He glanced at her. "I don't have to explain to you, do I? There's me, Ryan Hawthorne, and there's this person." He flicked the paper with a careless finger. "Sometimes I hardly recognize him."

"I don't recognize myself with that hairdo and those clothes."

He stared at her, frankly assessing, his golden eyes speculative. "This looks more like you than the pissed-off artist I saw at the Albert Hall last year."

She couldn't have been more astonished. "You came to see me?"

That concert had marked the start of her uneasy feelings, her realization that somehow her life had gone off-track.

His grin broadened. "Yeah. You were depressed. You played well, you did everything you were supposed to, but little things and the way you marched off right after your second encore told me something about you. You weren't happy, but you weren't about to short-change your audience. That works for me. I've been there myself, a time or two."

"I've wanted to change direction for about a year now. But Dad kept me busy and I didn't have time to sit down and plan until recently."

"And it's easier to carry on in the same old rut, isn't it?" He gave her a look of complete understanding. "Listen. You know my history." He grimaced. "Everybody does. Five years ago, after Maria died, I was a wreck, but I came around. I had to change my habits, my friends, the people who hung around me. They were all into the drug scene, and if I wanted to change, I needed to make the break. So I know a bit of what you're going through. And if you ever need somebody to talk to, I'll listen. If you want." The last sentence was so diffident

Corinne knew she was talking to the real Ryan, not the arrogant peacock who preened before the media.

"I will. Thank you." It felt good to have a friend.

Pure Wildfire took no prisoners at rehearsals. They corrected all her mistakes, however tiny, and the band halted while she corrected her bigger errors, pushing her through the pieces over and over again. The audition and the impromptu performance at Maiden were nothing. This was the real band, the heart of it all, where their reputation came from, and they were ruthless at getting their performance right. Fans might assume the band's stage performances were off-the-cuff, their reputation for great shows almost accidentally attained, but this was far from the truth. That kind of symbiosis was only won by playing together hour after hour, so that if one member of the band was a fraction off, the others could spot it first and take action to cover it up.

She wouldn't give up. When they took a break, they played her the rough cut of what they had so far for *Icefire*, so she could learn a couple of the songs from that and they gave her a CD to take with her. Homework.

Yet Corinne felt comforted and happy with the work. This was what she'd wanted, she realized as she sat with a steaming mug of coffee late in the afternoon. Musicians who cared about their work, people who strove for perfection. The fact that it was always out of reach didn't matter. Getting it might be more frightening than never getting there.

The postures, machismo and wild behavior the band was famous for never appeared at rehearsals. This was where the work started. All the rest was pomp and circumstance.

She didn't even want to make love when she fell into Aidan's bed later that day. She was too exhausted.

* * * * *

Aidan woke with a start, alone in the big bed. He didn't know what woke him—the apartment's windows were double-glazed, so outside noise didn't bother him. He stretched out his arm and met cold sheet. That made him sit up. Where had Corinne gone?

Checking with the clock told him it was four a.m. Where was she at this hour? His stomach tightening with apprehension, he sat up and slipped out of bed. When he opened the bedroom door, he heard it.

She was practicing. It sounded eerie, someone playing the guitar in his flat at this time of night. He was the only person who did that.

The flat was warm with the under-floor heating, so he walked out naked and took the stairs. The small light was on in the kitchen and he smelled coffee, but he turned the other way and followed the sound.

Beautiful. She could play when she wanted to, really play. She broke off and cursed, breaking the spell. When she began again, he recognized the tune. She'd repeatedly stumbled playing that one during rehearsals earlier in the day.

This was nuts. Four in the morning and she was down here playing the guitar.

As if he'd never done that! Smiling, he moved forward and pushed the door open. And caught his breath.

She'd donned a light silk shirt but hadn't bothered to fasten it, so it gaped open over her breasts. She'd shoved the sleeves up her arms to give her more freedom to play. It took her a few minutes to realize she wasn't alone, minutes he used by gazing at her and listening to the music she made.

She lifted her head and their eyes met. Slowly she scanned his body, from his eyes to his toes, lingering in certain places. He leaned against the door jamb and folded his arms, smiling at her. "Finished?"

"I think so." She paused, her hands draped loosely over the guitar. "For now."

He came into the room. "If you'd closed the door properly, I wouldn't have heard you."

She flushed, guilt stricken. "I'm sorry. I didn't mean to wake you. I went to sleep so early and this piece was on my mind, so when I woke up, I kept going over it in my mind and—"

"And you wanted to get it right. Okay, play it for me."

She took a breath, her hands poised above the strings. She looked graceful and beautiful, her breasts exposed, her head tilted to one side as she began to play. He tried to tell himself there was nothing sexual about his heated stare, but he was fooling himself. Already his cock stirred.

He moved behind her as she played, slowly so as not to startle her out of playing. He watched her hands moving over the strings and stood behind her. Then he saw a mistake. "Here."

She broke off and looked up at him, the ends of her hair gleaming in the dim light. He liked her new hairstyle. It didn't hide any of her gorgeous body. He dragged his lascivious mind back to her playing. "You're making the wrong shape on the bridge. Let me show you."

He sat behind her cross-legged and reached out to touch her arms. She wanted to play, not fuck, so his erection probably wouldn't be welcome right now. She relaxed against him and let him take her fingers and place them in the pattern he used on the bridge. "Try that."

She hit the chord and sighed. Her back moved sinuously against his chest. "You're right. I'm too set in my ways. I've never done it this way before, but it works better." She leaned back a little, allowing him more access to the guitar. "They're almost a part of me, the correct way to form the chords, how to bridge. You have more freedom. Were you taught?"

"By Jimmy Page, Alvin Lee and Eric Clapton. I played their albums over and over and broke a few tapes doing it. I used tapes because I could stop and start them, play phrases and licks over and over. I learned by copying them, then I started to do my own variations." Her back, even through the silk, felt wonderful against his. He shifted backward a little to adjust his insistent cock. It wanted in but Aidan wanted this interlude to last a bit longer.

She played a few notes, and since his hand was still on the fret, it was natural for him to begin to shape the chords. He knew the music. She played more. Before they knew it, they were playing together.

Opening his mind, he invited her in, delighted when she took it. Together, hands, minds and hearts. He'd never felt so close to anyone else, gently invading her mind, inviting her into his. After he'd put a few dark secrets away.

One day soon he'd tell her his secret, all of it. He wanted to tell her. This was for real, this was for keeps. Leaning over her to see her hands move on the strings, he knew he'd never have moments like this with anyone else.

He wanted—no, he *needed*—to be inside her now. He slowed the music, playing "Tearing Me Apart" at an unhurried tempo, forcing her to take her time. When he moved the silk robe aside, she tensed, then he felt her mind and body relax and accept him. She wanted this too.

Lifting her, he eased her onto his lap. His cock slid inside her pussy as if it belonged there, which in his opinion it did. His mind froze with the intensity of the sensation. When he drew her closer, she settled on him with a sigh. Everything in him melted at her surrender. She was his, if not forever, at least for tonight. And that meant he was hers.

He couldn't move inside her, their position didn't allow that. At her mercy, he leaned forward and seated himself deeper inside her. This was right, this was real. Deliberately closing his mind to the uncertain future, he made the chords for her while she played. His hair swept over her shoulder, stroking her breast when they moved, but it didn't stop them making music. He watched her, helped her but deliberately held back and let her do the creation. After her carefully constructed classical career, he thought she might find the improvisation difficult, such an important part of his kind of music, but he was fascinated by her approach to the skill. It was different to the instinctive, visceral method he used, but just as effective, and he learned as much from her as she was learning from him. But oh God, how he needed her!

They never got to the end of the song. When he fluffed a chord, he hauled the guitar away and eased her forward. Corinne fell on her hands and he gripped her hips, dragging her back against him. Her bottom nestled against his groin and he nearly lost it there and then. He cried out, past words now, not sure why Corinne Westfall affected him like this, not caring. He threw his head back, took a deep breath and drove his cock hard into the body of the woman he loved.

Glancing to the side, he saw them. "Oh God, baby, look!"

This room had once been a bedroom, and he'd forgotten the full-length mirror. Usually it was covered with music stands, but she'd moved them aside to get to the guitar and it was revealed. As were they.

He knelt behind her, back arched, hair streaming down in rivulets of fire, trailing over her ass, her beautiful, softly rounded ass. She leaned forward on hands and knees, swathed in ivory satin, flame-tipped hair flying around her head when she turned to look. "Oh!"

Her flush brought fire to her cheeks as well as to her hair. He caressed her hip. "Don't be ashamed, love. It's the most beautiful thing I've ever seen."

She laughed, making her contract around him, sending his excitement up another notch. "Egotist."

He breathed out slowly, trying to regain some control, but it was no good, he was lost in her. "Not me. Us. You. Me in you. It's wonderful. Miraculous. Oh baby!"

Dragging her back against him, he pressed deep inside her, opening his mind to her completely, uncaring what she saw or discovered. He was hers. All he was, all he'd been was hers, if only she continued to make him feel like this.

The sight of his cock, glistening with her juices, sliding in and out of her with just enough resistance to drive both of them wild, drove him to heights he hadn't known existed before.

His orgasm came like a tidal wave, bursting through him, into her, flowing through them both. She came at the same moment and would have fallen forward if he hadn't been holding her firmly around her hips.

He collapsed over her, trying to roll to one side, unable to resist the darkness that swept over him.

Chapter Ten

ھ

When Corinne woke up, she lay on the floor, Aidan's arm draped across her waist. They were still in the music room. He must have found a spare quilt from somewhere, because he'd swaddled them in warmth.

She glanced across to the mirror. In her mind's eye, she still saw them reflected there, him kneeling behind her, his cock fully sheathed in her body, his balls nestled against her upper thighs, slamming into her with every plunge, his face blazing all the desire and need she'd felt in his violent thrusting. He was truly beautiful, his body, with the light raking over it, revealing all the hills and valleys of a well-toned man. *Her* well-toned man.

Corinne swallowed. Did she want this? It seemed she'd belonged to someone all her life, while never being herself. Now he wanted her to belong to him. She wanted it too, but she needed to find herself before it was too late. Too late to be a person in her own right. Her father had taken over her life to an extent she'd only become aware of recently, tricked her into thinking she was making her own decisions while she was really dancing to his tune. Now Aidan wanted to help her break away so he could have her for his own.

She wasn't even sure she loved him. Their lovemaking was spectacular, the way he accepted her astonishing, but she needed to think, and while he was doing wonderful things to her body, it was too difficult for her to ever consider giving it up. He was beautiful, but he seemed so invulnerable, so sure in his life and career, she could be nothing but an accessory.

Sometime soon she would have to break away, but for now, she'd hold on. The marriage seemed the best practical solution to her current dilemma, and although he said he'd let her go, she might hurt him terribly when she asked for a divorce. She sighed and his hand stirred.

She knew when he woke up. Something stirred in her mind, like a blink, then he was awake. He swung up to look down into her eyes. "What is it? What's wrong?"

Corinne put her thoughts out of her mind. "Can you teach me to block my thoughts?"

He bent and kissed her, very softly. "Yes. And how to use them to incite. You can work up an audience that way, get them rocking in minutes."

"Is that how you do it?"

He shook his head slowly. "No. It's a point of pride with us. We do it with the music, though we do feed off the energy they send back to us. Every rock band does that, psychic or not." He caressed her cheek with his free hand, and she moved into it.

"Energy." She sighed again. "That was what was missing in my last concerts. I don't want to go back to that."

"You won't have to." He bent to her. His warmth was so seductive that she almost succumbed, but she put her hands on his shoulders and held him off. He looked at her enquiringly, one brow raised in an expression she found incredibly sexy, combined with the heat in his eyes—heat that was for her alone.

"I don't think it will work," she said.

"Why not?" He waited, leaning on his elbows over her. The hard presence between his legs nudged her pussy, but she refused to give in to the feeling, not yet.

"Our images. I've been thinking. That brawl at the roadside café on the way here, that was no fluke. Your fans own you, mine own me, at least they think so. They'll fight to the death."

He stared at her, bottom lip caught between strong, white teeth. "I know. I hoped you wouldn't realize it. The

Hammersmith concerts weren't fully sold out before, but they are now. Yesterday there was a rush at the box office, and I'd make a guess that they were your fans. There could be trouble."

Panic gripped her. "I'm not going back."

"Sweetheart, you won't. I promise we'll do everything we can to keep you away from that."

"Aidan, if we met in different circumstances, if we," she halted as if she was searching for the right words, "got together, would you have minded if I'd continued as the virgin princess of classical music?"

He never took his gaze from her face. "Not if you were happy. We could have worked something out. This is temporary, just to get you away from your father. After we marry, you can break that damned contract. Then the band has a break coming up after the concerts. We're not due to get together until later in the summer, when *Icefire* should be recorded, mixed and ready to go. That gives us time to deal with your father, and for you to decide what you want to do."

A surge of eagerness went through her at his words. "You don't expect me to carry on with the band?" She was so close to freedom, she could almost taste it.

"Not if you don't want to. We need someone for these concerts, but after that—we'll see how you feel."

"You mean it?"

He stroked her breast with a gentle hand and her nipple rose in response. "Of course I do. I can't expect you to bounce from classical to rock without a great deal of thought. Corinne, I won't even hold you to our marriage if you don't want to carry on."

She couldn't repress the spark of hope and pleasure she felt. "Will you teach me that blocking technique now?"

"Can you wait awhile?" Smiling wickedly, he pushed forward and sheathed his eager cock inside her waiting body, slipping inside as if it was coming home.

When he entered her, it was as if part of her was returning, the part she'd been missing all her life but not really been aware of before. She had to welcome him. It was what she was, what she was made for. He kept her wet, or she was always wet when she was around him. She'd never been like that before, not for anyone, but she started to dampen the minute she saw him or felt his presence. Her body needed him, ached for him.

She opened her eyes to see him staring at her face, his expression momentarily bleak, but warming when she looked at him. She had no idea what troubled him.

Familiar magic invaded her and she gave in to it, opening her legs wide and lifting her knees, the sound of their joining proving to them both how much she loved this. At this moment, this was all she wanted, all she needed. To feel him in her, on her, loving her.

"Oh yes, sweetheart, loving you, always loving you!"

He'd picked up her thought. She withdrew a little, shocked that he read her so easily. He stopped moving but stayed deep inside her. "When we're this close, I can't help it. We're one person. Do you mind?"

"A little."

"Then I'll have to teach you to block me, won't I?" He bent to give her a quick, invasive kiss. "But not now."

She had no more wayward thoughts when he shoved his hands under her ass and lifted her to meet his driving thrusts. He brought her to ecstasy swiftly, the tiny climaxes prickling her senses and her nerves. He kept her there, working her, his rhythmic thrusts driving everything out of her mind except him. He reached the spots of delight inside her, rubbing his cockhead against them repeatedly, concentrating on her pleasure, her needs. She rushed up to meet him, willing to surrender everything, no longer worried about maintaining any barriers. If she had any, she wouldn't be able to feel this good, feel what he was feeling, building the joy between them.

When they climaxed this time, it was together, her orgasms building and blending into one huge peak. "Close your eyes," he whispered.

She felt him reach inside her and take her up with him. She'd read books where people seemed to leave their bodies, but this time it could be true. "Keep them closed," he murmured.

He took her away from the world, soaring into the air. She saw dawn breaking over the Tower of London, a rosy glow turning the White Tower to a soft peach. She saw the great ship, the HMS *Belfast*, in the morning glow, the Thames, never still, churning in the wake of the small boats forever bobbing on its surface. "It looks better up here, doesn't it?" The words in her ears nearly made her open her eyes and break the spell, but she remembered to keep them shut. He soared higher, taking them up, up, until she thought she might break apart from the joy of being here alone with him, her man, her love.

She shattered and he scattered sparks of living fire around them, smoke rising to block her view, exalting her as she collapsed in his arms, boneless and spent.

She opened her eyes, trembling with exhaustion, to see him gazing down at her, gently tender after the wild passion of a moment before. "How did you do that?"

"Never mind. Put it down to a vivid imagination. Sleep now, darling. Rest."

As soon as he knew she was asleep, Aidan got up and went to the kitchen, knowing he'd taken a risk. He didn't regret it for a moment.

"Okay, what did you do?"

Aidan spun around to see Ryan sprawled on the sofa. Ryan had a key, but in any case, there was probably a window open somewhere. "Shit, man, you startled me. What are you talking about?"

"I felt the surge and I'm not talking sex, which, by the way, you reek of."

"Jealous?" Aidan headed for the bread bin. He was suddenly hungry. He wanted to keep the scent of their lovemaking—tonight they'd gone way, way past simple fucking—in his nostrils as long as he could.

"Absolutely. I've been celibate for—well, never mind."

Aidan shoved two slices of bread in the toaster, poured away the coffee dregs, refilled the filter and flicked the coffee maker on before returning to face his brother. "Not since Maria?"

Ryan flinched. "Five years? Are you fucking kidding? No. About six months. But there's something missing. The last time it was actually boring. Imagine that. I had two of them, supposed to be the best groupies around." He scowled. "Shit. You don't get me that way, brother mine. What did you do?"

Aidan shrugged. "Corinne knows about the telepathy, so she thinks I have a vivid imagination. I showed her what you can see when you're in the air. I didn't take her up." He turned his back and went into the kitchen. "But I will."

He restocked the toaster before returning with the coffee and buttered toast. As he expected, Ryan snatched a slice up and tucked into it, watching as Aidan slumped into a chair. "For God's sake, get dressed. You're putting me off my breakfast."

Ryan wore the clothes he'd left with his brother the other day after their visit to Corinne's solicitor. Aidan chuckled. "See to the toast." He went upstairs, returning in five minutes dressed in jeans and a fresh t-shirt. He was glad to see Ryan had piled a few more slices of toast on the plate. He needed the sustenance.

Ryan finished his toast before speaking again. "You'll have to tell her."

"Not yet."

"Before you marry her."

Aidan tensed and Ryan leaned forward on the sofa. "You have to, Aidan. You can't marry her before she knows what you are and what that means."

Aidan looked away. "She's not sure she wants to stay married to me. She needs to change her name, that's all. It's the only way out of that fucking contract, bar murdering her father, but she might not stay with me."

"You want her to stay."

"Oh yeah."

Silence fell. Ryan would know what that meant only too well. He'd told Maria, who had blurted out the truth to a photographer from *Rolling Stone*. The man, the only sober person in the place, fortunately assumed it was nonsense from a junkie, but Maria, stoned or straight, rarely talked nonsense.

Ryan was the first to speak. "Tell her. Trust her, Aidan. If I hadn't trusted Maria, I'd have felt worse after she died. I took her up for a flight, you know. She said it was the most beautiful thing that ever happened to her. I promised her I'd convert her after we got the cure." He paused and stared at his feet, his face working. Aidan pretended not to notice. "Do it, Aidan. It's not fair to marry her without telling her everything you are. If you were going to marry and then divorce, no connection about sex, then yeah, why not, but you want her to accept you. So tell her."

"Not yet." Aidan trusted her, he was sure of that, so he wasn't sure why he didn't tell her. No, he was lying to himself. He knew why he didn't tell her what he was.

He was afraid she might leave him. She was skittish as it was. She could hide nothing from him. Even after he'd taught her to hide her thoughts, she wouldn't be able to hide anything from him. He was the phoenix, the one and only, and his powers were immense.

He was tired of it. The only people who knew his secret and treated him like a person were the members of the band. Once he'd learned his skills and powers, he just had to—be.

People who knew, other shape-shifters, treated him with awe, which bored and infuriated him. Added to that was the awe many fans accorded him. He only wanted to play his music, he didn't want anything else. If Corinne knew, she'd recoil in fear or disgust. He couldn't bear it if she showed him any awe. "Let's get the wedding over with. Then I'll tell her, I swear it. She needs to get away from her father, needs it more than she needs to know about me." He paused. "Can you get me some Cephalox?"

Ryan studied him carefully. "Why should I?"

"Because you have some. Don't you?"

Slowly, Ryan nodded, his gleaming eyes dulling to yellow. "I have some left. I keep it to remind me never to take it again, to prove to myself I don't need it. I'll give it to you, but only enough to get you through the next full moon."

"I won't take it past the wedding."

"You bet you won't. That stuff is as addictive as heroin," Ryan growled, biting into another slice of toast.

Chapter Eleven

ॐ

Finally, Corinne understood why celebrities wore shades in dark nightclubs. It was so they could sleep. After a day's rehearsal and several lessons in mind-blocking, Corinne no longer cared where she slept. With Aidan's arm around her, she dozed fitfully against his shoulder, even though the music was deafening and the lights on the dance floor flashed wildly.

The other band members slouched on armchairs and sofas, obviously made of sterner stuff than she was. Jake had a groupie draped on each arm, leather-clad lovelies who were obviously going to end up in his bed. Corinne would end up in Aidan's bed, but she doubted they'd be making energetic love, at least not until after at least eight hours sleep.

They were only here to show themselves. Aidan consulted his publicist, who spread the word. In a recent telephone conversation, John Westfall declared himself delighted. "When we get back together for the new band with your sisters, we'll be on the front pages," he'd said. Not if Corinne had anything to do with it, they wouldn't.

"Well, hello!"

Corinne opened her eyes. Through the darkness of the lenses, she saw a familiar shape. Her heart sank. "Paige. What are you doing here?" She took off the sunglasses, pushing them up on her head, but didn't lift away from Aidan.

"Have you forgotten the TV program?" Uninvited, Paige sat down next to Ryan. "We have to be at the studio the day after tomorrow, so we thought we'd do a bit of shopping. Dad's come up to town too. Business." She made a wry face. Corinne's internal warning bell went off. Why hadn't her father told her he planned to come up to town when she'd spoken to him earlier in the day?

"Hi." Ashley and Tom had found them. Tom's eyes opened wide when he saw her, but she wasn't sure if it was the new hair and makeup or Aidan's suddenly wary presence that startled him. Ashley forced herself into the narrow space left on the long seat, forcing Tom to go and find a stool, dragging it up to sit next to Jake. This left him facing Corinne directly across the small table currently decorated by a collection of glasses and three pairs of booted feet, including Aidan's.

She peered at her sisters. Ashley and Paige made the groupies with them look classy. Their white jeans were so tight the clefts of their pussies were clearly visible through the thin fabric, and their tops, while opaque, fitted so tightly she could see the dimples around their nipples. Even though she didn't want to.

The music was too loud for a great deal of conversation, which Corinne thought was a blessing. She replaced the sunglasses and snuggled in to Aidan, ready for a little more dozing before they went home. "Why are you here?" Paige demanded suddenly, her voice loud enough to slice through a dozen sound systems.

"Why is anybody here?" Jake looked around at the crowded dance floor. They were sitting in a roped-off area meant for A-list celebrities, but the club contained a good sprinkling of the rich and famous from all the lists. It was the place to be, at least for this month, which was why they'd chosen this particular venue. "Dance?" He jerked Ashley to her feet and dragged her off in the direction of the dance floor.

Corinne watched them go, her sister's buttocks, cinched in the too-tight white jeans, working overtime trying to keep up with Jake's ground-eating strides. A smile curved her lips. "A combination of Jake and that outfit will kill her reputation as a sweet virgin."

Paige leaned forward across Ryan as if he wasn't there. "We've decided to take a leaf out of your book. We're going to behave like sluts for a while."

Her eyes opened wide in shock and she shot back as if someone had grabbed her collar and pulled. Nobody had, at least not physically. Corinne knew Aidan hadn't done it, though she'd felt his surge of anger at Paige's words.

Ryan smiled lazily at Paige. "She's not a slut," he said mildly, the timbre of his words contrasting enough with the loud dance music to make himself heard without having to raise his voice.

"No, I didn't mean that," Paige yelled hastily, pulling at her halter top to restore it to its rightful position after it swooped so low it threatened to become redundant. "I meant we aren't going to be eternal virgins like you were. We can dirty our image a bit. Daddy's seen how good it's been for you, so he gave us the okay. Your sales have gone up this last week or two."

Corinne sighed. She didn't want anyone to drag her back to her old life. The rise in sales would only make her father keener to get her back.

No chance of that happening. Aidan's communication came loud and clear in her mind.

She'd left herself open. She began to shield her thoughts from Aidan, then stopped. There was no reason to do so. Warmth flooded her mind when he caught her thought. He'd taught her how to shield herself from everyone else. It had been strangely easy to learn, as though she'd known once, then forgotten.

Paige eyed Chris across the table, lowering her heavily blue-mascaraed lashes to half mast. Corinne almost crowed with laughter and felt Chris' friendly presence in her mind. *Be careful, Chris. She wants you.*

You mean she's not a pure virgin? You disappoint me. I've not had one of those for a long time. Chris' communication came on a

167

different level to the one she shared with Aidan and she smiled at him. He sometimes phrased his mental messages in unusual ways, as though he'd lived when formality ruled. His surface image was perfect, hard, bulging biceps proclaiming his role as drummer in the band, language slurred and filled with curse words, but he'd never sworn in her mind or treated her with less than respect. He was an enigma to her, the most brutal in appearance but the gentlest in reality.

"The 'Diva' people want you to come along," Paige yelled. The music ended, immediately replaced by another track. "They want an interview with the new Corinne Westfall."

That was the real reason the twins had come tonight. She'd bet the farm on it.

Corinne didn't have to consider her answer. "No." No in-depth interviews, not yet. They all agreed on that. She would appear with the band, or with Aidan, but not on her own until the public accepted her new role. At least until the concerts were over. "We're too busy, Paige. Tell them to come back to me in a month."

The warmth Aidan sent her was replaced by a wariness she knew came straight from the heart. He wanted her to stay with him, to see what they had together, as he'd put it. She was sorely tempted, although she wasn't sure the love he said he felt for her was anything more than lust or infatuation.

What she felt for him was different to the days before she met him. Somewhere, the dangerous rock star had gone, replaced by a caring, gentle man with a dangerous edge, never turned in her direction but present all the same. Sometimes she'd sensed something else in him, a wildness she'd yet to explore and didn't really want to. When she touched that area of his mind, she felt pain, a sting warning her off. She wasn't sure if he knew it or not, because he never showed any awareness of causing her any pain and would normally go out of his way to prevent it.

Paige's mouth curled in a sneer. "Too busy? What are you doing?"

"Rehearsing." Corinne sat up. Rest was denied her now. She leaned forward and located her glass of whisky and ginger ale, more ginger ale than whisky.

Paige stared around the table, her sneer still in place. "It's only a rock group, Corinne. You can do better than that."

Corinne knew how deliberately tactless Paige could be. The hurtful words came from a sense of superiority and overweening selfishness. There was no more under the surface than there was on it. "I doubt it. Pure Wildfire is rock royalty, Paige. I'm lucky to be here. Each one of these musicians could teach you something important, if you were ready to learn. This band earns more in a year than we do in five. You can hear the music from Moscow to London. And they deserve it. They earn it."

Having said her piece, she snuggled back into Aidan's arms. She was really tired, otherwise she wouldn't have allowed Paige to get to her.

She watched Paige make a play for Chris and watched Chris accept her, but she couldn't bring herself to care. Chris would fuck her, but it was unlikely Paige would find herself in the inner circle. As she'd done, she realized with a start. Chris soon had Paige locked in a deep tongue kiss and Corinne lost interest and closed her eyes, feeling Aidan nuzzle her hair.

A low murmuring came from somewhere above her head and Aidan nudged her gently. "Hey, babe, I think we can go now. The paparazzi will be hanging about outside. Do you feel up to it?"

"Of course. If you hadn't kept me up half the night, I wouldn't be so tired in any case." When she sat up, she realized the music had, for once, stopped, and the table was once again fully occupied. Everybody heard her last remark.

I will not blush, I will not blush!

169

Aidan, damn him, threw his head back and howled with laughter. Punching him in the ribs only made him laugh more. Glancing around the table gave her three broad grins and three glares, especially from Paige. She sent a furious message to Aidan. *If you don't shut up, I'll set Paige on you. She fancies you, you know!*

What?

He stared across the table at Paige and Corinne knew he was probing her mind. He slumped back, his hand over his eyes. "Oh God! I wish you hadn't told me that!"

She heard Ryan's wicked laugh. "Would you like me to take over there, Chris?"

Chris put his head on one side, pretending to mull the offer over. "Not yet. I'll tell you when. You can have the other one."

Aidan got to his feet. "Let's leave these rakes alone."

"Rakes?" Corinne hadn't heard the expression outside a historical romance.

Aidan shrugged. "It's what they used to call them, isn't it?"

"Once upon a time, little brother," Ryan said. "Be careful people don't think you're living in the past."

Aidan clapped him on the shoulder on the way out. "Nobody thinks that about me. Only you and the other two. See you tomorrow."

"Nice and early."

Corinne suspected Ryan wouldn't bother going to bed at all. She turned to Paige. "When do you have to be in the studio?"

"Not until nine tomorrow."

Corinne shrugged. Why should she care? There had never been any room for her in the relationship between Paige and Ashley. They determinedly cut her out of any intimacy and constantly belittled her and her music. Their mother despised her mother, because Corinne's mother had been a nobody and theirs was a member of the English aristocracy. Corinne knew their mother encouraged it, and while she'd been living with her father, Corinne's life had been worse than at any other time, before or since. She'd coped. Now she didn't really care.

Or so she told herself, but before she left, she put a gentle hand on Ashley's shoulder. "Make sure she goes to bed soon," she murmured. Ashley gave her a sneer in return and sidled close to Ryan as Jake returned to his groupies, who weren't at all bothered by his temporary defection to dance with Paige. One of them shot her a sympathetic glance from under heavily mascaraed eyes as she passed.

Aidan and Corinne left, lingering outside the club to allow the photographers to snap a few pictures of them together. Aidan looked happy, Corinne looked tired but happy. It would give the impression they wanted.

Two days later, they sat with Ryan and Jake in Aidan's apartment and watched TV. "Divas" was an occasional series, usually done in blocks of six, when the presenters interviewed young women from the arts about their work. Corinne had done a program a few years ago, and now it was Paige and Ashley's turn. Corinne decided this was the best place to watch the program from—on the sofa, in Aidan's arms, instead of sitting in the studio trying to think up something interesting to say to the interviewer's vapid questions. "Paige looks tired."

Ryan chuckled. "Chris has been making sure she's short on sleep. Westfall's livid. I think that's why Chris is doing it, because she's not his usual type."

Corinne wasn't shocked. Ryan by now made some of his comments merely to provoke, not because they were true. Unlike the relationship between herself and Aidan, Paige and Chris had been discreet after that first meeting at the nightclub. Neither wanted to alert the press to the affair, though she had no doubt that if Paige thought the liaison would be useful, she'd use it.

The interviewer talked about their work, their father, whom he predictably called "Svengali", and their upcoming band, the Westfall Sisters. It was Paige who introduced Corinne's involvement. "Our sister is to join us, with Thomas Albright. Our father has booked studio time for next month, so we hope to begin working on the album soon."

"Corinne joined a rock band. Hasn't she turned her back on classical music?"

Ashley laughed. "Why should she? She's only taking some time out and helping the band. They were desperate for a guitarist." Ashley's spiteful remark bothered none of the members of the band, but it concerned Corinne. "That's not true!"

Aidan squeezed her hand. "I love your loyalty."

"Aidan!"

Ryan chuckled. "You think we don't know how he feels about you, little sister?"

"I-I—"

"We're family, Corinne. Whatever you decide in the long term, you'll always find friends with us."

Tears sprang to her eyes. She'd never met that kind of friendship in her life before. So casually explained, as if it was normal. Which it was for the members of Pure Wildfire. Just not for her.

The interviewer continued. "Do you expect your sister to return if the upcoming concerts at the Hammersmith Apollo are a success?"

Paige gave him a pitying look. "Of course she will."

"Not if I have anything to do with it," murmured Aidan.

"Oh Corinne's not going back," Jake said. He picked up his glass and tossed back the contents, reaching for the brandy bottle by his side. Corinne exchanged a grin with the blond giant. She'd not only found a lover, she'd found friends.

The interviewer asked the twins a few cursory questions about the new venture, then returned to the subject of Corinne. They watched Paige become increasingly annoyed, and when the camera widened to include Ashley, they saw how red her cheeks had become too. "Ashley only blushes like that when she's angry," Corinne commented.

She waited for the outburst, and sure enough, it came. "I thought you wanted to talk about us!" Ashley broke into a question about Pure Wildfire and their plans for the new tour in the autumn. "We're planning a tour, you know, and we'll get far more interest than Corinne. If you ask me, she's cheapened herself by taking up with a rock band, and her plans to marry Aidan Hawthorne are stupid, all her own imagination!"

With Ashley's explosion of rage came a picture. Behind her on the screen flashed a photograph one of the paparazzi had taken outside the nightclub, of Aidan and Corinne locked in a passionate, openmouthed kiss. They'd caught it when Aidan had drawn back a little, and the view of his tongue in her mouth spoke louder than words about what they'd be doing when they got home.

The kiss was staged for the photographers, but the usual magic happened and they'd forgotten everything except each other. Just after that moment, Aidan grabbed Corinne and almost threw her into the waiting car, eager to be home and inside her again.

The picture put the lie to everything Ashley said. Aidan's hand tightened around Corinne's. *God, you make me so horny, princess!*

At those heated words, Corinne became hot, just like that. She was no longer sure whether she fed her desire to him or the other way around. It didn't matter anymore.

Jake got to his feet. "Why do I feel we're not needed?" he said, grinning at Ryan, whose own smile was as wide as a Cheshire cat's.

"Because we're not. Come on, I'll buy you a drink in the piazza. We might get lucky ourselves."

As they let themselves out, Corinne heard Jake say, "Not as lucky as those two."

But by then she was in Aidan's arms, his lips on hers, his heated excitement feeding hers and enveloping them both. She returned the passion, no longer afraid to show him everything she felt, no longer wanting to.

He had their clothes off in record time and he was inside her even quicker. Only when Ashley's scandalized shriek came from the TV did he reach out a long arm for the remote. He managed to mute the sound, but by then they were lost in each other and he dropped the remote on the floor somewhere just after he found the off switch.

Corinne straddled Aidan, staring down into the depths of his amber eyes, driving him deeper within her. When he reached down to touch her clit, she sat straight up in shock, urged on by his moans of need. She plunged recklessly, taking every bit of his swollen shaft, wanting more. Every time she slammed down onto him, her clit touched his fingers, and he pinched and stroked, stimulating her inside and outside.

He gave her more, his cock growing inside her, reaching every part of her and flooding her with sensation. "Everything you want, I'll give to you, Corinne." He reached up with his other hand to trace her nipple with the tip of one finger, his long artist's fingers as fluent on her breast as he was on the guitar.

"I just want you, Aidan." The honesty she saw in his face gave her the courage to take the final step and tell him what she knew to be true. "I do love you."

She did, she was sure of it now. He treated her like a queen without smothering her, he knew what she needed and gave it to her quietly and without fuss. Except when they were making love, when he made her see fireworks. She wanted to give him everything in return.

She saw how much that simple statement meant to him by his dawning joy, the way his eyes blazed in response.

He sat up and took her in his arms, showering her face with kisses. *You won't regret it, my darling, I swear it to you!* Pushing hard up into her, he brought her to a quick orgasm, and when she shuddered around him, her body shivering around his ultrasensitive cock, he drove her to another one, holding on before he exploded inside her. Corinne surrendered, letting him take control and care for her as she knew he wanted to do. She'd resisted as long as she could, but now she gave herself to him, surrendered completely.

He knew and he rejoiced. She heard him in her mind, surrounding her with warmth and love, the love he'd been waiting to give her.

Drawing back, he framed her face with one hand. "You don't have to do that. We're together now, but your life is still your own. I know what it means to you. As long as you let me in far enough to love you, I'll be happy."

"Even if we live apart for a while?"

He smiled and kissed her. "Even then, my love."

He was still hard inside her. It would be a crime not to use it. More than anything else, she wanted to make him happy, so she pushed on his shoulders until he took the hint and lay down again. Tracing the muscles banding his chest, she watched him shiver in pleasure. Then she placed both palms on his chest and lifted off him, sinking slowly back down, watching him. His eyes drifted shut, and he let her pleasure him. She began gently, riding him with a gentle but sure rhythm, but built up her movements, each lift higher, each plunge harder, the sounds and scents of their lovemaking surrounding them with each other, and nothing else. She clamped her inner muscles around his cock to stroke him with each movement and it heightened her rise. He gripped her thighs hard enough to leave prints. She welcomed the pressure and it didn't stop her drive up to ecstasy.

They came at the same time, leg muscles locking together in a sublime moment of joy as the world spiraled out of control. Corinne gasped and cried his name, letting her orgasm blossom, encompassing everything she was in one of life's perfect moments.

She slumped forward onto him, totally spent, while his arms went around her in an unbreakable hold. His lips nuzzled her ear. "You're amazing, Corinne, you know that?"

With him still inside her, she slid into a light doze.

She woke up sometime later when he stood, still holding her. "Shower, my love? Just relax, let me do it all."

Happiness and contentment filled her and she reached up to slide her arms around his neck, pulling herself up a little so she could nuzzle her breasts against his hard, warm chest. He lifted her and climbed the stairs, the ease of his movements an effortless demonstration of his strength. He wasn't even out of breath.

Only after he carried her through the bedroom to the shower did he let her feet touch the floor, setting her carefully on the studded tiles before climbing in to join her. He turned the large knob to set the water flowing around them.

She reached out to touch the tattoo that only appeared when they made love, the glowing bird on his thigh, tracing the ridges gently. "How does this work?"

He gazed at her, studying her face gravely before he said anything. "Well—"

Before he finished speaking, he shuddered. His whole body quivered under his skin, as though it fought against his form, the muscles bunching and twisting. He threw his head back and groaned, but this time it wasn't ecstasy that moved him.

"Wait," he managed to gasp. "Wait here. I'll be back soon."

He pushed the screen aside and stepped out, hurrying into the bedroom.

Corinne stood under the streaming heat, transfixed with horror. She had no idea what could have made him react like that. Even classical music had its drug addicts, so she'd seen a few things she would rather forget. This didn't look like a simple case of flashback or withdrawal. Was he ill?

The thought spurred her into action. Grabbing a towel, she ran into the bedroom to a sight that filled her with horror.

Aidan was in the process of filling a syringe from a capsule, a strap bound tightly to his upper arm, the end held in his teeth. A box lay open on the bed, filled with capsules, spilling out on to the brightly colored bedcover, and another box lay open, showing a collection of spare needles.

They stared at each other, Aidan, hands frozen in action, the gleaming syringe touching his skin.

"You're an addict?" she whispered. "Oh Aidan, no! Or are you ill, do you have a condition—" She broke off, knowing she was clutching at straws. If he'd been a diabetic or been suffering from a condition that needed injections, he would have told her by now. Not if he was an addict. He knew how she felt about that.

He dropped the strap and let it fall loose. He opened his mouth to speak, but she saw it move and change, the nose lengthening to a strong, sharp edge.

With his remaining human muscles, he shrugged in a gesture of resignation. Then he seemed to relax, letting the filled syringe fall to the floor. He watched her, his eyes changing to a round, domed shape, but they were still his eyes, the man she loved residing deeply inside them. When she felt him reach for her with his mind, she slammed down her barriers in panic, a reaction she couldn't stop, nor did she want to.

What was he? What kind of creature had she just declared herself in love with?

Aidan continued to transform, the process accelerating until he took the shape of a great eagle. Golden feathers covered his wings, the color deepening to orange on his breast. His long, wickedly hooked beak looked like an eagle's, but he was far larger than any eagle Corinne had ever encountered or heard of and his feathers deepened in color.

When he lifted his wings, the span easily covered the width of the room and the movement freed Corinne from her paralysis. She ran.

Chapter Twelve

ℬ

After scrambling into a t-shirt and jeans, Corinne grabbed her jacket and raced out of the flat, only pausing to pull on a pair of sandals by the door. She needed to get away from this monster. Her whole world switched on its axis and she felt alone, spinning in a world she didn't understand. She'd just made love with something she didn't recognize, something she hadn't a word for. Fuck, she'd told him she loved him.

When she thought of Aidan, so loving, so talented, so utterly desirable, her heart melted, only to recall the moment he'd changed into something that terrified her so much her brain froze.

At first, she thought of looking for Ryan and Jake, but that was too dangerous. They were close to Aidan and they might know about this monstrosity. She couldn't quite believe what she'd just seen, but she had to.

Glimpsing a red t-shirt, she didn't take any more chances, in case Ryan and Jake were still in the piazza, so she left the main square of Covent Garden before they saw her.

Her mind went back to the conversation with her father, just before she'd left his house. He'd told her Aidan was something called a firebird.

Well, now she'd seen a firebird for herself. She wanted to see her father. Now. And she knew where to find him.

The Savoy was a short distance away from Covent Garden, at the end of South Street. She could get a room for the night. Her sisters were there and her father. She couldn't go back. She could never face Aidan again.

She had to know, had to be sure. Her father had shown her that book, called him a firebird. He already knew. She needed answers, needed to know what Aidan was so she could make her decisions and decide what to do next. Was she in any danger? Her mind revolved around the sight in the bedroom, half man, half bird. And still wholly beautiful.

Tears filled her eyes, spilling over on to her cheeks. Just when she'd given herself to him, trusted him with everything she was! Was that was he was waiting for? She should have remembered—she couldn't trust anyone. She already knew she couldn't trust her father, and now it seemed Aidan had his own agenda too. At least he'd taught her how to block thoughts, how to put up a barrier. She tested it now, making it as strong as she could. Nobody would contact her telepathically if she could prevent it.

She was sick of being drawn into other people's plans! Her tears dried when fury replaced her sorrow. Yes, she'd lost Aidan, but she'd make her own decisions. No more avoiding people, no more drifting. She'd take time out to make her own decisions, and whatever she decided, she would stand or fall by it. So help her God, she would. But she needed as much information as she could get and that lay ahead of her.

The Savoy's familiar blue neon sign glowed before her. Without pause, she walked in, daring the attendant outside the door to stop her. He did not.

Only to find they could only find a small single room for her. Despising the "Do you know who I am?" approach, she asked the clerk to reconsider. The man found a room he had somehow overlooked when Corinne flashed the Amex Platinum card from her wallet. *Quelle surprise.*

Upstairs in an overly fussy room with a pink-draped bed, Corinne picked up the phone and found the number of her father's room, after giving them the required codeword, the one her father always used when he stayed here. Back in the family fold. She headed down there, figuring that taking him off guard was a point in her favor.

She was right. His expression of surprise when he opened the door gave her some satisfaction. And she didn't let up, striding into his suite and standing in the middle of the floor, confronting him. "So what did you mean when you wanted me to get you a feather?"

He regarded her cautiously and used one of his usual delaying tactics. Walking to the mini bar, he asked, "Drink?"

"No thank you. Tell me."

"You've seen him?" No longer concerned with the bar, her father faced her. "You saw him change his form?"

The eagerness in his face gave her pause. For once, she was in control. "Why do you ask that?"

"It's the only way you'd believe me."

"Is it?"

He scowled. "Don't lie to me, girl, I know what he is. And you know what I want. That feather will give me power."

"What kind of power?" Her eyes narrowed in speculation.

John sighed. "Why does it matter to you? Just get me the feather and I'll make you the greatest star in the world."

"I'm not sure I want that anymore." Corinne studied her father anew. She'd become a new person since she'd seen him last. She no longer required his approval or his money. There was enough money in the bank to see her through for several years. She'd made sure of that along the way, opening new accounts completely unrelated to the ones her father had set up for her.

Her father only had her bound for five albums, and if she didn't want to make them, there was nothing he could do about it, as long as she didn't sign with anyone else. There were other ways of making music.

The realization gave her the bargaining chip she needed. "I don't need you, Dad. John." He'd insisted her daughters address him as "John" as soon as they'd signed their first contract. "I can get a job doing anything except recording albums and I will if you're not straight with me. What can you offer me?"

John Westfall regarded his daughter carefully. Corinne watched his speculative gaze, knowing what he was thinking.

With a shock, she realized she really did know. She could read his mind, or at least parts of it. He was going to offer her more money. She'd locked down receiving communications, but she must still be able to project.

"I'll increase your royalties per album."

Smiling, she shook her head.

John hissed through his teeth. "I'll make you the center of the new band."

It wasn't enough. It might never be enough. She needed to rethink her life, what she was or could be. The series of shocks had completed the process of galvanizing her out of her apathy and into what she always should have been—a powerful, independent woman making her own decisions.

"Never mind that for now. We'll talk deals later." Or not at all. She took a turn about the room, noting the green damask chairs, the oil paintings, the general air of wealth she'd taken for granted for most of her life. She didn't need any of this shit, but she could have it if she wanted it. "Tell me about firebirds."

A smile curved John Westfall's lips. "You want to know what you've been screwing?" He turned and went to the mini bar, pulling out a bottle of whisky. He cracked the top and poured himself a small shot. Corinne shook her head when he waved the bottle in her direction. "Well then, let's sit down."

She chose an armchair that looked as though no one had ever used it before, making sure it was far away enough for her father so he couldn't touch her. She wasn't sure she wanted anyone to touch her, ever again.

He rolled his drink between his hands, the cut glass glittering in the muted sunshine filtering through the lace covered windows. "Firebirds are very rare and they keep themselves hidden." He glanced up. Corinne watched him impassively. "There are other kinds of shape-shifters, but firebirds have great power."

"How is that possible?" Corinne wondered. "Was Darwin wrong?"

"No. Just not completely right. I don't know how it all works, but evolution wasn't in a straight line. It deviated, so there are species that are human in form, but not the same as us. We're linked, that is, the DNA is similar, but there are things they have that we don't." He paused. "Some species can transmit their gifts to us. They can make us like them. Others can't."

"So there really are shape-shifters?" Corinne breathed. She had to believe him now. She'd seen it for herself.

John took a sip of his drink. "Oh yes. And other, weirder beings. Some have died out and some are only just surviving."

"Are we at the bottom of the pile?"

John shook his head. "No other species has the drive ours has. We want more, always more. And we have the best analytical abilities of any species. Most are just happy to coast along." He shot her a speculative glance. "The mortal's real skill is our ability to reproduce. No other species of human can produce as many children as we can."

"Mortal?"

He shrugged. "Not accurate, but it's what they call us. We're all humans. We must be, because we can reproduce."

Corinne tried very hard to quell the natural skepticism she felt when talking to her father like this. For years he'd spoken of these things as though they were real and Corinne and the twins always derided him, refused to believe it. There were many reasons why this shouldn't be real, but she'd seen it now. She couldn't deny it forever. "Why do you want this feather? What have firebirds got that you want?"

John paused and finished his drink. When he looked at Corinne, his eyes were clear of deceit, so she knew for sure he was lying or, at the very least, holding something back. She didn't need to probe his mind to see that. Good old body language worked perfectly well. "They can live forever, or for a very long time, and they have the power to make people do what they want. I want those abilities."

"I've always been empathetic." She could always feel emotions around her, but until Aidan introduced her to it, she'd never believed in telepathy. "I could help you do that. And—perhaps a little more."

Her father's cold gaze sharpened. "What more? Has he given you a feather already? Have you accepted it?"

"What are you *talking* about?" He still hadn't told her.

He relaxed back in his chair. "Then he hasn't. Corinne, I want you to go back to him. Do the concerts, get that feather off him and bring it to me. I know how to unlock the power in it. I'll share it with you, I promise."

All this emphasis on one feather was very strange. The last time she'd seen Aidan, he was covered in them. "Doesn't he molt or something? Won't the feathers just be discarded?"

John grinned. "I've never known a firebird to molt, but sometimes feathers do get detached. They're worth nothing like that, apart from the rarity value. He has to give you this one of his own free will or it's just a pretty decoration. Only when he's given it does it mean something."

"If he gives it to me, doesn't that mean it's for me only?"

"No. You're free to give it to anyone you like."

Corinne looked away, staring sightlessly out of the window to the cloud-scattered sky above London. Her father wasn't telling her everything, but he'd told her enough to confirm that she wasn't going mad. She turned back to him. "How do you know he's what you say?"

John grinned. "All firebirds have a symbol tattooed on their thighs. A bird, or a feather, something of that nature. It's like a birthmark. It appears when they reach puberty. That's when they come into their full powers. It also means they're compelled to change form at the full moon."

"Have you seen the mark on Aidan?" she asked sharply. It was either that or he'd seen the marking on Aidan's thigh and how could he have done that?

"No." John answered too quickly. He was lying again.

Her shocked mind went back to the first time she and Aidan made love. In the rehearsal room at the manor. "Say you didn't spy on us. Say it wasn't then. Oh no, Dad, you couldn't have done that!" She leaped to her feet and made for the door, only taking in a little of his protestations.

"I'm no voyeur, my girl, never think it! I felt something— you're not the only empathetic member of the family, you know! I went to see—and I saw you both asleep. Very sweet." His mouth stretched in a sneer. "That's when I saw the mark on his thigh. He's a firebird, isn't he?"

"I don't know."

For the first time it occurred to Corinne that any other parent's first question, on seeing their daughter alone and distressed, might be to ask if Aidan had hurt her. If she was all right. Not John Westfall. His first thought was what he could gain from her. It was always like that—he never put his family over his business. She didn't expect it, so she hadn't thought it unusual until just now.

It had taken a bird to bring it home to her. A bird who showed her more love and care in two weeks than her family had in twenty-eight years.

She'd made the wrong decision. She should have stayed and talked with him. Whatever he was, Aidan would never hurt her. But when she thought of his transformation, her mind froze. It was too much for her to accept right now. "Dad, I have to think. I know I owe you five albums under the contract, but I'm thinking of giving it up completely. Or knocking out some crap in the studio."

"You won't do that."

No, she wouldn't. There was always an imperative to do her best, however pissed off she might be with the music her father asked her to play. She owed the people who bought her albums more than that. But she could give it up completely. "Does the contract say what kind of music I have to play?"

"No." John was watching her carefully. He leaned back in his chair, smiling expansively. "We might be able to renegotiate. Five might be a bit too much. We'll get a new contract drawn up."

He'd sacrifice one or two albums to secure her again, tie up the loophole. Well, she could be sneaky too. After all, she'd watched the best at work. So she gave him a conciliatory smile. "It would be nice. I want to study, Dad. It's time I brushed up my skills."

He considered, studying her through narrowed eyes. "It could be a good thing. We might be able to write it in to your career. Perhaps a year off would do you good." He leaned forward, steepling his hands, resting his elbows on his knees. "If I let you do this, I want something in return. Go and do the concerts with Pure Wildfire. I own their last album, *Sunfire*, and I want them to talk it up. And get me that feather. I tell you what. If you get me that feather, I'll tear up that contract, and this new band, the one with your sisters, can find another guitarist. I'll work at finding you a new niche. The old one's just about worn out anyway. How about that?"

He must be desperate. John bargained hard, and didn't give anything up without a fight. It was true Corinne's sales were going down, but that was from a high level, and the sales weren't plummeting, merely making a graceful swan dive into eventual obscurity some time in the future. He could milk the next five albums and use her to finance his newer ventures, which generally needed a higher financial output.

"I'll think about it. Give me a day or two to make my mind up. I might want to do those albums and take the time off instead." She stood up and faced the window, careful to keep her expression bland even then. There might be a mirror or her expression could reflect from the glass. Or there might be a hidden camera or two. John Westfall knew all about those. "I'll give you my decision by Wednesday, I promise."

"That's acceptable."

A knock came on the door and John barked his customary, "Come!" It was the twins, dressed in full evening rig, followed by Tom in black tie. A gala somewhere. Like her, they were garnering publicity. They glared at Corinne and she felt the hatred coming off them in waves.

"What are you doing here?" Paige demanded.

"I'm staying here," Corinne said. "Just for a few days."

"Love gone bad?" Tom sneered.

She lifted an eyebrow. "No. It's all for show anyway. Haven't you worked that out yet?"

"That's not what I saw the other night. You were all over each other."

"So were the paparazzi. They're lapping it up." She caught an approving smile from her father, which didn't warm her in the least. She kept her senses carefully blocked so he wouldn't pick anything up from her, but there was no need to worry about the twins or Tom. They had never sensed an audience's moods as she and her father could.

She tilted up her chin, regarding Ashley coolly. "You should really try to separate your working and your private lives."

Ashley glared at her. "You're not saying you didn't sleep with him."

Corinne's gaze transferred to Paige. "Wouldn't you?" Paige blushed and looked away. "If you want a date, Paige, I can probably set you up with one of the others when Chris has finished with you. You seemed particularly taken with Ryan. Let me know."

"Are you marrying Splinter then?"

This was hardest of all. The honest answer was that she didn't know. He might not want her anymore after she ran out on him and she needed to work through her feelings for him. She shrugged. "It gave the press something to write about, didn't it?"

Paige's eyes narrowed in dislike. "It certainly wrecked 'Divas'. That program was supposed to be for us, and all that man was interested in was talking about you! They even put it out early to catch the news about you. It was supposed to go out next month, to link up with our next gig and the news about the band, but oh no, the high and mighty Corinne has to have center stage. Even if she's not there."

Tom preened and stretched his arm out on the sofa behind Ashley's head. "I'm not sure we want you for the band, Corrie. I can see friction." He shot Corinne a quizzical glance, his dark brows drawing together before relaxing when he smiled. "I like your hair. It suits you."

"That means *so* much to me," Corinne said wryly, verbal acid dripping from her mouth. "I don't know if I'm interested in joining your band. I have other plans."

Paige's outraged gasp was all she'd hoped it would be. Strands of dark hair whipped around Paige's face as she turned to their father. "Dad, you promised!"

"There's nothing in writing," her father reminded his daughter. "And if Corinne doesn't want to join, it won't make for a comfortable relationship, will it? When she's finished with Pure Wildfire, she'll need a rest, so I'm giving her a month off after the concerts." His sharp gaze went to Corinne. "She has a favor to do for me, and then she may go and enjoy herself somewhere."

A chance to think. Corinne would have begged her father for that once, between the ages of sixteen and twenty, when he kept her working without a break. Now she was in a position to set her own terms.

Why did he want that feather so badly? What kind of power would it give him, exactly? Her father had a subtle mind, so the feather could be a blind. It might just be a feather. He might want something else entirely.

Her mind on the conundrum, Corinne made her way back to her room for some much-needed sleep. When she woke in the early morning light, the first thing she saw was Ryan Hawthorne, sitting on the edge of the frilly pink bed.

Chapter Thirteen

∞

Corinne sat bolt upright, only remembering at the last moment that she was naked. Flushing, she hauled the sheet up to cover herself. Ryan, dressed in one of the white toweling hotel bathrobes, tossed her another one and stood up, deliberately turning his back on her. Corinne quickly shrugged into the white toweling robe, tying the belt firmly around her waist. "How did you get in here?" she demanded, too angry to be afraid.

"I came in through the bathroom window." Ryan turned, the corners of his mouth turning up in a smile.

Corinne ignored the echo of the Beatles song, refusing to be amused. "You climbed up?"

"No, I flew."

Corinne clutched the robe to her throat. Ryan kept his distance. "Didn't you guess? We're all shape-shifters. I'm his brother, Corinne, and it runs in families."

All his rock star arrogance had gone. There was only the man—creature—left. He gazed at her, his amber eyes direct and honest. "Corinne, there are plenty of people who are different. We live among you. Just because our difference isn't obvious, it doesn't make us any stranger than Africans were when the Europeans first saw them, or Indians, or the Chinese for that matter. Don't treat us as if we're less than human just because we're different."

She'd not thought of it like that before. The idea came as a revelation. Just different kinds of humans. She bit her lip. "Sit down again."

He went toward the chair, but she patted the bed where he'd been sitting when she woke. She drew the covers up around her waist. Ryan obeyed her, but first crossed to the small table where the tea things were and clicked the kettle on. While it boiled, he came and sat on the bed, and stretched his hand out toward her.

She watched the feathers pop out of his skin, breathing deep until fascination replaced her terror. They glowed fiery orange in the early morning light. "How do you do that?"

"This time of the month, it's hard not to." The feathers receded, shrinking under the skin as if they'd never existed. "From what I understand, that's what scared you. Believe me, Aidan was doing his very best not to startle you."

"I was out of my mind with terror. I'd never seen anything like it."

He got up and went to the kettle. Corinne nodded when he lifted a brow, silently asking if she wanted a drink too. "That's the basis of bigotry," he said, dropping a tagged teabag into each cup. "Fear. People are afraid of what they don't understand and they instinctively recoil. Fear and anger are closely related, and the combination often adds up to bigotry. They close their minds and refuse to understand." He squeezed out the bags, discarded them and added milk. "Sugar?"

"No thank you." He was right. She'd closed her mind, the terror she'd felt had done that to her. She took a deep breath. "Then educate me."

Ryan crossed the room and handed her the cup of steaming, fragrant tea. She inhaled before taking her first sip. She always loved the first cup of the day. No other was ever so refreshing. Ryan seemed equally content, taking his time drinking his tea before he answered her. "We're different, that's all. We were born that way. It's best to keep it secret, because either bigots attack us or power-mad individuals are after our secrets. Bigotry and curiosity. They've dissected us to discover our secrets, treated us like animals. Worse than animals. Unfortunately, we're compelled to shape-shift every month, during the full moon, so if we're captured and imprisoned, eventually we'll reveal our natures."

"Is that what happened with Aidan yesterday?"

"Yes." He put the cup down on its saucer with a light click of porcelain. This being the Savoy, the cups were bone china, gold-rimmed and monogrammed with the hotel's insignia. "It's the first day of the full moon and he felt the compulsion to shape-shift. There's only one way to stop it—by taking a concoction our doctors have developed for us. It's called Cephalox, and it's only supposed to be used during medical operations or in dire extremity."

Realization dawned. "So that's what he was doing! I thought he was an addict."

Ryan grimaced. "That stuff is addictive and it helped get me into trouble. I started to use Cephalox and moved to heroin and other fun drugs. Aidan did it too, so it's hard for any of us to go back to it. We're at greater risk of getting addicted all over again. Aidan wanted to give you time before he told you, so he only planned to take it this month." He paused and looked away, staring into the sky. "I think he was afraid to tell you, afraid it might drive you away. And what he was afraid of happened. Didn't it?" He swung his head around and, for the first time, Corinne saw the bird in him. His eyes pierced her with their intensity and the way his head swung on his neck reminded her of a great bird.

She swallowed. "Yes. I was terrified. I stopped him taking the drug and he transformed—"

"Shape-shifted," Ryan corrected her.

"Yes, shape-shifted. He was as big as the man and he scared me to death."

"We can be larger. Or smaller. That's how I arrived today. Unless you looked closely, you might have thought I was a sparrow." He grinned. "You shouldn't have left your bathroom window open."

"Where are your clothes?"

192

He cackled, throwing his head back to enjoy the joke. "If we really need to, we can carry a few things with us, but usually we have something where we're going. This is the Savoy, so I knew there would be at least a towel for me, but it's for you, not for me. Think about it. Have you ever seen a robin in a jacket and pants? We get used to nudity, it means nothing—usually." He glanced at her, his eyes warm and wicked.

"How will you get back?"

"The same way I came. I think you should watch me shape-shift. Get used to it. If you want to, that is."

He went back to the table and made himself another cup of tea, allowing her a chance to drink her own brew and to think.

Ryan had given her a lot to think about. At first terrified by Aidan's change, she finally realized that whatever he was, whatever form he took, he was still Aidan. And she loved him. "Did he send you?"

"No. He took off—literally. We haven't seen him for a while. He contacted me to tell me the bare bones of what happened, then disappeared. He'll be back. He's a solitary bird, doesn't show his feelings easily." He regarded her coolly. "Corinne, he's my brother and I hate to see him hurt. I'm the older brother." He gave a harsh laugh. "Yeah right. And I love him. I can't make you do whatever it is you want, but make it quick. Don't hurt him more than you have to."

She began to speak, but he cut her off with a raised hand. "Whatever you decide, it's your business, not mine." He looked away and concentrated on making his second cup of tea.

"I also came on behalf of the band." He stirred the tea, the spoon clinking on the side of the cup rhythmically, and he returned to the bed. "We need to know if you're coming back, Corinne. You fit in well, but if you don't want to come back, we have to think about using the session man for the concerts." He sat down again. "We need to know and fast."

Corinne finished her cup of tea and put the cup aside. "I told my father I'd tell him my decision on Wednesday. Tomorrow. I never meant to leave you in the lurch, Ryan. I always intended to do the concerts, never thought of backing out. We've worked too hard for me to stop now."

"Good." Ryan's tones turned brisk. "We were planning a kind of dress rehearsal for you. We have a few ramps and stuff that we use onstage. You need to get used to the way things are set up, so we've hired a bigger room to block it in. We'll run through the set completely, just the bare bones of it and the nominal running order, just for you. Then we'll do it at Hammersmith, if we can get a slot." He cocked an eyebrow at her. "You know we improvise onstage. It's part of what we do. You look terrified, Corinne, but it's the way we work."

She swallowed. "That's not why I'm scared. Well, not the only reason anyway."

He grinned. "We'll try not to spring too many surprises on you. We can change the running order sometimes too, put different stuff in, but we won't do that." His grin broadened. "At least not on the first night. The mock-up'll be ready on Thursday. Will you come?"

She nodded, though her heart sank. If Aidan didn't want her back, she'd still have to be with him. That would hurt, but she was a professional to the core and she would no more withdraw from a commitment at this late stage than fly. "Ask the session man to come too, in case Aidan can't work with me anymore." She swallowed her sorrow away.

Ryan stared at her over the rim of his cup. She could see the family resemblance, especially in the eyes and hair, even though Ryan wore his short and spiky, but he would never come anywhere near Aidan's sheer, raw sexiness. At least, for her he wouldn't. She liked him. Watching the nervous energy of his performances, Corinne never imagined she'd ever be comfortable in the presence of such a man, but she felt a camaraderie with him and had since the second or third day of rehearsal. He worked like a madman, not stopping until he'd perfected a phrase or a piece of stage business, but offstage he relaxed completely, becoming a funny, likeable companion.

"We're going to have problems with my image, aren't we?"

He knew immediately what she meant. "Yes, we are, but I think we'll get past it. We've always put the music first and our fans know it. The first concert's going to be sticky, though I don't know if it will be your fans or ours who'll make the biggest stink."

"We'll have to keep them apart, like football supporters." Corinne's mood turned serious when she remembered the incident at the roadside café. "We saw it on the way to London. Some people saw us and it turned into a full-scale riot. We were lucky the press didn't get on to it."

"Yes, Aidan told me. Don't worry, Corinne. Unless the media really takes against you, we'll be fine, and so far they've been playing along."

He put his cup down by the side of hers. "We'd better wash one of those unless you want the hotel staff to imagine things."

She shrugged. "For all they know, one of my sisters has been up here."

His response was a visible shudder. "Ashley has been chasing me. Did you know?"

"I know she fancies you. I saw her watching you at the nightclub."

"A bit more than fancy. She came around to my flat yesterday, wearing a dress that showed more than it hid. When I offered her a drink, she virtually attacked me."

Corinne hadn't realized her sister was so desperate. "Did you take her up on her offer?"

He gave her a grin that was wholly wicked, clearly demonstrating the appeal he had for many of his devoted fans.

"What do you think? She's young, she's pretty—I'm not a monk, Corinne."

She should, she supposed, be scandalized, but she wasn't even surprised. "She'll want you for a while yet, I imagine."

"Nah. She can want. Though I might fuck her a few more times before I'm done." He frowned. "Do you mind?"

"No. The twins can be a bit full-on, and if she asked, she had it coming to her. Fuck her all you want, Ryan. Tom will hang on no matter what, and he'll turn a blind eye to Ashley's little affairs."

Ryan shrugged. "Tom or not, she's got no chance for anything long-term. Not unless she brings Tom with her. He has a nice arse I wouldn't mind exploring."

Now he shocked her and he grinned when he saw her reaction. "If it's pretty and it says yes, I'll fuck it. Sorry, luv, that's me." He finished his tea, holding the handle in the precise, pinky-stuck out way hardly anyone used these days. Weird. Just weird.

Ashley might have met her match in Ryan Hawthorne. Corinne certainly hoped so. The twins used sex both as a weapon and as a casual recreational activity, but she'd seen how keen Ashley was to get Ryan and she suspected he wouldn't be able to dump her quite as carelessly as he thought.

His eyes brightened. "Or she could bring Paige. Twins. I've never had twins. At least not at the same time."

She couldn't help laughing. "You really do live the rock lifestyle, don't you?"

He got up. "You'd better believe it." He turned to face her and, just for a moment, his eyes held a bleakness that echoed the hollowness of his soul. For an instant, his rigid self-control bent and she saw the agony he held inside, that he didn't want anyone to see. Not even Aidan. He hadn't recovered from Maria's death. He might never recover.

"Now I really must go. Do you want to watch me shape-shift or shall I go away and do it?"

She drew in a sharp breath. "Do it here."

He let the bathrobe drop to the floor. She kept her eyes firmly fixed on his upper body, not caring to see what was below his waist. "Get used to it," he said with a grin. "I do a few changes of clothes in the longer sets and you're likely to see this more often." She still didn't look farther down. Ryan bore a few tattoos, unlike his brother. The rose on his upper arm echoed the one Aidan had, the symbol of the band. The others were fading fast, faint lines showing a pair of RAF wings and a few nondescript lines.

She was about to ask him about the old tattoos when he began to shape-shift. She swallowed and watched, holding her breath.

Feathers popped out of his skin. Ryan extended his arms and she saw the feathers come, saw his body change shape. Seeing it for a second time was still shocking, but she could accept it because she was ready for it. She quelled her fear, knowing it for what it was now—fear of the unknown.

She thought of Aidan and knew she could stand it. If he was compelled to shape-shift every month, she would rather he did that than take the drugs Ryan said were addictive and dangerous. That Aidan would do that for her filled her with warmth and terror, mingled in equal measure as she watched her band mate and, perhaps, new friend change into a firebird.

Ryan was darker than Aidan in his bird form, his feathers a deep, dangerous crimson, the breast feathers more orange than golden. The lean body of the bird reflected his slender human form, his sharp nose echoed in the long, thin, hooked beak. His voice drifted in her mind.

I'll let the others know you're coming to the rehearsal. The rest is up to you. Call out to him in your mind and he will hear and come to you.

The bird changed in size, becoming as small as a swallow, the fiery wings flashing in the sunlight as they whirred. He darted into the bathroom and he was gone. Corinne felt his going, a spark of vitality leaving the room.

She sat for a long time thinking before her father rang, asking her to come down to breakfast. "No, not today, Dad. I have something else to do." She would skip breakfast, especially in a place as public as the Savoy, where people would see and take note of her presence, which was probably what John intended.

She wanted to go home.

Chapter Fourteen

ఈం

Aidan was frantic. He'd been for a long flight, living as a bird for a day and a night, soothing the beast within him that emerged each month, demanding that he take his other form. Some phoenixes never shape-shifted to human form—they preferred to remain invincible and unique. Aidan always felt more man than bird, though he'd never before longed to be just a man. Only a man, so he could love Corinne, give himself to her with nothing between them.

He sat on a tree branch and brooded, snapping viciously at any creature who ventured anywhere near him. He might be better taking his forebears' example and become wholly phoenix, leaving the man behind. He couldn't forget the look she'd given him when she'd seen him shape-shift—horrified, terrified even. Corinne would never accept him now. Perhaps if he hadn't been under the monthly compulsion, perhaps if he'd prepared her better…

It was no use. She'd left him. When he'd seen her, felt her and then seen the bird mark on his thigh, he'd known she was for him. Then, through his own carelessness and cowardice, he'd lost her.

For the umpteenth time that day, he cursed his own stupidity, but his mind was beginning to work again and he knew he had to go back. He had commitments, the bloody concerts for one thing. He couldn't abandon the band, not when he knew they'd started it for him, to give him something to do, an outlet for his talents and a way to belong to something.

He'd always been alone. When others of his kind met him, they treated him with deep respect. Respect he didn't feel he deserved. He'd been born the phoenix, given the gifts awarded the mythical bird. He hadn't earned a fucking one of them. When his brother and his cousins realized the way he felt, then discovered his talent, they worked to develop theirs, enough to form the band that had taken the world by storm in the last few years. One album and one live album down, so the next studio album was vital. They had all the world except the States, and they were working on that. *Icefire* should break them there too. No, he couldn't abandon them now.

He spread his wings, only then seeing the boy below. Aidan kept the phoenix large, hiding in the woods, not in the mood for coping with other creatures, knowing his sheer size would keep them away. He hadn't expected to see a human being this far away from civilization. But there he was, a tousle-haired boy, staring up at him, his mouth and eyes wide in amazement.

Aidan gave him a show. He lifted effortlessly up into the air and circled twice before he left for home. There was no harm in that. The boy would think he'd seen some kind of exotic escapee from a zoo or, if he had true sight, he might recognize what he'd seen. No one would believe him.

Glad to have made someone's day, Aidan made his way home, only just remembering to alter his size as he entered central London. Until then, he'd flown high and fuzzed his presence. He entered his bathroom as a small bird.

The shower was on and someone stood inside the frosted glass screen. One of the band, he thought, wondering why they would want to use his shower. He shape-shifted almost without thinking and reflected that he could do with a shower himself. He opened his mouth to swear at whoever was in the shower stall, so his mouth was still open when the screen was pushed aside and he got his first view of the occupant.

"Shall we carry on where we left off?" Corinne asked. Her delicious full breasts dripped water onto the shower floor, drops he badly wanted to taste, her smile invited him to join her. He could smell her, even over the combined scents of shampoo and soap, the arousal he'd evoked when he entered the room, when she looked at him.

He wasn't sure how he got across the room, but he climbed into the shower faster than blinking and the next moment she was in his arms, warm water cascading over them both. He took her mouth, sinking into the kiss as if his life depended on it, tasting her like a man dying of thirst. He brought his hand up to cup the back of her head, holding her around her waist, drawing her close. Almost frightened to hear what she had to say, he had to do this first.

Not wanting to end the kiss, he only drew back when he felt her tremble. He straightened, still holding her, staring into her eyes — searching for the terror he'd last seen in her.

He saw nothing but love. When he cautiously opened his mind to her, he felt her wholly open to him. Her eyes glowed warmly into his. "Say it," he whispered, unable to believe what he saw. "Say it before you kill me, Corinne."

"I love you, Aidan. Whatever you are, I love you."

"Oh sweetheart!" He pulled her close, held her for a full minute before he managed to blink back his tears and swallow the lump in his throat. The water rinsed away their differences, made them one.

He drew back and caressed her chin, then cupped her cheek. "I love you too. So very much."

"Aidan, will you promise not to hide anything from me anymore?"

"Gladly."

"Even if I run back to my father and tell him everything?"

He blanched. "Yes. Even then. I can't jeopardize what we have. I'll take any risk you want me to."

She caressed his back. He felt every stroke tenfold, welcoming her into his life. "I shan't do that. Make love to me, Aidan, so I can make love to you."

He lifted her, hardly noticing her weight, and felt her wrap her legs around his waist. It seemed so natural to slide inside her welcoming body, so right. Home. He'd come home. No other woman had ever felt like her, or evoked the same reaction with just a look, a sweet kiss or a touch.

She leaned back in his arms, smiling up at him. "Nobody feels the way you do, Aidan. I can't live without you."

"I can't live without you either." He turned her to prop her against the wall, giving him the leverage he needed to plunge deep into her weeping pussy. "Oh Corinne, you feel so good!"

Gasping, he thrust into her, joining her and letting her feel his pleasure, his delight in her. Every part of her was so well known to him that he'd missed her like a missing limb. Now, sheathed inside her, he knew where he belonged.

She gripped his shoulders, branding him with her touch, and he felt her pleasure rise, felt her juices flow for him. A drop trickled down his thigh, hotter than the water that cascaded over them. He took her mouth, since he couldn't lap the precious drop off his leg, and plunged his tongue into her mouth, tasting her pleasure that way.

He never wanted this to stop, wondered if it were possible to die of ecstasy. Her joy fed his but he refused to climax, held down the seed that threatened to burst out of him into her. Not until she'd come at least once. He stoked the fire and was rewarded when he felt her body stiffen.

When she came he watched her eyes close, feeling her body contract around his. He held on, pushed deeper. His wet hair fell across his shoulder, falling between them, and he lifted her closer to gain access to her mouth. He trailed kisses across her face, taking her mouth in a deep, devouring kiss, which she returned in full measure. Melded together, he withdrew only to plunge his cock deeper, take her harder. She gasped into his mouth and he sucked on her tongue while he felt her body rise toward another climax.

He'd never opened his mind to any other lover so fully, not even other Talents who knew what he was, never allowed anyone full access to his whole being before, but he couldn't stop now. He couldn't have closed himself off from Corinne if his life depended on it. He felt her accept him, felt her reciprocate, opening her mind, and then her orgasm sparkled like the finest champagne, tickling, inviting, intoxicating. It was too much—he couldn't hold back any longer. Much as he wanted to fuck her brains out for the rest of the day, stay here until they were both empty, his orgasm was too close.

He exploded, fireworks bursting in his head, his whole body melting with delight.

After an interval of who knew how long, he helped her lower her legs to the shower floor, holding her steady until she found her balance. He smiled and saw her beatific response when she beamed up at him. When he glanced to one side, he saw the soap and he picked it up. There was no need for words, mentally or verbally, so he worked up a lather between his hands and washed her.

Aidan delighted in the soft skin under his hands and the way the scented soap slid over her delectable body. She didn't flinch from his touch as she might have done a few days ago, but leaned into him, letting him see how much she enjoyed him. "What happened?" he said in wonder. "What changed your mind?"

"Ryan came to see me."

He might have known his brother wouldn't leave well enough alone. He would kill him when he saw him next. His hands slid over her breasts, slick with lather, and he tweaked her nipples to hard, wet points. No, he wouldn't, he'd kiss him. Fuck, her nipples felt like no others, the ridges and dimples all he wanted. She hissed and leaned against him. His cock took an interest again.

"Ryan wanted to know if I was walking away from the band. I said no."

"That all he said? Did he tell you anything else?"

"Not much. Just that you hid from view because people persecuted you."

Aidan grunted, much more interested in seeing just how hard he could make her nipples. He palmed her breasts, letting the stiff peaks push into his hands, and he groaned softly. He skated his hands over the curves, down to her navel, lingering to push the pad of his forefinger into the indentation before moving on to her hips.

Tears filled her beautiful eyes. "I was just as prejudiced as the worst type of bigot. I'm sorry, so sorry, Aidan. I just had to think things through." She touched his chest with the very tips of her fingers, melting him inside. "And I realized I couldn't live without you. Whatever you are, whoever you are, I need you."

He kissed her for that, long and sweetly. Their kiss didn't stay sweet for too long. Soon his arms went around her and she ended up flattened against the tiles again. But this time he slid down her body, licking the drops off her skin as fast as the shower replaced them. He curled his tongue into her navel, loving her gasp and wriggle and moved lower down to taste her more.

He parted her hair with his fingers, revealing her secrets, pink and glistening. Thick, dark curls covered her pubis, the ends tickling his mouth when he bent to taste her.

Her groan was better than any other music they might make together. Right now it was all he wanted to hear. He pushed her thighs apart and took as much of her weight against his body as he could. He wanted her, all of her, all the time.

You taste better than anyone else.

"Aidan, Aidan, please!"

Please what? More? Oh yeah!

Her juices flowed freer now and he drank them down greedily, working his tongue along the creases to get it all.

Tonguing her clit made her gasp and cry out, one short, sharp cry that might have been his name. It grew in his mouth, a little peak that hardened, just like her nipples, but it was slicker and it tasted of her, of the woman he loved more than life.

He slid his tongue down, opening his mouth to cover her clit and plunging his tongue deep inside her, as deep as he could go.

Soft, hot and slick with the juices he brought out, he wanted more. His brain stuck on the word and he filled his mind with it, pushed her to go higher for him.

More, baby, more!

Aidan! Her cry came from her mouth and her mind, every part of her filled with him. If any Talents lurked in the vicinity, her cry would drive them straight into orgasm overdrive.

She contracted around his tongue, pumped hot and sweet into his mouth. When she squirmed against him, wriggled her hypersensitive skin away, he followed. No way was he going anywhere until he'd taken every bit of her she could give, drunk every bit of her body's champagne.

When she sagged down onto him, he relented and drew away, sliding his hands up her sides to let her fall forward into his arms.

Onto his cock, which strained to reach her, a magnet heading for the hottest sweet spot in town.

With a groan, he pushed. He'd already grown outside her body, something that wasn't supposed to happen, but who cared, as long as he could get inside her without hurting her.

She was so wet, so hot, her folds swollen with need. For him.

He kissed her softly, closed-mouth, not sure if she wanted any more, but immediately she opened for him and folded her arms around his neck, pulling him close for a deep, tongue-twining melding of mouths.

When she slipped, he slid his hand down her body, gathering suds that had escaped the shower, and spread his hand over her beautiful ass. His middle finger, slick with the soap that he'd lovingly spread all over her, slipped in between and found her tiny opening. When he thrust, he felt his body in hers and the impact he made inside her. He wanted it all, every part of her, he wanted to fill every opening she had, so he slipped his finger inside. Her mouth, under his, tensed but then she relaxed and he pushed a little deeper.

Oh yeah. Her heat burned him, her body melted for him, butter against his skin, flowing over him, through him, until he couldn't imagine any other reality.

Slick, dark heat.

Aidan couldn't resist. He slipped another finger, his third finger, just inside and Corinne went wild.

He only just got his free hand behind her head to stop her knocking herself silly against the tiles when she pulled away from his kiss and threw her head back, gasping for air. "Oh no, baby, you don't get away from me. Not now, not ever."

He dragged her back and planted his mouth firmly over hers again, shoving her shoulder blades against the tiles so he could pump harder into her and tilt his body back so that his body hit her clit with every stroke.

Twisting his middle finger inside her ass made her lift her knees. He didn't think she was aware of doing it, but she lifted them, curled them up around his hips and he had to partially shape-shift so he could still hold her firm, using the bird's extra strength to support her while he fucked them both to oblivion.

He slid his hand back around her back and shoved hard inside her, sharing her orgasm, keeping it going. She sucked on his tongue then began to pant, the breath coming sharply down her nose since he wouldn't release her mouth. He loved the little pulses from her mouth, her breath hot on her lips and cheeks, his fingers inside her, feeling his cock relentlessly pounding her.

Surrounding him with wet heat, the shower still pounding them, he found rapture. In her, with her, gasping in his arms.

When he came around from wherever oblivion had sent him, he was sitting on the floor of the shower and she was washing him, using her hands instead of a sponge or a washcloth, gently running her hands over his chest, his arms and his back.

He took the soap and washed her, and where there had been searing passion, now there was tenderness and sweet servitude. Then, when he'd recovered a bit, he lifted her out of the shower, wrapped her in the softest, warmest towel he could find and carried her through to the bedroom.

They made love again, but slower, with a sweetness he could taste, lying side by side, neither dominant, but touching and loving in equal measure. He paused, deep inside her body. "I want to stay like this forever," he murmured, drawing her closely into his arms, savoring her presence.

She snuggled in, then wriggled on top of him, making him moan softly. She pushed him onto his back, following him so she straddled him. He helped her sit up and gloried in the sight of her. She lifted up and dropped, making him moan louder, and then did it again. "Aidan, I love you."

He'd never tire of hearing her say that.

He reached up to her waist, gripped her and helped her move on him. Soon they were lost in desire again, lost in each other. His cock in her pussy, where it belonged, where she belonged. She rode him, head thrown back in ecstasy, lost in him. He'd always prided himself in making a woman come before he did, even the groupies who only wanted to boast they'd fucked a star, hardly interested in the act itself, but he needed this woman to come, needed to make her happy.

Because it made him happy too, happier than any number of mind-numbing orgasms.

Although she was wet, her inner muscles still gripped him tight, still tapped into his deepest desires, the core inside him that flowed for her. Aidan gritted his teeth, trying to think of something else, anything else, to hold off his orgasm. He knew this time he'd flood her and that would be it, for another hour at least, and he didn't want that.

Remembering something Ryan had told him about, he released one hand from her waist and inserted his fingers between them. Corinne wriggled, and he nudged her clit on his way past. But this time he needed to do something else. Fast. She didn't stop moving, riding him hard now and he held his breath to stave off the orgasm welling through his body.

There. He pressed hard against the big vein going up the front of his prick, where it began at the base. That was what Ryan told him to do. Stopped premature ejaculation he said, although God knew it wouldn't be premature. It wasn't enough, would never be enough.

It was difficult to keep his finger where he needed it, and when it slipped, he couldn't stop it going up and in. Into her. Quickly he hooked his finger to prevent the nail scratching her. Corinne gasped and her eyes widened. "Oh Aidan!" she breathed.

He'd found a sweet spot. Or perhaps she was all sweet spot after his intimate kisses. Forgetting his own imminent problem, he entered the flow of their lovemaking. Feeling her convulsive plunges onto his willing body brought him higher, feeling the reality of their joining turned him on like never before. Chills chased each other up his spine, electrifying his whole body into the no-going-back phase and then he actually felt himself come.

His balls tightened and his seed surged up his cock. He felt his dick expand, then the hot gush of his seed, spurting hard and high inside her. Dimly he heard Corinne scream and then her walls contracted around him, pinching and squeezing every kind of response from him. His finger, still inside her, felt the extra heat and slickness of his seed, and when she finally, finally stopped coming, Aidan was no longer sure where he ended and she began, and cared even less. They were together. That was enough.

When she began to fall forward, he stopped her. "Baby, wait." His voice sounded weak and gruff, not that it surprised him. He slid his finger free and curved his hand around her waist again.

She fell forward and he eased her to one side. Although he felt his cock softening inside her, he couldn't bring himself to withdraw. Her pussy, still hot, but with their combined juices, held him in a loving embrace as their bodies twined together.

He felt her sliding into sleep and gladly joined her. The stresses of the last few days had culminated in an explosion of passion and now exhaustion took over.

* * * * *

When he woke, it was dark, starlight gleaming through the uncurtained window. He liked to see the sky. When she moved beside him, he reached for her with his mind and found she was awake too.

"I'm sorry for what I did. I should have told you, I know that now." He pulled her into his arms, and saw her eyes glint in the starlight as she looked up at him. "I nearly lost you through my cowardice."

She gazed up at him and her expression sharpened to concern. "You won't take that Cephalox shit again, will you? Ryan told me it was addictive."

He kissed the tip of her nose. "Yes, it is, but I reckoned I could use it about three times before I needed to worry. I figured that would be enough to see me through this month. I wanted to tell you, but I misjudged. I usually know when the full moon is coming. I can feel it inside, but this month I've had a lot of different emotions to cope with. I'm sorry."

"I've had a lot of emotions to cope with too. I never bargained for something as amazing as this." She snuggled in and he felt her shiver. Knowing it wasn't fear, not any longer, he reached down and snagged the tangled bedclothes, drawing them up to cover her. "Aidan, it was the shock of seeing you shape-shift, that was all. I didn't realize. And for years my father has chased the impossible. Or what I thought was impossible. I suppose I'm used to denying it all. He's never found any proof."

"We prefer to pass unnoticed."

"I know." She traced a line on his chest, circling his nipple with her fingernail and smiling when he shuddered with the exquisite sensation. "Why do you try to hide?"

"There are many different kinds of humans and one dominant species, *Homo sapiens*, the one we call mortals. The rest of us prefer to keep out of the way. It's better for everybody, at least for now. It won't always be like this, but we're a long way from revealing ourselves."

"Don't some of you try for it?"

He grinned. "Fame and fortune, you mean? Yes, but that's not the same as revealing my Talent, my true nature. Some mortals know—like you."

She traced his other nipple, refusing to look up at him, feeling foolish when she said, "Can you take me flying?"

She felt his chest move when he laughed. "Yes. We need to find somewhere quiet so I can shape-shift large enough to carry you. But you can fly for yourself, if you like." He took a breath, and she felt him tense under her hands.

Startled, she looked up at him to find him gazing at her, his expression grave. He was about to tell her something important. The air tingled with it. "I can make you like me," he said.

"What?" Her heart missed a beat—how could that be?

"I have a gift. Every shape-shifter has it. They may convert someone, just one person. Compatibility is rare, but it exists. Sometimes the phoenix has never found his mate, even in a whole rising."

"Rising?"

"Each reincarnation. Only that can be misinterpreted, so we call it a rising."

"Wait." She pulled away and sat up, blinking to clear her thoughts. "You're reincarnated?"

He watched her through narrowed eyes. "How much did Ryan tell you about me?"

She studied him. He lay before her like some delectable fantasy, flame-red hair spread over the pillow, limber body under the covers, warming her, and he waited for her to listen to him. "He said you were like him."

He took his time answering, keeping his gaze on her face. "I'm the phoenix, Corinne."

She bit back her startled comments. He lifted his hand and allowed a talon to form, sharp and lethal. "This is how I play the guitar. Not with picks or sharpened fingernails." He retracted the claw without effort. "I have power and I'm considered important by some people. I am a firebird, because the phoenix is a firebird. But I'm the phoenix. There's only ever one of those and I'm it."

For a moment only, the information stunned Corinne, but she could doubt it no longer. Ryan had been more slender than Aidan, his color darker. Where Ryan was deep crimson, Aidan was golden fire. His body as a bird was heavier and his eyes were pure flames. "Does that mean you're a prince or something?"

He smiled, just a ghost of a smile. "Some people call me 'my lord', but I don't think so. I just am."

"Do you have to do anything?"

"No. I sometimes attend the occasional meeting." He bit his lip. "I'm supposed to do more, but I refused. If I accept, I'll remember all my previous lives and take on responsibilities I don't know if I can perform."

"I didn't think the phoenix existed before I met you. Or firebirds, for that matter." She didn't move away. Whatever he was, he was Aidan, the man she loved, the man who loved her.

He chuckled. "You thought shape-shifters were perfectly ordinary animals in their other forms?"

"Yes, well, that is, I never heard of shape-shifters before."

"You've heard of unicorns, griffins, wyverns?"

"Well, yes, but—"

"All shape-shifters. They're not extinct, they're not legendary, they exist." He smoothed a hand over her back, unable to resist caressing her soft skin.

"How old are you?" She should have thought before blurting that out, but her brain recalled the legend of the phoenix—born of fire every five hundred years, only to return to fire and be born again.

He reached out and took her hand, interlacing their fingers. "I'm thirty, Corinne. No fancy stuff, just a thirty-year-old man facing the fact that he might have blown it with the woman he loves. I should have told you earlier, I know I should. Ryan wanted me to tell you at once, but I was too afraid of losing you. Well, I have to face it now and Ryan was right. He, by the way, is considerably older than me. He's nearly two hundred years old." She gasped and his hand tightened around hers, as if afraid she might run. "His family took me in as a baby, and we've never thought of ourselves as anything but brothers. But thirty years ago, my predecessor—my father—was killed in an air crash. When a phoenix dies, he's reborn, you know that from the legends. He is reborn as a baby and he has to learn again. My grandfather was a pilot in the Second World War and he was shot down and killed. If a phoenix dies through trauma, then the successor has the choice before rebirth to accept the responsibilities and the memory of past lives or start anew. If I accepted all the responsibilities that go with being the phoenix, I'd remember those lives and most of the ones that went before it. I don't think I can bear it and I'm happy as I am, so I leave it to people better qualified than me to do what they can." He paused, giving her a moment to assimilate what he was telling her.

Corinne sat completely still, listening and thinking, trying not to panic, opening her mind to everything he wanted to tell her. "Now all I can remember is this life." He paused, staring down at their hands, twined together. "I'm glad." His gaze lifted to her face again. "I'm glad now. I can't remember another love. There's only you."

"But you've had other women."

"Of course." He wouldn't lie to her now — she saw it in his eyes. "They've all been casual, friendly. Not like this."

"No, not like this." Whatever he was, she loved him. "Aidan, what do we do now? I'm tired of thinking. Just give me a clue."

He smiled and tugged her back down to lie in his arms. "We marry next week, as we planned. Then we do the three concerts, and you decide if you want to carry on with the band or not. If you decide not to, we have time to look around for somebody else after that. I'll take you away somewhere nice and hot, where we can lie on the beach and make love all day. While we're away, we close the contract with your father. We can leave it in the lawyers' hands."

"You really have thought about it, haven't you?"

He kissed her, very gently. "What do you think?"

"I think it sounds wonderful. Aidan, can we do this? What about — you know — the other thing?"

He chuckled. "The other thing? You mean that I'm a bird?" He laughed again then sobered. "I won't press you. I'll give you the feather when you're ready. If you ever are. We're in no hurry, are we?"

She latched onto his previous words. "Feather? What feather?"

He stroked her waist, his touch lifting her skin into instant awareness. "That's how it's done. I shape-shift and you take a feather from my breast."

Tension filled her. "A kind of ceremony?"

"Not really. We do it that way so you can see me in both my forms and accept me as both firebird and man."

"Why should I do it? Why can't we go on as we are?"

He lifted his hands in the bed and took both of hers. "Because, my love, my natural lifespan is much longer than the average mortal's. Five hundred years, with an extension if I go into the fire. If I *choose* to enter the fire, it renews me. You can live as long as I do. Once we've done this, we can decide to bond, body and soul. When I die, you die, and the other way about. It's a bond as strong as time, and once done it can't be undone."

"What happens after I take the feather from you?"

"You press it to your thigh or anywhere else you want the mark. I'm told it burns, but I'll help you. You'll end up with a mark like mine, but it only appears when we're turned on."

She gently withdrew a hand and touched his thigh, feeling the slight ridges and the extra warmth produced by the mark. He smiled. "I'm always turned on when I'm around you."

He leaned forward for a more passionate kiss, but although she participated, she withdrew afterward. "Aidan, my father sent me back for that feather. He said I was to ask you for it, to get it for him."

His face hardened, and glints of fire replaced his softened expression. "Is *that* why you came back?"

She spun away from him, tearing back the sheets, and would have got out of bed if he hadn't been quick to loop his arm around her waist. "Fuck, I am so fucking stupid, oh shit, Corinne, come back, please. I'm sorry. Please come back."

He had her in such a strong grip, she didn't really have a choice, but she resisted for a moment. "You're prickly, you know that?"

He sighed and his grip loosened. "I know. Come back, baby, please."

She slid back under the covers and his arms went around her. She wouldn't have gone far. He couldn't have let her.

"I don't get much rest from it," he confessed. He was holding her loosely so she could leave if she wanted to. She appreciated that. "In both my forms, people want something. People who know who I am want me to convert them. People who don't know want a piece of me anyway."

"I know how part of that feels," she admitted. "That charity recording, for instance. They jumped at the opportunity when John suggested it. We get those kinds of requests all the time. Dad protected us from that. Now I have to do it myself."

"I'll be with you," he murmured. "If you want me."

She did.

Chapter Fifteen

🔊

Corinne Westfall married Aidan Hawthorne two days before the first Hammersmith Apollo concert. The bride wore leather. White leather. The groom wore a suit from Armani, sharp, smart and totally unlike the rock persona he usually adopted.

Outside the register office, the media circus waited for them. After posing for a few pictures, they went inside to meet the rest of the band — and Corinne's father. He frowned at her tight, white leather sheath dress. Even more when Corinne paused to speak to him. "This might be the last time you ever see me in white, Dad."

She would have moved past, back to where Aidan waited for her, his eyes grave with concern at her speaking to John, but he touched her arm. Usually he wouldn't have had to do more than that to get her attention but this time she paused before turning back to him. "I've got to go and get married now, Dad."

"Yes, I know. I can't believe you're even considering it. Is there nothing you won't do for publicity?"

She gave him a look of disbelief. "That's you, John. You're the one who pushed me into this. But I found more than I expected and I want Aidan for myself now."

John's upper lip turned in a sneer. "Sex is paltry next to the power of control. Still, Corinne, we can use this. It'll help break you out of the classical virgin, into the wronged woman mode. I have a plan for your future career. I'll call you."

"Do that." She would have moved away again, but she felt an intrusion in her mind. Used now to Aidan's loving communication and gentle presence, she actually felt John enter her mind, menace and intimidation powering his presence. At the same time, he said, "I have a new contract for you to sign, Corinne. Call by the hotel tomorrow and I'll have it ready for you."

Deep inside her mind, Aidan snarled and as John sent the desire to visit him and sign the contract into her subconscious, he dissolved it, with a burst of mental energy exploding the attempt to control her into dust.

At the same time he stepped forward and curved his arm around her shoulders. "You don't get her like that, Westfall. Ever again."

For an instant she saw pure hatred in her father's eyes. And not just for Aidan. For her, that she had finally found someone who could reverse what he had done.

But all he said was, "She'll sign. You can't be with her forever."

Ignoring the other people present in the room, fellow band members, roadies, her sisters, Aidan drew Corinne aside and lifted her chin so their eyes met. "Are you okay?"

She bit her lip and smiled. "Sure."

"Corinne, I love you. Let's get married. Forget everything else. There's nothing we can do today but be in love. We're only going to do this once. Let's do it properly."

Warmth filled her, the warmth of Aidan's love and hers for him. He was right. "Yes. Let's get married."

The registrar smiled benevolently at them as they approached and with the words "Everybody stand, please," began the ceremony.

The marriage ceremony was simple, but Corinne and Aidan repeated their vows with clear voices and loving hearts. The room, a typical Victorian official chamber, but well maintained and decorated in light, cool colors, reflected their voices so everyone heard and understood this was more than a showbiz marriage, a quick exchange of promises to be forgotten after a year or two.

This was forever. Corinne would never forget the look on Aidan's face when he slid the broad gold band onto her finger and the way his hand trembled slightly when she pushed his ring on. She watched him and found love to match her own, and a devotion and understanding that humbled her.

They watched each other until the registrar said, "You may kiss the bride," and then Aidan took her in his arms and gave her one deep, loving kiss.

The first person to embrace them both was Ryan. Corinne had never thought that the energetic, powerful rock star could weep, but tears glistened in his eyes when he embraced her and then his brother. He didn't try to hide them either, but let them fall, one tear from each eye, trickling away down his cheeks like tributes. "I am so happy for both of you," he said, taking one of their hands in each of his. Then his sincerity turned into a wry smile. "I never thought to see the day anyone tamed my brother. But you've done it, Corinne. Welcome to the family."

Aidan shot his brother a cocky smile. "Your turn soon, Ryan."

Ryan's smile turned bitter. "Oh no. Not me, babe. Go and face your public now."

He turned away and they faced the congratulations of the others present. Paige and Ashley smiled, even they were swept away by her happiness, however temporary that might be, and wished her well, though she did notice they took the opportunity to grab Chris and Jake on their way out.

Outside the register office, the media waited. Cameras flashed, making the bright day dazzling, and they posed before answering a few questions, none of them too taxing. The press loved the reversal of roles, the rock star immaculately turned out, the classical babe raunchy in leather. Most of all, they loved the way Aidan swept Corinne into his arms and, after bestowing on her the hottest public kiss yet, tossed her into the Porsche standing outside the registry office, despite the double yellow lines that marked the road.

They left the screaming fans and picture-snapping media behind in a cloud of dust. Corinne tossed her bouquet over her shoulder as the car pulled away but didn't bother to look where it fell. The other members of the band exited through the rear of the building, leaving the Westfalls and the other members of the band to control the scene.

* * * * *

The first concert was the following Friday, so there was no time for a honeymoon. Aidan promised her a long, relaxing time in a villa somewhere, where she could learn about the firebirds and their ways and make what would be the most important decision of her life.

Aidan shape-shifted before her several times, so she could accustom herself to the sight, and after about three times, her terror receded and she began to see the beauty of the bird. In his bird form, Aidan could still talk to her through the mind link, aiding her acceptance. By the end of the week she'd made up her mind and on Thursday, when Aidan made the shape-shift for her, she accepted the feather that would change her life forever.

He stood before her, as large as the man, his breast feathers gleaming in the early morning light. He shook out his plumage and stretched his head, his beak a nightmare of hooked death. But not to her. Never to her.

Take the feather into your keeping, he said to her gently. *It's yours, whatever you decide. I want you to have something of me, something that means forever.*

I'll have you forever, she replied, anxiety taking hold.

His response was immediate and soothing. *I know. But take it anyway. Wear it tomorrow when we go onstage.*

Despite her long stage experience, Corinne worried about the concerts. The fans wouldn't just accept her. She had to prove herself more than any other new band member would have to do. She'd been unable to keep her anxiety from Aidan, who knew her better than anyone else.

Warmed by his efforts to reassure her, she stepped forward. She heard a rustle of feathers and a soft touch, and knew he'd curled his wing around her in a tender gesture of protection.

She tentatively touched the plumage, as soft as any feather bed, but alive, gleaming with strength and power. She laid her head against his breast and felt his responsive caress, stroking gently down her bare back. Power thrummed through the powerful body under the plumage of fire, like an underground electric generator, making every hair on her body tingle with awareness. *Are you very powerful like this?*

Very. His answer sounded a bit wry.

What can you do?

Start thunderstorms, drive lightning, blast fire.

What good is that?

Exactly. This time laughter echoed in her mind, but there was an edge of self-mockery she found hard to accept. *So can Semtex, and cloud seeding works well too.*

You can do it on your own. And you're beautiful like this. I've never seen a bird as beautiful as you.

The dawning sunlight slanting through the wide windows of the living room gleamed in rubicund blessing over his form, shooting red lights through the golden feathers on his breast, adding glints of fire to the lighter plumage. He was magnificent.

She could have stayed there longer, but his urging reminded her. *Take it, Corinne. Choose and take a feather.*

Corinne ruffled the feathers on his breast, lighter and softer than the ones on his wings and tail. She enjoyed the feeling before singling one, and holding it firmly in her hand. One sharp tug and it was out. She stepped back and watched him change into a man.

He held his hand over his chest. "I didn't know it would hurt," he admitted, allowing her to see the prick of blood just above his heart. "It felt like you dragged out a bit of my soul. You probably did." As she held the feather out to him, offering to return it, he took the step that took him to her and folded her hand around it. "You're welcome to it. You can have it all if you want it. Every feather."

"Thank you." The words sounded inadequate to her. "Aidan, are you sure? I can burn this or give it back to you, if you like. We've only known each other a month. Can we be sure this is all we think it is?"

"I'm sure." He folded her in his arms, just as he had in his phoenix form. "I've been inside your head, read everything you are, and I love every bit of it. The last three weeks have made up for everything else in my life."

"What else?" Looking up at his face, she saw an echo of pain etched there. "What do you mean?"

He kissed her forehead. "The phoenix has a solitary existence. I've been alone, Corinne. There is no one else like me. Ryan has his cousins and the other firebirds. They've never made me feel like anything other than family, but I wasn't, not really. I'm not my father's son. The man who brought me up isn't my real father. At the moment of my real father's death and rebirth, I entered my mother's womb as the phoenix, ousting whatever had been there before. I've had special education, all emphasizing what I am and what I have to be. But you accept me as a man. You fell in love with me as a man. Everyone else has fallen for something else, the legendary bird or the rock musician. You've brought me companionship and love, Corinne. For that, I owe you everything I can give."

She couldn't stop the tears. "I've been alone too, Aidan, but not as much as you. I do love you, so much!"

He picked her up and made for the stairs. "Then why exactly are we crying?" He bent to kiss the tears from her cheeks. "We should be celebrating. And you need your rest, love. Tomorrow's a big day."

* * * * *

They heard the crowd's yells even way backstage in the dressing rooms. Aidan, dressed in tight black jeans, cowboy boots and a leather waistcoat, stood in front of the mirror to tie his hair back. Partway through the concert, he would release it and remove the waistcoat, but only when he was nice and sweaty. Part of the act, and one he was used to. Corinne, silently brushing out her hair, suddenly shook her head so the static made her hair stand out in fiery tips around her head.

Aidan couldn't remember feeling so nervous before a concert before. Live shows were his bread and butter—the interaction with the audience fed his creative soul. A good audience drove him up as high as flight, even now, when he took no drugs and very little alcohol. He kept silent because Corinne needed it. He knew without her telling him, something that was becoming more common with them. He entered her mind and saw her going over the running order. She didn't need to, the list was pasted over various items onstage, the roadies could tell her and, in any case, Ryan was liable to change it. He probably wouldn't do that tonight, but Ryan onstage was even more volatile than Ryan offstage and it was difficult to predict what he would do next. If he felt the audience was hostile, he was quite capable of missing out the numbers the audience was waiting for—the latest single that had received acclaim even in the States, or the longer numbers which gave Aidan the chance to whip the listeners into a frenzy with his guitar solos.

The support act had been and gone, and the audience was watching the spotlight operators climbing the scaffolding to their posts high above. The sound engineer had gone to his desk. Aidan's Strat stood by the dressing room door, ready for the first number. His other guitars were in their usual place onstage.

Yet it was all different. The press had been kind to Corinne, all but the mostly hostile rock press. The rock world was still a chauvinistic one, depending as it did on macho performances and gallons of testosterone. Her background didn't help either. Other women successfully proved they could play rock, but the classical, pretty-girl image was a hard one to overcome.

Watching his wife in the mirror, Aidan saw little of the naïve innocence of Corinne's previous image. The hair made a big difference, as did the thick eyeliner and crimson lipstick, emphasizing the pallor of a face that had spent most of the last few days either in bed or in a windowless rehearsal room. She wore an astonishing pair of trousers she'd found in a boutique, made of soft black leather, fastened on the outside with a series of silver buckles, showing an enticing strip of skin from her ankles to her waist. A torn Led Zeppelin t-shirt, a black sports bra peeking through the tears and a pair of strappy sandals with three-inch heels completed her outfit. Privately, Aidan thought the sandals wouldn't last long, so he'd made the roadies check and triple-check the stage for anything that might hurt her. Luckily, the days of trailing wires had gone. Everything was digitally and radio controlled these days, so that was one less hazard to cope with. But he still thought the heels were a shit idea.

A sharp knock on the door heralded Ryan and Chris, ready to go. Chris wore his trademark bandana, bright red with orange streaks, which he threw to the audience at the end of the main show. Ryan wore a large white poet's shirt, open down the front over a pair of sprayed-on black hipster jeans that defied gravity, they were cut so low.

"Ready?" Ryan crooked a thin, plucked eyebrow. Corinne wasn't the only one wearing makeup, but Ryan's was deliberately asymmetrical, one eye redolent of the Clockwork Orange look, the other free of everything except a thin line of black circling it.

Corinne picked up her guitar. They could all see how much her hand shook, but nobody commented on it. Onstage they took no prisoners, and although Aidan was almost sure they didn't need him, the session musician was standing by, ready to take over if required.

Jake joined them during the trek to the stage. The Hammersmith Apollo was an old Odeon cinema, recently refurbished so it made a much better venue for rock than it used to, but it was still a building used for something other than it was intended for. "My wife arrived," Jake mumbled. "It's the first time she's seen us—the band."

Corinne spun around, nearly hitting him with her guitar. "Your wife?" Nobody had mentioned any wife to her.

Jake grinned. "She's an American. She needed a husband and I needed a wife. Now I tell all the women I sleep with that I'm married, so I can't get involved, and she got her funding." He chuckled at Corinne's expression of disbelief. "Her dad wouldn't give her a dime until she brought a husband home. That's why she picked me. The old man hated me on sight, but he'd made a deal, so he went through with it."

"Why didn't you—" Corinne shrugged. It was none of her business, really, but their recent long hours of practice had brought her closer to all the band members, even the taciturn Jake.

"We don't get on," Jake said, totally without rancor.

"Is she like you?" Corinne asked, meaning a shape-shifter.

Jake shrugged. "I haven't the faintest clue. Don't care enough to find out. But she's in the country, so she came to the concert. She sent me a note." He grimaced. "She hasn't changed. Body as sexy as hell and a tongue like a razor. If she's a shifter, she's a raptor." He nudged her, reminding her to keep moving.

Corinne followed the others to stage-side. The raw, open feel of the audience wasn't like the appreciative audiences she faced in the past. These people were rabid, ready for anything, volatile with violence, sex and edgy emotion.

The emcee began the introduction and the crowd responded with roars and screams.

She'd had her enthusiastic welcomes, but not like this.

Her station was on the far side of the stage. Chris entered first, began the first drum riff, and they would run on, already playing. Running and playing was a skill in itself, but that way the sound hit the crowd from the get-go, and if the members of Pure Wildfire were nothing else, they were fast and furious.

Corinne expected the usual surge of terror when she hit the stage, but what she didn't expect was the energy the audience pushed back at her. She wasn't sure if it was antagonistic or enthusiastic, but she didn't care. It gave her the boost she needed to get past the initial nervousness that always followed the terror.

She was in and she was playing. Aidan stood on the other side of the stage, all Splinter, and Ryan strutted center stage, taunting, preening, challenging.

Magic happened. They stopped being five people and became one entity, Pure Wildfire. The crowd shrieked and stamped, bodysurfers got busy at the front, keeping the security staff who lined the pit on their toes.

They played almost continuously, with the briefest of breaks between each number, riding the high, making it their own. Ryan controlled, calling out songs either vocally or with a mind link. When she touched Aidan's mind, there were no words. She heard music, times, but he'd gone beyond words, entered his world of whirling, sparkling music. Ryan, on the other hand, was all words, wringing every sense of meaning out of them.

When she proved she could produce the hard, driving backing, the base for Aidan to fly, she felt the audience relax. They came for a good time—they had paid good money for this, so unless she truly sucked, they were going to have that good time. She knew that—she'd felt it before, when she virtually sleepwalked through her performance. There was no sleepwalking here.

No longer needing Aidan to support her, she posed with the others, setting her own style as she felt her way through. *This* was where it happened, where all the rehearsals proved successes or failures, where she gelled or she didn't.

As the performance went on, she gained in energy instead of losing it as the Classical Princess had. By the time they reached the center of the evening and hit the long, winding version of "Tearing Me Apart", she was more than ready for the solo the band awarded her.

She felt Aidan in her mind again as they reversed roles and he began the hard, driving rhythm to back her solo. By now using her Gibson, Corinne strode to the front of the stage and faced the audience, holding the neck of the guitar high to emphasize her notes.

Her playing was very different from Aidan's. Where he was fire and energy, coaxing trademark riffs and impossible trills, Corinne was precise. As the band encouraged her to improvise, she found her voice, more jazzy in style than Aidan's pure bluesy rock. Her notes danced around the main tune, drawing the theme out and exalting it, spinning the listener up to the high scaffolding where the blue and pink spots aimed their light at her, and further still.

She hadn't realized she'd played for longer than they set aside for her until she heard Ryan's voice in her mind. *Brava, little sister!*

Brought back to herself, she glanced around. Aidan was closer than she'd thought, playing backup to her solo. The music sounded different somehow. Her backing was powerhouse, driving hard, but his was more delicate, indicating the tune, leaving Jake free to add the bass line and improvise on it. She wound the solo down and returned to her role, one she was beginning to love, shocked that she could become so carried away, shocked by the intensity of the response to her playing when the audience went wild.

At the back of the huge auditorium, the rock fans overwhelmed the Corinne Westfall fans. That gave her an idea. All her efforts had been to placate both sets of fans, to persuade the Corinne Westfall fans to come with her and the Pure Wildfire fans to accept her.

It was no longer enough. Finally, she realized just how stultifying her life had been. Forcing her into a mold had forced her talent, stopped her loving her work. She remembered the sense of exaltation she felt at the beginning and remembered the last time she'd felt it. Six years ago, when she'd mastered a tricky piece of Bach, her first love in classical music. Now here it was again, in a different milieu, playing different music. But she played both types from the heart. That was the real difference between this and the Corinne of the classical babe years.

Now that the first rush was over, Corinne had time to enjoy herself and enjoy the other performers. Ryan seemed tireless, twisting his body into expressive poses, screaming at the audience or seducing them with his lower, crooning tones. He taunted, he challenged, he made them weep, the perfect front man. When Ryan and Aidan moved in to perform an unaccompanied blues song, she nearly cried from the emotion they evoked. Her roadie was toweling her down at the time and it was only then she realized just how sweaty she'd become. It didn't matter, as long as she could still play. Her hair was stuck to her head, so she snatched the towel and rubbed it vigorously over her hair, shaking it to fiery tangles. Before the planned time, she stripped off her top. It was soaked. Cool air hit her as one of the roadies angled the fan toward her and she shot him a look of gratitude. When someone handed her a glass, she didn't care what was in it, as long as there was at least a pint. Iced water. Wonderful. She tipped the last quarter pint over her head, soaking her hair again, but shook it out.

Ryan was singing a heartbreaking blues number of loss and pain while Aidan ran the gamut of twelve-bar agony, bending the notes to suit his brother's anguished tones. When she listened to the words, they didn't surprise her. She wasn't a blues aficionado, not enough to immediately identify the composer, but it was Delta blues, basic twelve bar, lifted to sublimity by the emotion, pure and true, rarely heard in other forms of music.

She loved it. When someone shoved the strap of her Gibson over her head, it took her by surprise, because she'd become totally involved in the song. She nearly took a swing at the guy, but stopped herself, remembering who she was and what she was supposed to be doing. Her reaction shocked her. She'd always been the epitome of professionalism, hitting her marks, playing her part, but tonight she'd become someone else.

The next number was an explosion of sound and light, designed to take the audience by surprise. The roar from the pit told them it worked. In spades. For an instant, everything blazed brightly, illuminating the audience, the band and the banks of equipment behind them. Corinne saw the scene as though it was a photograph. The head bangers at the front, the ravers, the rockers, the sea of black leather punctuated by an occasional flash of white t-shirt, everything imprinted on her memory for as long as she lived.

Corinne concentrated on her work, purposely bringing herself back down. She saw Aidan, hair pouring around his body, head bent. As she watched, he swung around and faced the audience and took them into heaven. She'd seen him do it before, but not this close and never when she'd been a part of it.

Now she was. She drove the song, enhanced Aidan's playing, kept up the pace, playing just above Jake's thumping power bass and the scattershot of Chris' drums. When Chris shook his head, showers flew from his hair. He kept a jug of water next to the drum kit and occasionally doused himself or nodded at a roadie to do it for him.

Occasionally she stepped forward to share the mike with Jake, to add vocals, but on the whole, Jake sang backing vocals. His strong, gritty tones melded with Ryan's agile voice to perfection.

All through the performance, Aidan only approached Corinne when they crossed onstage. He seemed lost in his own world, but Corinne knew he was with her all the way. His presence never left her mind, or her heart.

She adored him. She adored this. She wouldn't willingly give it up now.

They played a two-hour set and two encores. In between leaving the stage and returning, Corinne took a long drink and exchanged grins with the others. There wasn't time for much else. Ryan managed to change, shrugging on a blood red shirt that contrasted strongly with the white shirt he'd started in, the shirt that now lay in a damp heap on a corner of the stage. When they left the stage after the second encore, the audience shrieking and screaming for yet more, someone grabbed her hand.

Looking up, she saw Aidan, hair whipping behind him as he dragged her in the direction of the dressing rooms. She couldn't see his face but heard the laughter of the band following behind her. It had gone well, so why was he agitated? She felt his surge of energy. Was he angry?

He got to the dressing room they shared and dragged her inside, slamming the door. He shoved her against the door and only then did she see his face. It blazed. She only had a glance before his mouth descended hotly on hers.

Oh baby, I couldn't wait!

They were the only coherent words she heard before she felt him pulling at her bra. It had no fastenings, so he shoved it up, exposing her breasts. His hands went to her, exploring as though he'd never felt her before, never touched her, cupping, squeezing, massaging her to a state of near oblivion, using her own sweat to send his hands slipping over her skin.

She burned with passion, opened up and let him take everything he wanted. There were no words for the way she felt, no way to convey her passion except to show him.

She grabbed at him, her hands sliding over his sweat-slicked back, inside the waistband of his jeans. She dragged them down, taking his underwear with them until his cock fell naked into her hands, hot and heavy with want.

His cock was huge, the size it became inside her. He tore at her clothes, but her leather pants stuck to her body, she'd fastened them so tight. She hadn't thought birds could growl, but Aidan definitely growled now, the sound reverberating through her to her very core. But he moaned when she pulled his foreskin back hard, exposing him to her ravenous attentions. She wanted to taste him, hold him, feel him fucking her, everything all at once.

Her jeans gave way and without giving him a chance to stop her, she dropped down on her knees and took him into her mouth, tasting his essence, glorying in this passion that fired them both and sent them into their own world of furious desire. She opened her mouth wide, sucked hard and felt his cock head hit the back of her throat. She wanted it all, every bit of him. She'd drain him dry.

Aidan's full-throated groan didn't stop her. "Jesus, Corinne, you have to stop, baby, stop, please! I want to be inside you, now!"

He caught a strand of her hair and yanked her to her feet, shoving her against the door. They ignored the thump her body made against the old-fashioned wooden door, and the bathrobes that fell off the hook above her head. He dragged her up his sweaty body to wrap her legs around him.

He was inside her quicker than thought. He ignored the slight resistance of her body at the entry of his broad, blunt cock, and moving hard, he shoved every inch of it inside her.

He pushed her against the wooden door with a series of thumps that became regular as they found the familiar rhythm. She dragged him closer so her mouth met his.

He broke away with a groan. "I can taste myself on you. Oh Corinne!" Then he returned to her, driving his tongue into her mouth to taste every part of her, lick the sides of her mouth, caress her tongue with his, smooth the sensitive roof of her mouth.

Aidan, oh Aidan!

She was past coherence, past thought. She pressed her shoulders hard against the door and tilted her hips forward to take all of him, down to the base. His balls slapped her ass with every stroke, hurtling her into a world of sensation that was for them alone. The elation she felt during the band's performance came back to her threefold. Her mind blended with his, as the music they made mingled, and notes and riffs shimmered through their minds. Words were beyond them now, but the music only enhanced their mutual joy. They could make music with their minds and their bodies, and the simultaneous delight of it was almost too much to bear.

With one hard, driving thrust, it ended. His essence flooded her, bathing her with hot, burning seed, and she came, screaming the ecstasy he forced into her willing body.

Aidan leaned his forehead against hers and she felt how wet they were. Her body trembled and he slowly lowered her legs to the floor, supporting her carefully. Tenderness and care returned now passion was temporarily spent.

Then he wrapped his arms around her and took her in a long, tender kiss.

When he pulled away, he was smiling. "I don't know how I kept my hands off you for so long tonight. I swear, watching you on that stage made me hornier than I've ever been in my life. I would have fucked you in front of the thousands out there if you'd wanted me. I wanted to. So much."

Corinne panted, catching her breath. "Nice to know when you're wanted," she managed.

He swept her up in his arms. "Shower."

It was only then that she realized he'd fulfilled one of her secret fantasies. Daydreams of hot, sweaty sex with a rock star had fueled her more tedious days, provided her with some entertainment during the long, lonely nights before she'd met Aidan. He fulfilled all her dreams, all her fantasies and this was all she needed.

"Shouldn't we go and face the press and the fans, or something?"

"After we've showered. And you have to change. I've destroyed those pants."

She looked down to where the sad heap of black leather on the floor. "What did you do?"

"I extended a claw and sliced them off you. There's not much left."

She chuckled, wrapping one arm around his neck as he took her into the small shower stall. "What a pity I didn't buy two pairs!"

The shower was marvelous, but they didn't linger. He wanted to fuck her again, but she'd heard Chris' disgruntled tone in Aidan's head before Aidan abruptly shut him off. "I know they're waiting for us. We have to go, Aidan."

"Sod them all. I want you. Nobody else." His eyes burned into hers, the truth they held unassailable.

"It wasn't just our evening, it was theirs too. Ryan is wonderfully organized for a man who is generally considered shambolic, isn't he?"

Aidan chuckled, his chest vibrating with the joyful sound. "So he is."

She found the denim jeans she'd arrived in and a clean white t-shirt. Aidan wore unrelieved black, which only served to enhance the blaze of his hair, now brushed to a gloss to hang down his back, slightly damp after his cursory use of the blow dryer. They left the room hand in hand, leaving shredded clothing and the sweaty smell of hot sex behind them.

Chris waited outside, his face cracked by a huge grin. He knew exactly what they'd been doing. "Ryan and Jake are holding them off. Come on, time you faced the hordes."

"Are there hordes?"

Chris shrugged, the movement emphasizing his bulky shoulder muscles. "Quite a few. Not all friendly."

Aidan glanced at Corinne and the connection gave her the courage to go and face whatever waited for them outside.

The large room was packed and noisy. Chris led the way and then a ragged cheer went up when the assembled masses saw that Aidan and Corinne followed behind them. Aidan's hand tightened around Corinne's as though he was afraid she would get away.

There was nowhere she'd rather be, no one she'd rather be with. In the corner, she saw Paige and Ashley, the ever-present Tom behind them. Her father strode through the crowd until he stood before them, his total attention on his daughter. "Have you got anything for me yet?"

She shook her head. "Nor likely to, Dad."

He saw the slender chain around her neck and reached out to pull it clear of the t-shirt, dragging her neck so she was forced to lean toward him. The feather lay in his hand, gleaming balefully. "I could just take it." His gaze didn't leave the feather until he looked up slowly to see Aidan watching him. "It's true then."

"What's true?"

"You. You really are a firebird."

Although he was standing at the other end of the room, Corinne saw Ryan's head jerk sharply as he spun to stare at them. A girl she didn't know stood next to him, her wide blue eyes as startled as Ryan's own. Corinne didn't need any extra sense to tell her that the girl was another shape-shifter. She saw it in the awareness, the poise of the girl's body.

Aidan grinned. "You're imagining things, old man. Getting too old for the job, are we?"

John Westfall glared at him, his gaze epitomizing hatred and envy. "How old are you?"

"Thirty. How old are you?"

Westfall stared. "I can't believe a thing you say, can I?"

"You never could." For a moment, the wild-living, gorgeously slouching rock star disappeared, replaced by sharp-eyed, intelligent Aidan Hawthorne. Westfall took a step back, dropping the feather that fell between Corinne's breasts. Corinne felt his malevolence just before Aidan shielded her from it, and then the sharp mental reprimand her husband sent to her father. It seemed effortless, the way Aidan controlled the powers of his mind.

Westfall sneered. "I know who you are. You can't hide forever. You know there are people after you. I know them too. Give me the feather, convert me, or I'll set them on to you and you'll never be free." Westfall said the words in a low undertone of pure evil.

Corinne felt sick. "How could you threaten such a thing? I want to stay here, with the band, with Aidan. Don't you know you'll make me unhappy too?"

John Westfall gave a sharp, mirthless laugh. "Unhappy? You'll get over it, girl. I can promise you world fame, people to do whatever you want. What's mere happiness compared to that?"

Corinne felt a sharp pain in her head, lancing through to the soft tissue. Before she could scream with the agony of it, Aidan pulled her close and pressed her face to his chest. To an observer, it would look like a loving gesture, but in reality, it was a protective one. She felt Aidan push out the pain, turn it back where it came from. She felt others, others she knew, but a barrier came down hard, separating Aidan and herself from everyone else in the room.

Over her father's sudden yelp of pain, she heard Aidan's voice. "Very clever! You wanted to bring anyone else out, didn't you? Well, no, you're not going there. I'm it, as far as you're concerned. And I'm stronger than you can imagine. You won't get anything from me. Neither will your filthy friends." Dislike tainted every word, words no one but her father would fully understand. Corinne wondered why. Aidan knew her father was power hungry, that he would do a great deal, but this hatred was deeper than that and held a menace darker than any she'd felt before in him.

"What is it?" she whispered into his chest. "What's wrong?"

Aidan only cradled her closer and continued to speak to her father. "I know what you are and I know what you do. At last. Why it took me so long, I don't know. Take my word for it, she is no longer yours."

A hush had fallen over the people nearest to them. The media was here, photographers and journalists. They might not be able to understand the words between her father and her husband, but the aggression, the attitude was unmistakable. The split between father and daughter would be all over the web and the news tomorrow. They'd deliberately courted the press and now was the time they had to face the consequences.

"You've made her your creature then?" John sounded controlled now and she knew he'd used his considerable self-control, as aware as she was of the listening media.

Aidan released his hold and she leaned back so she could look up at him. Although he still spoke to her father, his gaze was all for her, rich in promise and love. "She's nobody's creature. She's her own self, her own wonderful self."

Westfall made a sound of exasperation. "I made her mine years ago."

"I cleaned all your filthy prints from her. She's free to do what she wants."

Corinne smiled up at him. "I want you."

Aidan bent and kissed her, to a chorus of raucous catcalls and whistles.

* * * * *

An hour later, Corinne sat with the other members of the band in the lounge of the Covent Garden flat. Aidan sat next to her, her hand in his. It seemed that he hadn't let go of her since she left the stage, but he must have done so at some point. Not that she could remember it or wanted to.

She'd underestimated his strength and his resolve. His easy exertion of power that overwhelmed her father staggered her and then the way he'd dealt with the media. Yes, they wanted to split with Westfall, yes, Corinne had chosen husband over father. Feeding them without telling them anything new. Then he'd turned the conversation to the concert, the upcoming album and future plans. Ryan joined him, giving the press an exclusive about the next single, and John left. Interestingly, Paige and Ashley stayed on, though she wasn't sure what that meant. Still not entirely sure what all this meant, trying to come to terms with it all, she sat and listened.

"The bastard used compulsion on her," Aidan growled, controlled fury in his voice. "She's been under his control for fucking years."

Corinne thought back to the time when many of her contemporaries were going to university. It was the first time she'd considered resuming her music studies full-time. For some reason she couldn't remember, she'd changed her mind, decided to make another album instead.

Could it be true?

"He used me?"

"As much as he could." Aidan kept his inner thoughts shielded. She assumed they included doing something violent to her father from the grim tone she rarely heard him use. "When I realized someone had got at you, all I did was clean it out. I didn't do anything other than give you your free will back."

She turned to face him, seeing the man she loved, but also something else. A man of power. A man who could overwhelm her father with the strength of his mind. A man to fear. "I didn't want you to know," he said gently. "I knew what it would do to you." Aidan took no notice of anyone else, as if they were alone. "You thought you were weak and stupid for signing that contract with your father, but he compelled you to do it. I wanted to give you some strength before you confronted that and realized what the man who should have loved and protected you did to you."

"I thought I was stupid, yeah. But my father and I stopped even pretending we had anything other than a business arrangement years ago."

Aidan's face twisted in an expression of pity, pain, but the anger remained, simmering in the depths of his fiery eyes. "Fathers are for love and support. Not for exploitation. When I first met you, I wasn't sure you could ever leave that behind."

"You would have let me go rather than plant something in my mind?"

"A thousand times rather." He sighed and leaned back on the sofa, putting his hand over hers. "He learned some mind-control techniques, and every time you opposed him, he put up another block. Your mind was a complete mess when I first saw it."

"Does that mean I'm easy to control?" she asked, swallowing back the sob in her voice.

Ryan was the first to react, leaning forward to catch her gaze with his. "No. No one can resist once the techniques are in place. My guess is that he drugged you first to make you receptive to him."

"How can I believe anything anyone says?" She pulled her hand away from Aidan's, feeling bereft, but determined to put some kind of distance between them. She erected the barriers he'd taught her to raise and strengthen, praying he'd told the truth.

"You can use your instincts," Aidan said, his voice frighteningly controlled. "You can trust them now. I removed all your blocks, all the things stopping you from reaching your own memories. I did it soon after I met you, when you let me in."

She recalled the strange feelings she used to have, the slight nausea, increasing when she thought of forbidden subjects like her mother or her career. "I must be weak, stupid or something to let him do it."

Aidan left his hand on the sofa between them, where she could reach it if she wanted to, but he didn't touch her. "He compelled you to sign it. You're not stupid, Corinne, he controlled you. Anyone under those circumstances would behave the same way." He met her gaze honestly. "Yes, me as well."

"So he really is a Svengali?"

"Kind of, yeah. Only he didn't use hypnotism, he used a skill strictly forbidden to Talents. Never tell, never compel."

"There are changes that alert you when somebody is trying to use you," said Chris. He sat on one of the long sofas, stretching his arm along the back of it, but his lazy pose did little to hide the lethal strength of the man. And, presumably, the bird. "Your memory becomes fuzzy. It's a special kind of fuzzy, one that anyone who knows about these things can track. But you have to trust them enough to let them in."

"Her mind was full of it," Aidan spoke, his voice tight and controlled now, but fury still simmered underneath. "I knew it, but I didn't want to believe anyone would do it to their own family."

"That's my brother, always the romantic," Ryan commented. He leaned forward and clasped his hands in a tight fist before him. "Why shouldn't he? He had an asset who threatened to leave him. Easy, when you know how."

"Who could have taught him?" wondered Jake.

"My mother."

Corinne's words dropped into the conversation made them all stop and stare at her. "He always said my mother had power. I refused to believe him, thought it was part of his stupid hobby." She steeled herself for the question she'd never dared ask anyone else. "Could he have killed her? She died of a mysterious illness ten years ago. They said it was a form of food poisoning, and since half the staff went down with it too, that's what it seemed to be. She wasn't living with Dad by then, but she came back to see me sometimes. She fell ill shortly after one of those visits."

"I'm sorry, Corinne." Aidan's voice was soft now, the edge gone. "He probably did it. He'd have poisoned the rest of the staff to cover it up. Likely she refused to teach him more than she already had, so she stopped being of use to him and became a threat. If she found out what he was doing to you and she was a true sensitive, she might have threatened to take you away. He couldn't lose his little nest egg, could he?"

The pain of losing her mother swept up to overwhelm her yet again, but this wasn't the time, wasn't the place. She forced it back. "Teach me how to detect when my mind is being taken over and how to fight it."

"Willingly."

"No." She turned away from Aidan, toward the others. "One of you."

The three men seemed equally surprised, but all agreed. She chose Jake, just because she didn't know him as well as she knew the others. She wanted impartial tutoring, someone who would drive her hard so she could be sure of achieving her aim. Nobody would use her ever again. Nobody, not even the man she loved.

Cautiously, she let down the barriers she'd erected and found Aidan, waiting patiently for her.

Ryan stood up and shook himself, rather like a bird shaking out its plumage. "Time to go. You know Westfall will try something, probably during the other two concerts?" The others nodded and Corinne felt deeply ashamed that they were talking about her father. "I've increased the security. I've also contacted a few of our Talented friends and given them tickets for tomorrow night. They'll monitor the area. That's about all we can do."

The rest nodded grimly and Ryan headed for the downstairs bathroom, loosening his shirt as he went. Corinne knew that later she would find three sets of men's clothing there and the small window open to the early morning air.

It seemed almost normal.

Chapter Sixteen

ഔ

Corinne felt the extra tension as soon as she stepped onstage on Saturday night.

Pure Wildfire had arrived. Previously an up-and-coming rock band, they'd become the gossip *du jour*. Corinne brought them notoriety and the fame they needed to push up to the next level in the celebrity firmament.

The press had been kind after the first concert, but tonight the big guns were on board. The international music press, the TV news reporters and the big Sunday newspapers. Not only that, but a few Corinne Westfall fans had made some banners. "Come back to us, Corinne" and "Corinne stinks in rock!"

This was it. Make or break time. A new rock band with everything to prove, everything to lose.

She'd expected that and steeled herself for it. What she hadn't expected was the extra element—the paranormal power that swept and surged through the building like a tidal wave. It was raw, undiluted and impossible for her to tell which force was friend and which foe. The energy was primal, without morals, without sense.

Her roadie was new too, burlier than Ted, who'd looked after her so far. This one was tall, built like a battering ram, and she suspected that if he was a shape-shifter, he was some kind of bear. With her newly enhanced senses, Corinne knew he was certainly something paranormal. Her skin prickled with awareness when she'd first met him. She only hoped he knew a Gibson from a Stratocaster.

She needn't have worried. In the first half hour, the banners disappeared and they had the audience rocking. Ryan took the added tension and used it, spiking his performance up to new levels, uncomfortably forcing the audience to share in his private nightmares and dreams, with the band dancing, enhancing, flying around him.

Halfway through the set, they were running about ten minutes overtime. Corinne stripped off her t-shirt and received some whistles for her pains. Tonight she'd abandoned the heavy sports bra in favor of a black satin bra with push-up cups. Although earlier in the day she'd tried it out, jumping and twisting until she was quite happy she was safe, the audience didn't know that and it showed its appreciation with whistles and whoops. Her jeans didn't hide much either. Low-slung hipsters topped by a studded black leather belt. She'd allowed the belt to ride lower than the low jeans. She wore no jewelry except her wedding ring, a silver slave band high on her upper arm and one long, trailing chain earring. She abandoned the heavy eye makeup of the night before, which had worn off halfway through the set, deciding instead on heavy shadow, mascara and lipgloss.

Despite that, halfway through her solo, something black dripped into her eye and she had to blink to make it go away.

A sharp pain lanced along her right arm, freezing her hands on the strings. She cried out before paralysis gripped her right arm, and then total numbness replaced the pain. She couldn't feel her arm anymore.

Corinne was right-handed, so she couldn't pick the notes anymore. Her nerves were completely frozen, the muscles paralyzed. Panic gripped her and she felt Ryan in her mind. *Start again. Keep going if you can. Do you need us to take over or get the session man to cover you?*

This was a deliberate attack. To make her look inadequate and stupid, to drive the press against her. She couldn't recover from it if she gave up now. Whatever the band thought, she'd always be the woman who'd fucked up their biggest night.

No! This would *not* happen. She managed to hit the strings with her now completely frozen hand and used her left to bend and twist the sound, discordant and angry. It was the way she felt.

A familiar presence appeared in front of her. Aidan, sans guitar, topless and gleaming with sweat. She felt his hair caress her shoulder when he moved behind her and leaned over her. *Remember the nights we've done this? Do it now, Corinne. Let go, blend your mind with mine completely. Put your hand on my thigh and let's give them a show!*

When she turned her head, he took her in a deep, passionate kiss, and at the same time reached over to touch her guitar.

He was right. They had practiced this, at first to learn techniques, but it also turned both of them on. She leaned her bottom against his crotch and felt his erection, hard and needy, pressing into her through her pants. That night in his flat, when he'd lifted her onto his cock, returned in force and reminded her of the passion they shared. His response was to shove himself hard against her. When he released her mouth, they stared at each other for an instant before she turned her head away to concentrate on her playing.

Together they played, moving from one melody to the next, teasing the audience with a carillon of bright notes, then turning dirty, twisting and bending the notes to deep, despairing oblivion. The mood turned sexual. By now aware of no one but each other, their minds fully merged, they played as they felt—needy, horny, their bodies tingling with awareness, the attack that caused this temporarily forgotten in their blaze of passion. Aidan thrust forward in an instinctive movement and Corinne heard the audience roar its approval. From somewhere behind them, Ryan laughed, and they took his sound, twisted it, enhanced it and made it theirs. Corinne felt Aidan's hand caress her breast, hold her steady, and she pushed back in return, ground her buttocks into him until she heard him groan with frustrated desire. Using the Gibson and his gift, he showed her what he wanted to do to her. In her mind, she saw them both completely naked, his body driving hard into hers, sweat flying from his body as he worked to continue to play and to satisfy his body. Every Talent in the audience must have seen the graphic pictures and Corinne felt her body melt for him.

More powerful than the most blatant floor show at a sex club, they openly flaunted their love and craving for each other. And still the guitar wailed on, screaming in release as Corinne felt the music, heard him begin to wind down in her mind. She followed, but teased him with little tweaks of her fingers, pulls at his heart.

When the solo completed, he spun her in his arms, and took her in a deep kiss, careless of the thousands of spectators. Ryan came forward and finished the song, Jake and Chris filling in. When Corinne finally opened her eyes she saw Chris, standing to one side, grinning at them. *Way to go, sister,* she heard in her mind, and then a tinge of anxiety colored his voice. *You feeling okay now?*

Yes, thanks. But that was an attack, not me freezing up.

Silence before Ryan's anxious communication. *Can you pick up where it came from? Did you get a signature?*

No, nothing.

I did, Aidan put in. *I got a fix on where it came from and sent someone up there, but I bet whoever did it is long gone.*

Ryan swore. She saw his lips move and he moved instinctively to block the direct view to her, a useless gesture now, but one that warmed her heart, showing, as it did, that Ryan cared for her.

Aidan pressed his forehead against hers. "Do you need to go offstage? I felt your hand as soon as it happened."

Corinne flexed her fingers against his thigh. "I've got it back. It came back about halfway through the last few bars. All of a sudden."

"Somebody was made to release you," he murmured. "Come on, take your applause."

"Our applause," she reminded him.

They turned to face the audience, which was going collectively insane.

* * * * *

The next day, Aidan went out to collect the papers, leaving Corinne luxuriating in bed. True to his word, he'd made love to her for most of the night until she'd pleaded exhaustion, and only then did they sleep.

They made the front page of *Music for Rockers*, commonly known as MFR. Aidan was leaning back in the shot, his hair streaming behind him, his groin welded to Corinne's backside, while her mouth was open, her eyes half closed, her hair in her eyes and plastered to her cheekbones. "We might have to do that again," he commented. "In public, I mean." He tossed the heavy Sunday paper onto the bed, leaving a scattering of magazines, inserts and freebies behind, and stripped off his clothes to join her under the covers again.

Startlingly, they made the front page of many of the Sundays. The faux moralistic right-wing *Sunday Review* had a headline that screamed "Should We Let Our Children Watch This?" With a side view of Aidan, hand firmly on her breast, an expression strongly like sexual ecstasy on his face and bliss on hers. They couldn't have better publicity if they'd paid for it.

They'd beaten it, turned imminent disaster to triumphant success. Later in the morning, the TV executives began to call, filling the answer machine with requests to appear on news programs and arts programs. Even the producer of "Divas" called.

"Shall we do it?" Aidan asked her.

She sat up in bed to shove some of the papers clear. "We need to work out what we're going to say. I won't do 'Divas', because they'll want me without you, but we could do some of the others."

"What we need," he said thoughtfully, "is a good manager."

Squealing in indignation, she turned on him, leaping on him to pummel him into the mattress. He laughed as he fended her off, then caught her hands in his, holding her upright. She saw his eyes flash and darken into desire before he tugged her down.

She landed heavily on him, her breasts squashed to his chest, her hands spread above their heads. He wasted no time, taking her in a deep, sumptuous kiss while wriggling his body into position under her. Still in the kiss, he slid home as though he'd never been away, his cock easing into her wet, needy body, making them one. Only then did he finish the kiss and open his eyes, watching her as they moved together. She smiled down at him. "Don't you ever get tired of making love?"

"What a stupid question! No, and I never will. I love you, Corinne, and that's for keeps too."

She sat up, watching his face, and they both looked down to where they joined. Raising her body, she stayed there until the slight chill of the morning invaded the space between them, then she slammed down on to him and he cried out and arched up to her. "Baby, you are something else! Fuck me, never, ever stop!"

So she didn't, riding him hard and deep, impelling him deeper inside her with every stroke. He howled under her, his strong body taking everything she gave, responding to every downward plunge with an upward thrust of his own. Deep, deep and deeper, holding her orgasm back by sheer willpower, making it last, making it theirs.

Until he caught a place inside her, his cock head rubbing slickly over it, and she exploded, yelling his name like a plea, a prayer.

Aidan didn't stop, but swung her down and then rolled over, turning a fierce, hot fucking into intense loving.

He took his time now, sliding deeply in and out of her, until she sighed, long and luxuriously, relaxing into his strokes. "Now close your eyes, my darling, and let me take you flying," he murmured.

Corinne closed her eyes and at once felt his arms go about her. Her body tingled with awareness and she felt him draw her up and seat his consciousness firmly in hers.

This is what I see when I fly. She saw London, just as she'd seen it before, when she'd thought it an illusion, but they were swiftly over it and they glided over the countryside, toward the sea. *There's my house.*

A small cottage perched on a cliff, nothing else for miles except a narrow dirt track. It looked solitary, a place she could really be alone with Aidan. *Can we go there?*

Soon. I promise. We'll be completely alone.

I want to convert, Aidan. I want to be with you always.

His mouth descended hotly on hers and he ravaged her in a passionate kiss, fucking her stronger and harder, unrelenting until she cried out and arched up to him. His head descended to her breast and he drew her nipple into his mouth, sucking strongly to send chills racing through her body until she came again, erupting in pleasure, screaming his name. His hair brushed her skin, falling freely around her, tantalizing her with its soft touches, and he continued to drive her up to the clouds until his seed spurted hotly deep inside her body and he cried out her name over and over.

Aidan gave Corinne all she ever needed, all she ever wanted. She opened her eyes to crumpled bedding and crushed newspapers and Aidan. He wouldn't let her look away, lifting his hand to grip her chin. "You mean it? You want me to convert you?"

"Yes. I want all the time I can have, if it means spending it with you."

He kissed her, gently this time, then slid to one side, holding her close. "Are you sure?"

"Will it hurt?"

He nodded. "I'm told it does. But I'll be there with you. All the way." She lifted the feather on its chain around her neck, but he enclosed it and her hand in his bigger one, surrounding her in warmth. "Not yet. Conversion can make you weak, so wait until after the concerts. Next week. We'll go away. When we're done with business, how about we go a bit farther afield than the cottage?"

Keeping one arm about her, he rolled onto his back and reached for the drawer in the bedside table. He took out an airline pouch. "I was going to give these to you after the concert tonight, but it might as well be now."

He gave her the pouch and watched her open it. She read the first words and then her glance flicked up at his face, warm and happy. "The Bahamas!"

"I've hired a villa. We can be completely alone and you can have all the rest you need. If I can keep my hands off you, that is." He growled, close to her ear.

She swatted him with the pouch, laughing. "It's perfect!"

"We go as soon as we can get away and stay as long as we like."

"When do we have to be back?"

He slid his hand around her waist. "Not for a month, at least. We can do a quick interview and go. *Icefire* is going to be remixed, although I have some ideas about that."

She turned a questioning eye on to him. "About all those new tracks I've learned?"

"I want your input, not Matt's. I want to re-record his parts with you there instead. He violated more than his contract, and as long as we pay him enough, he won't object."

"Are you sure? What will the others think?"

"After the last two concerts, we're on a roll, sweetheart. The press seems to have taken you to its heart, and putting you into the album can only do us good. Even if you decide not to stay." He paused. "You don't have to, you know. You can still study, if that's what you want."

She slid closer. "I want to study with you. I've found what I need, Aidan, and it's you."

"Woman, do you ever want to get out of this bed?"

She shook her head, laughing. "Not until we have to."

* * * * *

They had to, later that day. When they arrived at the Apollo, the crowd was notable for its increased size—word had got around and the delighted fans greeted Aidan and Corinne with wolf whistles and shrieks of delight. The Corinne Westfall supporters, there for the last two nights, had gone, probably in disgust. While Corinne was sorry to upset anyone who found pleasure in what she did, she had no intention of continuing in the same old rut just for them.

The others had arrived and a raucous cheer went up when they went through to the narrow corridor that contained the dressing rooms. "You'll be asking for red only M&M's next!" one of the roadies called.

"I don't like M&M's!" Corinne called back, to a muttered "I'll have yours" from Jake.

The atmosphere was euphoric. The papers, whether condemning or congratulatory, hadn't ignored them. While the only music paper yet to report on the concerts was MFR, the others wouldn't be long in coming, and MFR assured Pure Wildfire of humungous attention.

Corinne met the new manager for the first time, the man they'd chosen to take over after the contract with Westfall ended, which would be immediately after the concert tonight. A bear of a man, Randy Norwood was American and highly experienced in his job. He wanted to take them to the States and had planned a careful campaign. "We need to make a quick video," he informed them. "We'll take something off the cameras at the concert." At her look of surprise he chuckled. "I had the concert videotaped, not for general release, but for us to see how it went. But I should be able to get something interesting from them. Not your highlight, we'll keep that for later. But we need to keep this news going." He studied Corinne and Aidan shrewdly. "You're newlyweds, but I hope you're prepared to keep this up for a while. That stuff you did last night was something!" His face broke into a broad grin and he reached out to slap Aidan on the shoulder. "Great stuff. You've been touring since you started, but we're ready to take the next step up. A few of the better clubs left in the tour, but more larger venues. With the publicity you've been providing recently, they'll be slavering for you by the time I get you over there!"

Although he seemed intimidating, Corinne found Randy a lot less daunting than her father. Large in build, expansive in nature and an ex-wrestler, Randy held a great deal of shrewdness and savvy, more than most people gave him credit for, but he must have, to have piloted his bands to success.

Tonight she wore a waistcoat deliberately made like the ones Aidan liked to wear. His were too large for her, but they wanted to give the impression of wearing each other's clothes at times. Tight jeans, the slave bangle and a long earring consisting of several trailing fine chains with different symbols at the end of each completed her outfit. Despite the band's skepticism, the high-heeled sandals remained and she intended to keep them on through the whole performance.

They met up with the others when they were ready and headed for the stage when the word came. Everyone was happy, the spirit of end-of-term infecting everyone, together with the success of the last two concerts. After this, everyone was off on holiday somewhere, even if it meant, as in Chris' case, going home, closing the door and disconnecting the phone.

Corinne still felt nervous, but she always had. She didn't expect that to go away. But she loved being part of a band instead of holding everything on her own shoulders. She'd never known camaraderie like it before, especially when her sisters had joined her onstage. They would be there tonight. They sent word that the Westfall family would be there. No doubt her father had received the official notice of cancellation of her contract, as well as the band's, by now.

When she ran onstage, she felt the atmosphere, extending her empathy to sense it. For a brief moment, she sensed hatred piercing through the wall of ecstatic welcome. But they were already into the first number, and she had no time to worry about it. In any case, the feeling was gone almost as soon as she'd become aware of it. No doubt one of the psychic crowd. They were still there, in force. The electric atmosphere wasn't just the high voltage engendered by the power sent to the amplifiers. The air crackled with it, both good and bad. Tonight they'd prepared for the sneaky assault Corinne received the night before and she was sure that wouldn't resurface. Shape-shifters had emerged in force and were present tonight. The shape-shifter community didn't take attacks on its members lightly, and Corinne, although not yet a shape-shifter, was a member.

She didn't need to force herself to concentrate on the music. It was still new to her and she was still getting used to the way one of the band would use the music as a springboard for something she hadn't heard before, a variation on a theme. That was how she recognized that Aidan was nervous. He was sticking to the riffs she knew, for the most part, still giving the audience what it was screaming for, but not taking off like the previous night. She felt his mind in hers and roving the auditorium. What did he sense that she didn't? Stretching her empathetic senses, the ones she was accustomed to using, Corinne felt nothing she hadn't spotted in her first sweep. She touched the minds of the other band members, and discovered them on full alert, but not unduly alarmed. Perhaps Aidan was being more careful because of their relationship.

That must be it. Keeping her senses alert, Corinne turned the bulk of her concentration to the music. When "Tearing Me

Apart" began, she remembered Aidan was to come to her. At first, she thought he wouldn't, but after a few bars of his solo, he looked up and smiled at her.

He took his time crossing the stage, while the audience whooped in delight, knowing what he was about to do. She tried not to smile. The song was about the agony of losing somebody and knowing it was your fault. The solo was an anguished wail, recollecting the grief of losing and the bliss of having. She looked down and felt rather than saw Aidan's arms go about her. She relaxed back into them and felt his gentle kiss on her neck.

He put his hand over hers on the strings and she dropped her hand, leaving him in control of them, while she kept the bridge and the frets. They could do this either way, after they discovered it was easiest, and far more interesting, for him to sit behind her and demonstrate. If he could have read and written music, it wouldn't have been necessary, but she was delighted it had been.

She felt the picture in his mind and opened herself to him. He showed them both naked, with her sitting in his lap, playing and loving. It was a beautiful picture and they would never make the music they played together at those times public. It was theirs alone.

She followed where he led, although she knew he would let her lead if she wanted to. Tonight, when she wanted his mind off the peril and on the concert, it seemed better to allow him the lead. The basic melody left behind, they rose together to a climax both saw in their minds and she felt his free hand cover her breast over the thin leather of the waistcoat. Warm and loving, she felt the tingle as her nipple peaked for him. He groaned softly in her ear and pressed a kiss to the rim. All the time they were playing, driving up the intensity, winding the music up to its climax.

When she heard his gasp, she thought he was about to lean back and create the pose featured in most of the newspapers that morning. Instead, she saw a horrific vision in her head, and knew they'd taken a wrong step. They'd expected the attack to be psychic. They hadn't expected a sniper.

Before she could collect herself, Aidan picked her up and spun her around, broadcasting the picture to all the psychic readers present. She didn't hear the shot over the roar of the crowd and the commotion added by the psychics, all racing toward the sniper. A man, but she'd seen no more.

Aidan fell on top of her and she knew the heat she felt was more than sweat. It was blood.

Chapter Seventeen

ꙮ

Aidan lay heavily over her, but then groaned and rolled away, allowing her to get to her knees. Someone started the dry-ice machine, the only way to obscure the band from any more shots, and people were screaming. She felt hands on her shoulders and turned to see Ryan, looming at her out of the fog. "Did you see?"

Pale-faced, Ryan knelt down on the other side of his brother. Two roadies arrived, but Jake and Chris shouldered them aside.

Aidan's eyes flickered open and searched for Corinne. He forced a smile and lifted his hand. She took it in hers. "We'd better get you to a hospital." She spoke quietly, all too aware of the growing pool of blood under her knees.

He shook his head, wincing with the effort. "I'm dying."

"No!" Her shriek was louder than Ryan's voice ten minutes ago, when everything had been right with the world. She took a breath, deliberately controlled herself.

"Truly, sweetheart. I'm dying. I need to go to the fire."

Ryan reached over and touched two fingers to the center of Aidan's forehead, closing his eyes. Puffs of clouds created by the dry ice drifted between them. Ryan opened his eyes. "He's right."

A movement caught her eye when Chris stood up and quietly left the group.

Aidan opened his eyes, straight on to Corinne's face. "My only regret is not meeting you sooner," he said. "I love you, Corinne. You've made the last few weeks the best of my life."

"Aidan, fight it. Don't go!" She kept her voice low and soft, leaning close, uncaring of the blood that was now seeping out, making the floor under her knees slippery.

"I won't go yet."

She glanced up at Ryan and then down at the man she loved. The man who had just saved her life at the cost of his own. How she wished he had not!

"The phoenix knows when he will die. It gives us time to get him to the fire." Ryan's voice came as low as hers, but calmer. "I was there before, when what remained of his father went into the fire. I know what to do. Just stay with him, Corinne. Be there for him."

Two men bearing a stretcher emerged through the clouds of mist and Corinne became vaguely aware of what was going on around them. Shouts and yells came from the auditorium, but although the noise was loud, it didn't hold the air of panic. She felt the calming atmosphere and she knew the psychics massed in the audience were working to maintain it. Someone was making an announcement, but she didn't bother to listen.

The men lifted Aidan on to the stretcher, and he cried out in pain. She reached for him with her mind, but she couldn't connect. He wouldn't let her. She guessed it was the pain, but she so wanted to share his last moments with him. She took his hand and walked by his side, shielded from spectators and jostlers by Chris and Jake. "Please, Aidan, let me in. Please." She didn't know if he could hear her. "Don't waste your energy shielding me. I need this time with you."

As though he'd breathed out after holding his breath for a long time, she felt him open up. The pain was there, but muted, probably by the shock. He flooded her senses, filling her with love and a reassurance that broke her heart.

She saw the certainty of his death and knew it for what it was. Not a warning, not a premonition, but a certainty. She saw what he had to do and determined to help him do it. Whatever it cost her. Ryan, walking on the other side of the stretcher, caught her eye, and she knew he was there too, helping and supporting.

They went outside where an ordinary-looking ambulance waited. Only Ryan, Chris and Jake followed them inside, with an attendant. As soon as the doors slammed on them, the attendant got busy, padding the wound and stanching the blood.

Aidan was shot through the heart. There was no way of saving him and only the first-aid and the combined wills of the shape-shifters present could keep him alive long enough to go into the flames. If he died, he would go into the flames anyway, but she felt his need to spend as long as he could with her. She felt the same way. Forcing her private grief away for the present, knowing she would have the rest of her life for that, Corinne concentrated on giving him all the love in her heart.

The ambulance took off, the siren wailing.

"Where are we going?"

"A private field near Epping Forest. They're preparing everything for him. There will be no delay."

She felt Aidan's relief. He spoke in their minds, easier for him now than dragging breath into his laboring lungs to speak. *Know that I love Corinne more than life. Look after her.*

We will, Ryan promised.

She mustn't go back to her father. He set the attack, didn't he?

Probably. Chris, laconic as usual, whether mentally or verbally.

The attendant moved back and sat down. Corinne knew without being told that this wasn't a normal ambulance. This was more in the nature of transportation. She sat on the bench where Aidan lay, holding his hand as though she would never let go.

She saw a faint smile crease his lips. *You know suttee isn't required, don't you?*

I would do it, if it was.

No! The response was vehement. *You have so much to offer. Don't waste it. Don't waste what I did tonight, Corinne. Promise me you won't take the easy way out.*

I promise, she replied without hesitation. *I'll never, ever forget you, Aidan.*

The ambulance siren stopped, presumably past the built-up areas, the driver no longer wanting to draw attention to their presence.

"You need to know what happens now, Corinne." She nodded to show Ryan she was listening, not taking her gaze from Aidan's beloved face. "Before he is put on the pyre, Aidan will shape-shift. He can't go there in human form — he has to go as the phoenix. This won't be private. There will be others there, people anxious to witness the rebirth. It's a great thing and it doesn't happen very often. Usually. He will not be able to communicate with us once he has shape-shifted for the last time."

"How will he be reborn?"

Ryan hesitated. She reached for his mind, but it was closed to her. That hurt.

"It might be through you," Jake said softly. "It won't be Aidan, Corinne, but it will be the phoenix."

"But I'm on birth control!"

"Accidents happen," Jake said softly.

"Corinne, he won't come back as Aidan," Ryan said. "He will be someone else."

Corinne swallowed. That much was clear to her. This was a violent death and Aidan had already told her the new phoenix would be without memory, a new being. "Is there nothing anyone can do?" She'd grope at any straw, do anything to get Aidan back.

"No."

She was glad they told her directly. She needed to know. Her mind was numb, all but for the reality she saw before her. Aidan, the pad under his body now soaked with blood, was leaving her. And she might have his child, who would be another phoenix. But it would also be Aidan's child. She couldn't be sorry about that. There would be something, however small, to bring back the man she loved so much.

I'm sorry we didn't have more time.

She saw his eyes close, and was afraid he'd slipped too far away from her, but then he opened them again. *I'm sorry too. But we made the most of it, didn't we?*

Yes, we did.

I love you, Corinne.

I love you, Aidan.

* * * * *

The field was on a private estate. Corinne saw two lodges and a great black iron gate, which opened before them, and then the ambulance took them over the grass to a field.

When they got out, they saw a crowd assembled around something she couldn't look at—not yet. Jake and Chris carried the stretcher now and a path opened before them. She wouldn't let go of Aidan's hand. The crowd was as different in atmosphere to the one at the concert as it was possible to be, but it contained many of the same people. However, this crowd was almost silent, communicating on private mental paths or in low murmurs. Some held blazing torches, lighting their way to the pyre.

Corinne looked up to see a great tower of brushwood, like the largest Fireworks Night bonfire she'd ever seen. Birds hovered above and animals raced over the grass to reach them, all shifters, come to witness the amazing event of the phoenix rising from its own ashes.

Aidan's hand lay cold in hers, but the fingers still exerted a slight pressure, so he was still with her. He was past talking, past communicating in words now. Only warmth came from his mind, to her and anyone else who cared to eavesdrop. He was seeking to comfort her right up to the last moment. She wanted to weep but wouldn't disgrace him in front of all these people. Despite his public profile, Aidan was a private person, keeping his world to himself. She knew he wouldn't want a public display of grief. She called on all her training, all the years she'd smilingly played for crowds of people when inside she was despairing of every finding a true meaning for herself, found that mask and put it on. Not smiling, but grave and clear eyed. She would give him honor and love. It was the only thing left for her to do now.

When his hand slipped away from hers, they put the stretcher down on the ground and she felt him withdraw. He shape-shifted.

Ryan stood next to her. "This happens even if he can't do it himself. It's a force of nature."

She watched the great bird emerge. In its natural form, the phoenix was larger than a man by about a foot. It was large, glittering with golden red plumage, its beak an angry hook, its eyes flashing red fire.

It got to its feet, the bloodied garments Aidan had worn in rags on the ground. There was no sign of the terrible wound that had killed Aidan, but there was no feeling in the great bird either. Nothing emanated from it, good or bad. It just was, a force of nature. Its gaze swept the crowd, acknowledging them, before it turned to the fire.

The torchbearers ringed the bonfire and thrust blazing torches into its base, stepping back when the fire flared up, brightly burning.

The phoenix faced the fire and, as the people stepped back, he stepped forward. Without warning, he spread his wings and launched himself into the air. He circled the fire, the flames licking at the beautiful plumage, lighting it into blazing colors of gold, red and orange. Then he flew straight up into the air.

Corinne felt for Ryan's hand and found it. She hung on. Her grief didn't prevent her appreciating the sheer beauty of the sight, the creature and the element it was made from. She wanted to remember everything so she could tell her son, if that was how the phoenix would return.

"You know he won't be able to come back for you." Ryan's voice was calm, but inside she felt the terrible sense of loss he felt. "He will forget and come back as someone completely new."

"Aidan is dead. I know that." She couldn't think past that one, terrible fact.

A woman's voice, someone whose voice she found hauntingly familiar came from behind Corinne. "Don't turn around, my love, my daughter. I have seen this twice before and I have read about it in hidden texts. Have you anything left of him?" Corinne turned her head, but the voice reminded her, "Don't turn around! You can't see me, my love, or I will have to leave you."

How could her mother, dead ten years, be here?

Corinne remembered the feather. She dipped into her waistcoat and dragged out the chain. "Should I put it into the fire?" She dropped Ryan's hand and took a step forward.

"No!" Her mother's voice sounded unnaturally loud in the silence. "Hold it with both hands and wish and remember. Wish for the thing you want most, however unlikely you think it might be. Wish, my child, use all the power I invested in you, not the power your husband has taught you. Reach for it, feel it and wish!"

Corinne did as her mother told her, remembering Aidan, the way he'd loved her and the bond they'd made freely, a bond that had strengthened in the time they'd known each other. She called to him, held the bond tightly, knowing this might be the last time she could ever do so.

She watched the great bird circling in the sky, spiraling higher as the fire took hold and the flames reached up, searching for company.

She wanted him back. She didn't want this to happen. *Make it go away, make it all go away, bring Aidan back to me!*

With a sharp cry, the first she'd ever heard from the great bird, the phoenix closed its wings and plummeted into the fire.

Corinne caught her breath and the crowd cried out. Head first, the bird dived, plunging without hesitation into the flames, lethal beak gleaming with wicked intent, red eyes flashing.

The flames roared up, flaring into renewed life. They changed color, from orange-red to deep crimson, then back to orange and finally rich, pure gold. The flames illuminated the faces of the people closest to it, revealing awe and total absorption in the scene before them.

Then Corinne realized what was missing. Cameras. When Pure Wildfire performed, the audience was strobed with flashes from cameras, but not here. Nobody forbade them, but nobody was using them either.

Corinne's mind tried to avoid the tragedy playing out before her. The loss of the man she loved, the man she was born for, was too much for her to handle all at once. She couldn't manage it. No doubt it would come, haunting her for the rest of her life. Not that she cared anymore. If she hadn't made a promise to stay, she would have been tempted to follow him into the flames.

The fire began to die down, the blaze growing duller and smaller. They must have built the fire in a particular way, because a solid bonfire would have continued to burn for some time, but this did not.

Corinne felt someone touch her hand and only then did she remember that Ryan was Aidan's brother. Tentatively, she opened her mind to him and felt him waiting. When turned her head cautiously, only the members of the band stood close to her. The woman she'd heard, the voice of her mother, was nowhere in sight, and she knew from searching Ryan's mind that he hadn't heard her. Her message had been for Corinne alone. Ryan's grief was great but controlled, helping her to control her own, to keep her dignity intact, as Aidan would have wished.

Would have wished. The words held a finality Corinne found difficult to comprehend. While her reasoning could see he'd gone, could go through the steps of his death, her body remembered him, caressing, kissing, deep inside her. It would not let go. Not yet.

She still gripped the feather with both hands, enclosing the relic as she wanted to hold the memories in her heart. *I miss you. I will always miss you.*

Aidan Hawthorne was dead.

Chapter Eighteen

ஐ

Dawn came slowly that day, as though reluctant to appear. Most people sat on the ground. Some shape-shifted, so they could roost in trees in bird form or curl up cozily on the ground in animal form. Little heaps of clothing lay around — these people weren't shy at displaying their natural forms to each other. Corinne stopped wondering. She dozed, supported by Chris, who had lifted her into his lap and wrapped her in his arms with a brotherly kindness she was too weary to refuse.

They waited for the next phase. The birth of the new bird. The fire had died down and was now a heap of gray ash. Occasionally a small fall of debris made everyone look up, but it had been quiet for some time now.

Corinne had never felt so alone in her life before. She'd shut herself away, refused to share her mind with anyone except Ryan, and then not all the time. She couldn't bear the reminders, and every time she lowered her mental barrier, she expected something that wasn't there. Would never be there again.

She'd stay around for a while, then she'd go somewhere she could be completely alone. To think, and in time, to plan. Now she was numb. Unthinking.

The next stir was an event, not a mere shifting of debris. Corinne lifted her head and Chris sat a little straighter. Ryan, sitting next to them, lifted his head. Ash fell away from an object, until now obscured by charred debris.

An egg. A large, crimson egg, veined in gold. A disturbance ran through the crowd. People stood, creatures shape-shifted and reached for their clothes. The crowd had grown in the night when people arrived from farther away, who couldn't reach the spot in time for the death of the great bird. Corinne climbed off Chris' lap and stood, pulling the blanket someone had given her closer around her body. Dawn spread its fingers across the sky, bleakly announcing the new day. No golden or red streaks marred the gray light. It seemed appropriate.

The light muted the colors of the egg, the green grass and the browns of the trees. Everything seemed covered by a veil of drab material. It seemed right to her that her first day of the rest of her life without Aidan should begin with a dull, gloomy, overcast morning. She would watch this because they expected her to, and then retreat. If, as Ryan suspected, the new phoenix re-created in her body, if she bore Aidan's child, then she would have to live in his world and get used to the gaping wound caused by his absence. If the phoenix appeared elsewhere, then she could turn her back on it all; this life, Pure Wildfire, her father—everything. She hadn't accepted his Gift and now there was no reason to. The thought of more than fifty empty years ahead filled her with such despair she didn't know if she could bear it.

The egg moved, rocked gently. The new phoenix had woken. Cautiously, as though peeping out from behind a physical barrier, Corinne lowered her shields, opened herself to the egg and to Ryan, who would guide her through the experience. She felt his acceptance, but nothing more. Nothing from the egg.

The great egg rocked more violently and, within five minutes, cracks fissured its shell from a point where the creature's beak must be breaking the obstruction between the old life and the new.

We will watch it go through its life cycle until it is a mature bird. It won't take long. Are you tired?

No. She might be fatigued, but she didn't feel it. Grief gave her a sharp edge.

The egg broke open, revealing a large chick covered in gray fluff, its beak unwieldy and too large, its feet stumbling on the broken shards. No one stepped forward to help. People hardly moved, everyone intent on the drama unfolding before them. Almost everyone was in human form now, on their feet and waiting.

Ryan spoke quietly to her. "Sometimes the phoenix chooses its family, or even its mate at the moment of maturity. Usually it takes longer, but people always hope."

That explained the group of attractive women standing together on the other side of the crowd. Corinne choked down her emotion when she thought of the magnificent creature giving himself to another person. "Will he look like Aidan?"

"No. I swear it, Corinne." Ryan must have picked up on the great lump of grief settling on her stomach. "He will have red hair, but this can vary from golden red to dark mahogany. He will have a different build, be a different person. Unless he appears within you. If it's possible for him to do it, I think that will be what he will do. He died violently, Corinne. He will have to learn everything over, so it is best if he returns as a baby."

I couldn't bear it if Aidan came back and didn't know me.

That won't happen. I promise.

The gray chick staggered around in the ashes, finding his balance. His beady black eyes surveyed his audience, no sign of humanity about them. Corinne breathed out, relieved. Any trace of Aidan would have sent her into such anguish she doubted she would have been able to bear it. In other circumstances, she might have called the creature "cute", the stubby wings flapping in an effort to keep the bird upright only adding to the effect.

It changed visibly as they watched. Within ten minutes, sharp feathers disturbed the gray fluff, growing through the down, in the familiar colors of red and gold. Corinne watched the breast feathers develop, smaller than the longer, stronger, darker wing feathers. The body elongated and grew larger.

Within half an hour, the phoenix stood before them. This phoenix was darker than Aidan had been, the wings more crimson than flame orange, the gold only fully glowing on the breast and, when he spread his wings, underneath in the tender areas where the wings met the body. He was still wholly bird. When Corinne stretched out her senses, she found no humanity there at all, not yet.

The great bird spread his wings and launched upward. Corinne was close enough to feel the breeze created by the wings when he soared upward, straight up into the sky.

They watched until the clouds obscured their view, the bright spot of crimson covered by gray morning clouds. Dawn passed and the new day was upon them.

People watched the sky expectantly, waiting for the reappearance of the giant creature.

Corinne doubled up, gripped by a sudden pain in her stomach.

* * * * *

With Chris' and Ryan's arms around her, Corinne straightened up. The pain had been sudden and sharp but went away within a minute. At first, she thought it was a cramp, brought on by spending the night in a damp, cold field. Then she felt something stir inside her.

"Corinne? Are you all right?"

She couldn't remember a time Ryan's voice came to her unpracticed and cracked with emotion. She turned her head to meet his gaze. "I don't know, Ryan. Something has entered me, I can feel it."

"May I?" At her nod, Ryan pressed his hand gently over her stomach. He withdrew it sharply then brought it back. "You're pregnant," he said flatly.

The shock was immense, although Ryan had done his best to prepare her. The joy she felt overwhelmed her for a moment, the knowledge that Aidan hadn't died leaving nothing behind him. She would have part of him with her and she knew with a certainty what she would do. She would have this child and give it all the love she could. There was only one kind of love, after all, and she felt it in its purest form for the being growing in her womb.

Her reaction hadn't gone unnoticed. People stopped staring up into the sky and stared at her instead. Ryan nodded to the nearest one in confirmation.

Word spread quickly, low murmurs passing through the crowd, a ripple of awareness growing to a stream. Corinne realized she would never be alone again, not while her son lived. For if he was to be the phoenix, it must be a boy. A child with flaming red hair and a smile that reached every corner of her heart.

"I never expected to feel like this," she said. "I'm glad, so glad."

"So am I." Ryan took her hand and she felt the gentle spark of hope inside him.

A rush of wind distracted them and, to her amazement, she saw the new phoenix swooping down to land right in front of them. She'd thought she wouldn't see him again, not for many years, not until her child had grown. Did this mean she wasn't to bear the phoenix? In a way, that made things better, because he would just be a baby. Her baby and Aidan's.

The phoenix shape-shifted. She watched the wings melt, the feathers blur until they were gone from view, replaced by long, strong arms. One of the arms had a design near the shoulder. A burning rose.

I thought that was Aidan's tattoo?

It was.

She watched, shocked to see the familiar chest emerge from the feathers, the legs with the glowing feather marked strongly on one thigh, and finally, the head. The blazing red hair reached to his waist, the amber eyes gazed into her own.

Ryan had betrayed her. "I thought you said he wouldn't look like Aidan?" she cried, her heart breaking.

Before Ryan could speak, the new phoenix stepped forward and folded his arms around her. "They let me come back," he said, in the tones she knew and loved. "I have unfinished business."

Chapter Nineteen

ဢ

As bewildered as everyone else by this miracle, Aidan felt Corinne dissolve into tears, the tears she'd suppressed since he'd been shot. He felt memories inside him fade and disappear and knew that had to be, as the phoenix never remembered his rebirth, but there were other memories that had not been there before. He knew the price he had to pay. He remembered crashing and burning in an airplane. Not once, but twice. An accident thirty years ago, and when he was shot down thirty years before that. Then an unbroken two-hundred-year stretch of memory, of being the same person, contriving to be reborn in different places as he reached the human lifespan. Before that—he didn't care to search. Some of the memories were painful, of loves born and lost, of lives lived too recklessly, of early death and scandal and loneliness.

The phoenix was too often alone. Fear and awe from followers drove him into solitude, sometimes literally. He'd lived in the desert for many years, not shifting into human form, just to get away from the relentless worship and requests, most of which he couldn't fulfill, wasn't worthy of.

Someone threw a blanket around them, but he wouldn't let go of this woman, this miracle. His wife, his love. Never would he allow anyone to hurt her again, to damage that fighting spirit.

"Corinne." Gently, he tilted up her chin. "Corinne, it's me, Aidan. I won't leave you again."

"If you do, I'll kill you," she said illogically, her eyes streaming. When he reached out a hand, someone handed him a tissue, which he used to blot her tears.

"Don't cry anymore, Corinne. I'm back."

"Why?" The voice beside him reminded him there were more people who were glad to see him back.

He turned, one arm holding Corinne tightly, to face his brother and his cousin. Jake approached them, his eyes suspiciously reddened. That would explain why he hadn't been here with the others just now. Jake didn't like others to see his emotions.

Aidan exchanged a grin with his brother, redolent with meaning and love. "I can't remember. I don't know. As soon as I shape-shifted, I felt the memories going. Then I heard a voice, a female voice, but someone I didn't know, telling me to hold to my bond with Corinne if I wanted to stay, to think of her and nothing else. So I did. Instinct guided me. I plunged into the fire thinking of Corinne and held her in my mind until I shape-shifted just now."

Someone thrust a pair of jeans at him and, grinning broadly, he obeyed the unspoken request and released Corinne just long enough to pull them on. He was glad to thrust his feet into the sneakers dropped next to him. The ground was chilly, much too cold for bare feet.

Which reminded him. He needed to get Corinne into a bed soon. A warm, soft bed, preferably their own. He would get the next part over with quickly. "I'll talk to everyone and then we'll go. Have we got a car or something?"

"An ambulance." Ryan's grin welcomed him back with full force. "Do you remember it all?"

"I remember being shot." Aidan stroked Corinne's hair, unable to stop himself touching her. "I remember the journey in the ambulance. I remember them carrying me here, and then it all goes fuzzy and I went inside myself."

"God, I wish the fans could have seen that!" Jake exclaimed, clapping Aidan on the back with a force that made him stagger for a moment before regaining his footing. "We'd be the greatest band on the planet!"

"And the biggest spectacle. I can hear it now, 'Oh Aidan, shape-shift for me'! What chance has music over that kind of sight? Better call it a circus." That was from Chris, thinking of the band as always.

Aidan turned his head to grin at the drummer. "Back to work then?"

"Back to work," Chris confirmed.

Corinne hadn't spoken, but the way she opened her mind to him, fully and without reserve, humbled him more than anything else that had happened. He let himself enter her, feeling her welcome and her joy, knowing he reflected it back to her.

The gentle murmur of the crowd reminded him there were more people here. He lifted Corinne's chin and kissed her gently, a tender, closed-mouth kiss. "I need to do something before we go."

She nodded and would have stepped back, but he took her hand and walked forward with her.

By the ashes of his funeral pyre, he addressed them. "Thank you for coming to witness the rebirth. I am, as I was before, Aidan Hawthorne. I am the phoenix and I have been given leave to return. I can't tell you anything about the rebirth, you could probably tell me more, so I know no more about the secrets of the world to come than any of you. Don't ask. I can't answer. However, you know who I am, and if you need me, I will try to help you."

A murmur went around the crowd. In this, Aidan knew he was different. Before, he tried to do everything he could to avoid his destiny, what he was. He didn't know what he was, he hadn't grasped the full meaning of it. Now he knew what he could do and what he could not, and the experiences residing in his mind told him which were wise and which were not.

"As you know, I was assassinated. As you might not know, it was by someone who wants to use the power we have for his own selfish ends. A man who is using compulsion to bind people to him and make them do things they don't wish to do. I intend to bring this person to justice. The future is ours to use wisely and try to bring humans to an understanding of their fellow beings. Thank you, everyone."

He stepped back. The applause was spontaneous and meant more to him than any other. Acceptance by his own kind. At last. It had always been waiting for him, waiting until he was ready to accept it, as he was now.

"If you don't stop crying," he murmured to Corinne, "we're going to drown." Her watery chuckle rewarded him. "The sooner I get you into bed, the better. Come on, sweetheart. Let's go home."

* * * * *

It seemed to Corinne that they had been away from the flat for much longer than a night, but here they were again, back in the bedroom she was beginning to think of as theirs, and here was Aidan, gently removing the clothes she hadn't taken off since the concert last night. He seemed no different, but when she entered his mind, she saw a new gravity and new understanding.

She wanted to tell him her news before he discovered it for himself. "I'm pregnant."

He looked up from where he knelt at her feet, in the act of sliding her panties down her legs. "I know." Her heart sank that she couldn't be the one to tell him. "That was my choice—to return to you as I am or to start again inside your body. I was only given the choice because I love you so much I couldn't bear the thought of leaving you."

"I thought you said you couldn't remember anything?"

He remained kneeling at her feet, gazing up at her, love openly displayed in his marvelous amber eyes. His attention shifted lower and he lifted his hand and touched her stomach, splaying his large hand over it. "I can't remember it properly.

Not all of it, and there are a few points where there's no memory at all. This is a boy."

"I know." She felt the warmth seep right inside her, a soothing, gentle warmth from his hand. "Can I still convert?"

"Do you want to?"

There was no hesitation in her response. "More than anything else. I don't want to watch you die again, Aidan. I can't. You said that if I convert, we can go together."

He gazed up at her face, his hands loosely clasping her waist. "We can."

"Aidan, I don't want to wait. Not now. Can we do it now? Will it hurt the baby?"

He shook his head. "The baby can adapt to the change."

Fear gripped her. "What will I have? A baby or —"

He grinned. "An egg? No, love, the child is born in the form in which we conceived it. Once born, he won't be able to shape-shift until he reaches puberty. I don't think I deserve to be so happy." He leaned closer and pressed a gentle kiss to her stomach. "I promised not to run again. That was the price."

"What do you mean?"

He got to his feet and put his arms around her. "For the last three rebirths, I've been running away from what I am, refusing to accept responsibility. I'm special, not alone."

"What are you?"

"You know." He bent his head and kissed her. "I'm Aidan, the phoenix. No more nasty surprises, I promise. But that means I'm an Elemental. And I'm a leader, born into it. I never wanted it, but it's mine. For the first time in my life, I know why I'm here and what I should do."

"I don't understand."

"Nor do I, not properly, but I'll learn." He smiled and leaned his cheek on her hair. "I can't wait any longer, Corinne. I want to be inside you. Now."

When she lifted her head, he took her mouth, raw desire flaring instantly between them. He pulled her closer, pressing her body against him, eager to feel all of her against all of him. He released her mouth only to gasp, "Are you ready? Dear God, you have to be ready, Corinne!"

"As ready as you are." His cock burgeoned between them, strong and hard.

Passion blazed high, plunging them into their own conflagration. She felt his hands under her thighs and when he pulled, she jumped into his arms. She wrapped her legs around his waist and felt his cock head nudge her pussy. His mouth covered hers, his tongue stabbing deep as he drove deep inside. A step brought them in contact with the bedroom wall, giving him the resistance he needed to withdraw and drive deep, deeper into her body with each luscious stroke. The scent of sex rose around them.

When she began to spiral up into her climax, he followed, driving inside her until all she could do was clutch him and cry out, her head thrown back against the wall behind her. He bent to lick her nipple and circle it with his tongue before opening his mouth wide and taking her in, sucking hungrily.

No one except Aidan could bring her this joy. He shared his passion with her, entering her mind as he had her body, to encourage her, to take her joy and give his in return. *You look unbelievable*, he crooned in her mind. *Nobody has ever looked as sexy as you do.*

To you, she responded wryly.

Nobody would be able to resist, seeing you like this. He rose up, pressing into her hard, his lips parting with delight when he saw and felt her helpless response. *Come on, love. Come for me, one more time. Come on, Corinne, you can do it.*

He held her tight and slammed into her, relentlessly forcing her against the wall. Corinne gasped, feeling him nudge her womb and slide past, every stroke encountering a spot inside her that drove her wild. He didn't lessen his attack until she'd cried out for him twice, her body convulsing about his, her hands grabbing at him, to hold on to something, anything. He lifted her and her hands touched his shoulders. She held on. Together they rocked, pushing her up again until he threw his head back and roared his release.

A still moment followed, when they just existed, in and with each other. It was enough. It was more than enough.

His chest heaved as he drew a deep breath, and unable to resist, Corinne reached forward and tweaked his nipple. "Hey!" Laughing, he eased her legs from around his waist and held her steady while she regained her feet. His face was without shadow. None of his recent experience showed in the eyes, glowing with exertion and love, or his delicate, mobile mouth, the corners turned up in a beatific smile. "Shower, my lady?" He gave her an exaggerated bow.

She slanted a suspicious look at him. "How far back can you remember?"

He laughed again and wrapped one arm about her waist, guiding her to the bathroom. "Beyond a hundred years, the emotions seem to be gone. They're like stories."

"So you'll be able to send me to sleep at bedtime with a story?"

"I can think of a better way," he murmured, bending to kiss her shoulder. "Get into that shower, wench, and let's clean up."

She didn't want to be apart from him, not for a moment. At the back of her mind was the thought that he might go away. Irrational, but it niggled at her, made her want to touch him, be with him all the time.

They washed each other, lingeringly, enjoying the sensation of scented soap sliding over each other's skin. Neither used a cloth or sponge, preferring to use their hands, occasionally they exchanged a kiss. The shower was a sensuous delight, their touches healing, their glances delighting in the sight of their bodies, coming together in gentle caresses. She washed his hair for him, that long, thick mane of pure fire. That hadn't changed. He rinsed hers, much easier to do now that she'd had it cut shorter. *I love your new haircut. It doesn't hide any of your beautiful body.*

The thought skimmed her mind before he leaned over her to switch off the water, stealing another kiss as he did so. By the time she stepped out, to be enveloped in the large, warm bath towel, he was bone dry and so was his hair. "How did you do that?"

He grinned. "Good, isn't it? I heated up for a moment."

"Can you do it for me?"

He wrapped the towel around her, patting her dry. "Not yet. Soon, if you really want to convert."

She turned around to face him. "Yes, yes I do. When you left, I realized how deeply I need you. Want you. I thought I could live without you. I can, but I don't want to."

He gave her such a tender kiss that she thought she would melt with it. She couldn't embrace him until she'd shaken free of the towel, but when she reached for him, he pulled away, desire deep in his eyes. "Let's do this thing first, shall we?"

Naked, she followed him into the bedroom, where he stood clear of the bed, lifted his chin, spread his arms and shape-shifted.

Now that she was used to it, Corinne appreciated the beauty of the sight. She watched the feathers form and grow through the skin, the body bulk up and the claws with the wickedly sharp talons lance through his fingers.

When he had shape-shifted, she stopped to examine this new bird. His plumage was darker on his back and his wings, while the delicate, soft feathers under the wings and on his breast were a true, bright gold. He was beautiful.

Thank you. Inside, he sounded exactly the same. *Come, my love. Make your choice.*

For the second time in her life, Corinne had the privilege of taking a feather from the breast of the legendary phoenix.

She stepped closer and touched his breast, running her hand down the soft, thick plumage.

That feels good.

She did it again and he rewarded her by chirruping low in his throat. *You're not afraid anymore?*

No. There are worse things to be afraid of. I lived with a monster for most of my life without realizing it.

My love. Sorrow suffused his words.

She pulled out a feather with a quick jerk of her hand. It lay on her hand, golden, gleaming with richness. It would probably be worth much more than its weight in gold if she could prove its provenance. She watched the feather while he shape-shifted, and by the time he touched her on the shoulder, she'd blinked her tears away.

"What about the other one? The feather you gave me before?"

"It won't work. Its owner is dead. Keep it as a souvenir."

She looked up at him and held out the feather. "What do I do now?"

He placed his hand under hers, supporting it, and guided her hand down to her thigh. "Is this where you want the mark?"

She nodded. "The same place as yours."

He glanced down and touched her thigh, tracing the skin with the edge of his finger, still holding her hand. With a sudden gesture, he pressed her hand with the feather in it to the place he'd just touched.

Instantly, it burned like a brand. Corinne blinked and braced herself against the pain. He'd told her it would hurt. She just hadn't imagined how much. It must be like a red hot poker held against a wound instead of being pulled away.

"Did it hurt this much to die?"

"Worse."

The terse word was all she needed. She would bear this alone. Her pain, not his. She blocked his attempts to help her bear the pain. He'd had enough of his own recently.

"Let me in, Corinne. Let me help you."

Beyond words now, she shook her head and lowered her eyes. He wouldn't see her pain, he wouldn't feel it. She felt him probing at her mind, looking for a way in, but he'd taught her too well. She erected her strongest shield and refused to let him in.

Corinne needed all her willpower to keep her legs locked so she could stand upright. She wanted to sink to the floor, curl up in a ball of misery. The burning heat penetrated to her bones, surged through her body. She felt as though she'd been petrified. The pain was so bad that it penetrated everything. There was no escape, nowhere for her to hide. Still, she refused to let him in. He'd suffered his own trial—now it was her turn. Her pain, her trial of strength.

"Corinne, please!"

She ignored him, going inside herself, drawing out every ounce of strength she had.

* * * * *

Ryan!

Aidan, I'm here. What's wrong, bro?

It's Corinne. She's inside herself, she won't let me in.

What's going on?

She's converting. We're pressing the feather to her leg, but she hasn't moved for fifteen minutes. She's so hot, I'm afraid she's burning up from the inside!

Hey, hold on while I ask somebody.

Aidan was terrified. His free arm held Corinne up, firm despite the blazing heat she threw off. He waited for Ryan to get back to him. Suddenly his voice came, clear and true.

She'll be okay. I just spoke to one of our doctors. This is what happens. Protect the baby. Go into her and shield the baby. Good luck!

Aidan aimed all his thoughts on her womb, on the baby inside. He was surprised to slide in without resistance. He found every other part of her body closed to him, but not this. He searched and found the speck inside her, the speck that formed their child, and he enclosed it in protection, restoring the temperature to normal, ensuring the blood vessels that fed it were open and working.

He sent this being, less than a week old, all the love in his heart. He would do this right. His child would never feel alone, never feel rejected, isolated, unwanted. His son. He knew it was a boy—the phoenix was always male, and if he'd made his choice otherwise, he would now be inside her body for the next nine months. For a moment he allowed himself the luxury of experiencing Corinne surrounding him, of her warming and nurturing him, and a shadow of memory came back to him. He could have been part of her, at least for a while. But he couldn't have loved and cared for her as he wanted to. That would have been lost to him. And he couldn't cause her so much pain. When she'd told him she loved him, he knew he couldn't leave her alone.

Aidan's panic passed. This was the only way for a firebird. There was no escaping it and there was little he could do to ease her changing. Her body was reshaping, the bones becoming lighter, the blood changing and the immune systems building. At the moment, Corinne was a shell, her mind in stasis, protected by nature from the violent changes happening in her body. He knew that if he forced his way in, he would suffer too, and could do nothing to alleviate her pain. All he could do was wait.

Aidan forced himself to remember this, to remind himself that he was helping to protect her, not to harm her. His heart stopped beating so fast and he assessed the situation.

This phase of the conversion could take up to half an hour.

After twenty minutes, he felt a change under his hand where it covered hers and cautiously moved. The feather had gone and the tattoo glowed vividly on her thigh. Pure gold, it heated his hand when he touched it. He anxiously inspected Corinne's palm, but it was clear of any mark. She was still lost to him, eyes closed now, and when he moved his arm away, she sagged a little, so he swept her up and carried her to the bed, laying her down gently on the cool sheets.

It meant he could leave her momentarily to fetch water. She would need it when she woke.

He threw on a robe and went downstairs, only then remembering how hungry he felt. Tension kept him from feeling it before, he supposed. No time to cook anything. He grabbed a plate and piled it with bread and a hunk of cheese from the fridge, adding a knife. He made two jugs of iced water and found two glasses to go with them. Although he eyed the kettle wistfully, he knew he'd no time to make tea. He had to get back to her. He shoved all the items on a butler's tray and made his way back upstairs.

Only to come precariously close to dropping it when he saw her eyes were open.

"Corinne, oh Corinne!" Aidan put the tray on the floor by the bed and leaned over her, careful to take his weight on his hands. "I was so afraid!"

"Were you? What happened? Am I a bird now?"

She looked the same except for the reddish glints deep in her dark eyes. They sparkled at him. He smiled, brushing a kiss to her forehead. "If you want to be. We'll deal with that later. I protected the baby. He's all right."

"Oh yes. I'm not quite back yet, Aidan. I'm tired, but I feel fine. Can I get up now?"

When he probed her mind gently, he found the remnants of pain and a deep weariness. The terrible heat had gone. He knew she was being brave for him and his heart ached for her. "No. I'll come and join you. I brought bread and cheese, but if you like, I can make us something better to eat."

The lids drooped over her eyes. "No, not yet. Come and hold me, Aidan. I need you more than I need food." Her eyelids rose a fraction. "I am thirsty though. Very thirsty."

He laughed, but the laugh cracked at the end. "Sweetheart, if I'd known you were going to go through that— I mean, I read about it, I knew, but to see it—" He turned away and poured a glass of iced water.

Corinne sat up and took the glass, letting the covers fall down around her waist. His body responded to the sight of her perfect, full, uptilted breasts with the deliciously milk chocolate-colored areolas. She managed a chuckle but said nothing, tipping the glass up to her mouth and not lowering it again until she'd drunk all of it. He refilled it for her, and she emptied it again but refused a third glass. "In a little while. Thank you." She didn't just mean the water. Aidan lifted the covers and slid into bed next to her. When she snuggled close, he sent up a brief, silent prayer of thanks. They had both survived. For now, it was enough.

"Corinne, I didn't know how bad it was going to be. I'm sorry."

"I'm not. There's nothing between us now, is there?"

"There never was," he said, pressing a kiss to her brow, and when she lifted her head, another to her mouth. He kept it sweet and tender, savoring her response. "If you hadn't wanted this, I would have lived my life with you and gone to the flames after you died, without any regrets."

He stroked her hair and twisted a curl around his finger. It was still tipped with fire. He wondered if that would stay permanent now. There was a definite red tinge to the undyed hair, where it had been ash brown before. "You won't be able to shape-shift after the third month. The baby will need a stable environment. Until then, you'll have to shape-shift every month, but the urge is suspended for the rest of the pregnancy."

"Like my periods?"

"Like that."

She stroked his chest and opened her palm flat on his stomach. "How long will I live, Aidan?"

He smiled against her hair, relishing the thought. "About five hundred years."

She caught her breath in a sharp gasp. "What does a five-hundred-year-old woman look like?"

"Very beautiful. You'll be immune to disease, but not to violence and accidents, like a plane crash."

"Or a shooting."

"Yes." They had to talk about it sometime. He'd hoped the conversation wouldn't lead that way, not just yet, but it had.

After a long pause, she said, "What are we going to do about my father? He set the sniper on us, didn't he?"

He heard the shake in her voice but didn't pull her closer, didn't try to comfort her. Gently in her mind, he sent a soothing mood, but that was almost involuntary. He couldn't have stopped that. "Yes, love, he probably did. Jake made enquiries. The sniper is dead. He was sent such a hard psychic attack he dropped dead as soon as he'd fired."

"Will the police find out?"

He knew she hoped they would sort it out that way. "No. There was nothing to connect the man with your father. We know from our own sources, but our proof would mean exposing ourselves to public scrutiny. You know we can't do that."

"Yes." There was no hesitation in her voice or in her mind. "He has to be stopped. What will you do?"

Nothing but the truth would suffice. "I can't kill your father. He did at least one thing right in his life." He kissed her forehead but drew back afterward. "I'll go to see him and remove all the knowledge from his mind. I have everyone's backing for that and their help, but I won't need it."

"Isn't that compulsion?"

"Yes, but I have agreement and permission. As the phoenix, I don't need it, but I prefer to work within the law."

"Won't he be ready for you?"

Aidan's mouth firmed into a thin line. "It won't help him. Not now."

"I want to go with you." Her voice softened. Despite her resolve to talk, he felt her weariness. She had to sleep soon.

"No, love. Best I go on my own."

"No." She roused and lifted her head, lifting her hands to enclose his face. "Aidan, no. I want to be there."

"It won't be very nice, Corinne."

"No. I want to go. It would be cowardly to do anything else." She forced her eyes open. Her exhaustion battered at his mind, forced him into submission.

He knew she was right. She had to face her father. Anything else would be cowardice and his Corinne was anything but a coward. "All right, we'll both go. As long as you sleep now."

She dropped her hands and curled one around his waist, settling her head on his chest. At last, she relaxed, sliding into sleep.

Aidan watched over her.

Chapter Twenty

ဢ

Two small birds winged their way across the sky. The kestrel saw them but recognized one of the birds. He'd rather starve than go for them again. No more little yellow birds for him. They were off his diet for good.

Landing in the small glade, Aidan shape-shifted quickly and watched Corinne do the same, his heart filled with love and pride. She'd taken to her new life with alacrity, loving the small flights he'd taken her on before this day. Below them, Mike and the SUV traveled on the road. As soon as she'd completed her transformation, he stepped forward and took her in his arms.

As he'd suspected, she drooped, not immediately able to find her balance. That was one of the hardest things to manage at first. They were due to leave for their honeymoon the next day, to a hot country where they could practice and rest. He intended to put all this behind them, to help her to recover from the ordeal to come and the one she'd just suffered. Not to mention his own sufferings. Rebirth took it out of a shape-shifter.

When he tried to lift her into his arms, she laughed and pushed him gently away. "No, Aidan, I can do this. I love flying, especially with you. It's the best thing I've ever tried!"

"Better than playing the guitar?"

"It makes me feel the same way. Free and joyful."

He pulled her close for a quick kiss before leading her out of the glade to where Mike waited in the SUV on the little back road behind the wood. To all intents and purposes, Mike was deep into his newspaper. Aidan blessed his tact. While his kind looked on nudity as a natural state, Corinne still had the shyness inherent in her origins. He rather liked it. It meant nobody saw her nude but himself and he found he had possessive instincts where she was concerned.

Inside the car were clothes. Mike pulled smoothly away in the direction of the main gates of the manor. When they were dressed, Aidan slid aside the screen between the driver's section and theirs. "Thanks, Mike. Don't forget what I told you—there might be trouble, so don't let your guard down. Be ready for a quick getaway, will you?"

Mike grunted in reply. A human, one of the few who knew that shape-shifters existed, he'd proved invaluable to Aidan and the rest of Pure Wildfire. Mike was nothing if not taciturn.

"I'm going to tell Westfall we've signed with somebody else. He might not want us to stick around after that."

This time Mike chuckled. "He won't like that. Yeah, I'll be ready." Smiling, Aidan went back to join Corinne. If Corinne hadn't reminded him, he wouldn't have remembered the sling and bandage. They told the media that the sniper had shot him in the shoulder, but he wasn't badly hurt. Randy was handling it, but they had a news conference scheduled for later in the day. Then they would fly out, and to hell with everything else for at least a month.

Corinne stared out of the window, but she couldn't hide her apprehension from him. Aidan sent her soothing waves, knowing she would feel like this. "I wish you'd stayed at home."

"Will you hurt him?"

"Not unless I have to."

That was all they had time to say before the car pulled up in front of the door to the manor. Aidan shoved his arm into the sling and stepped out.

Miss Grantham, Westfall's secretary, met them in the hall, her crisp suit and neat hairstyle just the same as when he'd seen her last. "Mr. and Mrs. Hawthorne, Mr. Westfall has asked me to convey you to his office immediately."

"I need to go to my flat first, Miss Grantham. I want to collect a few things. I think I told him."

"Your belongings have been packed. There is no need for that. They will be sent to you." She glanced at Aidan's sling but said nothing.

Aidan took Corinne's arm when he felt her surge of anger. "Tell John Westfall we'll be with him soon. Corinne wants to check her apartment." *Let him wait. It'll wind him up nicely.*

Wicked man!

He followed her up the stairs. Corinne's rooms were at the end of the long corridor at the top of the stairs. Another door opened as they passed it. "Corinne!"

She turned and smiled. "Hello, Ashley, are you well?"

Ashley scowled, and her gaze flickered over them. Like Miss Grantham, she didn't ask Aidan about his arm. Too taken up with her own troubles to think about anyone else. "That bastard Ryan won't answer my calls."

"Ryan has never been one for long affairs," Aidan drawled. He lowered his eyelids a little and lifted his chin, looking down at Corinne's sister with a stare he knew was arrogant. "I've never known him to have the same girl for more than a week. And usually more than one at a time."

"Can you believe he wanted me to do that?" Ashley said. "Share him?"

"He often does." Aidan couldn't see Corinne's face, but he felt her triumph. Good. She deserved a little payback. He hadn't spoken to Ryan about Ashley recently, but he knew if a girl offered herself, Ryan usually accepted. "He likes girls in quantity. Says they're all so good, why should he restrict himself?" Ashley didn't deserve to know the real Ryan and she never would.

"Bastard!" said Ashley viciously and slammed the door in their faces. Aidan wasn't sure who she'd aimed the last epithet at, but he didn't much care. Corinne turned away, and he followed her into her rooms.

Corinne had four rooms—a lounge, bedroom, bathroom and small kitchenette. There was nothing remarkable about any of them. Decorated tastefully, but with nothing personal about them. A packing case and a large trunk sat in the middle of the floor.

"Oh!" Paige came through the door leading to the bedroom, a Perspex guitar in her hands. "Hi. Your arm better, Aidan?"

Hallelujah. "A bit, thanks."

"I didn't think you'd come up here today, Corinne," Paige said.

"Why not? Why are you packing for me, Paige?"

"I decided to move in here," Paige said. "Your living room faces south and mine is always cold. Do you mind?"

"Not at all." Corinne tilted her head to one side. "As long as you don't mind being watched." She crossed the room to the TV and picked up the remote control. With her enhanced senses, she could find the sensors easily. She opened the back and used her fingernail to ease out the added ingredient. "See that, Paige? That's a listening device. Dad's been bugging this place for years."

"What?" Paige's initial outrage passed when she saw what Corinne held. "Is that what that thing is? How could he? Are you sure?"

"Oh yes, I'm sure."

Aidan slouched to the kitchen and found the kettle. He needed coffee and it gave Corinne a chance to tell Paige about her father's nasty little spying activities. Whatever he thought of the sisters, no one should be watched the way Westfall watched his prize investments.

287

When he heard Paige's outraged shriek, he knew she was as furious as her sister had been. He waited a few minutes before making the coffee and loading it onto a tray. He strolled through to find both sisters staring at him.

"She says you spotted it," Paige said.

Aidan put the tray on a side table and stood up, facing her. He allowed the rock star persona to fall away and met her gaze squarely. "I did. Probably because she was so used to seeing her apartment, she didn't notice the odd things about it."

"Will you check my sister's apartment and mine? Please?"

He nodded. "Sure."

He crossed the room and kissed Corinne on the cheek. "Are you okay here?"

"Yes. I can collect what I want while you're gone."

Aidan followed Paige out of the room and Corinne watched them, her gaze thoughtful. Perhaps Paige and Ashley might be interested in Randy Norwood's services. Abruptly, she turned and went into the bedroom. The wall safe in there contained her mother's jewelry, her only contact with the woman who had left her life all too early.

When she came back into the lounge, the small box in her hands, she nearly dropped it. "Oh! You startled me!"

Tom Albright grinned. "I used to come in and out of here all the time. How are you, Corinne?"

Corinne put the box down on the table by the door. She couldn't think why she felt so uncomfortable. "I'm fine. How are you?"

"I miss you. Ashley isn't half the woman you were." He moved closer. "Your father thinks your marriage is a sham, that you've only done it to break the contract with him. Is that true?"

"No."

She took an involuntary step back when Tom came too close, deliberately shortening the difference between them. She smelled his cologne, heavy and sweet. She hit the small table and remembered the coffee. The cups were still on the tray, abandoned when Aidan went with Paige to examine her apartment for bugs. Turning, she picked up a cup. "Coffee?"

"No thank you." Smiling, he took another step. Corinne lifted her chin and gripped the cup. "I know what he is, Corinne."

Her heart missed a beat. "Aidan? He's a rock star. He doesn't do drugs anymore, he's completely straight these days."

"I don't mean that. You know it too, don't you? He's a shape-shifter, isn't he?"

One look told her a blank denial wouldn't get her anywhere. "So what? What difference does that make?"

His dark eyebrows went up in exasperation. "You know, you must do! These people are a threat to normal people! Don't you know that?" He loomed over her, his black brows now set in a fierce frown. "They want to take over, Corinne. They think they're superior and all their efforts are to pervert us to their twisted ways!"

With horror, Corinne recognized the face of bigotry. Fear and anger warred in Tom, spiced by jealousy. She didn't need anything more than empathy to spot them. The emotions seethed from him, filling the air around them, making her shiver. "No, Tom, you're wrong. They just want to be left in peace."

"That's what he said, is it?" Tom's full mouth curved into a sneer. "You must be cracked, Corinne, to believe that! They have powers you can only dream of, powers that should rightly be ours too." He put a hand on her arm and she flinched back, but then faced him boldly. "Corinne, they can live for centuries! They don't get ill. We need some specimens, so our scientists can find out what makes them tick."

Corinne swallowed. She no longer wanted Tom to stop. She needed to find out what he knew. Opening her mind, she contacted Aidan.

What is it, baby? Do you need me?

Don't come in, Aidan. Just listen.

"What do you mean, Tom, they don't get ill? How do you know that?"

He glanced around and crossed the room to close the outer door. Corinne heard the lock snick closed, but wasn't afraid anymore. Tom's approach had startled her, but she was back in control. She was glad he'd moved away. She took a deep swallow of coffee and turned to put the cup down.

Tom lowered his voice. "We've been watching them for some time. Your husband is one, and perhaps the other members of the band too. We're pretty sure Ryan Hawthorne is one. They're birds really, did you know that?"

Corinne gazed at him. Tom had wooed her with charm and humor, none of which was present today. "Who is 'we'?"

Tom grinned, and a vestige of the old charm flashed in his eyes, just for a moment, overlaid by triumph. "We call ourselves the PHR. We're dedicated to destroying the abominations that call themselves Talents."

Jesus! The PHR people are brutal bigots. They kill people like us because they think we have no right in their world.

The charity album was for the PHR. I thought they wanted to eliminate poverty.

No, just Talents. With a sinking heart, she realized the album she and Aidan made the track for had been for the enemies of what she now was. How ironic! They would make money for the organization intent on destroying them.

Corinne gasped. She should have known! Before today, she'd accepted the ambitions of the charity were to eliminate hunger and suffering in the world, as their manifesto stated.

We'll withdraw the track.

She felt the anger in Aidan, anger she felt for herself.

Tom noticed nothing. "Once we have the key to the powers, we can incorporate them into human DNA. We won't need the mutants after that."

"So you don't want them, but you're willing to steal from them?"

"It's not stealing. Somewhere along the way, a mistake happened. They got the gifts we should have had. It's obvious, Corinne. If they have these gifts, then why haven't they done more with them? Why haven't they taken over?"

"Why should they? They believe in free will, Tom. Freedom of thought, freedom of action."

"No they don't. They want to make us their slaves." Tom strode about the room, a dervish of furious action. "They want to use us. We can't have that, don't you see? We need to beat them before they beat us. And we need those gifts. Longevity and immunity to disease. If they are so benevolent, why haven't they shared their gifts with us? Why don't they work with us instead of against us?"

Corinne was astonished at the perverted ideas pouring out of Tom's mouth. At the time of Aidan's rebirth, she'd not been a shape-shifter but a mortal, one of a handful of humans there. She hadn't felt threatened, had been made welcome by these people, people, she now understood, who had good reason to mistrust her. "What if they can't share their gifts? If that is just how they are?"

"Bollocks to that." Tom must have been agitated. It was rare to hear any kind of cursing from him. "There must be a way. We have the same origins. We've captured a few specimens and their anatomy is similar to ours. There are different parts of the brain and some minor differences we can't explain. Our scientists haven't analyzed all the substances we took and we're hoping there's an enzyme or something like that. It's evolutionary, so there must be a way."

Has he ever thought that humans have something extra? We lack the barriers most humans have built against psychic communication. Perhaps they built another barrier against shape-shifting. Aidan's tone turned cold, and Corinne knew it wasn't on her account. *Have they ever used vivisection on a human to discover the difference? I think not.*

They cut them up alive? Whatever temptation Corinne had to share something with her old fiancé disappeared like smoke up a chimney. These people were evil, greed and jealousy fuelling their approach. That and the fear of the unknown that sparked most bigotry. "Tom, I can't help you."

"Yes you can!" Tom's eyes narrowed in speculation. "What's he done to you? Are you under his control?"

The lock clicked open and Aidan walked in. His arm was still bandaged, but he'd discarded the sling. He didn't walk across to Corinne but stood against the open door, watching Tom. Tom took a step forward, smiling expansively, none of the hatred Corinne knew he felt evident on his face. He stuck out his hand. "Congratulations, old chap. The best man won."

Aidan glanced at Corinne but made no other move, keeping his hands by his side. With a sudden, explosive gesture, he kicked the door closed and took a step into the room toward Tom. "I will not compel you to do anything. It is against everything we believe in. This hampers what I would like to do. To be frank, I'd like to kill you, but I won't."

Tom looked from Corinne to Aidan and back again. "You forgot the part about shape-shifters being telepathic," she told him.

Shock registered large. "You're siding with him?"

"There are no sides, unless you make them, Tom." Keeping his attention, she lifted her arm, allowing her hand and lower arm to begin the change. Feathers sprouted on her hand and wrist, and the fingers began to elongate, ready for their transformation into wings. Corinne stopped the shape-shift and returned to human form. When she lifted her gaze to

Tom, she saw the beads of sweat on his brow. It wasn't a particularly hot day.

"I'm sorry, Tom. You can't believe this nonsense. Shapeshifters are different, that's all. We can't teach you to fly, because you haven't any wings. We can't teach you to live longer, because we just do. Humans have their advantages. Why not concentrate on them instead of wishing for something you can't have?"

"Fuck!" Tom took a step toward the door, but Aidan got there first. Reaching out, he put the tips of his fingers on Tom's temples, exerting no pressure. "Look at me, Tom."

"Aidan, what are you doing? You said compulsion was banned!"

Aidan didn't take his gaze away from Tom. "It is. I won't compel him to do anything he doesn't want to do. I don't like doing this, Corinne, but Tom Albright is a danger to all of us. I'm going to stop him going against us."

"How?"

"By removing everything about this organization from his mind. He will think that the PHR is a charitable organization, one he donates to from time to time but one that doesn't mean anything in particular to him. Listen to me, Tom." He paused, and although neither man moved, Corinne felt the arc of electric power that surged between them. "Are you listening?"

"Yes." Tom's voice dulled. Despite what she'd just learned, Corinne hated to see this. She would hate Aidan too, but she felt the sorrow in his mind, the regret he felt at having to go even this far down the path to compulsion.

"Tom, the PHR is not important. The PHR is just another charity. You will lose interest in its activities. After all, what it does is insane, right?"

"Right."

"Nothing like the creatures it describes ever existed. They don't exist now. I'm just the man who has married your ex-girlfriend. You don't like my music, so you don't care about me. There is no connection between me and the PHR. I don't even donate to them. Understand?"

"Yes."

"After a few months, you'll take them off the list of charities to donate to. You think they're mad and you'll tell them so."

"Yes."

"Close your eyes." Corinne watched Tom's eyes flicker shut. Aidan didn't close his but lifted his fingers away and touched a point at the center of Tom's forehead. Tom's head went back as though he'd been pushed, but Aidan still exerted no pressure. When Aidan removed his finger, Tom remained frozen in the same position. Aidan turned to Corinne and met her accusatory stare with a grave one of his own. "That's as close as I dare go. I could make him go against the PHR, but that would be compulsion. There is nothing in him naturally that would make him do that, so I won't. But I can't leave him to work against us. You understand that, don't you?"

Mutely, she nodded.

"Please, Corinne. I promise I will never, ever do that to you, unless you ask me. I have never done it to you, not ever. I swear it."

He didn't make a move toward her, though she felt his need to touch her. He was right. Seeing how easily Aidan made Tom slip into his trance had worried her. "I've always fancied you, so it wouldn't have been compulsion to make me want you more. Did you do that?"

Aidan shook his head slowly. "The only thing I did was show you my own need. I can't say I've always wanted you. It was when I saw you in person and felt your presence that I fell in love. And I did, Corinne. Instantly and irrevocably. I love you and I'll do anything for you, even undo what I just did to Tom if you want. Do you want me to?"

Corinne stared at him, going back in her mind on the things he'd done. He'd removed all the clumsy mental blocks her father put in place. He'd also loved her more than she thought anyone would ever love her. And now this. For her, he would put his own people in danger, would walk away from it if she asked him to.

She'd be mad to ask that of him. He was right. Tom was dangerous to all shape-shifters and rich enough to provide the funds their enemies needed. "No. I trust you, Aidan. Am I a complete fool, have I gone from one man to the next, just a puppet?"

"No!" He took the few steps that separated them and put his hands on her shoulders. "No, all I did was give back to you the things you lost. Your free will and your gift for music. They were yours, they always were yours. I swear I've put nothing into your mind that wasn't there before, planted nothing. If you can't believe me, perhaps we'd better spend some time apart."

Her sense of loss she felt now was hers alone. She'd felt it before, after her mother died. "No. I want to stay with you. Aidan, I don't care about anything else. I love you. What's the point of living by myself if there's no happiness or joy in it? You gave me that back. Even if I didn't love you, I'd be your friend forever because of that."

He leaned forward and kissed her, softly and tenderly, the embrace pure love. When he drew back, he murmured softly to her, "I love you too, Corinne. I'll never do anything to hurt you, I swear."

She swallowed her tears—this wasn't the time for them. She turned away to pick up the jewelry box. "Then we'd better get on with it. We should see my father, then go. I want to get you home, Aidan, and naked."

When she turned back, she saw his smile had changed and now held a wicked edge. "You read my mind, baby. Let's go."

He woke Tom with a snap of his fingers, shook his hand and left.

Chapter Twenty-One

ജ

John Westfall waited in state in his office. It was the same as always—the large desk with its computer screen and neatly stacked, slim files, the books on the shelves looking as though no one ever read them, the glass cases with the valuable grimoires and magic texts, the walls adorned with presentation gold discs.

Her father looked the same as well. Immaculately dressed in black, short, dark hair combed back from a square forehead. His slight smile was in place, which could change to questioning or a serious mien. Corinne wondered if she'd ever known this man at all. She chose not to probe his mind. She left that to Aidan. After today, she wanted never to be in his presence again.

John rose to greet them, his smile turning affable, but his dark eyes dead, except for a gleam deep down. He walked around the desk to them. "Nice of you to finally appear."

"I went to get Mother's jewelry and put it in the car," Corinne said, then wished she hadn't. She'd always rushed to explain her actions and it put her at an immediate disadvantage.

John shrugged. "I thought you'd already taken those. You should have sent for them."

"Perhaps I should have."

John turned his attention to Aidan, who had not, for once, adopted the rock star pose of half-closed eyes and slouch. He stood tall, amber eyes wide open, fixed on John's face. "Have you brought her back?"

"That's up to Corinne." Aidan didn't touch her, didn't look at her.

"I'm staying with Aidan. I won't come back, I'm not joining your girl group and I'm not playing classical music in public."

Aidan touched her hand. "Don't say that. I have plans for that Bach transcription."

She smiled, but it faded when she looked at her father. "How could you? How could you spy on me like that?"

John shrugged. "It wasn't personal. Just business." His gaze sharpened. "Have you got what I asked you for?"

"The feather?" John's gaze went from Corinne to Aidan and back again. Corinne smiled. "Yes. Do you remember what you promised me? I want out, Father. I want you to sign me off, free and clear, no comebacks, no court cases. We have a new manager for Pure Wildfire and I want to go to him."

"Give me the feather and you can have all that."

Aidan interrupted, his voice clear and precise. "We have an out, as no doubt you know, but that would take time and you could always challenge it in court." John shrugged. Aidan continued to speak. "Also, we want the track for the charity album withdrawn. You can use it, but not for that charity."

John lifted an eyebrow. "You discovered what that charity did then?" He smiled. "I'd planned to taunt you with it, but if you give me what I want, you can have that too. Besides, I'd be nuts to throw that away on a charity, any charity. Now that you two are an item, I can make good money from that track."

"Don't you want to give money to the PHR?"

John made a sound of exasperation. "That narrow-minded bunch of bigots? They can't see what's in front of their noses. No, convert everyone, that's what I say. Or enough of the people who matter."

"What would you do if we decided to do that?" Aidan sounded merely curious, his words totally without heat, but Corinne felt the anger simmering under the cool surface.

"We could control the world. Or, at least, that part of it we cared about." John stared at Aidan, his gaze razor sharp.

"Not unless you made people do what they didn't want to do. You know what that's called?"

"No. I don't care much."

"You should. It's called compulsion. We don't allow it."

"Tcha!" John strode up to Aidan, his whole body burning with energy, the energy that drove so many worthless acts up the pop charts, the energy that worked for genuine artists with equal passion. "Unproductive, gutless thinking! Why not use what you have?"

"What do I have?" Aidan still didn't respond.

"You have communication skills far above the ones I have! I had to develop mine, work for them, but you're born with yours! You can transform into wonderful, powerful creatures. Invulnerable." John swallowed and Corinne knew he was salivating.

Aidan smiled easily and moved to the desk. On it lay her release, mailed to him the day before. They had a copy in the car, just in case this one hadn't arrived. Aidan flicked the pages, skimming for alterations. He must have found none, because he picked up a pen and handed it to John. "Sign. Both copies, please."

John's glance flicked up to Aidan's impassive features. "And I get the feather?"

"Do you know what to do with it?"

The thin lips curved into a smile. "Oh yes, I know what to do with it. Some of your compatriots can be very vocal, if we persuade them the right way. That charity is useful for something, after all."

"So you don't subscribe?"

"I give them money and lip service, yes. They had the information I needed. That fool Tom Albright is completely under their spell, but I've always said charity begins at home."

"With you."

"Who else?" John took the pen but paused, the instrument millimeters from the paper. "Let me see the feather."

Silently, Corinne reached inside her pocket and drew out the feather on its chain. It gleamed wickedly in the spring sunshine streaming through the windows, in fiery golden splendor. John's eyes gleamed. Pure avarice. "You want this, Dad?"

He licked his lips. "You know I do."

Behind him stood Aidan, impassive to all appearances but seething inside. This was what they had agreed and, so far, it was working. "Sign, Dad. Let me go."

"This is all you want?"

"Yes."

John signed. Aidan took the document and John signed the one underneath. Corinne stepped forward and signed both copies. Only then did the tension in the room begin to subside.

She handed him the feather. "Here."

John touched the feather and smoothed his fingers down each side. "So small," he wondered. "Now I put it on my body and ask a shape-shifter to touch me while I do it."

"That's about it." Aidan sounded conversational.

Pushing up his sleeve, John took the feather and pressed it to his forearm. "Can you do the honors?"

He put the feather on his arm and placed his hand over it, all his attention on Aidan. Corinne leaned across the desk and put her hand on top of her father's, pressing hard.

His head whipped around and he grinned, baring his unnaturally white teeth. "You've converted?"

"Yes. I love Aidan too much not to do it."

A slight rumble showed her Aidan's appreciation. For a bird, that sounded too much like a purr.

A minute of tense silence ensued, a minute where very little happened. John looked up. "Isn't it supposed to burn?"

Corinne took her hand away. "It is. It does. Why did you set the sniper on us, Dad? Why did you try to kill me?"

He growled low in his throat. "I didn't. That was the fucking PHR. If you hadn't done away with the sniper, I would have done it. I don't wish you harm, I just want what you have."

"This?" Aidan suggested quietly and put his fingers to John's temples, just as he had to Tom.

This time the effect was instantaneous. Before his mental barriers slammed down to shield her, Corinne felt Aidan pour power into John. "Is this what you want? Is it?" He pulled his hands away and lifted his head, breathing deeply. Then he looked down at the manager again. "You won't be able to do to anyone else what you did to Corinne, and when we leave the room, you won't remember anything except the contract you just signed. Our kind abhors compulsion and you won't be able to do that again. I've burned it out of you." John gaped. "The feather is one of mine. Or it was. There is one thing you don't know about me, Westfall. I'm not just a firebird. I'm the phoenix. The sniper killed me, or would have done had I been human. I've been reborn. You know what that means?"

John slowly shook his head, not taking his gaze away from Aidan. Corinne had never seen her father so taken aback, so totally off balance. "It means I'm a new bird, and anything from my past life is useless. You wanted the feather and you have it. Hang it around your neck as a souvenir."

He removed his gaze from John Westfall and walked around the desk to Corinne. "We're done here. Let's go home."

He took her hand and led her from the room.

* * * * *

Randy Norwood took the signed papers from Aidan the next day. Corinne and Aidan were in the flat, relaxing before the next stage in Pure Wildfire's career. They hadn't been out of contact with each other for more than five minutes and Corinne had been surrounded by love, physical and mental. Exhaustion wasn't far away, but Aidan wanted this part of the business over.

The big man got to his feet. "We're all set then." He glanced at Corinne. "After your news, we'll keep a guitarist on retainer. The band wants you, but your health has to come first." He grinned. "Don't tell me you planned to get pregnant."

Corinne grinned back. "No. It was one of those things."

"Not to worry. If you're well, there's no reason you can't do the American tour, or some of the dates anyway." His grin widened. "A pregnant rock guitarist! We're going to sweep the board with that!" Whistling to himself, he nodded to them and left. The click of the door closing echoed in the silence.

Aidan got up and came across to Corinne. She put both her hands in his when he held them out. "You look tired, sweetheart. How about a nap?"

Her one-sided grin was knowing. "A nap?"

"In a little while."

"Okay, I'll settle for that. A nap in a little while." She let him pull her to her feet and fold her in his arms. "Dad's furious. He can't understand why he signed the contract. The answering machine's full of his messages."

"Not anymore. I changed the disc."

Corinne snuggled into Aidan's broad chest. "He might still join the PHR. You didn't remove his yearning for power."

"He's just your ordinary, everyday megalomaniac now. He doesn't remember anything of the power he stole from your mother." He bent to lift her up into his arms. "Come and have your nap. In a little while."

She smiled up at him. "Sounds good to me."

Also by Lynne Connolly

ℰ

Icefire

Moonfire

Thunderfire

About the Author

℠

Lynne Connolly has been published for 5 years and in that time has won two Eppies and a number of other awards, Recommended Reads and other acknowledgements for her paranormal romances and her historicals.

While these are very gratifying, that isn't why she writes. She wants to bring the stories in her head to life and share them with others, in the hope that then she might get some peace.

Writing is what she was doing while she was working, bearing children and doing the other boring things that constitute living. Her favorite writer's motto is "I can use that."

She lives in the UK with her husband, children and cats, and her doll's houses. Creating worlds, miniature or otherwise, seems to be Lynne's specialty!

Lynne welcomes comments from readers. You can find her website and email address on her author bio page at www.ellorascave.com.

Tell Us What You Think

We appreciate hearing reader opinions about our books. You can email us at Comments@EllorasCave.com.

Why an electronic book?

We live in the Information Age—an exciting time in the history of human civilization, in which technology rules supreme and continues to progress in leaps and bounds every minute of every day. For a multitude of reasons, more and more avid literary fans are opting to purchase e-books instead of paper books. The question from those not yet initiated into the world of electronic reading is simply: *Why?*

1. *Price.* An electronic title at Ellora's Cave Publishing and Cerridwen Press runs anywhere from 40% to 75% less than the cover price of the exact same title in paperback format. Why? Basic mathematics and cost. It is less expensive to publish an e-book (no paper and printing, no warehousing and shipping) than it is to publish a paperback, so the savings are passed along to the consumer.

2. *Space.* Running out of room in your house for your books? That is one worry you will never have with electronic books. For a low one-time cost, you can purchase a handheld device specifically designed for e-reading. Many e-readers have large, convenient screens for viewing. Better yet, hundreds of titles can be stored within your new library—on a single microchip. There are a variety of e-readers from different manufacturers. You can also read e-books on your PC or laptop computer. (Please note that Ellora's Cave does not endorse any specific brands.

You can check our websites at www.ellorascave.com or www.cerridwenpress.com for information we make available to new consumers.)

3. *Mobility*. Because your new e-library consists of only a microchip within a small, easily transportable e-reader, your entire cache of books can be taken with you wherever you go.

4. *Personal Viewing Preferences.* Are the words you are currently reading too small? Too large? Too… ANNOYING? Paperback books cannot be modified according to personal preferences, but e-books can.

5. *Instant Gratification.* Is it the middle of the night and all the bookstores near you are closed? Are you tired of waiting days, sometimes weeks, for bookstores to ship the novels you bought? Ellora's Cave Publishing sells instantaneous downloads twenty-four hours a day, seven days a week, every day of the year. Our webstore is never closed. Our e-book delivery system is 100% automated, meaning your order is filled as soon as you pay for it.

Those are a few of the top reasons why electronic books are replacing paperbacks for many avid readers.

As always, Ellora's Cave and Cerridwen Press welcome your questions and comments. We invite you to email us at Comments@ellorascave.com or write to us directly at Ellora's Cave Publishing Inc., 1056 Home Avenue, Akron, OH 44310-3502.

COMING TO A BOOKSTORE NEAR YOU!

ELLORA'S CAVE

Bestselling Authors Tour

UPDATES AVAILABLE AT

WWW.ELLORASCAVE.COM

erridwen, the Celtic Goddess of wisdom, was the muse who brought inspiration to story-tellers and those in the creative arts. Cerridwen Press encompasses the best and most innovative stories in all genres of today's fiction. Visit our site and discover the newest titles by talented authors who still get inspired - much like the ancient storytellers did, once upon a time.

Cerridwen Press

www.cerridwenpress.com

Discover for yourself why readers can't get enough
of the multiple award-winning publisher

Ellora's Cave.

Whether you prefer e-books or paperbacks,

be sure to visit EC on the web at
www.ellorascave.com

for an erotic reading experience that will leave you
breathless.

2163631

Made in the USA